# BOY *of* ruin

UNWANTED
BOOK 1

## K.V. ROSE

For more information, please contact authorkvrose@outlook.com

Cover design © Arijana K. at Cover It! Designs

Edited by: Amy Briggs

ISBN: 978-1-989954-02-7 (ebook)

ISBN: 978-1-989954-01-0 (paperback)

*To the one I left.*

# PLAYLIST

Available on Spotify.

*Comedown* by Bush, along with *Another Life* by Motionless in White were key to writing this book. But the playlist is over 100 songs so we'll save that space.

As with every book in this series, this is a *dark* romance. It does not get lighter. Proceed with caution.

# PROLOGUE

## JEREMIAH

*SEVEN YEARS AGO*

Her eyes are the brightest blue, and in this moment, full of fucking horror. My hand around her throat feels good, and so does the way she scratches at me, struggling beneath my body.

So much bigger than hers.

There's nothing she can do to get me off of her.

*But there're a few things she can do to get me off.*

"Look at me, bitch."

She swallows beneath my hand, her face slowly turning pink, tears welling up behind those ocean eyes as she averts her gaze. She's the ugliest one between the two of them, but her eyes are hard to look away from. Especially when they're full of so much goddamn pain.

Reluctantly, she stares up at me, stilling beneath me, her nails still dug into my forearm. My hand starts to shake around her throat, and another wave of rage crashes over me, my adrenaline spiking all over again.

I try to tame it back, try to draw this out.

I smile down at her, my knees on either side of her hips, one hand planted beside her head.

Glancing past her, I see her father trying to crawl to her.

Crawl to *me*. But I broke his fucking legs, and that pain renders him nearly mute, small whimpers clawing their way up his fucking throat like his bones are piercing their way through his pant leg.

The smell of iron and gasoline is sharp down here in the basement, and I can almost taste the fucking fear. This girl's mother and her sister are dead now, naked and on their backs just past her father, in a dark corner of the basement, lit only by the light spilling down the stairs.

I've lived in this darkness for two weeks.

And it's not the first time.

My throat tightens as my grip loosens on the girl beneath me and I close my eyes tight, breathing in and out through my nose, trying to keep it together.

*"Jeremiah,"* her father croaks out, and I know he's almost gone. He won't make it over here in time to save his daughter because he's got a goddamn bullet lodged somewhere near his heart, but he's going to watch me fucking defile her.

*It's the least he could do.*

My stomach growls, hunger groaning through me painfully. I take a sharp breath in, forcing back the feeling. The ache.

"Jeremiah," my sister whispers beneath me, "I'm so sorry."

My eyes fly open with those words, surprise steeling through me. She rarely spoke to me, save for one thing. One thing she said over and over, and I've known her since I was eight. Nearly a fucking decade. I tighten my fingers around her throat and reposition myself between her thighs. She's wearing a white dress like she's a fucking angel, but we both know that isn't true. I'm going to stain it with red to show her just what she really is.

A demon, like the rest of them. Like what they forced me to be.

"Why didn't you help me?" I ask her, and I hate that the

words come up at all. I hate that I'm asking. *That I want an answer.* I jerk my head toward her father, still struggling to get to us, *to her.* My throat is so fucking dry from dehydration, I don't know how I manage to get my next words out, but I do, because my hand is shaking around her throat and it won't be long before I eat her a-fucking-live. "He never loved you."

A crease forms between her brows, her fingers loosening on my forearm.

"They never fucking loved you. Why didn't you *help me?*" My words are jagged, hoarse, and I close my eyes again as I lean down toward her, pressing my forehead to hers. "You could've saved me. You could've…"

She lets go of my forearm, brings her small hands to my back, almost as if she's holding me close. As if she wants to comfort me, when I'm about to *kill her.*

"Sicher," she whispers, her breath soft against my dry, cracked lips. "Sicher."

My heart twists with that one word. The only word she ever consistently spoke to me, *all these fucking years.*

"Sicher," she says again, choking on it, and as I open my eyes to meet hers, I see the tears pouring down her face, her nostrils flaring as she chokes up. "*Sicher.*"

A lie.

It was always a fucking lie.

I pull my head back to take her in, feel her pulse point flying beneath my index finger, but she doesn't stop hugging me. Doesn't stop holding my gaze.

Her father is closer now.

I consider, for one single second, the possibility that I might regret this. That she was fucked over just as I was.

But then I think of Sid Rain.

I think of *her* in that cage. In the darkness. Beating her head against the iron bars hoping to split her skull. Sleeping face down in her own piss because moving was too much of a burden, it cost too much precious energy. I imagine all the ways she might have wanted to kill herself. Did she ever try to use a bandana, like I did, to hang herself in a space that she couldn't even sit up in? Did she ever find a sharp point of her crate to dig into her wrists? To bleed out, starving, and alone?

Did she ever have her hands bound so tightly, she suffered permanent damage?

What else did they do to her?

*Did they rape her?*

The moment of pity I feel for the girl beneath me is gone. She was fed. Clothed. She wasn't the favored sister, but she was fucking *cared for*.

A manic smile curves my lips, because I know I'm not going to stop.

I'm naked as it is, as I've been for most of the near decade I've been in this house of horrors.

*They all deserve to fucking burn.*

I let go of her throat, reach for my cock between us as I turn to stare at her father.

He's crying too, those dead eyes full of grief. All these years, I never saw a single fucking emotion on his face. Not until this moment.

"Yeah," I taunt him, smiling as I push against her entrance and she whimpers, "you feel something now, fucker?"

# CHAPTER  One

SID

THE RAIN IS the only thing that makes me feel alive these days, and tonight, it's like a fucking tsunami. My hair is plastered down my back, running shirt stuck to my drenched skin, rainwater and sweat mingling in the black, soggy fabric. Fat, warm drops fall from the night sky relentlessly, and off in the distance, I hear thunder rumbling, see lightning spark above the canopy of the forest.

I know I should turn back, but I've been running until I can't breathe lately and right now, I'm still fucking breathing.

A few nights here recently I've wished I'd stop altogether.

I splash through a puddle, my sneakers instantly soaked, water spattering up my exposed calves. It's been too hot in North Carolina to wear pants even though it's only April. I imagine the summer will be torture.

Especially if I'm still pregnant when it comes.

I shake my head trying to rid the thought, my wet ponytail whipping the side of my face as I do. Wiping my wrist over my brow, I blink, trying to clear my vision. It's hard enough to see as it is on any given night in the dark woods behind my new home, and with a downpour like this, it's nearly impossible.

Still, I don't stop.

My heart is racing, chest heaving, and my calves start to ache, but I keep going, rain pelting every inch of me.

The constant onslaught is more than an attack. It's a reminder.

*I'm alive.*

I can still *feel.*

Speeding up, the forest flies by in a blur and I have to duck around a low hanging branch at the last minute, nearly twisting my ankle in the process as my sneaker slips in the mud. But I correct myself and keep sprinting until I think I might fucking faint and white spots pop in front of my eyes.

I tip my head back and open my mouth, letting the water fall onto my tongue as I slow to a fast walk, my lungs near bursting, my pulse so loud I can hear it in my head, even past the storm.

Lightning strikes again as I close my mouth and dip my chin, my hands on my knees when I come to a stop.

The sparks illuminate the trees overhead, forking violently through the blue-black sky. But it illuminates something else too, and suddenly, I really can't breathe.

I straighten, my hands in fists by my sides as I take a step back, fear crawling down my spine. The rain is so loud around me that I can't hear my own voice when I shout, "Hello?", wanting the figure I saw in that flash of light to know that I saw them.

There's no response. Even if there had been, the storm would've drowned it out. Still, I have this strange feeling whoever it is isn't here to fucking talk.

*Fuck.*

I take another step back, reach around for the zipper at the top of my shorts in the back, trying to tug the pocket open with slippery fingers. I feel clammy. Cold.

I shouldn't have fucking done this.

Every night, I've disabled the alarm of the house and snuck out the back where I know the guards aren't positioned because Jeremiah wanted to give me some semblance of a normal life.

He wanted to trust me.

Some nights he works late, his schedule is erratic, so I have a key in my pocket too, in case he locks up and accidentally locks me out, not knowing I'm out here.

But it's not the key I reach for now as I manage to get the zipper open.

It's the switchblade.

I thumb the latch, gripping the handle tight as I take another step back, my hand trembling.

Fuck, Jeremiah is going to kill me if I die out here. Bring me back from the dead just to slit my throat and say, "*I told you so, sis.*"

I glance over my shoulder as I keep retreating, refusing to turn my back completely on the hunter. I can't see shit in the darkness, even toward the house. There're no lights on and Jeremiah wasn't home when I slipped out this time.

He had a late night "job" he said before he told me goodnight.

Lightning crackles across the sky again, and the hairs all over my body stand on end. For a second, I'm motionless, scanning the forest in front of me. Beside me. My knife is held aloft, the handle slick beneath my wet fingers, and I grip it tighter, biting my lip and holding my breath as I use that half a second of light to find the person watching me.

But I see nothing.

No one.

They vanished.

I start to think maybe it was just my imagination. Sometimes I have hallucinations, stemming from my recovering memories. Usually I know when it's happening, because Reverend Wilson is dead. The men who touched me, they're all dead.

The ones I didn't get, my husband killed.

But this didn't feel like a hallucination.

It felt so real.

Still feels real, like I'm being watched.

Taking a breath, I go to spin around, but before I can, strong, sure fingers circle over my wrist, an arm banding across my chest and prying the knife from my grip, holding the blade to my throat.

The hand on my wrist moves to clamp over my mouth as I gasp, trembling and momentarily mute with fear, my heart seeming to stop beating altogether.

Someone's hard chest is against my back, the blade's sharp edge to my neck as I stand motionless, my mind telling me this is real but another part of me wanting to believe it's all in my head.

*Is it all in my head? Am I crazy too? Just like my husband?*

"You're all wet, sis," a voice says in my ear, trailing the point of the knife lower, ripping into the fabric of my running shirt. I gasp beneath Jeremiah's hand even as I reach for him behind me, gripping his shirt in my fists. He keeps dragging the blade down, slicing through my shirt, my sports bra, freeing me, the tip of the blade grazing my skin.

"Jeremiah," I say beneath his hand, my chest heaving, voice low, and I don't know if he's heard me. "Stop—"

He tightens his hand over my mouth as the blade cuts through the hem of my shirt, the scraps of wet fabric in pieces, my chest and belly exposed. But he doesn't stop with the fucking knife. Instead, he skims the sharp point softly over my low belly, up my ribcage, my sternum, before coming over my left breast.

I can't breathe, my knees shake beneath me and I have to lean back against him for support. When he circles the flat side of the blade over my nipple, hard and tight from the rain and the cool steel, the irony isn't lost on me that I'm looking to him for protection from…*him.*

"I think I told you not to come out here alone," he whispers against my ear as a shiver slides down my spine.

The onslaught of rain has slowed to a light shower, but I hear thunder rumble in the distance. I see another flash of lightning making the dark forest eerie with the brief spark of light, and the outline of trees become unnerving. Haunting.

Jeremiah slides the blade across my chest, circling my other nipple and I close my eyes, fear, anger and lust warring within me.

He knows better than to touch me like this. But with his erection pressing into my back, a knife to my chest, *I* know better than to try and fight him right now.

With my foster brother, you choose your battles, or you end up fucking dead.

Still, when he finally drops the knife and I can breathe again, taking in great gulps of air, I relax marginally into his touch. Into knowing it was him out here, and not someone else.

He might be the scariest monster who could ever stalk through this forest, but as his hand softly cups my breast, his thumb smoothing over my nipple, I know that he's *my* monster.

Even still, I grab at his hand, trying to pull it off of me.

I can't do this.

I *cannot* do this.

Not to my husband.

I can't break his heart more than I already have.

I start to struggle in Jeremiah's grip, and I swear the hand over my mouth trembles.

For a second, I pause, my fingers latched around his wrist.

Is he shaking from anger?

Restraint?

Was that...something else?

But then his hand stills and he says, "Do you really want to fight me, after you disobeyed me?" He squeezes a handful of my ever-growing breasts—one perk of pregnancy I've discovered in my second trimester—and licks the side of my wet face. "You taste like a fucking brat," he murmurs against me, "and brats need to be punished."

He pulls at my nipple and I gasp against his palm, my eyes flying open, still trying to yank his hand down, but it's impossible. The flex of muscle and tendons beneath my fingers is all that gives, and I know I can't fight him that way. My brother is a fucking beast.

I raise my foot, ready to stomp on his, just like he taught me in our self-defense lessons, when lightning strikes again, flaring the thick of the woods in bright purple light.

I lower my foot, my mouth falling open, my pulse racing all over again.

Jeremiah runs his hand over to my other breast, kneading my flesh, but he notices my trembling and pauses.

"Sid," he whispers. "Baby…"

"Jeremiah." This time he moves his hand from my mouth and this time my fingers aren't circled around his wrist to keep him off. Instead, I'm holding on tight as his arms band around me, to protect me. Because that wasn't a hallucination.

It was the same hooded figure I'd seen the first time. The one I thought was my brother.

"What is it, baby?" he asks, concern threaded through his voice.

I take a shaky breath, feeling dizzy with fear as I whisper, "There's someone out here with us."

And I can't help wondering…*Is it him?*

# CHAPTER Two

## JEREMIAH

LIVING UP TO MY NAMESAKE, I love the fucking rain. Thunderstorms, lightning strikes, I could watch a storm for hours if it'd let me. But as I turn away from the pane of glass that stretches from one end of the living room to the other, I catch sight of the most volatile storm I've ever seen in my life perched on the edge of the leather couch and huddled beneath a white towel.

Sid is shivering, her brown hair made darker by the rain and plastered to her head. Twenty-one years old, and since she was a toddler, I've been tracking her like a storm chaser, coming ever closer even when she's a fucking danger to the thing I thought I lost all those years ago. My heart.

Her silver eyes lock on mine as she looks up, her pale pink lips parted as she stares at me. Her perfect nose is slightly upturned, and I watch a bead of water drip from the end of it.

"Did you see anything on the cameras?" she asks, wiping absentmindedly at her nose. Her husky voice is so fucking sensual, it's an arousal all on its own.

I run my hand through my wet hair, then slip it back into my pocket as I cross the stone floors of the living room to stand in front of her.

She rears back with my nearness and I roll my eyes, taking a seat on the black coffee table, hear it groan beneath me.

"No," I tell her, then jerk my head toward the window. It looks out on the in-ground pool, currently being pelted with rain, then beyond that, the forest that surrounds this house. Still in Alexandria, but away from the city core, it's the perfect hiding spot.

Perfect, except Sid Rain is the target of many powerful men, and if she doesn't learn to listen to me, she's going to get herself killed.

If she does, I'll have nothing left to live for. I told her once I couldn't live without her. She has no idea how much I meant that.

"They're still looking." My men, including Nicolas, are out there with flashlights, getting thoroughly soaked. I pay them enough to make it worth it.

My eyes lock on Sid's as she pulls her lip between her teeth and I bite the inside of my cheek to keep from groaning. Three weeks she's been here and three weeks I've tried to give her space.

But I haven't slept with anyone since I gave up Brooklin for Sid, and my hand isn't cutting it anymore.

I need her. I've always needed her, and I've had her in every way except one. *Almost*, but that doesn't count. And thinking of that night, when I made him watch…I feel a wave of nausea roll over me, but I push it back. Down.

My eyes find her dry cotton tank beneath the towel, her black sleep shorts and bare feet, toenails free of polish. We both changed when we came to the house and I sent my guys out, but now I kind of wish she was back in those running clothes I nearly cut off of her. It amazes me, how used to my bullshit she is.

We're perfect for each other, if only she'd get that through her fucking head.

"You can't do this anymore, baby," I tell her softly, even as her eyes narrow on mine. I know she doesn't like being told what to do, but she'll learn to like it. Eventually. *It's for her own good.*

I lean forward, my knee knocking into hers as my hands find her thigh, circling my fingers over her leg. Her muscles flex beneath me, the skin soft and smooth, and she looks like she might get up and put more distance between us, but her throat bobs as she sees my fingers against her pale skin, and she stills.

I trace circles over her knee with my thumb, taking in those long lashes nearly grazing her cheekbones as she stares at my hand on her.

I avoid looking at the small scar over her brow. I asked her about it. I'm pretty sure she fucking lied to me.

"I want to keep you safe. I want to take care of you." I slide my fingers higher up her thigh and feel a tremor run through her body. It's a reminder of my own, and reluctantly, I pull my damaged hand away from her, ball it into a fist on my lap. I've always been careful to avoid showing her my weakness. "But I can't do that if you're always defying me."

She clenches her jaw, eyes meeting mine. "I was going for a run—"

"Close to midnight in the middle of the fucking forest." I can't stop the anger in my own words as I cut her off.

Her eyes flash as she sits up straighter, letting the towel fall back on the couch and exposing her lean arms and collarbone, stark against her pale, olive skin. "I won't be a prisoner here too, Jeremiah. Not again." She makes to get up, but I shoot my other hand out, gripping both of her thighs and holding her down.

Standing in a crouch, I lean over her as she backs against the couch, and I marvel at how small she is beneath me. I'm over six feet tall and since I left that fucking cage when I was seventeen—seven years ago—I've never let myself be in anything but the best shape.

Sid is a runner, and naturally, she's petite, short, and slender.

She can't fight me, even with all the lessons I've given her. She can't outshine her master.

I plant my fists on the couch, against either side of her head as I loom over her, caging her in beneath me.

She holds her palms to my chest, trying to keep distance between us like she always does. But I felt her tits in my hand out in that forest, and I've seen how she looks at me. That night in the club too, before Lucifer Malikov tossed us both in a fucking cell, I know she wanted me.

She's spent so long trying to fight it, I think she's having a hard time remembering that it's okay.

She can want me.

I'm not really her brother, even though I've looked after her in all the ways a brother should care for their little sister.

I press my brow to hers as she backs herself against the couch.

I can smell her lavender scent and I inhale, my mouth inches from her own.

"You're not a prisoner," I tell her, angling my head so my lips are aligned with hers. "But you're mine to look after." I brush my mouth over hers and hear her sharp inhale. "Just *let me*." I move one hand to her low belly, slipping my fingers beneath her shirt and splaying them against her soft skin, her rounded belly. "Let me do my fucking job."

Her eyes are searching mine, wide and open, as if she's considering it. As if, for once, she doesn't hate me. She isn't just here for protection from the fucking cult and her fucking psychotic husband who she ran from. As if she might...love me.

I run my mouth over hers again, my fingers digging into her skin. She parts her lips but doesn't kiss me back and I think about grabbing her chin and forcing her to do just that when I hear footsteps at my back.

I curse under my breath and reluctantly pull away from her as I straighten, turning my back to Sid and blocking her from view.

Nicolas comes into the living room, his blond hair damp, black shirt clinging to his lean frame. He opens his mouth then closes it as his eyes drift from me to Sid, then back again. There's a furrow between his brow as he puts his palms together and clears his throat.

I hear more footsteps down the hall that leads toward the downstairs entrance, and more men file in behind Nicolas, all dressed in black and armed with flashlights and weapons.

Arching a brow in a silent question, I look back to Nicolas, trying not to think about the muddy footprints in my house, even though it makes me feel physically ill.

It's why I have house staff, I remind myself. They'll deal with it.

"We searched the forest," Nicolas says, glancing toward Sid at my back, then down at the floor. He clears his fucking throat again and I want to slit it because I'm running out of patience. It was only a matter of time before *he* came looking for her. "We checked all of the cameras, including the ones you've been watching her from."

I hear Sid snap my name at my back, as if she thought I didn't know about her little midnight runs. As if she thought those cameras were décor.

Silly girl.

"And?" I press, ignoring her and clasping my hands behind my back.

Nicolas brings his dark eyes to mine and I feel my stomach flip with that look. Like he's trying to tell me something without words.

Like he's trying to tell me that my sister is insane.

"There was nothing out there."

▼

I INHALE FROM MY JOINT ON THE BACK DECK, LOOKING OFF into the darkness of the forest. Three in the morning, the sun hasn't yet risen.

The air is hot, humid with the storm now passed.

I exhale through my nose and grind the rest of the joint against the wooden railing, pocketing it to throw away inside the house. I keep my left hand in my pocket, clenched into a fist.

The marijuana is the only thing that stops the tremors. Never for long enough, but it helps. *If only it took away the memories too.*

I clench my teeth together with that thought, pushing it back along with all the other nightmares of my childhood.

There's no use feeling sorry for myself over them. I'm glad I had to claw my way out of that goddamned cage. If I hadn't, I wouldn't be who I am today. Someone respected. *Fucking feared.*

The man Sid Rain runs to when she needs *real* protection.

The 6 won't come for her here. The Unsaints are a fucking joke, and in this little pocket of Alexandria, an hour from the downtown core, our home surrounded by forest on all sides, she's safe.

*Safe.*

I hear the sliding glass door at my back and tense, standing up straighter, sliding my other hand into my pocket. I don't turn around, because I can tell by the slow, heavy footsteps it's Nicolas.

His birthday is tomorrow, and I'm throwing a party. I don't give a fuck about birthdays and I don't like parties, but I want to try a different tactic with Sid.

I've been nothing but nice to her since she's been here.

I don't think she really likes *nice.*

Nicolas comes to stand beside me, leaning his elbows on

the railing, clasping his hands together as he looks down at the inground pool below this deck and the gate around it which Sid has been sneaking in and out of to run at night.

I've had Nicolas watch her on the camera every fucking night, but three hours ago, I happened to get home in time to see her leave myself.

She's a fucking brat.

I love her for it.

"So," Nicolas says as I lean my hip on the rail, angling toward him so I can read his body language when he speaks. The tremor in my hand is worse tonight than it usually is, and I should've finished that joint, but I know that's not why it's so bad.

It's the stab wounds.

My target tonight just didn't want to fucking die, so I over-worked myself, and I had blood on my black shirt to prove it. Doesn't help I hit an arterial vein, didn't move out of the fucking way in time. But the rat that was talking a little too loudly to the cops is out of his misery.

I need to shower. But when I saw Sid slipping away in the night, glancing over her shoulder but not catching sight of me upstairs watching from the window as I started to change, I couldn't resist the urge to follow her.

Now, I can't sleep.

Thinking someone is out there. Watching us. *Her.*

*Is it* him?

"Do you think she needs to see a doctor?"

I arch a brow at Nicolas. "I had the midwife come last week." We listened to the strong, fast heartbeat together as I held her hand. I clench my jaw as I think about the fact it's not *my baby* she's carrying, but one day.

One day it will be.

Nicolas hangs his head, his shoulders curving inward as he does. "Not that kind of doctor," he says softly.

I grind my teeth together before asking, "Then *what* kind of doctor are you fucking talking about?"

He lifts his head up, his eyes searching mine, but he doesn't say anything.

Heat flushes through my body with the way he's looking at me.

"She's not crazy," I bite out.

He runs his thumb over his bottom lip, slips his hand into the pocket of his running shorts and looks away from me as he straightens from the railing. "I'm not saying she is. But she's had a lot of trauma in a short period of time and—"

"Don't talk to me about trauma. Me and her both know trauma. We were born into fucking trauma, Nicolas." I glance at the cigarette burns on his arm, visible in the lights from the porch, and I see a muscle strum along his jaw. "You might've had it rough, but us? Me and Sid? What we went through makes hell look like fucking Disneyland." I turn my back to him and feel my hand tremble in my pocket. Rage lights through me all over again and I have to bite it back before I break Nicolas's fucking neck. "She's not crazy. If she said she saw someone, she fucking saw someone. And *you* missed them." I head toward the door, desperate to be near her. To touch her. Hold her. If she'd let me, fuck her.

"And what about you?" Nicolas asks quietly at my back. "Did you see anyone?"

I clench my jaw and close my eyes for a second. I don't bother answering him as I pull open the sliding glass door and step inside. But before I can slam it closed, he speaks again.

"Maybe she didn't imagine it, but if she didn't…" He takes a breath, and I tense, a whirlwind of anger and pain blowing through me. "You know Ignis is coming, right? You know he isn't going to let her out of it? In his own way, he wants to keep her safe too."

I ignore his last sentence because it kind of makes me want to shoot him, but just like that, with the name of one of the many fucking ceremonies the idiots do, all those memories I try so fucking hard not to dwell on, they come rushing back, nearly crippling me. My hand shakes violently in my pocket and I want to fucking cut it off. Rip apart any piece of me that's connected to *them.*

I can't wait to get my hands around Lucifer Malikov's neck so I can pay him back for everything he ever did to me. Everything he ever let happen. *How he took her from me.*

"He's going to die before then," I answer Nicolas. "And after that? We're fucking leaving this place behind." I slam the door closed after me and head into the house to find the only girl I've ever loved. The one whose heart I'm going to have to break when I plunge a knife through her husband's fucking brain.

I watch her sleep through a crack in the door, marveling at how she could pass out so fast after being stalked through the forest.

She must be exhausted.

Or maybe she's just grown used to monsters.

There's a soft blue glow in the room from a nightlight I got her, and I see her arm slung over her brow, watch as her fingers slowly unfurl. I catch sight of that X on her palm.

I tense, grinding my teeth as I stare at it, visible in the dim light overhead. *Coagula.*

*Bullshit.*

He doesn't even fucking know her, and he's already tried to own her. A forced marriage, but where was he when she was in California? Where the fuck was he when we were both starving, neglected, driven further into misery and poverty with each passing day because of his piece of shit father?

*And mine.*

But I refuse to think of Lazar Malikov as having any relation to me.

I don't have a father.

I never did.

But me and Sid?

We always had each other.

*MOM BRINGS HER IN, COOING AT HER AND SMILING AND SWAYING her in her arms. I'm sitting on the sticky kitchen floor.*

*There's a knock on the door.*

*Mom's eyes find mine. I don't know what she sees when she looks at me, but she seems nervous. She always has around me.*

*"It's okay, Jamie. Mommy will be right back, okay?" She squats down, her long dark hair falling over one shoulder as she sets the gray-eyed toddler down. The knock gets louder. "I love you, Jamie. Mommy loves you."*

*I grab my red fire truck. There's a wheel missing but I don't care. I've always liked broken things. The stuffed bear Mom gave me for Christmas is missing an eye. Mom said she could fix it. I tore the other eye off and threw the shiny, smooth plastic into the trash. I prefer the teddy broken, too.*

*The baby with the weird eyes crawls to me as fast as she can. She has brown hair, to her shoulders. Her skin isn't as tan as mine. It's because Mom lets me play outside a lot in our backyard with the small plastic pool. It's supposed to be a sandbox. One of Mom's friends told me so before he locked me out of the house. It's shaped like a turtle.*

*But Mom says it's a pool and I prefer the water anyway.*

*I hear Mom's voice rising at the front door. A man answering her in a deep voice.*

*The baby grabs my truck. I yank it back. She bats at my face. It makes me laugh.*

*Mom is crying.*

*The man is yelling.*

*The baby crawls into my lap. We both hold the truck, but I don't touch her with my hands.*

*Mom makes a sound like I did when I jumped from the stacked washing machine and broke my leg.*

*It's so loud.*

*My heart hurts and I don't know why.*

*I rub my chest.*

*The door slams. Mom is still crying.*

*The baby looks up at me. Her eyes are silver, like a nickel.*

*She pats my cheek.*

*I touch her hair.*

*She kisses my face.*

*Mom is still crying.*

*She ends up doing that a lot.*

*But me and my new sister never do.*

*I keep her with me, never let her go. I don't want her to ever cry like Mom.*

For a long, long time, I wasn't able to keep track of her. Protect her. But for the past three weeks, she's been right here. *With me.*

And this time? I'm never going to let her fucking go.

# CHAPTER *Three*

## SID

"YOU'RE A SKINNY BITCH, you know that?"

I jerk my chin up at Ria's voice, see her standing in my doorway with her hand planted on her hip, a lock of her dark, curly hair wound around her finger. Pulling down my black T-shirt to cover my belly, I glance once more at the floor-length mirror in my spacious room. Spacious, but nearly empty. A queen bed at my back, gray and black sheets with black curtains blocking out the morning sun, covering my own personal balcony. There's a walk-in closet on the same wall the mirror is on, and a bathroom adjacent the bed. But this is a new house, not lived in, no clutter. A safe house that Jeremiah bought specifically to keep me hidden.

Protected from all the things I ran from.

I'm grateful for it, but it doesn't take the ache away.

For my husband. The father of my child.

I run my hand absentmindedly over my low belly, even though the bump is only just starting to appear. Just shy of nineteen weeks and I'm barely showing, but Jeremiah had a midwife come by last week. We listened to the heartbeat—fast and strong—and Jeremiah's pale green eyes lit up as he snatched up my hand, pressing his mouth to the back of it.

"You ready to be a dad?" the midwife had asked, the wand of the Doppler in one hand, the other on the little machine.

Neither of us bothered to correct her.

I run my fingers through my hair, long enough now that I can do neat tricks like put it up in a ponytail.

I'm ready to cut it off again.

"Shut up," I mutter to Ria, biting back a smile. "What're you doing up here so early?" I glance at the alarm clock on my nightstand. It's not even seven in the morning. Tonight, there's a party for Nicolas, and I'm thinking of skipping it altogether, sleeping the night away right in here.

Ria folds her arms, leaning against the doorway. She's dressed in pale pink shorts and a white tank. There's a smile on her lips, but something else in her golden eyes. She's found solace with Nicolas here, but I know she's still being held against her will, even if she's an accepting prisoner.

Jeremiah is guarding her family, unbeknownst to them, and they think she's studying abroad for her last semester at Alexandria University before she graduates with a history degree. Little do they know, she's getting the biggest history lesson of her life by being here, stashed away from the families that have lorded over the city in secret for years.

I swallow down the lump in my throat that comes when I think about him. *Lucifer.* Even thinking his name makes it hard to breathe.

But we need space.

And I had to leave.

Sometimes in the night, I feel those hands on me again. Hear their whispered threats. Taste the fear coating the inside of my mouth. They would've never let me leave Noctem alive.

If it wasn't for my brothers—and I can't stop including Jeremiah in that category, as if thinking it will keep me from giving into him, giving him what he wants—I would be dead.

Lucifer might hate me, but I hope he's at least grateful I'm alive.

Knowing him though, he'd probably rather I be a corpse than here with Jeremiah.

"The birthday boy told me to come keep an eye on you," Ria says, smirking.

I roll my eyes, turn from the mirror and walk to the night-stand, snatching up my knife and stowing it in the back pocket of my black, ripped jeans. "Aren't there enough eyes on me? Why do I need yours, too?"

A beat of silence that seems a little too long passes and I turn to face Ria again, seeing her brow furrow as she averts her eyes to the polished wooden floors.

My pulse picks up speed as I tense. "What?" I press her. "What is it?"

She clears her throat and glances over her shoulder, into the hallway. Jeremiah's room is opposite the house from mine, and the one Nicolas and Ria hole themselves up in is on the first floor, so I assume she's looking for prying eyes in general. Turning her gaze back to me, squeezing her fingers around her arms, she says, "I don't know if I'm supposed to be the one to tell you but—"

"But what?" I press, stepping closer, growing impatient. *Did something happen to my husband? Where is he? Is he okay?*

"They checked all the cameras." She chews her lip, furrows her brow.

I can't breathe, my throat is closing up, my body frozen as I stare at her, waiting to hear it wasn't him. Waiting to hear he's okay. I want to run past her, shove her aside and leap down the stairs just to see with my own eyes. To know he's still breathing. Still living. Still whole.

"I heard your brother," she cringes with that word, real-izing her mistake, but thankfully she doesn't correct it, just keeps talking while I struggle to breathe, "talking." She swal-lows. "With Nicolas. They didn't find anything…and Nicolas thinks you might have…" She shifts from foot to foot. "Might have imagined it."

Oxygen fills my lungs as I inhale, letting my eyes flutter closed. I'm nearly dizzy with relief knowing Jeremiah didn't get to him. I feel lightheaded, but I force my eyes open, and see Ria's concern as she makes to step into the room, but I hold up my hand, letting her know I'm fine while I breathe in through my nose, out through my mouth.

Then her words register in my mind.

I drop my hand, the momentary relief replaced with anger. I can see the figure in my head. Wearing a dark hood. No facial features, and it was dark, in the middle of the forest, but I know *I saw someone.*

"I didn't imagine it," I say through gritted teeth.

I watch Ria's throat bob as she swallows, averting her gaze. "I believe you." Her voice sounds rough with those words as she meets my eyes again, and a shiver runs down my spine. "They took me too, you know." Those words are barely more than a whisper.

Before I can say anything though, we both hear footsteps coming down the hall, sure and quick.

Ria straightens immediately, turning to face the hallway, and I hear my brother before I see him.

"Are you ready, Sid?" He sounds impatient, tense.

When he comes into view, he stops short, glaring at Ria. She might have run into his arms at Noctem, because she knew he was better than the 6 who kidnapped her after letting her free for a few weeks when she ran from Mav, but there has been no love between them. I don't think she's quite forgotten how he held a gun to her head that night in the car, all those months ago.

He's done far worse to me.

I haven't forgotten, either, but I guess I've come to expect it from him.

He slides his hands into the pockets of his gray basketball shorts, a white T-shirt stretched across his broad chest. I realize I should be in workout gear because we train every morning, but for some reason, after what happened last night, I had assumed we might skip it this morning.

I should know better.

And if no one fucking believes me, if there's no evidence, maybe he doesn't even think there's a cause for concern.

We're just onto business as fucking usual.

Even with an erratic schedule, my brother is a stickler for routine. I think it helps him feel in control, when he spent so much of his life being out of it. I know that feeling, because I did too. But I don't desire control.

I crave freedom. *Escape.*

*But there was someone out there.*

"What are you doing?" Jeremiah asks Ria, his voice low as he cocks his head, a lock of his dark brown, wavy hair just above his pale green eyes.

Ria steps back but runs into the door frame. "I was just—"

"She was telling me that you and Nicolas think I'm delusional," I butt in, coming to stand closer to them, to protect Ria from my brother's horrible temper.

Slowly, his jaw clenched, he turns to face me. "I never said—"

"You don't believe me?" I demand, locking eyes with my brother, hating that my words come out hoarse. Hesitant. "Why didn't you come to *me* with that?"

He stares at me a second, biting his lip as his gaze sweeps over me, from head to toe and back again.

A flush runs through my body with his stare, and I hate that I feel something when he looks at me like that. Like he wants me.

I cross my arms over my chest, knowing he knows what he's doing to me by that slight smile on his full lips. "I never said I didn't believe you, Sid."

Ria scoffs, and Jeremiah's eyes narrow, but he doesn't look away from me. Shaking her head, Ria walks past him, muttering something that sounds like, "I'm out."

We listen to her footsteps retreat, then echo down the stairs.

"Don't play those fucking games with me," I tell Jeremiah, stepping closer. I catch his clean scent, like fresh laundry and a hint of his cologne or deodorant. He smells so damn good and he looks even better. He's becoming impossible to resist. But my heart doesn't belong to him. At least, not all of it.

*At least...that's what I try to tell myself.*

"I'm not a child you need to keep in a cage." I snarl the last word and see his jaw tick. He refuses to talk to me about that fucking cage, so I refuse to tiptoe around what happened to him. "*Talk to me.* Let me be equal to you—"

He reaches out a hand, grabs my arm and yanks me flush against him. My hands come to his chest as he glares down at me, and I can feel his heart beating strong and sure beneath my palm.

"You want *equality?*" he asks, condescension in his tone. "Never mind bullshit about your *mental health.* Get out of these fucking clothes and into the right ones, then come down to the gym. If you can finally fight me off, I'll treat you like an equal." His words are whispers against the shell of my ear as his hand comes to my back, slipping up my shirt, pressed flat against my spine. "If you can't, then you'll stop fucking questioning me."

▼

"No, baby, that's not...that's just not right." Jeremiah shakes his head, sighing, but there's a smirk pulling on the corners of his full lips. He bows his head, hands on his hips as he steps back from me. He's shirtless, drenched in sweat, and I see it glistening down his hard body. I see the scar too, not quite healed, still angry, red, and raised.

Right under his ribs.

The scar from my husband.

It's a miracle Jeremiah survived. Then again, he's always believed he was a god. I guess it makes sense he's nearly immortal.

His mood has lightened since he's kicked my ass over and over, and I know the feeling. Workouts help me forget all the heavy stuff.

For a little while.

"I don't wanna do this anymore," I tell him, wiping the back of my hand over my brow. I'm sweating too, in a sports bra and running shorts, my feet in black sneakers. We've been in the basement gym for the past two hours.

He picks his head up, his jade eyes full of amusement as his gaze meets mine.

"Your form is just all...wrong. Your legs are what's free, right? You can't expect to squirm your way out of my grip. It just won't happen, Sid." There's a double meaning to those words, and I see it in the way his eyes light up as his gaze slides down my body.

I ignore the warmth spooling in my core with that look. His words. Instead, I tighten my ponytail and turn my back to him, headed to the stairs at the corner of the room, ready for breakfast. I've read, in the baby book that Jeremiah bought me and left on my nightstand one night, that I'm lucky I don't have morning sickness.

Still, I'm fucking starving, all the time, and after our *disagreement* in the doorway of my room, I didn't eat, ready to shut his ass up.

I haven't.

"I don't need to fight. I'm good at running, if you haven't noticed by now."

But before I can take two steps, his arm bands around my chest, yanking me back against his sweaty body.

His other hand finds my throat, and my breath leaves me in a rush, just like it did last night.

I'm frozen, my heart pounding so loud in my chest it *hurts*.

I can't breathe, especially as his hand trails down to my bare waist, his fingers light against my skin. His grip on my throat is tight, but not painful.

*Not yet.*

His breath is against my ear, and my eyes flutter closed as I relax into his touch, hating the way I don't hate it at all. Hating that I can feel his erection hard against my back, and while I haven't so much as kissed him in the three weeks I've been here, some part of me...*some part of me wants to.*

"I'm good at catching you, *if you haven't noticed by now."* His words cause goosebumps to crawl up my skin, and my throat feels tight beneath his fingers. I can't swallow. Can't move at all.

I'm not even sure I want to.

"You need to know how to defend yourself, baby. If someone was following you last night...they could do it again." His tone is laced with anger. "So," he whispers, "get away from me. *Right. Now."*

I think about the knife by my bed. The gun in this very room, on one of the weight benches. Nicolas upstairs, along with my brother's other guards.

Because I snuck out, they couldn't have protected me. If Jeremiah didn't get home at the right time, and Nicolas hadn't looked for me, it could've been *them* that came for me.

I grit my teeth and take a steadying breath.

I can practically hear Jeremiah's smirk against my ear.

My first instinct is to do exactly what I've tried the past few hours. Squirm free. Or grab his arm, still banded around my chest, his calloused fingers still grazing my bare waist. But I fight back on that urge, try to listen to what he said.

*My legs are free.*

There's nothing stopping me from kicking up and back and—

Just as I try, he wraps his leg around mine, keeping me in

place, his hand tightening around my throat. "Try again," he instructs me, his tone not mocking. *Helpful.*

I try to kick my other foot up, backward, but he's faster, sweeping my steady leg to the side and throwing me off balance. *Both of us* off balance. We fall backward, and a scream leaves my throat, not from concern about me, but *him.*

Surprising me, though, he doesn't make a sound and as we come crashing to the ground, I realize he landed on the padded mats he has scattered around the cement floors.

He laughs, a delicious sound that I don't hear nearly often enough. And just as a small laugh of my own bubbles its way up from my mouth, he's spinning me around so fast I'm dizzy as my back hits the mat and he's on top of me, his hands planted on either side of my head.

My breath catches in my throat, the laughter dying on the tip of my tongue. I reach for his forearms, corded muscle hard and slick with sweat beneath my fingers. I don't know why I'm holding onto him. I don't know if I'm trying to keep him away or if I want him…closer.

His knees are on either side of my hips, and I'm just thankful he's on them instead of flush against me.

My eyes trail down from his, over his handsome face, his full, parted lips, the sweat dripping from his defined jawline.

I see the muscles in his neck, his shoulders, down his body. He's built, tall, so much bigger than me.

Being underneath him like this is something I shouldn't crave but can't help but…like.

"Jeremiah," I whisper, my fingers tightening around his forearms. "What are you—"

He leans down close to me, cutting off my words, his lips inches from mine. I can smell him, clean like fresh laundry even as he's drenched in sweat. Everything about my brother is perfectly polished and neat, almost as if he needs it that way to hide the rot that is his soul.

"I like you underneath me," he says softly, his breath—like

toothpaste, warm against my mouth—caressing me. Drawing me in. Causing me to clench my thighs together. Close my eyes so I can't see him. So I can pretend this isn't happening.

He's my brother.

*My brother.*

"I like that you aren't fighting me." His mouth is closer, nearly touching my lips.

I dig my nails into his forearms, and he huffs a small laugh, but doesn't move back.

"It's a step, huh, baby?"

I don't speak. I keep my eyes closed, holding my breath. Hating myself for this. For…wanting it.

"Good try today, Sid." I can feel the absence of his mouth over mine and relief floods through me, but it's short lived. Instead of my mouth, he trails his soft, full lips over the side of my face. "But remember you'll never be able to fight me." His mouth finds my throat, and instead of shoving him away, instead of telling him to stop…I just arch my neck back, giving him better access.

He laughs against my skin at my submission. His teeth scrape above the hollow of my throat. "Not because you're not strong enough." He closes his lips in a kiss, sucking me into his mouth.

I bite back a moan, gripping him so tightly I know it's got to hurt. His muscles flex beneath my fingers but he doesn't tell me to let go.

"You're the strongest girl I've ever met," he says softly, his words vibrating against my throat.

Butterflies jump in my stomach, desire coursing through my veins.

"But you don't want me to stop, do you, baby?" He closes his mouth again over my skin. "I'll wait, though. I'll wait until you give in. And when you do?" He picks his head up so he's staring down at me. "When you do, I'll make you the happiest fucking girl in the world." His smile is wicked, and I know he isn't done. He brushes my hair from my face, tucking a strand that came loose from my ponytail behind my ear. "But *equality is earned, baby*. And until you get there, you're going to let me keep you safe." He runs his tongue up my throat and I close my eyes, feeling the little goosebumps down my body with the warmth of him against my hot skin. "Let me take care of you, because *that's what brothers do.*"

# CHAPTER Four

**JEREMIAH**

I COUNT out the money on the table in the expansive back room of the club, where we decided to have Nicolas's party, as a safety precaution. In case Sid *isn't* losing her mind.

Five grand, fifty bills, the going rate for a hit on a nobody dealer. If he'd kept his fucking mouth shut about walking in on a body drop that he should've never seen, he'd make it to his daughter's second birthday next week, and I'd save myself five thousand dollars.

He didn't, and his kid is probably better off. He's not exactly winning father of the year, despite his "anonymous" tip to the cops.

Glancing up, I see my sister perched on the leather couch edged against the opposite wall, her legs crossed, arms too, her expression is one of polite interest as Roman Torres takes a seat next to her, holding out his hand to introduce himself.

I've still got one hand on the stack of bills, one on my thigh, and that one clenches into a fist as I see Sid and Roman shake hands, an easy smile gracing Roman's face, dimple flashing in one cheek. Their contact lingers, and when Sid finally pulls away, crossing her arms again, Roman leans in close, lacing his fingers together over one knee.

"Second thoughts?" Nicolas asks, sitting opposite me, but I don't answer him as I stare at Roman, my driver. Not personal. *For business.* Getaways, transportation to and from kill sites, occasionally filling in when a runner has to bow out.

He's here now waiting to deliver the cash to my newest mercenary. Found him on the dark web, where all the good ones are, and I've got a job for him if this goes well. He's already delivered valuable information to me on the 6. Almost too good to be true, and sometimes I wonder if it's someone on the inside. Then again, that's exactly what I need.

But if Roman keeps looking at my sister like that, I'll have to find a new fucking driver.

I see Nicolas twist around on the couch, looking over his shoulder and watching as Sid laughs at whatever the fuck Roman is saying.

"Ah," Nicolas says, his voice low, "I see." He blows out a breath, twists back around, but I'm still staring dead ahead as Roman's knee knocks against Sid's.

*I'm going to fucking kill him.*

"I told him she was off limits. He just likes to talk, let it go." Nicolas slides the cash from under my hand and I straighten, pressing my palm flat against my thigh.

It's my left hand, and it's starting to tremble.

The marijuana is wearing off, and my vape is in the car. I hadn't planned to be here long. I own a few clubs, and I enjoy the scene every now and then, but I thought I'd show up for Nicolas, deal with the piece of shit dealer, then take Sid home. Still, with the thud of the bass booming from the door of the back room—*Fuck You* by Yo Gotti—and the green and blue lights edging under the crack of the door, I'd almost wondered if Sid and I could enjoy the night out.

I wouldn't mind her fine ass dancing on my lap.

But now I think I'll have to call in a cleanup crew to get Roman's blood out of my furniture.

I stand, Nicolas too, wrapping a rubber band around the

bills and tossing it in the black bag on the couch. He shifts a step to the side, trying to block my view of Roman and my sister, but I'm taller than he is, so that's not really going to work.

I glance at the door, see my bouncer with his eyes on them, too.

Everyone knows my girl is *off fucking limits.* Nicolas shouldn't have had to tell him.

But now Roman wants to fuck with me.

*I'm not really in the mood to be fucked with.*

I graze my fingers over the gun on my hip but think the better of it. Instead, I keep staring at him while I roll up my shirtsleeves, to my forearms.

I see Sid turn toward me, her gray eyes wary as she watches me with Roman—oblivious—still talking in her ear. She brushes back her bangs from her face, raises her chin, arches a brow, as if to ask me what the fuck I think I'm doing.

She knows how I am. More than anyone else in the world, she knows me. And now that I've finally got her here, *with me by choice,* she should know I'm not about to let some fuck boy with a nose ring mess that up for me.

"Come on, J," Nicolas mutters under his breath. "Take it easy."

I ignore him as Roman's hand comes to Sid's arm, and she jerks her head his way, her eyes narrowing into slits, glancing at him touching her.

*That's my girl.*

But I'm not waiting for her to open her pretty little mouth to tell him to fuck off. I step around the table and Nicolas, cross the room in a few strides, hands in my pockets.

Roman keeps fucking talking, but as I stand directly in front of him, he looks up, his fingers still around Sid's forearm, bare beneath her oversize black tank, a lime green bra visible beneath.

His charcoal eyes, a shade darker than hers, are wide with

surprise, but he still doesn't move his damn hand. He usually picks up the supply around back of the club, and he came recommended to me through a guy that works under Nicolas. I know, rationally, he doesn't know me very well.

But when it comes to Sid Rain, I've never really been *rational.*

"How's it going, Roman?" I ask him politely.

He blinks up at me, as if he's startled.

I run down his facts in my mind. A year younger than me, he's twenty-three, worked up a little name for himself at the dragstrip in high school, been dealing pot since he was in middle school, and he doesn't have a rap sheet. Not yet.

He smiles, dimples flashing in his smooth, boyish face. "Good, Rain," he says, glancing at Sid. "I was just talking to *Sid*," he says her name in a way that makes me want to sew his lips together, "and she was saying the club is only open tonight for the party?" His smile widens. "Mind if I deliver that cash a little later?" He looks back at Sid, sidling closer.

Their thighs are touching.

Sid is trying to pull her arm from his grip but he's not fucking paying attention as he turns back to me. "I'm sure Lazarus won't mind."

*Lazarus.* My new employee's code name. *Absurd.*

"You think he won't?" I question.

Roman shrugs. "I think it's a *she,* but no, five grand now, five grand later, it's all the same, right?" He laughs, and just as he turns to Sid, finally realizing she doesn't want him to touch her as his grip loosens enough for her to pull away, I shoot my hand out, drag him up by his throat, and shove him against the wall adjacent the couch.

His head collides with the brick, his hands coming to mine around his throat as his eyes water.

"What the fuck, man, I was just—"

With my left hand, I reach for that metal hoop in his nose

and see his eyes widen, his breath leaving him in a rush, his words lost.

Aside from the music from the dance floor beyond the closed door, it's so quiet it seems like no one is even breathing in here.

"Did Nicolas tell you about her?" I ask him, cocking my head as his dirty nails scratch at my hand.

I tug on the nose ring in a warning. I'd hate to cut off all of his fucking fingers for touching me like that. It might ruin his driving career for good.

He stills but doesn't drop his hands. His eyes dart past me, to Sid, and I hear her boots echoing on the concrete floor.

"Jeremiah," she whispers quietly, but I ignore her, give this fuck's ring another tug.

"A-about Sid?" he asks, and I pull harder, hating him saying her fucking name. I feel his throat bob beneath my hand as he swallows. "H-he just said she was your s-sister and—"

I knock his head against the wall again, and he cries out, panicking now as his nostrils flare, his eyes going to my fingers around that disgusting piercing, sweat beading along his temple.

"You think you should touch my sister?" I ask him quietly, arching a brow.

Tears well up in his eyes and I feel him trembling beneath my hand. Pathetic.

"No, no, I just…me and my girl just broke up and I just thought I'd try to—"

I yank hard on his piercing, twisting it as I do, ripping through his skin, dragging the metal all the way to the end of his nose. Blood gushes everywhere as I release him, the metal hoop between my fingers as he screams, sinking to the floor, his hands over his nose.

I turn to look at Sid, see her complexion turn a strange gray color as she looks at Roman on the floor, still howling, then my fingers, circled around his hoop, blood dripping down my wrist.

She has her hands in fists by her sides, and she shakes her head. "Jeremiah, you didn't have to do that," she says so quietly, I can barely hear her over Roman's howls.

In the distance, Nicolas is zipping up the black bag, pretending not to pay any fucking attention.

I shrug. "Would you like to kiss him better?" Closing the space between us, I drop the ring, circle my fingers around her slender wrist as I drag her flush to me, his blood against her skin. I bow my head, thread my fingers through her hair and grip the back of her skull. "Wanna practice being a mommy with him now, baby?"

"Fuck off, Jeremiah." She tries to jerk away but I grip her tighter, pressing so hard against the bones in her wrists I feel them rub together.

"Should've told him that when he came to sit beside you, sis." I brush my lips along her cheek, to her ear, bite the tip of it gently, enough that she stiffens against me, one hand pressed against my chest. "You know I don't like when people touch you. People that *aren't me.*"

Roman is still sniffling at my back, but I ignore him as I run my bottom lip over Sid's ear, feel her shiver even as she tries to back away from me. I don't let her go.

The idea of someone touching her, hurting her, of anyone besides me *having her*, fucking *eats at me.* I let her go for too long. Long enough for him to knock her up. *Marry her. Hurt. Her.*

I can't let that happen again.

The past two decades have proven over and over again how *she belongs to me.* And I can't imagine spending my life with *anyone else.* When I'm with her, my nightmares are quieter. I have a reason to breathe.

Someone taking that from me?

I'd do more than rip out a fucking piercing.

I bite my lip, my cheek still against hers, my mouth over

her ear as I try to tamp down on the warmth coursing through me with her nearness. With hurting someone, *for her.* I'd do it again and again. All of her nightmares, I'd fucking silence them.

"We're going to go enjoy Nicolas's birthday, sis. But if you let someone that close to you again…" I trail off, pressing her closer to me, hand still in her hair, fingers wrapped around her wrist, hoping to Satan the tremor doesn't start. "I'll rip their fucking eyes out."

# CHAPTER Five

## SID

THE LIGHTS from the club are overwhelming, flashes of blue and green that make my head spin, my anxiety spike. The music is loud, ROCKSTAR pounding a rhythm in my temples.

But I'm not so sure it's any of that shit that's making me feel so edgy.

Instead, I think it's the fact that despite what he did to poor Roman in the back room of the club, Jeremiah seems perfectly content right now. In the worst way. I see a woman perched on his lap, her arms wrapped around his neck as she laughs at something he says, nuzzling her face against his chest in the giant circular booth we're in, at the end of it, lots of space thankfully between us.

My throat feels like it's closing up as I watch them, and I bring the bottle of water to my lips, wishing I could drink something stronger. Wishing, not for the first time, I wasn't pregnant.

I'd had an appointment. An abortion scheduled. I was going to be done with it, after I ran from Noctem. Straight into the arms of another man who wants to eat me alive.

But the day of the appointment, I woke up in a cold sweat,

imagining how my husband would feel. Thinking of his heart breaking.

No matter what he did to me...I can't do that to him.

Jeremiah's eyes are locked on mine as he tips his beer up to his lips, the woman's hands pawing at his gray dress shirt, the sleeves rolled up, showing off his corded muscle.

The scars on his wrist.

*Scars for me.*

But it's not me in his lap. It's a dancer at the club, a very pretty woman with tan skin, a lithe body, and long black hair. She's wearing a silver dress, her tits nearly spilling out of it, the hem of it hiked up to just under her round ass, where Jeremiah's hand is resting against her.

I kind of want to kill her.

"Hey," a voice says from my left, the booth seat shifting as I turn my head to meet Ria's golden gaze while she settles in beside me, "you okay?"

I force myself not to look back again at Jeremiah.

I know what he's doing.

He's treated me like gold since I've been back with him, in his hideaway on the outskirts of Alexandria. Similar to gold mixed with psycho like he was with Roman, but that's Jeremiah.

He's been nice, for him. Nicer than I've ever known him to be.

Nicer even than my husband. Then again, my husband is an asshole.

I don't know if Lucifer knows I'm here, but if so, as far as I know, he hasn't come by. Hasn't tried to call or contact me.

I hope he's getting help.

Thinking of it, I run my hand absentmindedly over the scar above my brow. So small, Jeremiah didn't notice it until the third night I was here, and he was closer to me than he should've been.

He'd asked how I'd gotten it.

I'd lied.

Just like I do to Ria, now. "Yeah," I tell her, speaking up over the music, forcing a smile I don't feel as I glance around the club. "Are you enjoying yourself?"

The place isn't packed, but the DJ has an audience on the dance floor, and about half of the private booths are filled, too, for Nicolas's birthday. I haven't seen him since Jeremiah snapped his fingers and had his bouncer deal with Roman, still sobbing on the floor.

Ria runs her hand through her curly brown hair, tucking a lock behind her ear. She's dressed in a white, cut-off tee that shows off the flat planes of her stomach, her brown skin contrasting beautifully with the white shirt. She's got on distressed jeans, burgundy booties. She looks good, and I feel like a blimp next to her.

I haven't been sleeping well either and I know I look tired.

With the person I know I saw in the woods—but no one else seems to fucking believe existed—I won't sleep well tonight either, which is why I don't mind being out so late. It's either stay here or toss and turn in bed like I did before I ran.

I don't know if it's the pregnancy that's kept me up, or the fear.

Sometimes I dream about Lucifer.

Sometimes I don't.

I'm not sure which is worse.

I run a hand through my greasy, brown hair, down to my shoulders now. I had my bangs cut, blunt across my forehead, just above my eyes. I haven't gained much weight according to the scale, but according to my bra size—I had to order a few online since I got here—I've gained quite a bit.

It's why I'm in a tank a few sizes too big over black leggings. Actually, no, that's part of my regular attire.

Still. The leggings are tight, and the shirt is straining against my new boobs.

Lucifer had been in love with that.

But he'd been in love with a lot of things that weren't really me.

*I STEP OUT OF THE BATHROOM, STEAM WAFTING FROM THE shower at my back. Pammie's blood went down that drain, and with it, all the ways Maverick and I hurt her.* Killed her.

*I wonder if I should feel some type of remorse.*

*I don't.*

*I can only hope that's how my husband feels when he thinks of what he did to his father.*

*I can't hear the music up here, and as I towel dry my hair, standing in front of the floor length mirror, checking for any flecks of blood, I'm glad. I'm exhausted, and I'd rather believe it's because I'm pregnant and not because I don't sleep at night, thanks to the nightmares that have come back. But I know better.*

*Then there's the fighting.*

*We're always fighting.*

*I drop the towel on our bed behind me, wonder where my husband is. Last I saw him, Ezra was dragging him away from the kitchen, from another shot of vodka, and I let him go, because me and Maverick had to take care of his tormenter.*

*Now, though, I wish I knew where he was.*

*My eyes are heavy with sleep as I pull on one of his black T-shirts and a pair of shorts from the dresser. I rake my fingers through my wet hair and glance toward the door of our suite here.*

*Still closed, and I don't hear anyone coming.*

*Sighing, I grab the fluffy white towel from the bed, hang it up in the bathroom, then brush my teeth, checking for any lingering blood on my face or neck. The black bandana is in the hamper with the rest of my clothes. Eventually, of course, I'll tell him. But maybe when he's sober, which I know won't be tonight.*

*I rinse out the toothpaste, flip off the bathroom light and head to the bed, pulling back the soft white sheets and climbing under the covers, closing my eyes in the dark as I lie on my back, thinking of my husband.*

*Of Maverick's rage on his behalf.*

*Mine, too. Listening to Pammie take her last breath. Choking on her own blood, before I wrapped that bandana around her throat.*

*A smile curves my lips, and a disturbing thought bursts through my brain.*

*I'm not much different than Jeremiah.*

*None of us are any different, taking pleasure in another's pain.*

*Not for the first time, I feel a stab of my own pain at missing him.*

*I roll over on my side and try to push it from my mind. If it makes my husband happy, I'll let it go for now. Eventually, when our emotions have cooled, I can bring it up again, and maybe then he'll understand. Maybe, if we're living in a fucking alternate dimension, Lucifer will even want a relationship with his half-brother.*

*Or maybe that's just asking for too fucking much.*

*I scoff into my pillow, hands slipped beneath it as I try to get comfortable. It's cold in here, and I love it, but damn, I want the warmth of my husband.*

*After a while, I drift off to sleep, only to be awakened by the sound of a door slamming shut.*

*I sit bolt upright, gasping, making to grab for the knife on my nightstand.*

*"What the fuck, Sid?" Lucifer's raspy voice settles my nerves, but the tone…he's angry. Fucking pissed.*

What the hell?

*"What's wrong, babe?" I ask him quietly as he walks into the bath-room, takes a piss, then flicks on the light. I blink as I turn my head to him, see his blue eyes narrowed on mine. His arms are folded across his chest, and he looks as angry as he sounds.*

*My heart thunders in my chest as I clench the sheets in my fists, fore-boding making me feel sick. Not another fight.*

*Not right now.*

*It's like one in the morning.*

*I want to sleep. I want to sleep with him.*

*"Where were you?" he growls at me.*

*I frown up at him, running a hand through my still-damp hair.*
*"What are you—"*

*"Where the fuck were you, Lilith?" his voice is a snarl as he steps closer to the bed, the light in the bathroom framing his silky black curls. His face is pale, circles beneath his red-rimmed eyes.*

*I wish he'd climb into bed.*

*I wish he would save this fight for the morning.*

*I sigh, knocking my head back against the headboard and closing my eyes. Someone told him. Of course, someone told him because the Unsaints are the fucking brotherhood from hell.*

*I know Mayhem didn't. He promised he'd give me until at least Sanctum to tell him myself.*

*Fuck.*

*"She deserved to die," I say, exhaustion evident in my every word. Maybe he'll hear that and let me sleep. "We both know she did."*

*"That wasn't your call."*

*I pick my head up and turn to lock my eyes on his. "Oh yeah? You wanted her to suck your dick again, baby?"*

*His eyes widen, his arms falling by his sides, the blue veins straining against his pale skin. "What the fuck did you just—"*

*"I mean," I shrug, throwing up my hands, pissed off right along with him now, "that's the only thing I can figure from this." I gesture toward him. "You must miss her mouth on your cock, is that it? I'm not doing enough for you? Want mommy back in your bed?" I fling my covers, my feet hitting the floor, my back to my husband. So much for getting some sleep tonight. "Get the fuck over yourself," I mutter under my breath, crossing the room to the balcony.*

*Before I can pull back the floor-length curtains, a hand is on the back of my neck, jerking me around and shoving me against the wall. Lucifer is in my face, his fingers curled around my throat.*

*"You know what I wanted tonight, baby girl?" he asks me, his voice low. I smell the vodka on his breath and a sense of unease crawls down my spine.*

*My hands are by my sides, and I don't feel like fighting him. Not tonight.*

"What, Lucifer?" I ask, trying to keep my tone even.

He dips his head and runs his mouth over mine. My own lips part for him, but he pulls back, smirking at me. "Not you," he tells me, flicking his eyes up and down my body. "I didn't want you."

My heart twists with those words, and I dig my nails into my palms.

"Guess since I'm not related to you, you didn't want—"

He lets go of my neck, steps closer to crowd me against the wall, where he plants his forearm beside my head, his other hand pressing against my sternum.

I can hardly breath with that pressure, but I like it. It keeps me together. Stops me from falling apart.

"You're one to fucking talk." He shakes his head and my face heats. "Fucking my best friend? Your fucking brother? You got an incest fetish, baby girl? Wanna roleplay with me as your foster dad, huh?" His eyes rake over my body before meeting my gaze again. "You been a bad little girl, Sid? Need daddy to punish you?" He presses harder against my chest. "Need me to fuck you up, baby girl?"

There's venom in those words.

I swallow, hard, wanting to get back into bed. I'm not even angry anymore. We've fought this fight before. He obviously isn't over me fucking Maverick, but I can't take it back and neither can he.

"Nah, beautiful, the reason I didn't want you is because there was someone so much fucking better in Ezra's bed. A hot blond with a fat ass and big tits." He bites his lip, looking down at my own chest, covered by his T-shirt that's far too big on me.

My face flames with his words, my chin quivering. I don't have big tits and we both know it. I never knew it bothered him.

I didn't think he cared about that. I thought he loved me...

"Kinda reminded me of Ophelia's. Or Julie's, when she was pregnant." He groans, even as he steps closer to me, the bulge in his pants against my low belly. Where I'm carrying his fucking baby. "God, her tits were so swollen, I couldn't fucking get enough of her in my mouth. And when she squeezed them around my dick—"

My hand comes up fast, and I slap him as hard as I can, the sound seeming to echo in the quiet room. His head spins, his jaw clenched.

*He doesn't move his forearm from the wall or his hand from my chest. But he turns slowly back to me, a scowl on his face. His lip curls up into a snarl, and he says, "You can hit me all you want, Lilith. Doesn't change the fact that tonight my dick was hard for a girl that wasn't you."*

*"Get the fuck off of me." I shove him, but he doesn't move. "Get the fuck off of me now, Lucifer. Get the fuck out of my face!" I'm screaming the words, pushing at his chest. He clamps a hand over my mouth, spinning me around and dragging me backward, until he comes down on the bed, lying on his back, me on top of him, my back to his chest.*

*I squirm in his grip, but he moves his hand from my mouth and bands his arms around me.*

*I keep kicking and clawing at his arms, his chin on my head as he whispers, "Shh, stop fighting me, baby girl."*

*My throat tightens, pressure building behind my eyes. But I'm so, so tired, and if I was strong enough to say it out loud, I'd just ask that he hold me, so we can sleep. So we can pretend tonight never happened. That none of the bad shit ever happened, and that we were whole and perfect for each other.*

*"Why do you do this?" I ask him instead, my words coming out broken. I hate that, too. This weakness I have with him. I'm not used to people seeing me weak, but it seems like all he wants to do is break me down. "Why do you act like you hate me?" I whisper in the dark, trying to hold back my tears as he holds me. "Did you...did you cheat on me?"*

*For a long moment, he doesn't speak, and I take a shuddering breath in, my chest heaving as I try to hold back my sobs.*

*But then he flips us over, pushing me back flat on the bed, propped up on his elbow as his warm, lean body comes over mine, his hand on my cheek.*

*"Open your eyes, baby girl," he whispers, stroking his thumb over my mouth.*

*Slowly, I do as he asks, feeling unshed tears pooling in the rim of my eyes.*

*He shakes his head. "I didn't," he tells me. "I didn't cheat."*

*I feel something like relief with his words, my hands fisted in my shirt as I bite my bottom lip, his thumb brushing over my teeth, too.*

*Then his hand slides down my throat, over my chest, to my low belly, his fingers splayed wide. Protective.*

*"I'm so sorry," he says, like he means it, and a tear falls down my face, warm and hot. Uncomfortable. He grips my tummy tighter, angling his head as he stares at me. "I'm so fucking sorry, I just…with you, I just feel like I'm going crazy every second you're not with me."*

*He dips his head down, presses his lips to my brow and holds them there for a long moment. Then he exhales a warm breath, pulls back to look me in the eyes again, his fingers still splayed over my belly, beneath the shirt I'm wearing, his thumb just under my shorts.*

*"I didn't mean what I said," he tells me quietly. "I fucking…I fucking love everything about you." He bows his head again, and his mouth drops over my nipple, his teeth closing around it over my shirt.*

*I gasp, my back arching with his touch.*

*We know how to love each other this way, even if we fail at every other way.*

*My hands find his back, and he groans against me, picking his head up after he tugs my nipple with his teeth.*

*"You drive me crazy, baby girl," he whispers, leaning down and opening his mouth over mine. Our kiss is wet, raw,* passionate. *"I just want you all to myself." He slips his hand down my shorts, runs his middle finger down the length of me, then curls two fingers inside of me.*

*I tighten around him, my nails digging into his back as I stare up at him, his warm breath against my mouth.*

*"I want you to always be mine, because no matter what shit you throw my way, Lilith, I'm always gonna be yours. Even when you hate me."*

RIA SIGHS, REACHING FOR THE DRINK THE WAITRESS SET ON our table. She finishes the rum and diet and I feel a stab of annoyance that I can't have the same.

I hope it's not a sign that I'll be a horrible mother already, that I don't feel any attachment to the life growing inside me.

Because I don't.

If it wouldn't kill my husband, I'd end it, even now.

"More or less," Ria says, glancing around the club, and I almost forget that I asked her if she was enjoying herself.

I force back the memories of my time with Lucifer, follow her gaze around the room. There're a lot of women in short dresses, men in tailored pants and shirts, expensive watches. Guards with guns.

This isn't the usual Saturday night crowd. This is for Order of Rain.

"I'd enjoy myself more if I could go home, but we both know that's not going to happen." She laughs, but it's forced. No humor in it.

She was supposed to graduate this spring, a history major. She's the reason I even know about my past. What happened to me and Jeremiah. How we were used. But that's also the reason she's on the shit-list for the 6. The reason she ran from Maverick's basement when Ella accidentally let her out.

She went home.

Told her parents she'd been away, studying abroad. She had a few weeks looking over her shoulder, paranoia shadowing her every move.

Then they came for her.

The same fucking night they came for me.

She told me it'd been much the same as it had for me. Ripped away from our own homes. Used as bait for the boys.

Thinking about the whispered threats sends a chill down my spine. I was already planning to run.

I couldn't stay in that house another day, not after all of the fights, and the screaming and the women and fucking coke.

I brush my thumb over my scar again, above my brow, then drop my hand, not wanting to draw any more attention to it.

I force those memories away. I'm good at it. And since I'm

stuck in limbo here, afraid to move forward, backward, *anywhere*, there's no fucking use thinking about any of this.

"Has Nicolas said anything?" I ask Ria quietly, aware that even with the music and all the noise, most of the people here can't be trusted completely.

In fact, I don't trust *anyone* in here completely.

Lucifer destroyed that for me.

Actually, they both did.

Ria shakes her head, looking down at the glass in her hands, her bronze rings tapping against it. "No." Her brows pull together, a grief I can understand darkening her eyes. "We both know if I leave here unprotected, they'll come for me." She looks up at me through her lashes. "And Maverick…"

My mouth goes dry as she trails off. I want to reach for Ria, place my hand on her knee or something, but I'm not good at that. Comfort.

I'm good at fighting. Destroying shit. Breaking my husband's heart.

I have no business trying to be a good friend.

But I know what she's thinking. *Maverick is with Ella.* He chose her, in that cave at Noctem, right before I shot Maddox Astor.

I wonder if he's dead.

I haven't asked Jeremiah, not wanting to talk about it.

I hope he is.

I might not deserve much, but my brother, my *real* brother, deserved much more than having him as a fucking father.

"We'll figure it out," I lie to Ria. I chew on my lip, circle my fingers around the plastic bottle until it flexes in my hand. "Maybe Nicolas could—"

"I don't want to be with someone because I'm forced to," Ria says, her words sharp as she glares at me. "I know that you didn't have a much better life before any of this shit," she gestures around the club with one hand, and the words sting, but there's nothing but truth in them, "but *I did.*" She drops her hand, closing her eyes a second. "My family loves me," she whispers, almost to herself. Almost as a reminder.

I wish I knew what that felt like.

"And I want to get back to them." Her golden eyes meet mine again and I nod, not knowing what to say, but understanding her all the same. I don't have a family to go back to. The only *family* I have is a man who wants me dead, sold me into a pedophile ring, and my half-brother who might have agreed with my decision to leave Lucifer but probably wants to kill me now that it's been nearly a month and I haven't come back.

In my defense, I don't know if things are different.

I don't know if they ever could be. Lucifer's demons could eat him alive. It seemed the more he was around me, the bigger they grew. Like he couldn't take care of himself because he was so busy watching out for me.

I wanted him to be able to breathe.

To heal, without trying to heal me too.

And that scar over my brow…I resist the urge to touch it again.

Ria shakes her head, swallowing, clasping her hands around her empty glass again, just melted ice inside. "Anyway, I know you're going through your own shit," she says on an exhale. Her gaze slides past me and just as I go to tell her I'd much rather deal with her shit than have to look at my own, she adds, "Satan is watching you."

A small smile pulls at my lips at the nickname. I always thought Lucifer was the demon, personally. But I guess it's just a matter of perspective. "I know," I tell her without looking at Jeremiah behind me. I have no doubt the dancer is still in his lap.

He's not even a man whore, so I don't know why he bothers pretending to be. He's been with a lot of women, but he hates people in general. Having them sit in his lap, flirt with him?

I know what he's trying to do.

And sometimes…it almost works.

"You wanna go stop him before this chick fucks him right here in front of everyone?" Ria asks me, looking back at me, her face flushing red with whatever is happening at my back.

I shrug, even as my spine stiffens, my blood warming. "Nope," I tell her, popping the p. I didn't come here to cheat on my husband.

I came here because Jeremiah can protect me. Because he's…security.

And I needed that. Even from Lucifer himself.

But I won't break his heart by involving myself any other way with Jeremiah. I can't. He would never forgive me, and until I know there's no way to fix what's broken between us, I'm not going to even think about crossing that line.

Ria laughs, but it has a nervous edge. "Looks like you won't have to," she murmurs under her breath, so quiet I can barely hear her. Her eyes go up, tracking someone behind me, and I feel his presence the moment before she starts to slide out of the booth, bringing her glass with her and says, "Excuse me." She hesitates, then adds, "Maybe when we're done here in hell, we can head back and get in the hot tub?" She arches a brow but doesn't wait for my reply before she walks off.

*Fuck.*

Jeremiah's hand comes to my shoulder, his fingers digging into my shirt as the seat of the booth shifts behind me. "Having fun?" he asks at my back, his voice low.

I inhale, breathe in his clean scent.

"Loads of it," I tell him, rolling my eyes, unseen by him. I'm still angled away from him, my fingers squeezing the cold water bottle, feeling the condensation against my skin. I set the bottle between my thighs, feel the chill through my leggings and try to hold onto that. To calm the warmth under my skin with Jeremiah's nearness.

"Why won't you look at me, baby?" he whispers, and his mouth is just over my ear, drowning out the noise of the club.

I stiffen, bite my tongue and squeeze my eyes shut a second.

*Because I'm worried if I do, I'll melt for you. Give in to you.*

But before I can say or do anything, his hand leaves my shoulder and comes to my chin, fingers splayed against my jaw as he turns my head toward him, pulling me back against his chest as he does.

I grit my teeth, crinkling the plastic beneath my fingers again as I stare up into his eyes, his dark brow arched as he looks down at me.

His left hand is in the pocket of his tailored black pants, and I wonder at the scars on his arm.

But I don't let myself think about it.

If I do, if I think of all the ways he's hurt because of me... it'll make it that much harder to remember all the ways I could hurt my husband if I cave.

He presses his thumb into my bottom lip, tugging it down as the corners of his full lips pull up into a soft smile. "You okay, baby?"

I swallow hard. When he calls me that, *baby*, it's a little hard to breathe. "Yeah," I lie, my mouth moving beneath his thumb. I think of the knife shredding through my shirt last night. Jeremiah's strange, sick sense of humor.

How much it doesn't bother me, even though I know it should.

He brushes his thumb across my lip, slides even closer so I'm pressed flush against him. I see the muscles of his shoulders shifting beneath his dress shirt. I've seen him shirtless so many times lately, in our training in the mornings, I should be immune to how fit he is.

*I'm not.*

He angles his head, his eyes dipping down to my mouth. "You lying, baby?"

I take a deep breath, my heart flying in my chest. "Nope."

He narrows his eyes, still staring at my mouth. "I saw you watching me," he says softly, his lips brushing mine as he keeps his eyes on my mouth, his long, dark lashes making me envious.

"I wasn't," I protest, narrowing my eyes as his finally meet mine again. "I don't care what you fucking do—"

His grip on my face tightens, his thumb pulling down my lower lip. "Watch that mouth, Sid."

I blink at him. "Are you fucking kidding—"

He groans, pulling his hand from his pocket and winds it in my hair, tilting my head back, my neck arched upward as I'm forced all the way against him. He presses a soft kiss to the hollow of my throat, his mouth open as he does. I can smell the alcohol on his breath, and my eyes flutter closed as I dig my nails into my leggings.

I know I should tell him to fuck off.

Move.

Cause a scene.

But his tongue runs along my throat, up toward my jaw, and I can't breathe, let alone fucking move.

"I'm trying to wait for you," he whispers against my ear, the hairs on the back of my neck standing on end as he slips his thumb into my mouth. It takes *effort* not to suck on him, but I don't do it. "But you keep fucking tempting me. And if you keep talking to me like that, I won't be able to stop myself, baby."

He presses an open-mouthed kiss to that sensitive spot just under my ear, then releases me, pulling back and sliding his hands into his pockets.

I dip my chin as I twist around to face him, try not to feel where his full lips lingered. "Stop yourself from *what?*" I slam my water bottle on the table where I leave it before I slide out of the booth on the opposite end, standing. He does the same, the dancer nowhere to be seen as we confront each other.

He's over six feet tall and I'm not even five fucking four, but I'd rather face him on my feet than on my ass. "Force me? Don't you think you've done enough of that?"

Hurt flashes in his eyes, and it stuns me. I expected him to snap back. Maybe even slap me. Fighting is what we do best.

But hurt? Pain?

All the fight seems to leave me, and my shoulders sag as I bow my head, taking a deep breath. "I'm going to see if someone can give us a ride back—"

He steps closer, brings a hand to my face again, but his touch is light. Soft. "Please don't," he whispers, his other hand coming up too as he cups my cheeks, brushing his thumbs over my lips. "I'm sorry, Sid, I just…" I watch his throat bob as he swallows, averts his gorgeous eyes for half a second before he's looking at me again. "It's hard," he admits. "It's hard being so close to you…but…"

*But not being able to have me.*

He doesn't need to finish that sentence. I know what that's like. It's how I felt throughout my entire marriage to Lucifer, as short as it's been. He was unreachable.

He became someone I couldn't talk to.

Couldn't even *breathe* around.

It's not quite the same, what's happening between Jeremiah and I, but I know what it's like to feel alone even when you're touching someone else. It's like holding a ghost.

My heart hurts for him.

I bring a hand to his chest and his face softens with that touch.

"I know," I whisper, stepping closer, forgetting the noise. The people here. The music. For a moment, it's just me and him. His hands slide down to the sides of my throat, just holding me gently. "Thank you for…trying."

With those words, I drop my hand from his chest and after a moment, his eyes searching mine, he lets me go too.

He looks down. "I'll take you back."

I open my mouth to object, wanting to be alone, away from him, but he adds, "I'm closing this place down. It's nearly three," before I can say anything else.

THE DRIVE HOME IN HIS MERCEDES IS SILENT, RIA AND Nicolas following behind us. Jeremiah glances my way a few times, but I drift off into an uneasy sleep until we arrive home and he carries me up the stairs and starts to pull my shirt over my head as he sets me on the bed, his fingers brushing my sides.

I lean away from him and his jaw clenches, his grip tight for a second, but then he lets go, stepping back.

"I've got it," I tell him quietly.

He stares at me a long, long moment, and for a second, I worry he won't leave.

But then he nods, walks out, shutting my door softly behind him.

After I grab the phone he bought me from my nightstand, I roll over in bed, exhausted. Only the soft glow of the night-light on.

I send Ria a text, tell her I'm too tired for the hot tub. A second later, before I slide my phone under the pillow next to me, she responds.

**Ria: Don't let him suck the life from you. He doesn't deserve you.**

I wish I believed that, but as I set my phone down and roll onto my back, staring at the fan whirring high overhead in the dark, I think we might deserve *each other*.

I close my eyes, and don't sleep. But I think about *him*, and it's almost like dreaming.

# CHAPTER Six

## LUCIFER

*"YOU WANT TO FUCK HIM, again, is that it? You didn't get enough the first time he put a fucking belt around your throat?" I grab her arm, yanking her away from the door she just walked in through.*

*It's still dark out, and she smells like him. Like fucking marijuana and leather and all the things she should never smell like again because... She's. Fucking. Mine.*

*She puts her palms out, flat against my bare chest, and even though I'm fucking pissed and sometimes I think I really do hate her, her touch is electric. It ignites something in me, and I have to hold onto it. The anger. If I didn't, I'd let her walk all over me.*

*I already have.*

*Not anymore.*

*Not after I just caught her in the middle of the fucking night walking back from Maverick's house.*

*"Huh? Fucking answer me, Lilith."*

*She grits her teeth, her silver eyes full of hurt and anger and... exhaustion. She hasn't been sleeping well. She's barely sleeping at all. And even though she's carrying my baby, she's so...frail.*

*She needs to take better care of herself.*

I need to take better care of her.

*"What the fuck were you doing over there?" I ask her, getting in her*

*face. She concedes a step, her back against the door. "You fucking* smell like him. *It's disgusting."*

*I can't stand it.*

*I just can't fucking stand thinking of her with someone else. Ever since that night she was dressed as Lilith for Halloween and I met her at that intersection, she's been just that to me. My other fucking half. I wish she felt the same about me. It's why I was with that girl at Liber on New Year's Eve. I never really would have touched her. And even when Mav had Ella over, her in his lap, her thighs spread, her pussy there, so close to me I could fucking smell her...even then, I would have never done it.*

*I would never cheat on my wife.*

*But I'd tell her all about the times I almost did, because she seems to forget. While she pushes me away, confides in everyone but me, looks at me like she's scared of me or some shit, she forgets other women want me.*

*They fucking adore me.*

*I would never hurt her by having a goddamn affair, but I just want her to notice me.* Love me *like I love her.*

*I put one hand on her chest, keeping her flat against the door. My other is still wrapped around her arm, and she's taking shallow breaths, her breasts rising and falling rapidly beneath my palm. I can feel her pulse under my fingers, flying like she's terrified.*

*Or pissed.*

*"Lucifer," she says, her voice low, that one word—my goddamn name—on her tongue, and I start to deflate. I feel like I'm coming undone when she speaks my name. I feel like I'm losing my mind most of the time around her, being with someone who doesn't really want to be with me. But when she says my name...everything is just so much...*better*. I force myself to loosen my grip on her arm and she takes the first deep breath she's taken since she walked in here. Her silver eyes search mine beneath her long lashes. Goddamn, she's fucking beautiful.*

*"Are you high right now?" she asks me, and the expression on her face...it fucking hurts.*

*It hurts, and it breaks me.*

*I swallow hard, thinking about the line I bumped before I came downstairs looking for her. If she was up, I was going to be up. If she needed me, I'd be there.*

*I didn't expect her to be fucking gone.*

*I look down between us, her in her combat boots, me in black socks. I'd been about to put on my shoes and go looking for her. If I'd seen her actually in his house, I'd probably have killed him.*

*I take a breath.*

*I feel my own pulse racing, from anger, from hurt, from...fucking blow.*

*Her hands are still against my chest, and she slides them around my ribs, to my back, bringing me closer to her small body.*

*I look into her eyes again as I let go of her arm, moving my own hand from her chest and pulling her close to me in an embrace.*

*She seems to deflate against me. Like she knows I'll always hold her up. I'll always be what she needs me to be, even if I do it all...wrong.*

*"I'm worried for you," she says, her words vibrating against my bare chest. "I love you, you know that? I love you, and I'm scared for you."*

*My heart cracks in two with those words as I slide one hand up her back, to her hair, threading my fingers through the soft strands.*

*My chin is on her head as I speak. "I love you so fucking much. I'm terrified to lose you. I'm scared someone is going to take you from me."*

*She doesn't say anything. She just holds me tighter.*

*"I'm scared you're going to leave." I can barely breathe with that admission, especially as she doesn't say a word. She's the only good thing I've ever had in my life. The only thing that makes it all...bearable. "I'm so scared you're going to run again."*

*She keeps clinging to me.*

*But she doesn't say a word.*

*As if she's going to do exactly that.*

*Run.*


IN THE PASSENGER SEAT OF MAV'S CAR, I INHALE FROM MY cigarette, watching the cherry glow bright in the darkness of the night, made ever darker by his illegally tinted windows.

Pinching the butt between my thumb and forefinger, I toss it out the crack in the window and hear Maverick scoff.

Turning my head and exhaling through my nose, I arch a brow in a silent question as he stares at me.

I try to let it go. The anger I feel when I look at him. What he did to me. *To us.*

He's got one hand on the wheel of the Audi—far less conspicuous than the McLaren—and one on the gearshift, even though we've been parked outside of this fucking house for an hour now.

Probably aren't going anywhere for at least another hour.

"You shouldn't leave your DNA everywhere," he mutters, jerking his head to the window I just tossed the cigarette out of. "And you shouldn't smoke in my car."

I just stare at him a second, his light blue eyes eerily bright even in the darkness. Then I lift my hips and reach behind me, pulling something out of the back pocket of my black jeans.

Settling down in the seat again and waving the little baggie so he can see it, I say, "In that case, I'll just rail a line." Shrugging, I start to open up the bag, but he snatches it from my hand, tosses it into the pocket of the driver's side door without taking his eyes off of me.

A flood of anger rushes through my veins, because I really do need that shit, but before I can say anything he snarls, "Pay attention, Luce, goddammit." He grinds both hands on the wheel, tearing his eyes from me and glancing at the ranch-style brick house we're parked two doors down from at the end of a sleepy suburban cul-de-sac. "You need to get some fucking help." He doesn't look at me as he says those words, which makes my throat feel like it's closing up.

It's like he means what he's saying. A hard truth that he'd rather not really face right now.

I laugh, a hoarse sound, devoid of humor. Running my palms down my jeans, I stare at the front door of the house we're watching, too. A man with more information than he should have lives here. Hacked through a firewall he should've never been able to get into. Works for a tech company that could help spread some information he should've never seen.

Obviously, he's going to die tonight.

But the 6 need him brought in, so they can figure out who he said what to.

A quick glance at the clock on the center console, and I see it's nearly three in the morning.

After this shit, we're supposed to meet at Sanctum for Council.

I'm getting that coke back from Maverick, even if I have to break his nose to do it.

"I don't need help," I mutter, clenching my hands into fists, thinking about the scar slashed across my palm in the shape of an X. *I need her.* I don't say those last words, because he already knows. He knows, too, that the longer I spend without her, the more likely Jeremiah is to kill her, *my fucking baby,* or…worse.

*Make her his.*

But my brothers won't let me go after her. Drag her pretty little ass out of his mansion at the edge of Alexandria. I know they don't want to start a war with Order of Rain. Like it or not, he controls a lot of underground crime in this city. But more than that, they won't let me, because right now, they claim, she's better off with him. They think I'm fucking losing my mind.

I lost that a long time ago.

Still, I'm supposed to wait until Ignis. Four weeks from now, when we can't wait anymore.

That's not gonna fucking happen.

Maverick rolls his eyes and turns his head to me, but before he can speak, his phone rings through the speakers, making us both flinch.

"Fuck," he swears under his breath, answering the call from the steering wheel. I see Elijah's name on the dashboard console, and I lean my head back against the seat, turning to stare at nothing out my window.

"What's up?" Maverick asks quietly.

"Get to Sanctum," Elijah's deep voice rumbles through the car.

Maverick is already starting the engine, putting the car in drive, but he still says, "We don't have the fuck. What's going on?"

There's a pause as Maverick cruises through the quiet, sleepy street and I imagine what it would be like to have a life like this. A normal one. Free of Satanic rituals, cult secrets, and a goddamn wife that would rather fuck her foster brother than *me*.

It would be nice, I think.

It'd be really fucking nice.

I hear Elijah blow out a breath and I tense, reaching for the skeleton bandana around my neck. A nervous habit made worse when I'm in withdrawals.

"Just get here." Elijah ends the call without another word, and Maverick floors it out of this nice, normal subdivision, away from the type of life I'll never have.


PULLING THROUGH THE GATES AT SANCTUM, MY STOMACH flips. I thumb the lighter in my hand, watching the flame spark, then go out, over and over. A distraction from that cemetery behind the church. From the unmarked grave I never want to do anything to except take a fucking piss on.

Maverick double parks behind Cain's Camaro, cutting the engine and turning toward me.

I don't look at him.

Just keep fucking around with my lighter, gritting my teeth, as if grinding my molars to dust will keep everything in my head *back*.

Mav sighs and I tense, watching the light spark up.

Go out.

"You ready?" he asks quietly.

I bring my thumb over the dented ridge. Spark up. Go out.

Another loud exhale from the driver's side. "We have to go in."

I go to ignite the lighter again, but it's just a ghost of a flame. Shaking it, I try one more time.

Nothing.

I curl my fingers around it and turn to look out my window, at the expansive lawn of Sanctum, dark and brooding. No light, three in the morning is the devil's hour.

I can feel it, even now. The hairs on the back of my neck standing on end. My heart shooting out of my chest. Could be left over from the blow I did back before Mav picked me up, but I doubt it. My body has probably already burned through that.

This is dark magic I feel, on this desecrated ground.

*Memento mori.* Like the reminder of death calling.

Beckoning, really. Sometimes, I think it'd be for the best.

*Especially if I never get her back.*

Thinking of deep graves, I wonder if I should've had my father cremated. Burned to ash and buried far, far from here. I think his bones might poison Sanctum. Taint even the unholy grounds of the place that's been my sanctuary and torment for over two decades now.

I think I first learned to walk here. My father told me that. Or maybe it was Pammie.

Maybe when she was deep throating my cock and tears streamed down my face as I pretended to hate it. Tried to lose myself in burning incense and better memories.

But I didn't really have those.

There was nothing to hold onto.

Nothing until *her.*

"Luce, we have to go in—"

"Shut the fuck up." I snarl those words, just like I said them to my wife a few weeks ago. I had her backed into a corner, my fists planted against the wall on either side of her head. She was scared of me.

I liked it.

I wonder if she thinks about that now and laughs.

I wonder if he scares her, too. Does she like it? Why does she always want him at his worst, but she needs me to be on my best fucking behavior?

Was I always supposed to let her go to him?

*Why didn't Maverick let him fucking die?*

"Watch how you talk to me," Mav says, his voice low. "I know you're hurting, but we need to go to Council and find out what Elijah—"

"Why'd you do it?" I cut him off, leaning my head back against the leather seat, turning to glare at him, the lighter still in one hand, the other resting against my thigh. "Why'd you let her run to him?"

Maverick's pale blue eyes are locked on mine, and he's still got one hand on the wheel and another on the gearshift. I see the top of that one, my wife's name etched across it.

Big, bold letters.

He's got his dead brother's name inked against the side of his hand, down his wrist. *Malachi.* And his sister, Brooklin, is over his chest.

Ella's name is the biggest, on his hip, leading down into his pants.

I saw that at Noctem, right before he put his dick down my throat. I saw the letter too. From *Jeremiah*, to my fucking brother.

"I think you know the answer to that," he says slowly.

I offer him a small smile, running my thumb over my bottom lip before I drop my hand back to my thigh. My scarred hand. *Coagula.*

I almost laugh, thinking about it. About how only Sid

Rain could take something so perfectly holy and run away with it, ripping my heart out as she did. Sometimes I want to cut that fucking hand off, getting rid of any trace of her.

But I've got her scar on my thigh, too. Over my Unsaint's tattoo. There are others from the Death Oath, but I know hers.

She's got a matching one, and yet I can't help but to think with Jeremiah Rain, she might have more scars. Bruises, maybe.

I wouldn't put it past him to break her fucking bones either.

"I don't, though," I tell Mav, holding his gaze. "I don't fucking know."

I watch his tattooed throat bob as he swallows and averts his eyes to the stone cathedral ahead of us. "You could have killed her."

My mouth goes dry with those words coming from his mouth. It wasn't that bad. It wasn't like *that*. I would have never—

"You're coked out of your mind more often than not, you refuse to let her breathe, and you think that *she's* the problem?" He turns back to look at me, tightening his hand on the wheel, his jaw clenched. He's angry now. For her.

Everyone is always trying to protect her, but when *I* do the same thing, *I'm* the fucking villain.

"You two needed some space."

"I don't want space," I counter, picking my head up from the seat, twisting to glare at him, gripping the lighter so hard my palm starts to sweat. "I want her back, *now*. And I'm going to fucking get—"

He shakes his head, arching a brow. "You're not safe. This shit right here," he jerks his thumb to the door panel, where my baggie is, "you gotta cut that shit out. She didn't run because she loves him. She doesn't *want* him—"

I slam my fist on the center console and Maverick's jaw

jumps. "My wife is a fucking liar," I snarl at him, "and if you didn't know that about her, then you're not nearly as smart as I thought you were." Without another word, I throw the lighter at his window and hear it clatter against it as I undo my seatbelt and get out of the car, slamming the door closed behind me.

ELIJAH IS IN THE SANCTUARY.

I don't expect that, to see him in the front row pew, his head bowed, fingers clasped together, the 6 ring—a snake curved into the shape of the number—glinting on his dark brown finger.

I slow my steps down the red carpeted aisle, glancing around the expansive room, lit by sconces flickering in the wall. Cain, Ezra, and Atlas are seated on the opposite pew, Atlas with his head tilted back, eyes closed, skin paler than usual. Ezra is staring straight ahead, hands in the pocket of his hoodie even though it's too fucking hot outside for one, and Cain is watching me, his coal-black eyes tracking my move-ment as I hear the heavy double doors thud closed at my back after Maverick walks through.

"What?" I ask Cain, taking in the black eye he got at his last fight.

He's dressed in a gray button down, tailored to his fighter's frame, and he's got his hands in the pockets of his slacks. "Sit down."

My heart picks up speed in my chest as I hear Maverick coming up behind me. Unease races through me, and I clench my hands into fists as I get to the front of the sanctuary, my back to the pulpit as I turn to face my brothers, Elijah ignoring me, his head still bowed.

"What's wrong?" My voice comes out hoarse, nervous. I don't care. I *am* nervous. I'm thinking about her. What he could've done to her. Our baby.

Cain dips his chin, jerking his head to the space beside him, between him and Atlas, who adjusts the backwards cap on his head and sits up straighter, opening his eyes. "Sit down," Cain says again.

I glance to Maverick, level with the pew Cain is on, his eyes narrowed as he stares at him, waiting too. He, like me, is wearing a fitted, black T-shirt, and I see the muscles in his inked arms flex as he stiffens.

"Tell me what the fuck is wrong," I tell Cain, stepping closer to him.

He's got his feet flat on the floor, knees spread, taking up way too much fucking space, and he doesn't bother sitting up straighter as he says, too calmly, "Sit the fuck down and I'll tell you."

Elijah sighs, dropping his hands and looking up, his dark green eyes on mine as I freeze, halfway to the pew.

Elijah runs a hand over his burgundy button-down shirt, his muscles shifting as he does.

"Is someone gonna tell me what the fuck is happening?" I ask him, swiveling to face him fully. Cain and his seat can go fuck themselves. My blood is pounding in my head, and my patience is almost non-existence these days.

These days *without her*.

Elijah sighs, casting his eyes up to the ceiling and clenching his jaw, as if he's praying for patience. But we don't pray to anything that might be up above.

Finally, his gaze shifts back to me and he clears his throat. "We have a problem."

I tense, biting my tongue.

My blood runs cold as I turn to my brothers, who are all watching me carefully, because they already know.

Maverick is stepping closer to me, but I hold up a hand, halting him as I look back at Elijah, wondering where Callum and Adam are. Where Maddox fucking Astor is.

"I'm not fucking stupid. I figured that out." My voice

comes out shaky as I drop my hand, curling it back into a fist. "Is it her? Where is she? *What happened?*"

Elijah clenches his jaw, and I know I shouldn't speak to him like that. But I kind of no longer give a fuck what I should or shouldn't do. I spent my entire life following my father's orders, only to drive a knife through his skull. In the end, he ended up not actually being the immortal god I thought he might be.

We're all flesh and bone. We can all fucking snap, and if Elijah doesn't start talking, I'm gonna prove it to him.

"Someone got to my guard."

I frown, murderous thoughts suddenly leaving my brain as I dart a glance at Ezra. He shrugs, looking bored, and I know he probably wasn't close to his father's guard. We aren't close to our fucking families at all, guards are nothing to us. But even still, if someone got close to a Van Damme personal guard, then someone's *too close.*

I turn my gaze back to Elijah. "Who?"

Elijah shrugs, his shirt pulling tight against his muscular frame as he looks up at me, his eyes lined with red. "We don't know," he admits, clasping his hand. "It was a drive-by. I was at the governor's mansion and Cory was in the car. There are no cameras around the back of that building."

Just like there aren't cameras here.

I always told my father that was fucking stupid. Sometimes he'd hit me for that. Snarling shit about me never being able to take his place when he was gone.

*You're gone now, dick, and you're right. I'll never be like you.*

"What the fuck does this have to do with me?" I don't give a fuck about Elijah's guard, or Governor Phil, if I'm being honest. And I know Elijah has already replaced Cory, because attachments are not things the 6 *do.*

Seems I'm the only person in this fucking cathedral who gets too close to people.

Elijah narrows his eyes, but he reaches for something

beside him on the red pew. For the first time, I notice a manila envelope. He unclasps it, slides out a glossy photo the size of a sheet of paper and hands it to me.

With a sense of unease, I take it, looking down at it as my stomach twists into knots.

It's blurry, and the first thing I see are trees, dark shadows behind each gray trunk. Then I notice a smudge in one corner of the photo, like a droplet of water on the camera lens. I don't even see her for several long seconds, but then I do, and I freeze.

She's running.

Her hair is back in a ponytail, and she has a bandana around her neck, her body slanted forward, one foot off the muddy ground, black shirt clinging to her lithe frame. I see her pert nose, those full lips. The details aren't clear in the photo, but I know my wife. I have her entire body burned into my brain. Every morning we went for runs together, and she insisted we wear the fucking bandanas.

Even if we hated each other come nightfall, in the mornings, we were together.

A team. Us against the world.

I bring a shaky finger to her face, and I realize, little hairs standing on end along my body, that she's not facing the camera.

Whoever took this…she didn't know they were there.

And she's alone.

*She's alone.*

I snap my head up, dropping my hands to my side and clenching the photo in my fist, wrinkling it as I do. "Where did this come from?"

"Might wanna sit down," Cain says softly.

I ignore him, rage lighting through me.

Elijah sighs. "Found on the guard's lap."

My breath catches, blood running cold. "How would anyone working with the 6 know about *my fucking wife?*"

Elijah scoffs, scrubbing a hand over his face as he clenches his jaw and looks away, his hands clasped together on his thighs as I glare down at him, still seated. He doesn't say a word.

My blood is boiling. "How do they know about her, and who the *fuck* did this?" I haven't even told Julie about her, wanting to keep her as safe as I can. I knew one day I'd have to *out* her, but I wanted to give her secrecy. Carrying my baby, especially, I wanted to protect her from the world.

Maybe I made her feel like a prisoner instead. Add that to my many fuckups.

Elijah stands, glaring at me. "We operate in secrecy, not in solitude, Lucifer. Unfortunately, in order to *do our goddamn jobs*, we have to work with many agencies, many people. They know more than we'd like them to, but that's just how it is." He exhales through his nose, smoothing down his shirt. "Adam and Cal took one of the photographs to a lab to dust for prints and check the geography. I assume this is at…Rain's mansion. Right now, we know nothing but what I've told you."

"Where's Maddox?" I ask through clenched teeth, ignoring the mention of my fucking half-brother, balling up the glossy photograph tighter in my hand. I glance at Maverick, and he's staring at Elijah, too, waiting for a fucking answer.

My wife shot him. Her and Mav's father. She fucking shot him, and that motherfucker still lived.

*He should be dead.*

Elijah clasps his hands together. "It wasn't Maddox, Lucifer. If he knew who did this, he'd—"

"He'd what, Elijah?" I ask, tilting my head and stepping closer to the new Dominus, given that title since I killed my father, in this very room. "He'd tell us, is that what you're saying?" I taunt him, another step closer.

I hear Ezra growl my name, no doubt angry that I'm in

his father's face, but I think he should know by now I don't give a fuck about anything, much less *fathers.*

Elijah's eyes narrow. "Back up."

I don't. I grip the photo so hard my hand shakes, but I do not *back up.* I step closer, and Elijah has to look up at me, because I'm fucking taller than he is, and if he thinks I'm going to let Maddox Astor off the hook, he's delusional.

He's insane, right alongside *me.*

"No, I don't think so," I tell him, so close I catch the dark scent of his cologne. "You trust Maddox? You think he doesn't deserve to fucking *die?*"

Elijah's jaw ticks. "Maddox Astor is not your father, Lucifer," he says, his voice strained, like he's trying to reason with me. Trying to remain calm, so he doesn't snap, like I feel I'm about to do.

"Did you know, Elijah?" I ask him instead, thinking about what my wife went through. All the men that put their hands on her without her permission. All the people that were supposed to care for her but hurt her instead. Fucking betrayed her. Made her the kind of girl that runs away from someone who only wants to love her. "Did you know what was going to happen to her?" *To him?* I don't ask, because I don't care what happened to Jeremiah fucking Rain. He's a piece of shit. But my wife? My wife is *everything.*

Elijah shakes his head. "Lucifer, there are things you don't understand—"

"Then *make me* understand, because if what you're telling me is that this fucking pedophile ring is still alive and well and you *knew,* then I think you might need to die, too, *Dominus.* Because that's why they're after her, isn't it?" I shake the photo in my hand in front of his face. "To keep their dirty little secret *buried?*"

Elijah's chest is heaving as he stares at me, trying to hold back from what he really wants to do with me. Probably punch me in the fucking face.

I don't care.

I hope he does.

It'll give me an excuse to go at him.

"Lucifer," he says softly, dipping his chin and arching a brow, "there may be things we have to look into within the 6. But right now, our priority is figuring out who shot my guard, and who took this." He glances at the photo in my hand, and I tense. "She could be in danger, because you're right. Whoever it is likely knows about her, about her connection to the 6, and about her...past."

I try to hold onto his words, but it's all rushing back to me.

"We have our own watchdogs, and if more people learn she's not under your protection, they could kill her before we get the chance to bring her back. This is not a good sign, as it is." He blows out a breath, runs a hand over his short, dark hair. "We're going to need to work with Jeremiah Rain. He might know something."

My stomach churns.

He keeps talking, but I'm not seeing him.

Barely hearing him.

Instead I'm thinking of that night.

Jeremiah's hands around her throat, the smile on her drunken lips, because she thought he was me. The way I screamed, how the rope cut into my flesh. Warm blood trailed down my torso, seeping into my pants, but he didn't stop.

His hands were all over her.

He was straddling her, pinning her down, but he didn't even have to. He didn't need to go to the trouble.

My wife is a fucking slut, and maybe she didn't think it was me at all. Maybe she knew it was him or someone else, and she didn't care.

She's spread her legs for anyone who's wanted her. Anyone who's shown her the slightest bit of attention.

Before I know what I'm doing, blinding pain shoots

through my fist and someone is at my back, their arms tight around me as they speak something in my ear.

I realize I'm not holding her photo anymore, and my fist is against the wall beside the pew, the drywall split and cracked like my knuckles, but I don't care about *that* pain.

*That* pain doesn't hurt.

That pain is…survivable.

It's this other, the fucking hole in my chest…it's *that* I'm not sure I'll make it through. I need to get myself together. I need to think about what Elijah just said.

But the room is spinning, and I can't think, and I can't breathe and I…*can't.*

I need her.

I need my wife back. *My goddamn wife.*

"*Respirare.*"

Maverick's voice. Over and over, the same Latin word. *Breathe. Breathe.*

*Breathe.*

I close my eyes. Inhale. I can smell Maverick, like leather and something else. Darker. His scent is soothing. His arms are tighter around me. He's still speaking in my ear. Over and over and over.

I sink against him.

He's holding me up, and I turn in his arms, throw my own around him, aware everyone is watching us.

I don't care.

I rest my head on his shoulder, tears burning behind my eyes.

*Don't cry. Don't cry. Don't you dare fucking cry.*

"It's okay," Maverick says in my ear. "You can cry, Luce."

And then I can't hold it in anymore.

# CHAPTER Seven

## JEREMIAH

I TAKE A COLD SHOWER.

So fucking cold, I'm trembling as I plant my hands along the tile, hang my head and close my eyes, letting the water sting my skin. Bring about that numbness I've been craving lately.

Usually, it's easy to slip into. Indifference. Unfeeling. *Cold.*

But lately, with her around, so close but so fucking far from me, it's become increasingly harder.

My teeth are chattering, my left hand shaking violently, my right has just a soft tremor. I grind my teeth together, pressing the side of my face against the black tiles. I inhale deeply, trying to breathe through the cold. To take it. To drown in the pins and needles of it all.

I can still feel Cindy on me from last night. Her fingers digging into my shirt. I can still hear her moans as she grinded against me. Her begging me to take her home and fuck her.

But I couldn't do it.

I've slept with her before, and she's the best dancer I've got at Remorse, a club in Virginia, she came down just for me. But we aren't friends, and I'm not fucking any other girl while Sid is under my roof.

Thinking of her, pregnant with *his* baby, it makes my fucking skin crawl, but at least I know she's done with that shit. She's not fucking anyone in my house.

I'd never do that to her. Maybe at the hotel, when I knew she wasn't ready for me. When she wasn't ready to hear the truth, and I didn't want to tell her, because I thought if she knew we weren't *really* related, she'd run from me, no excuse to stay by my side.

But now, I can't do that.

Besides, the only woman I want is her. I want to own her. Brand her. Bruise her. *I just fucking want her.*

And in the three weeks she's been here, since I gave Brooklin up for her, nothing has touched me but my own hand.

I slam my fist against the shower wall, pick my head up and curse under my breath, reaching for the silver handle, switching off the water.

I always do the wrong thing.

Cutting her shirt off.

Trying to make her jealous.

*Always fucking wrong.*

I know something is wrong with me, *but I don't know how to fix it.*

For a second I just stand there, fist still against the shower wall, staring at the clouded over glass doors. There are four shower heads in here. Plenty of room for Sid, too, and I'd probably give anything to get her naked in here.

I've seen her naked before.

Once.

After that night a year and a half ago. After I...

I close my eyes tighter, slamming my fist so hard against the tile, it hurts, and I know I need to be careful. With the injury to my hand, the nerves there, breaking my fingers in the shower could fuck up my hand completely.

And I need that hand. I'm left fucking handed, and of

course, thanks to fate or Satan or what the fuck ever, it's my left hand that was permanently injured from my time in that...*house*.

I open my eyes as I shove open the glass door of the shower, stepping out into the large bathroom, grabbing a white towel from the rack and dragging it over my face, blinking the water out of my eyes.

Blinking away the memories too.

Of darkness. Hunger. *Pain*.

My stomach twists into knots, and I stumble over to the marble sink, letting the towel fall, my hands planted on the counter as I try to force it all back. What they did to me there.

What happened after.

*What Lucifer fucking Malikov did too.*

An inhuman cry leaves my mouth, and I snap my head up, staring into the fogged-up mirror, wanting to bring my fist against it, letting the glass shatter, my skin bleed so I can fucking *feel something*.

I'm only ever able to do that with *her*. It's like she's a poison beneath my skin, crawling ever closer to my heart, circling in my veins. One day, I'm pretty sure she just might fucking kill me.

I glance at the bobby pin on the white marble countertop, and it's the only thing that calms me. And just barely, at that.

Startling me out of those thoughts, there's a soft knock on the door and I tense, turning to the black door, double-checking the lock is on.

I clear my throat, my pulse racing. It's either Nicolas, or *her*. Only those two would fucking come into my room, knock on my goddamn bathroom door. Besides, a quick glance at my matte black watch on the counter beside one of the gold double sinks, I see it's not even six in the fucking morning.

"What?" I call out, not bothering to keep the edge out of my words. I like to have my mornings to myself. Truth be told, I like to have *everything* to myself.

I see the gold handle of the door wiggle and I curse myself for not grabbing the gun that's in my nightstand. I have guards and a locked gate, but with the 6 and the Unsaints circling around, waiting to fucking strike and try to get my sister back, I should be better prepared.

Still, I stand up straighter, stride to the door. "Who the fuck is it?" I growl.

"It's me, you fucking—"

I flip the lock, yank the door open before Sid can finish her sentence. I kind of like when she talks shit to me. She's the only person in the world who has never been afraid of me, but I'm not in the mood to deal with her bullshit right now.

*I don't think.*

Even still, there's a smile on my face as the cold air from my bedroom hits my naked body, one hand against the door, the other by my side as I tilt my head to take my foster sister in.

But when I do, her silver eyes wide as they trail up and down me, my attention gets caught on something around her throat, snagging like skin against a rusty nail.

My pulse pounds in my head.

I can't even hear her, her mouth opening and closing as she takes a step back, her chest heaving, some excuse coming to the tip of her tongue about why she interrupted my time in the bathroom.

But I'm not listening.

There's an edgy, twitchy feeling in my hands, and before I can stop myself, I close the space between us, grabbing that black bandana around her throat and backing her up against the wall in my bedroom.

Her nails come to my forearms, clawing at me.

I don't feel it.

I don't feel anything.

See anything.

*But them.*

. . .

*I DON'T MIND THE DARKNESS.*

*For Noctem, it's a requirement, they told me. Dark spaces. Three nights of no food or water.*

*I almost laughed when they said it, thinking of my time in that fucking cage. But Lucifer was watching me carefully, and I thought about when he came to see me down there.*

*I didn't laugh.*

*He was smiling.*

*Now, though, he's not around. None of them are. It's just me, my knees curled up to my chest, arms around my shins. It's a cave of some sort, and we were blindfolded and led in here. The rest of them split up. No one asked me to go with them. They pretended I wasn't here at all, save for Ezra, whose dark hazel eyes connected with mine in the glow from his flashlight.*

*One second.*

*Just a split second, and I thought maybe he'd want me with him. I thought about the bobby pin. The box of matches. His whispered words.*

*But I didn't do as he asked, and the look he gave me wasn't one of kinship.*

*It was fucking hatred.*

*Sometimes, I think he knows what I did to Kameron.*

*Doesn't matter. It's better for me this way.*

*I'm not sure why I bother keeping up appearances. I've got a house. Money from the family I fucking slaughtered. I could cut ties with them all.*

*I saw on the news they reported I shot the Forgues.*

*I huff a small laugh in the damp, wet underground of this cave, thinking about it. I did shoot them. Three of them, anyway.*

*But I did so much fucking worse than that.*

*The house burned down afterward. After I got out. I started that blaze with the matches from Ezra, but it was Lazar Malikov that finished it. He was waiting when I ran out of the house.*

*Right into his arms.*

*He didn't hug me.*

*Didn't hold me.*

*His eyes—so blue they seemed unnatural—were on the fire. The house engulfed in flames in the night, on a street that I'd never seen.*

Ever.

*When they ripped me away from Sid, I'd been blindfolded when they put me in that car.*

*And it wasn't until I was clinging to Lazar, my fists clenched around his dress shirt, my head buried in his chest, that I realized it had been nearly ten. Fucking. Years. Since I'd been* outside.

*I cried harder.*

*He'd shoved me away, held me at arm's length, his eyes trailing up and down my naked body, covered in blood, his lip curling in disgust.*

*I knew I smelled bad.*

*Looked bad.*

*I knew my head was so, so fucked. But under the full moon in that night sky, on the private street, I didn't care.*

*I was free.*

Free.

*He had dropped his hands from me as if I were diseased. He stepped back, jerked his head to a black Lincoln pulled up on the curb. "Go."*

*That one word.*

*I went.*

*Then I was inducted.*

*In the darkness of the cave, I close my eyes, forcing myself not to think about that. The initiation. It wasn't proper. Just...pain.*

*My mouth goes dry, and my bones* ache.

*My face burns, thinking of their humiliation.*

*Their taunts.*

*How it hurt.*

*I clamp my hands over my ears, rocking back and forth, humming softly, a way to drown out the memories. A habit I took up in that...cage. I sleep that way, in my own big, empty house. Sitting up, against the wall. Rocking.*

*For a while, here in the cave, it works to calm me.*

*My mind goes blank. I lean my head back against the rocky wall, drop my hands to my knees and keep my eyes closed, hoping to sleep the next three nights away.*

*I grew used to that in the Forgues house.*

*But just as I feel like I'm nodding off, drifting away into that bliss of nothingness, I sense someone beside me.*

*At first, I think it's in my mind.*

*That happened all the time in the cage. I made friends with dozens of people. Lovers. Parents who cared. Sid even came to see me.*

*I had it all inside my head.*

*So, I don't even open my eyes at first. But then I hear a clinking sound, smell something like smoke.*

*My eyes fly open and my breath leaves me in a rush as I flinch, startled by the sight of someone kneeling beside me, a small flashlight positioned against the wall opposite me in the tight space, illuminating Lucifer from behind, that hood over his head casting his features in shadow, a bandana around his throat.*

*He has demon eyes.*

*Just like his father.*

*The cherry of his cigarette glows orange in the dark, and I tense with his nearness as he exhales through his nose, my hand shaking around my shins as I curl tighter into a ball.*

*"Hi, J," he says in his hoarse voice, raspy even though he's younger than me. It's the cigarettes. I wonder when he started smoking.*

*"H-hi." My face warms as I stutter, but years spent being isolated made words difficult, even with my language classes. Sometimes I swear I speak German better than English, even though English is my first language. I wasn't degraded in German, and when the voices in my head started to speak, they never spoke to me in English.*

*I learned German because of* her, *and I force myself not to think about it.*

*About that whispered bullshit she gave me.* "Sicher." Safe.

*Lucifer inhales again, sits with his back against the wall. There isn't much space between our feet in this cramped crevice of the cave.*

*"You doing okay?" he asks me, his voice full of a strange cheerfulness.*

*As he turns his head to exhale again, I catch sight of his eyes in the glow from the flashlight, still leaning against the rocky wall.*

*His pupils are huge.*

*Far too enlarged to be…normal.*

*My skin pricks at the sight of it.*

*"Y-yeah." I swallow, try to think of something else to say. To ask. "Are you?" I finally croak out.*

*He turns back to face me, brushing the hood off of his head, running his hand through his black hair. He holds the cigarette between his thumb and forefinger, and glances at my shaky hand.*

*A smile curves his pale face.*

*My stomach flips.*

*"Your hand is shaking," he points out.*

*I think about the rope biting into my flesh. About him, prowling around my cage. How I begged him. Pleaded.*

*There was a lock on the crate, always. But he could've helped. If I could do it with that fucking bobby pin, he could've done it.*

*I close my eyes, swallow down my fear and curl my hand up tighter, putting it on my lap, between my legs and my stomach, hiding it from his view. "Y-yeah," I say softly, "i-it does that s-sometimes."*

*He doesn't say anything for a long while and I feel pressure building behind my eyes, my nostrils flaring as I try to breathe normally. Try not to cry in front of him. I'm older than he is, but he's the leader.*

*I want him to like me, and I hate that. Because I know what he did to me.*

*I haven't fucking forgotten.*

*I hear his shoes scuff against the dirt, sense him lean closer to me, but I don't dare open my eyes.*

*"Does it?" he asks softly, and for a moment, I forget what we're talking about. All I know is that he's too close, the smell of nicotine too much. Nicotine and pine, and I can almost feel his breath against my mouth.*

*I don't open my eyes, breathing hard, my pulse going haywire. I bring my knees closer to my chest, crushing my hand in the process but I don't care.*

*I don't want to show him that weakness.*

*"Yes," I whisper, that pressure behind my eyes growing stronger, that lump in my throat bigger.*

*"What did you do to those girls, J?" he asks softly, and I feel his legs bump against mine.*

*Feel a cold sweat break out along my neck.*

*"Did you* fuck them, *buddy?" He laughs, but it's cruel, causing the hair on the back of my neck to stand on end. "You come inside of their tight cunts, listen to them scream for you to stop?"*

*My stomach hurts. He can't know what I did. How would he know that? The papers said I shot them. I shot them, and my attorney took care of the rest. My lawyer, and the money, and Lazar...*

*Suddenly, his hand goes to my throat, knocking my head back against the wall of the cave. My eyes fly open, but I don't move to defend myself and I see the burning tip of the cigarette held just above my face as Lucifer looms over me, on his knees, his fingers biting into my flesh.*

*"You wanna scream for me now?" he growls, his hand going to my jaw, fingers splayed along my cheek, his thumb on my chin. He brings the cherry closer to my eye, and I whimper, gritting my teeth as I start to tremble. "Ah, that's it," he whispers, "I like that sound. Did they sound anything like* that?"

*I open my mouth, but nothing comes out but another fucking whimper.*

*His smile widens. "You sound like a little bitch, J," he says softly. "Just like them, huh?" The cigarette comes closer and I blink, darting my hands out, curling my fingers around his arm, trying to force him off of me, but he's stronger. A year after getting out of that cage, and I still haven't built up my muscle yet.*

*He leans against me, and I can't fight him off, his scent overwhelming me, the heat from the cherry too close to my eye. It starts to water, and my hand trembles against his forearm.*

*He laughs. "Stupid fucking idiot," he says in that hoarse voice. "Can't stop shaking, huh? I scare you that much?"*

*He moves the cigarette away from my eye, and I exhale with relief.*

But his fingers are still on my face, and when he says, "Stick out your tongue," I start shaking all over again.

"No, L-Lucifer, p-please don't——"

"That what they said to you, prick?" he growls.

I don't answer him, my fingers still curled around his forearm as I shake my head.

"Answer me, you piece of shit."

Then it happens.

My bladder loosens. A habit from being in that cage.

Warm urine coats my sweats, seeping through my boxers. I pray in my head that he won't notice. That if I just do what he says, he'll leave me alone.

He'll go away.

I start to open my mouth, my face flaming with humiliation, but then he wrinkles his nose and leaps to his feet, backing away from me.

"You pissed yourself?" he asks, incredulous as I squeeze my hands around my shins, rocking in a ball all over again, humming to myself, pretending I'm not here. "You fucking pissed yourself?"

I hear someone else in the distance, someone calling his name.

He laughs and turns his head, cupping his free hand over his mouth. "Mav, this asshole fucking pissed himself!" He laughs, drops his hand and turns back to me. "You're fucking disgusting." Then, when I think he's going to walk away, to go to Maverick, he steps closer to me and I hold my breath.

Waiting.

Shaking.

Still rocking.

Before I can even think of what he's doing, his foot collides with my stomach, pain reverberating through my ribs.

I go down on my side, curled up in a fetal position, my face against my own urine.

Just like in that cage.

I close my eyes and he laughs, then I hear a zipper.

His footsteps coming closer.

No. Please don't. Please, please don't.

*He laughs again, and I feel something hot against my face, dripping into my eyes, my mouth.*

*"We've got some faulty fucking plumbing in here, Mav," Lucifer calls as his urine coats my mouth. "But at least there's a goddamn toilet."*

"Jeremiah!" Sid is saying, her voice high-pitched. Scared. *Unnatural.* Her nails are still digging into my arm, my hands are around her throat, my thumbs against her windpipe, but that *fucking bandana* is touching me.

I release her, holding up my hands and stepping backward on the dark hardwoods of my room, breathing hard and gritting my teeth as I try to focus on the silver of her eyes.

Her long lashes.

Those swollen pink lips.

Her growing tits visible beneath her low-cut white tank. *Those* are getting bigger with every week that passes. And I want to touch her, and bite her and fucking *hurt her*, especially as my eyes rake over that bandana again. But I won't.

*I won't.*

It's not her fault.

*It's not her fucking fault.*

I swallow hard and drop my hands, aware that I'm completely fucking naked and I don't get naked for anyone. Clothing is an armor.

A shield.

I long to disappear into my walk-in closet, to the right, to don a suit and fucking cufflinks and maybe even a goddamn tie, just to cover up. I work out without a shirt, I'm comfortable enough in my own skin.

But being completely unarmed, I don't like it.

Especially as Sid's wide eyes rake over the scar slashed across my ribs. From *him.*

I curl my hands into fists. "Do you need something?" I ask her, trying to calm my temper. To hold back.

For her.

Always doing every fucking thing for her.

She's got her palms flat against the dark gray accent wall at her back, her spine pressed flush with it, too, but at my question, her eyes narrow. I see shadows beneath them, but they're better than they were when she first came here.

Then, she was frail. Almost…sickly. Like she was when I first found her that night. That night they could have fucking killed her. The night she wanted to kill herself.

"Yes," she says through gritted teeth, "Nicolas wants you."

I arch a brow. "Then why didn't Nicolas come up himself?"

At this, she bites her lip, looking down at her combat boots. It's fucking April in North Carolina, hot as hell outside, but she insists on wearing those fucking boots. Her closet, in the room down the hall from mine, is packed with clothes I bought just for her. Her usual shit, hoodies and band shirts and ripped black jeans, but also…*tasteful* shit.

She hasn't worn any of that.

"I was just going to tell you I made breakfast."

My mouth drops open as I blink at her, stunned. I don't think anything she said could've surprised me more than that. My sister, *cooking.*

She doesn't cook.

I learned that in the year we spent together in that fucking hotel. We have staff to do it for us, but I enjoy making my own meals. Sid is a vegetarian. I thought she might enjoy it, too. Vegetarians always seem to want their hands and noses in the business of the fucking kitchen.

But not Sid Rain. She was content to dump a handful of spinach on a plate and call it a fucking salad.

Besides that, last night, I let another girl grind on me, right across from her. Despite our goodnights when I carried her upstairs after we got home, I was pretty sure she was still annoyed with me.

I kind of hoped she was.

*Does she really not care?*

But no. She was jealous. She was fucking jealous. I know she was.

*Did she poison me?*

"Why?" I manage to ask, raking a hand through my wet hair.

Her jaw tightens, those silver eyes clouding with anger. "You're fucking welcome," she spits at me, then turns on her heel to stride to the bedroom door. Her temper has gotten worse since she's been here and I don't know if it's the pregnancy or *me*, or what but...*I don't fucking think so.*

I grab her wrist, yanking her back to me. She spins around, shoves me off, her small hands planted against my chest, sparking that electric touch in me at her nearness.

I grab her bandana, twist it in my fist, trying not to vomit as I do.

But her fingers dig into my chest, and she willingly comes closer to me, her lips parted as her breath comes out in a rush while I choke her.

*This is what she likes.*

And it's what I like, too. I like fighting with her. I fucking get off on it. Hurting her feelings, having her scream at me. Defy me.

She's it for me. She's always been it for me, even if, sometimes, I want to rip her apart, limb from fucking limb.

"You want to lose that fucking sarcasm, baby?" I whisper against her ear, pressing my body to hers. My cock grows hard with her nearness, with pulling that bandana so fucking tight that she can barely breathe.

With her nails raking against my chest.

How she doesn't back off from me.

"Fuck. *Off*," she hisses, the words coming out hoarse.

I huff a soft laugh, run my mouth against the shell of her ear. "You want me to *fuck off?*" I bring my free hand to her throat, still twisting the bandana in the other. "You wanna play with me, baby?"

She's stiff against me, and I feel her throat bob as she swallows.

"Let me go, Jeremiah, I was just coming up here to—"

"Taunt me?" I ask her, then I spin her around, yank her back so she's against my chest. Before she can move, I grab the ends of the bandana again, wrap it tighter around my fist. I hear her gasp, her fingers flying up to the edge of the material under my hand around her throat, trying to tug it off so she can breathe.

I angle my head next to hers, so we're cheek-to-cheek. "I don't like this shit on you."

She's jerking on the bandana, frantic, trying to pull away from me. But she *can* still breathe, because she says, "Get the fuck off, Jeremiah," but her words are hoarse.

I release my hold on her throat, trail my hand down to her tank top, brushing my thumb over her nipple, circling it until I can feel it pebble. She's not wearing a bra.

She drops her hands.

Stands perfectly still, except I think she leans back *into* me.

Her breath comes out in a rush as I squeeze her tit, a whole fucking handful now.

"I like what's happening here," I tell her, turning my head, so my mouth is against her skin. I squeeze her harder, let go of the bandana at the back of her neck and wrap my arm around her waist, my fingers splaying against her bare skin, under her shirt. "You're growing, huh, baby?" I inhale her lavender scent, my cock aching with how close she is to me.

*How close she is to giving in.*

Her hands are down by her sides still, but she says, "We can't do this."

My body feels heavy with those words, and I want to push her away from me. Go back in that cold shower. Be alone.

"Why can't we?" I ask her instead, through gritted teeth.

She sighs, tries to walk away. I squeeze her tit tighter, dig my fingers into her skin too, just above her running tights. "We aren't… Just fucking let me go," she snarls, the last sentence angry.

I close my eyes tight, reminding myself she needs time. She just needs time. I mean, I've known her since she was fucking two years old, but I guess nineteen years for her hasn't been enough goddamn time for her to figure out I love her more than I'll ever love anyone else in the world.

But I can't do it.

I can't let her go.

Not yet.

"Sid," I whisper in her ear, feel her shiver in my arms, against my chest. I trail my hand up, dip my fingers into her shirt cupping her soft, smooth skin, feeling her hard nipple against my palm.

She still doesn't fight me off. I'm not even sure she's fucking breathing.

"Give in to me." My voice is hoarse at that plea, and for a long, long moment, we don't speak. I keep kneading her flesh, pinching and pulling at her nipple. She whimpers, a sound caught in her throat, and I can *feel* her pulse under my hand.

She's nearly shaking with her restraint, and fuck, I just want her.

*I fucking want her.*

But then she jerks out of my grip, spins around, and before I can say a word, she slaps me across the fucking face.

I grit my teeth, balling my hands into fists as I flex my jaw, turning back to glare down at her. "What the *fuck* was that?" I want to go for that fucking bandana on her throat. I want to pin her down and make her scream and cry. I want to hurt her, just as I want to protect her from everything in the world.

Everything except me.

Her chest is heaving, her brow furrowed. "You can't do

that," she says, her words laced with rage even as her eyes flick down to my hard cock. "You can't do this to me."

I bite my tongue, close my eyes. Then I see *him*. I feel him. Fucking pissing on me in that cave. I see him leaving me in the fucking cage. My eyes spring open and I take a step toward her, satisfied when she flinches. But she doesn't step back.

She's the only girl in the fucking world who isn't afraid of me. Most of the time, I love that. Sometimes, though, I fucking hate it.

"Why not?" I demand, throwing up my hands, knowing what she's thinking about. *Who* she's thinking of. "You think he wants you back? You trying to be a good girl, for *him?*"

Something like pain flits across her face and I want to slap it off of her.

"Where is he, baby? Where the *fuck* is he? He hasn't come for you. He hasn't called. He's just fucking fine without you." I drop one hand, the other closing into a fist that comes to my heart. "But I'm not Sid. Without you, I'm *not fucking fine*. Can't you see that shit? Are you that fucking stupid?"

I drop my hands, waiting for her to say something.

*Anything.*

I see the anger in her eyes. I know something bad is coming. I know it, and yet when she says, "We aren't *lovers*, Jeremiah. I'm not...we're not fucking like that."

When she steps closer, her finger going to my chest, on my bare, wet skin, I feel my heart already cracking, preparing for what's coming next. "You know I love you. I fucking love you, but not like that." Her voice breaks on the last words, and her finger turns into her palm flat against my chest as she hangs her head. "I'm not the one to save you, even though I want to. God, I fucking want to."

I grab her waist, pulling her closer. She looks up, startled, but she doesn't try to get away. And I mean every fucking word when I tell her, "You can. You have. You do. Without you, Sid, I wouldn't still be here. And we can *be like that*."

Her silver eyes search mine, and I wonder what she sees when she looks at me. With her hand still flat against my heart, mine around her waist, I wonder if she sees how much I love her.

As much as I can love anyone, anyway.

I wonder if she knows I've always tried to save her. From Lucifer, from the Unsaints, from every bad thing in the world. I've killed for her. If I thought she'd be safer, I'd die for her. The things I've gone through? If they had happened to her...

She's already been through too much.

"Let go of me."

Her words make my blood run cold. My mouth opens, but nothing comes out. She drops her hand, tries to step away from me.

I don't let go.

"Jeremiah, *let go of me.*"

I don't.

Even when she lifts her hand and slaps me across the fucking face again, I don't let go of her. I turn my head back to face her, fingers digging into her waist as I pull her closer still.

Her jaw clenches, her hand still raised like she might hit me again.

"Do it," I tell her. "If it makes you feel better, do it again. I want you to fight me. It's why I've tried to teach you."

Just as she goes to do just that, to show off what she's learned, I catch her hand, spin her around so her back is to my chest, both of her wrists gripped in one of my hands, the other over her mouth.

She stills in my arms.

"If you were another girl, Sid Rain, I'd have already fucking killed you," I tell her, my mouth against her ear. "Be careful what you do to me." I kiss her neck, feel her shiver in my arms. "Be careful what you say to me." I kiss her again and she relaxes into my touch because I know Sid Rain, and I know she's a sick fuck, just like me. "Be careful how you treat me, baby, because I don't play games. I'm not *him.*" My hand over her mouth slides down her throat, over her chest, to her stomach. She tenses beneath my touch. "I'd never *want* to hurt you, you know that, Sid?" My fingers slide under her tank top, hot against her smooth skin. "But if you keep fucking playing with me, I'll have to show you all the things I don't want to do."

# CHAPTER Eight

## LUCIFER

*"YOU DON'T WANT THE BABY." I don't phrase it as a question because I already know the goddamn answer.*

*She looks down at her bare feet, and I see her swallow. "I don't think now is—"*

*I brush a lock of hair behind her ear as she lifts her chin, her eyes silver slits as she looks up at me, gaze wary. "Now is the perfect time." I drop my hand, gesture around the living room. This fucking stone mansion that's hers now, just as much as it's mine. This entire street is ours. The fucking world is ours. But that doesn't seem like enough for Sid Malikov. "I'll take care of you, like I've always done. Of our baby." I glance at her belly, definitely not showing yet but still. There's a baby in there. "Why isn't now the right time, Lilith?" I try to keep my tone soft, but I'm feeling edgy, my fingers twitchy.*

*Her hands are balled into fists at her side as her gaze hardens. "Because you do fuck all but get high and lose your fucking mind whenever I try to open up to—"*

*I slam my fists on the wall beside her head, caging her in and making her flinch. I hate that, but I can't…stop. Nothing I do is enough for her.* It's just never fucking good enough. *"You mean when you try to tell me how much you miss the man that fucking raped you?"*

*"He didn't—"*

"Yeah, because he realized you were his fucking sister. Are you stupid, Sid? I always thought you were the smartest person I ever knew, but lately I've been wondering if—"

She slaps me. I should see it coming. It's her thing. She does that. Especially with me. But I don't see it coming, and my head spins to the side as I flex my jaw, my heart pounding so hard in my chest I can hardly fucking breathe. Anger lights in my blood, and it takes a fucking effort to keep my fists against the wall and not on her as I turn back to face her. I don't want to hurt her. Not like that. But my blood pressure is skyrocketing, and it's the fucking blow that I can taste in the back of my throat. She isn't wrong, the things she's accusing me of. She isn't wrong, and I hate that all the more.

"Don't talk to me like that, Lucifer. Get out of my fucking face." She glances behind me, the sun not even up and we're already fucking fighting. She couldn't sleep well and I decided, one more time, I'd try to be there for her. Clearly, that was a fucking mistake. "I want to be alone."

I bite my tongue, trying to hold it all in. All the hurtful things I want to say. The shit that's been boiling in my blood for a couple of months now. She's hurt that I stabbed him. The man that made her life a living hell. The one who never belonged with us and has no place in her life. I know what he did to his sisters. I know how they suffered. My father told me that. The 6 claimed it made him one of us. They didn't even find one of the bodies and I feel sick wondering what he did to her.

Now, Sid is mad because I did the right fucking thing.

Fuck that.

I don't hold it in anymore.

"Nah, I'm not moving."

Her eyes snap to mine.

"You're fucking testing me, Sid. You're pushing me and I've been nothing but patient with you. The coke? The fucking…women? All of that is your goddamn fault for pushing me away—"

She shoves me, and I step back, my hands going to my side. "Don't put that on me. I've done nothing but exactly what you want me to do." She throws her hands up. "I've stayed in this house and haven't gone anywhere to please you and—"

"*Shut the fuck up.*" *I wipe my hand over my mouth, regretting the words as hurt flickers in her eyes, but I can't stop myself. It's true, about the coke. It's true, and when I got up this morning, it was true as I bumped a line then, too. But I need it. I can't keep up with her mood swings. With the fact that no matter what I do for her, it won't be enough because I'm not him.*

*And the things I'm seeing, the voices in my head…it's getting worse. They're getting louder.*

*I need her, but I can't figure out how to talk to her.*

*I drop my hand. I still regret those words. She pled with me to stop hurting her, weeks ago. And I haven't. I fucking haven't.* "*I just…I'm sorry. I want to keep you safe and I love you, and I don't—*"

*She doesn't wait. She just walks off, heads down the hall and up the stairs.*

*A moment later, I hear the door slam.*

*I wonder how long it'll take for me to put my hands on her, because I meant what I said, despite my apology. She's fucking testing me.*

*And when hours pass and we decide to talk again, it gets worse.*

*I throw a glass against the wall, watch it splinter into pieces.*

*She misses him. This morning, she told me she doesn't want our child, and just now, she's fucking telling me she misses him.*

*Over and over and fucking over.*

*Now she's standing beside the wall I just threw my rocks glass at, her face pale, her body stiff, every muscle in her small frame coiled with tension.*

*That could've hit her.*

*We both know it.*

*Doesn't matter that she's thrown a wine bottle at my head before. That was…*before *we were together. Before we were married. That's a line I shouldn't have fucking crossed but I can't seem to stop.*

*I glance at the lines of coke on the table that she started yelling at me about. Then I hear it again, in my head. How much she misses him. How she just wants to* "*check on him.*"

"*Sid, I'm sorry, I—*"

"*This is why now isn't the right time,*" *she snarls at me, her eyes narrowed, throwing back her words about wanting an abortion in my face. "We can't have a child. We can't even have a fucking conversation. Fuck you, Lucifer."*

I HEAR HIM IN THE DARK.

His voice, so like mine, whispering words of damnation to me. To her. To our child. My fingers tremble, clenched tight around my glass, the ice clinking against the sides. I downed the drink moments ago, but I need another one.

*I need another one.*

I need her.

Her, her, *her.*

It's always fucking been her.

But he's here. Whispering to me. And it isn't real. I know it isn't real. He's dead, buried in an unmarked grave behind Sanctum. But right now, it doesn't matter that he's a fucking corpse. Right now, he's in my head and he's in my fucking room at *our* house, and I—

"Luce?" a voice whispers in the dark.

I flinch, sloshing the ice and the dregs of my drink over the edge of the cup as I leap out of bed, my heart racing. My eyes try to adjust to the darkness, but I can't see anything and now I hear him all over again.

*"You're nothing. You are* nothing. *You will never be anything. Pammie never touched you, Lucifer. What woman in their right mind would want* you, *when they could have* me?"

"Lucifer?" that other voice whispers and I back against the bed, my hand shaking so violently that the glass slips from my fingers, hits the floor with a thud, ice spilling across the hardwood.

But it didn't shatter.

At least it didn't shatter like that glass I threw at Sid's head.

My chest caves as my father's whispers grow louder. I

clamp my hands over my ears, my pulse thudding too fast in my chest. The blow, and the memories, and the fear and disgust have my heart palpitating.

*Stop.*

I say it in my head, over and over, trying to hold onto something that's real. My wife. Her love for me. *She loves me.* I know she loves me. She ran because she loves me. Because she loves our child and she won't let him...she would never let him take that from me. From us. She'd never...

"Lucifer!" Someone's fingers are around my arms and I flinch, dropping my hands from my ears and shooting them out, knocking into someone solid. Real.

I hear a feminine cry, a gasp of shock.

My eyes snap open and my vision seems to clear. I'm in my room, a light on in the hall, spilling past my doorway.

Illuminating Ophelia.

*How did she get here? Why is she at my house? How long have I been home?*

I'm breathing hard and I glance over my shoulder, see light streaming in through the blackout curtains of mine and Sid's room.

*What fucking time is it?*

"Why are you..." I turn back to O, shaking my head, taking in what she's wearing. A white, low cut top tucked into her jeans, high-waisted, showing off her thick thighs. Her blond hair is up in a braided bun, tied with a red bandana, matching the lipstick on her mouth. "What are you doing here?"

I run my fingers through my hair and realize I'm not wearing a shirt. I'm in black basketball shorts, bare feet. I take in the rocks glass, the spilled ice. The bottle of vodka tipped over on its side, thankfully capped.

*What the fuck?*

Glancing at my black nightstand, I see coke residue, and

my fingers twitch, wanting to get to it. Dab it up, place it on my tongue.

But O is watching me.

And I still don't know why the fuck she's here.

"You called me," she says quietly, darting her eyes past me.

I turn to see what she's looking at. Oh. My cell phone, in the middle of the rumpled gray sheets. I don't remember calling her. When the fuck did I call her?

*Why?*

Last night…it was late when we got back. Mav drove me here. Told me him and Ella would stay the night if I needed them, but I told him to fuck off. I don't need him.

*I need her.*

Then it all comes flooding back to me. The fucking photo. Elijah's guard. *Dead.*

*Someone is following Sid.*

Mav said Elijah and the 6 are going to try to talk to Jeremiah fucking goddamn Rain this morning, but I can't be there.

My fingers curl into fists and O takes a step toward me, her white sneakers squeaking on my polished floor.

I even hired a housekeeper for Sid. She didn't want one, told me it was a waste of money, but I insisted. I was gone a lot, odd hours, working for the fucking cult.

She still ran.

She didn't appreciate *shit.*

I smell O's floral perfume as she gets closer, looking up at me through her long lashes. I think they're fake.

I don't care.

They look good.

Her green eyes are two big pools of concern and blood rushes to my dick at her nearness.

I waited a year for Sid once.

A fucking year.

But she's with him.

*She's with him.*

It's hard to breathe, my pulse racing, thinking of her, underneath him. Of her moaning his name. Him coming inside of her, her dragging her nails down his back.

Him, choking her. Fucking her from behind while he pulls her hair.

I want to vomit. I'm going to fucking be sick.

"Hey," O says softly, her voice meant to reassure me.

I take a step back from her, flop down on my bed, run my fingers through my hair again and pull, trying to get all of those horrible thoughts out of my fucking head.

She wouldn't.

She needed space. She needed...to breathe. She missed him. But not like that. She wouldn't...she wouldn't fucking do that to me.

She knows I could never forgive her for that.

*She wouldn't.*

"You're okay," O is saying, and that's fucking bullshit, but as my nostrils flare, snot dripping down into my mouth, the taste of blood in the back of my throat from all the fucking blow I can't stop doing, I don't say anything.

She steps even closer, her hands going to my shoulders as I start to shake, a sob clawing its way up my throat.

*She left me. My wife fucking left me. We were going to have a baby. She's...the baby...they're mine.*

"It's okay," O says again, massaging my shoulders, then wrapping her arms around me, holding me close.

I yank my hair harder, tears falling faster now.

The sobs grow louder, my chest fucking heaving, but I try to swallow it down. Bite it back. Clear my fucked up head.

"You're okay," she says again, and I pick my head up, dropping my hands, covering hers with my own as I pull them off of me, between us, letting her go.

There's a crease between her brow and I think of all the

mornings I'd go over to her house, watch cartoons together while we ate cereal.

She's always been there.

In pharmacy school now at AU, I don't know how she can afford to be here right now, but I'm grateful for it.

*For her.*

I pick one hand up, run the back of it over my nose and swallow down the blood and mucus trailing down my throat.

"I'm sorry I called you," I tell her, my voice hoarse. "I'm sorry I…"

She sinks down to her knees, kneeling in front of me, threading her fingers through mine. But I can't do that.

*I can't do that, because my wife likes to do that.* She didn't care much for most romantic shit, but holding hands was *our thing.*

I disentangle mine and O's hands, clench mine into fists, thinking of the scar on my palm. Sid's matching one.

That meant something to me.

Coagula.

It fucking *means something to me.*

But did it for her? I don't think so.

"Don't be sorry, Luce," O says, rubbing my leg, comforting me. She offers me a small smile, flashing her white teeth. "Why don't we get you some food?"

I swallow down the lump in my throat. Think of how Sid hated cooking. She tried, though. Whatever she made usually tasted like shit and I'd get notifications on my phone that the fire alarm went off more often than it should have, but she tried.

Usually, we'd have cereal for dinner, or I'd order something in. I thought about hiring a chef. It would be nothing for me. But I know how she felt about strangers in the house, and really, the less people to see our secrets, the better.

Still, thinking of her in the kitchen, cussing out the smoke alarm…I feel myself smiling, despite the tears still blurring my vision.

"Yeah," I tell O, nodding, wanting her hands off of me. My dick is still hard, morning wood, and I just…I can't think with her so close.

She smiles at me, her hands trailing higher up my shorts and just as I clench my jaw, about to tell her to fuck off, we hear footsteps, coming down the hall. Heavy, fast, then a familiar voice barking my name.

O's fingers dig into my shorts as she turns, still on her knees, to look over her shoulder.

Maverick looms in the doorway, stopping like he's shocked, just outside of it, pulling up short, his bright blue eyes going to Ophelia on her knees, to her hands on my thigh, then to me.

That inverted cross on his face tugs upward as his eyes narrow and he slips his hands into the pockets of his shorts.

He's not wearing a fucking shirt, his tattoos on display, the muscles of his forearms flexing as he keeps glaring at me like I fucking ate all of Ella's cookies or some shit.

"The fuck are you doing?" he growls, and O awkwardly stands, stepping back against the bed, wrapping her arms around her chest and shifting from foot to foot. I can feel her staring at me, but I don't look at her.

Mav doesn't either.

"What's it look like?" I ask him, holding up my hands and shrugging. Him and Ella have been by every morning since Lilith has been gone, Mav dragging me into the shower, Ella setting food on the table.

Sometimes she'd leave, sometimes she'd stay.

I wanted to hate them for it. For thinking I can't take care of myself without her. For thinking I'm…fucking insane.

But I'm not sure those things aren't true.

"Looks like you were about to get your dick sucked by someone that's *not your goddamn wife.*"

A small gasp escape Ophelia's lips and she shifts closer to me, still standing, but her thigh brushes against mine. "It wasn't like—"

"I don't think I'm fucking talking to you," Mav snarls, but he doesn't even look at her.

Him and O have never been friends, but he knows she's *my friend*. And he should know I could really fucking *use* a friend right now.

I gesture toward my crotch. "My dick look like it's out to you?"

He glances down, his lean jaw clenched, the muscles of his core flexing as he takes a step into my room. "Looks like you're fucking ready to go."

I drop my hand and roll my eyes. "Maybe get Ella in here. She'd know all about—"

He crosses the room so fast, his hand going to my throat as he shoves me backward on my bed, I don't even have time to fucking take a breath. He climbs on top of me, caging me in beneath him as my hands go to his forearm, pushing him off.

But he's got one hand planted beside my head, and all his weight is leaning against the one wrapped tight around my throat as he glares down at me, those blue eyes full of rage.

"Don't fucking go there. Stop acting like a piece of shit."

Ophelia calls his name—"Mayhem,"—but he ignores her, circles his fingers tighter around my throat.

"Maybe you forgot someone is stalking your fucking wife, but I haven't. And you might not give a fuck about her anymore, but she's my sister, and she's carrying my niece or nephew," he leans down close, his mouth over mine, his fingers closing tighter, "and I fucking do," he snarls, the scent of toothpaste hitting my nose.

I wonder what my own breath smells like.

I can still taste iron in my mouth.

Probably not great, but right now I'm barely fucking breathing so I guess it doesn't matter.

"Get the fuck up. Get a fucking shower, get dressed, and meet me downstairs." He glares at me for a long moment, then shoves me away, releases his grip on my throat and gets off the bed, ignoring Ophelia completely. Instead, he turns away, his huge Unsaints tattoo on his back facing me, smoke through one eye, a U through the other.

I sit up slowly, my hand going to my throat as I massage it, flexing my jaw, my blood pounding in my temple.

Just as he walks through the doorway, barely clearing it, he glances over his shoulder at me.

"If you'd get your goddamn head out of your fucking ass, you'd know that you've got a long drive ahead of you."

I narrow my eyes, swallowing hard. I'm not fit to drive. *I'm not going to drive, unless it's to my baby girl, and I'm pretty fucking sure she doesn't want me around.* If it was up to me I'd go anyway, but the 6 have other plans. They don't want to start a war, so apparently, I can't go burn down his house and drag Sid out by her hair.

Mav's voice breaks through those thoughts. "Julie called. Someone's been fucking around her property."

I freeze, drop my hand as my throat tightens. I haven't been to Julie's in a long, long time. Not since Sid and I got married. I wanted to give her space, to let her adjust to the idea that I was financially supporting a kid that wasn't fucking mine from a girl I fucked that meant nothing to me.

Sid never did seem to warm up to the idea. Still, she never asked me to stop paying, either.

"She got Finn a kitten?" Maverick is saying, arching a brow, his tattooed face particularly sinister like that.

He scrubs a hand over his face like he's tired, drops it by his side, and I catch sight of my wife's fucking name on his hand.

I swear to God, one day I just might cut it off.

I nod, vaguely remembering Julie texting me some shit about that. A white kitten. There was a photo.

I didn't give a fuck.

"What about it?" I ask, waiting for him to get to the

goddamn point. I can't even take care of my wife, no way in fuck am I taking in a kitten.

"It's dead," Mav says, his tone emotionless. "The head was found on her doorstep."

Ophelia gasps, her hands flying to her face as Mav turns on his heel and walks down the hallway, and I hear his heavy footsteps on the stairs.

My blood runs cold, my eyes closed tight as I think about it.

The possibilities.

Could be a fucking coincidence. Nothing at all.

Except for the fact Julie lives in Acid City, which is the middle of fucking nowhere Virginia. She keeps to herself since her break up with Finley. I don't know much about her anymore, but I know she's a good mom.

She wouldn't make enemies that would do something like that.

But me? The Unsaints? The 6? *We fucking would.*

# CHAPTER Nine

## LUCIFER

*I CAN'T BREATHE.*
*All I can see is the letter in my head.*

We both know that as of now, I'm the best place for her and
the child.
Oh, you thought Lucifer's psychotic break was a 6 secret?
I have eyes everywhere.
I can promise you if that happens again, you won't need me
to wait for Noctem.
Pedicabo vos et irrumabo.

*ALL I CAN HEAR IS MAVERICK TELLING ME SHE'S GONE.*
*She's gone.*
*She's. Fucking. Gone.*
*Ella's mouth is on my neck, and I'm in the bed of an upstairs room*
*in a house I've never seen before, staring up at the ceiling but I take in*
*nothing.*
*Nothing.*
*Ella leans back, sitting on her heels, on top of me, and she unbuttons*
*her white shirt with sure, quick fingers.*

*Maverick is on his knees beside the small bed, one hand going to my throat, his fingers tightening around my neck. He leans down toward me as tears blur my eyes, and his mouth is over mine. "She had to go," he whispers, his breath against my lips. "She had to go, but she'll be back, Luce. She loves you so much." His mouth comes over mine and I part my lips for him, tasting marijuana on his tongue.*

*I groan against his mouth, my hands on his shoulders, wanting to push him away. To hate him for betraying me. For letting him take her, but I don't want to breathe. To feel. I just want to taste him.*

*Ella is on her hands and knees over me, her fingers going to the button of my pants and my instinct is to break her fucking hand.*

*That's not hers.*

*I'm not hers.*

I'm not fucking hers.

*But Maverick moves his hand from my throat, instead pins my arms over my head as he pulls away. I bite his lip, wanting him back as I taste blood in my mouth. But he gets away, glares down at me, blocking Ella from view as she pulls down my zipper, my boxers, my pants, just to my knees.*

*My throat feels tight as her slender fingers circle around my dick, and I look at Mav, narrowing my eyes, but I'm not fighting Ella, and we both know it.*

*"We need to find her," I whisper, my words hoarse.*

*Ella strokes me, her grip firm. Skillful.*

*I bite my lip and let my eyes flutter closed as Mav keeps my arms pinned down to the mattress. I inhale his scent; leather, and marijuana, and something else too. The underground of this house. Where she left.*

*She left.*

*"We need to fucking find her—"*

*But Ella's mouth is on my cock, and my words are drowned out in a groan even as I try to sit up, straining against Maverick's grip.*

*"That's it," Mav whispers against my ear, tightening his hold. He nudges my head to the side with his nose and bites my ear lobe. A shudder runs through me as Ella deep throats my cock and I hear her choking on it. "Just relax, Luce. Okay? Just relax. Let my girl take care of you."*

*My back arches, and I bite my lip hard enough to taste my own blood. It feels so fucking good and hearing her choke...fuck.*

*But no. No, no, no.*

*"Maverick, we need to find her. He could hurt her. He could fucking—"*

*Maverick clamps his hand over my mouth, moves onto the bed so he's straddling my chest, his weight making it hard to breathe.*

*He lets go of my mouth, pulls down his own pants, and I see tattoos on his torso as his shirt brushes up, exposing every line of his abs.*

*Then his tattooed fingers circle around his hard cock.*

*My eyes lock on his as Ella's mouth leaves me and I almost cry at the loss of it.*

*"Open your mouth, Luce," Maverick says softly, a smirk pulling on his lips. He has circles under his eyes, and I know he was tripping, too, and I think maybe he still is with that glassy look in his blue irises.*

*But he has to know I can't do this.*

*I can't live without her.*

*And she's pregnant.*

*She's pregnant with my baby...*

*Unless it's fucking his.*

*My eyes narrow, rage surging through me as I try to sit up again, but with Mav on my chest, holding down my arms, and Ella on my lower half, I can't fucking move.*

*"We have to fucking find her!" I scream at him, but he just lifts his hips, leans over, and pushes his dick into my mouth at the same time I feel Ella's tight pussy sliding down my cock after she pulls my pants all the way off.*

*Fuck.*

*I think about biting Maverick, but he grips my jaw, staring down at me with narrowed eyes. "She'll be okay. She's my sister. I won't let her get hurt." Ella moans behind him and I see her hands coming over his shoulders, her nails digging into his shirt as she uses him as leverage to ride me.*

*She feels so good.*

*My eyes nearly roll back in my head as Maverick says, "She's safe, Luce. Let us take care of you, okay?"*

*Ella rides me faster, the entire bed shaking as she does, and Maverick seems angry as he thrusts his cock into my mouth, making me gag.*

*She left me.*

*I try to hold onto that thought.*

*She...left me.*

*But with the taste of Maverick in my mouth, his cock hitting down my throat, and Ella's tight, wet pussy clenching around me, I can't think.*

*I can't do anything but feel.*

*Maverick shifts his hips as he fucks my mouth.* "Fuck, Luce," *he groans, drool dripping from the corners of my mouth as I stare up at him, barely able to breathe.* "You're so good at this."

*Warmth rushes through me with his words, with him dominating me, Ella making me feel like a fucking god.*

*But she moans again, calling Maverick's name even though it's my fucking dick she's riding.*

*Maverick must see something in my eyes because he smirks down at me, his cock still lodged in my throat, saliva dripping down the sides of my mouth, my chest heaving beneath him straddling me.*

"Oh, now you want to act like the big boy that you really are?" *he taunts me, but he pulls his dick out of my mouth, traces his thumb over my lips, his hands planted by my head as he leans over me.* "That was good, lover boy, but I think my girl can do better." *Before I can say anything, he's off the bed, watching as Ella rides me, her fingers digging into my hips as she bites her lip.*

*Mav leans down, takes her nipple in his mouth, tugging with his teeth.*

*One of her hands finds his hair, digging in as she moans and my hands come to her inner thighs, gripping her hard enough to bruise as she rides me.*

*Maverick's hand is around his dick, stroking himself as he releases Ella's nipple with a pop. He grabs her breast, hard, and she moans his name. His mouth comes to hers as my thumbs brush against her pussy lips as she rides me faster, wrapping her arm around his neck to balance herself.*

"You like fucking my best friend, pretty girl?" *he whispers against her mouth before he devours her, his tongue down her throat. He pulls away and she whimpers, letting go of me and grabbing her breast, riding me faster.*

*I push a finger into her, beside my cock,* and she moans his name *again.*

I'm getting kind of tired of that shit.

*He grabs her throat, lifts her chin and her green eyes are locked on his like she's worshipping him even as I'm the one fucking her. "Yeah, you like him filling you up?" He presses her lips together as he squeezes her face. "You're a dirty little whore, pretty girl." He spits in her mouth, then bites her lip, releasing her throat, his fingers coming to her clit, so close to my own inside of her.*

*She gasps, digging her nails into her chest.*

*"Ride him," he tells her, "for me. Don't stop until I tell you to."*

*I groan, biting my lip, and Mav turns his head, his eyes locked on mine as Ella fucks me faster and Mav's fingers are circling her pretty pink clit.*

*"You feel good, Luce?" he asks me, a smirk on his face. "Or do you want your cock down her throat, too?"*

*My breath catches as I sit halfway up, one hand still on Ella's thigh as she rides me, the other beside my dick, inside of her.*

*"Answer me, handsome," he says, still smirking at me, still rubbing her.*

*And I know she's coming, the way she clenches so tight around me, a sudden gush of warmth all over my dick, my fucking finger.*

*She says both of our names, over and over, and I don't look away from Maverick as his girl comes on my dick.*

*"Yes," I finally say when she's coming down, slowing her movements. "Yeah."*

*He drops his hand from her pussy, turns to face me fully, pushes his fingers into my mouth. I taste her as he leans down close, shoving those fingers into the back of my throat. His mouth comes over mine, his lips half on me, half on his own hand.*

*"You like how she tastes?" he whispers.*

*I suck his fingers, my mouth brushing his.*

*"Or do you like how I taste?" He pulls his fingers out of my mouth, kisses me again.*

*Then Ella pulls off of me as he straightens, grabbing her arm, yanking her from the bed.*

*I catch a glimpse of her bare, smooth pussy as she stumbles barefooted on the wooden floors of this room.*

*"Get on your knees," Maverick growls at her, staring down at her as he strokes his cock.*

*She does, glancing at me and wiping the back of her hand over her mouth.*

*Her red hair covers her breasts as I sit up, and Maverick pulls her hair back, exposing her big tits to me, her nipples peaked, bite marks around her pale skin.*

*I stand, cross the room until I'm beside Mav, both of us in front of her, on her fucking knees, her thighs spread so I can see her pussy. Where I just was.*

*I circle my fingers around my dick. "Finish what you started, Ella."*

*She doesn't move, her green eyes glued to Mav.*

*He threads his fingers through her hair and jerks her head back. "You heard him, pretty girl. Do what he says."*

*She licks her lips, smiling up at him, then turns to me, opens her mouth and lets me push my dick down her fucking throat.*

*Mav guides her head, slow at first as he strokes himself, then faster, until her face is turning red and she's fucking gagging, slobbering all over me.*

*My fingers find her throat and I feel her trying to breathe. Trying to swallow.*

*I'm so fucking close.*

*Mav turns to me, trails his tongue over my throat, releasing her and grabbing my face as he pulls away, twisting his head to me.*

*I gasp against his mouth, and he groans too, the both of us tasting each other's pleasure as I come in Ella's mouth.*

*"Goddammit, Ella," he says, lips brushing mine.*

*My eyes flutter closed as he finishes all over her perfect tits, slapping one as he does, and I spill down her throat, my hand coming to the back of her head and grazing Mav's fingers as I force her all the way down on me.*

*I don't let her go even when I'm done, and Mav licks the seam of my lips, bites me again before he pulls back, letting me go.*

*"Get off her," he snarls.*

*I blink my eyes open, feeling dizzy as I release Ella's head, pulling my dick out and seeing strings of saliva connecting me to her.*

*Her chest heaves as she tries to catch her breath, and Maverick sinks to his knees, cupping her face in his hands. He leans down close to her as she blinks up at him, looking scared.*

*"You did good, pretty girl." He tilts his head, his mouth claiming hers in a noisy kiss. I see the Unsaint's tattoo on his back, watch his shoulders flex as he holds onto her face, pulling away from their kiss. "You did so good, baby. I fucking love you."*

*And with those words, the pleasure leaving me, I remember.*

*And my heart breaks all over again.*

PEDICABO VOS ET IRRUMABO.

*Jeremiah signed his letter to Maverick that way. A Latin line in a Catullus*

*poem. Roughly translated to, "Suck my fucking dick."*

*I'm going to fucking kill him.*

THE DRIVE TO JULIE'S DOES NOTHING TO GET *HER* OFF OF MY mind. The lines I did before I got in the car does nothing to get her off of my fucking mind. Maverick's threats to keep my hands to myself, his insistence he'd be looking for my ass if I'm not back tomorrow, that doesn't do shit to help clear my head.

And Ophelia in my passenger seat, wearing a dress she changed into that hits at her upper thighs, riding up further as she's sitting in the leather seat of my M5? Fucking nothing.

"Who do you think did that?" she asks, her tone guarded

as she drums her manicured nails on the center console. The windows are cracked, and she bitched about it messing up her hair.

I wasn't going to roll my fucking windows up because it's a gorgeous day outside, just past noon, and while I don't exactly love the sun, I hate using AC.

Sid used to sneak down in the night to turn it down.

I told her there was an app on her phone she could use.

She said the fun was in crawling out of bed without me noticing. I'd laughed at that, pinned her down on the couch in the living room, flipped her over, and fucked her in the ass.

And every time I heard her get out of our bed, I'd pretend to sleep until she crept back up the stairs and I'd fuck her again.

Thinking of it now—a time when we were happy in the night; not when I woke up hurting her, dreaming of my fucking father—I can't hide my smile.

O stops drumming her nails, reaches for my hand on my lap.

I stiffen as she tries to thread her fingers through mine.

*That's for my fucking wife.*

I casually pull my hand away, go for the stereo even though I could turn the music up on the wheel.

O sighs, getting the point, and slouches back in her seat. She's on spring break from pharmacy school she told me, and being a spoiled asshole like I was, she doesn't work.

Perfect for now, when I need someone to distract me from the nearly all-consuming thoughts of my fucking wife, although this drive to Julie's is for just that. I spoke to Julie on the phone and she was freaked out. I don't really think I'll find anything driving up here, but I own a house not far from her I can stay at, and it's good to clear my head.

Except it's the fucking house where Sid found out that *I* wasn't the one who assaulted her.

I grit my teeth, thinking about it. About her. With him.

Even after that, *she still chose him.*

O blows out a breath. "You think you'll be able to find out anything, going here?" I know she isn't pumped about going. Her and Julie didn't exactly get along, probably because they both wanted my dick. I don't care, I didn't fucking force her to come.

But it is nice not being alone. It seems the voices in my head are quieter when I've got another voice to hold onto. I think that's why Maverick didn't give me shit about her coming.

"Who fucking knows," I mutter, glancing over at her. She's glaring at me, her green eyes narrowed.

"What's going on, Luce? Why did Mayhem pin you down this morning? Why'd you let him?" She asks it in a way that makes me think she's trying to put me down.

*Watch yourself.*

"You shouldn't let him do that to you. Sid left *you.*" O doesn't know why, of course. She just knows she's…gone.

I shift lanes, pass a slow-moving car on the highway, on the right side, then yank the wheel back to the left lane.

A startled breath leaves O's big fucking mouth, and she holds on tight to the door handle. I don't say anything, just keep driving north to Virginia.

Maverick is with Cain doing some fucking surveillance for the 6, bringing in that hacker we had to leave, or he'd be with me. Ezra and Brooklin are probably getting fucked up some-where, and I realize I haven't asked Mav how he feels about them spending so much time together.

I haven't asked Brooklin, either, how it was. *With him.* Did he hurt her? Is he…rough? Is he going to hurt my fucking wife?

*Lie to Me* by 12 Stones is blaring through the speakers, and the wind streaming in through the cracked windows is loud as fuck, but none of that is enough to get Ophelia to shut the hell up as she keeps talking from the passenger side.

*Why did I bring her?*

*Oh, that's right. Because I fucking called her when I was high out of my goddamn mind and she came to my house.*

I could've told her to stay at her house when she picked up some clothes from there and we dropped her car off. Should have. But I thought having her with me would prevent me from doing something fucking stupid with Julie. The more time that goes by that my wife doesn't call me, doesn't look for me, the less upset I am.

The more *pissed the fuck off I get instead.*

"What's going on with you and Mayhem, anyway? And are you getting a…divorce?"

I almost run off the goddamn road at that question, my jaw ticking, pulse flying. I run my hand over my nose, which seems to have developed a steady stream of mucus lately with all the fucking blow I've been doing.

Tightening both hands on the wheel of my car, I try to keep my tone even when I say, "No." I'm not getting a fucking divorce. Those things don't *exist* with the 6. Sometimes, I think my dad had my mom killed. I think that single car wreck was all bullshit. I think someone ran her off of the road because he got involved with fucking Pammie.

Too late to ask him that now.

Too late for too many fucking things now.

A flash of how it felt, driving that knife into his head, hearing his inhuman screams—a sound I've heard many times before with all the bullshit I've done for the 6, but not from my father—it all echoes in my head. I want to punch myself to get it out of my mind. I want to drive off the fucking road. Cross the median, hit a tractor trailer head on.

"Then why are you—"

"Can you please stop talking?" I cut O off, digging my hand into the pocket of my shorts and grabbing my lighter. I clench it tight, not wanting to smoke in the car because I've tried to stop doing that. For Sid.

I can feel O glaring at me, feel her anger, too. I don't care. I've never given a fuck about anyone's anger except my wife's. Nothing has changed.

Again, I glance at the traffic across the median.

So tempting.

O's voice is laced with anger when she starts with, "You want to use me for—"

"How the fuck am I using you?" I snap back, knowing I'm doing just that. "I haven't even kissed you. You haven't fucking sucked my dick, O. Please explain how the *fuck* you think I'm using you? I thought we were friends—"

Her hand comes to said dick, cutting off my words.

She palms me, and I'm not hard yet but if she keeps running her hand up and down me, my basketball shorts not leaving much to the imagination where the feel of her touch is concerned, I'm going to get there.

I keep my eyes on the road. Fumble my fucking lighter, dropping it down into the crease between the seats. *Fuck.*

I put both hands on the wheel as I suck in a breath. Hear O unbuckle her seatbelt, see the sign indicating its undone flash on the dashboard.

I can't do this.

I cannot do this. Not to my wife. Not to what could be my...*family.* That word feels thick in my head, too heavy. Weighted down.

I don't know what a functional family is like.

None of my brothers do, either.

We were given the world on a silver platter, but love? That was something we had to figure out on our own, and no fucking surprise, we only found the worst forms of it.

But Ophelia is stretched across the seat now, her tits spilling out of her dress. I can see her hard, pink nipples as she looks up at me through her lash extensions, licking her plump lips. I think she gets filler, just like her mom does.

Like Pammie did.

Her fingers curl around my dick, her mouth open. "Let me help you," she whispers, her head in my lap as I try to pay attention to the road, clenching my jaw as I do.

Wrestling with myself as I glance down at her, then back up.

She keeps stroking me, my dick growing harder with her touch.

I can't believe I waited that year for Sid.

A year. *An entire fucking year.*

Me.

Maverick wouldn't leave that shit alone. Cain is the biggest whore out of all of us, but I wasn't far behind.

Still, I couldn't get it out of my head.

I couldn't get *her* out of my head. What he did to her. What we promised each other. The fucking Death Oath never meant shit to me before her. A ritual with no heart. An illusion of control. A practice for the responsibility we'll all eventually carry.

The scars, the blood, the fucking sex in the asylum? That didn't mean a fucking thing to me until I met Sid Rain at that intersection.

I was supposed to kill her.

I was supposed to bring her to my father.

But instead, I fell in love with her like I was a fucking boy. A child.

I swear to God, it took me two fucking minutes. That's it, and I was hooked. Addicted. Before that, I never gave in to anyone. I didn't let my girls fuck around because I didn't *have* girls. I fucked them and I was done. I thought, sometimes, when I was alone, or blasting off into fucking outer space high on shrooms, I thought I was broken. That the gene to love, to feel compassion for someone outside of myself, I thought I didn't have it.

The psychedelics helped. Helped me *feel*. But when I came back to earth, I was broken all over again.

Numb.

*Until her.*

But she left me. *She fucking left me.* Things were bad, and Mav encouraged her, and yeah, I didn't act like husband of the fucking year, but she wasn't exactly wife material, either.

But there was that night…that night I know she decided to do it. It wasn't my fault. *It wasn't my fucking fault.*

I slam my hand against the wheel and O flinches, startling in my lap.

My throat feels tight, and I'm about to tell her to stop when she whispers, "You can pretend I'm her," and starts to pull down my shorts.

*Pretend she's her.*

I almost laugh at that. Sid wouldn't be so hesitant. Sid would be all over my dick, fucking choking on it. She was so skittish about so many things—opening up to me. Letting me in her heart. *Learning to cook.*

But she had no problems with sex.

"It's okay," O says softly, picking her head up and trailing her open mouth down the side of my neck. A shiver slides down my spine as I keep my eyes locked on the road. O doesn't smell like my wife. Feel like my wife.

*She's not my wife.*

And that's who I really want. That's who I really need.

*But she's not here.*

"Let me make you feel good," O whispers, sucking on my neck.

I don't breathe for several long moments, my foot shaking on the gas pedal, my fingers tapping against the wheel. But Ophelia dips her head and keeps stroking my dick, and I keep seeing it in my head.

Him on top of *her.*

Pinning her down.

His hands all fucking over her. That drunken smile on her

face, her glassy eyes. The moment he realized *who the fuck she was.*

But I see something else too.

Her legs wrapped around him at that club. Her arms threaded around his neck, his dick grinding against her as he held her, shoved up against the wall of the bathroom.

She had been drinking, but she wasn't drunk.

She knew what she was doing.

And if I hadn't walked in...*she would've fucked him.*

I think about another thing. About the fact that we have the pregnancy test, the positives, her missed period, but that baby might not even be mine. She avoided going for an ultrasound. She wanted an abortion. Wanted to pretend *my baby* didn't exist.

But maybe that's because it isn't mine.

She fucked Maverick, too, and he doesn't use condoms. He told me he pulled out—my skin crawls thinking about it—but who fucking knows? My wife is a goddamn slut and—

I shift my hips, let O pull down my shorts, tears blurring my vision as I try to get myself together because I'm doing twenty over the speed limit and I'm *not* in a good place right now.

She left me.

She fucking betrayed me.

And if she's fucking with him—and how can she not be, when she's wanted him ever since she found out he wasn't her brother?—I can never forgive her for that. He scarred me.

We hated each other long before her, and he fucking scarred me and made me watch him assault her.

I could never forgive her that kind of pain.

Besides that, I've let her do whatever the fuck she's wanted, and I'm running low on forgiveness right now.

It's my fucking turn.

I thread my fingers through Ophelia's hair as she pulls down my boxers, wraps her fingers around my cock. Her mouth isn't Sid's, and she's tentative at first, hesitant to take all of me down her throat, but when I shove her head down and she gags, trying to get away from me, her nails digging into my thigh, I don't care.

It feels good all the fucking same.

And when I come in her mouth, biting my lip and thinking about my wife's beautiful eyes looking up at me when she's on her knees, my hand wrapped around her throat, it feels the fucking same.

# CHAPTER Ten

## JEREMIAH

"DO YOU ENJOY HURTING HER?" Nicolas asks me, his arms folded over his chest, chin dipped down as he stares at me.

I roll up my shirtsleeves, my throat tightening as my hand trembles.

Another morning murder, another fucking spasm. When I'm done fucking with my sleeves, I lean back in my office chair, fingers under my chin, one elbow propped in my opposite hand.

"I'm a bit of a sadist." I shrug. "Do you care to elaborate?"

Nicolas's dark eyes throw daggers my way. "You're taking her to Virginia."

I nod once. "Ah, good. You got the schedule." Because I fucking emailed it to him before I drove into the city today.

"They've requested a call with you," Nicolas says through clenched teeth.

I nod. I got his email, too. Glancing at my watch, I shrug. "In about ten minutes. What about it?" Looking beyond him, I take in the morning sun. I was out of the house at four this morning. Sid will be waking up any minute now, and we have training to do. Bags to pack.

Her piece of shit husband is already in Acid City. I'd hate for her to fucking miss him.

"Elijah Van Damme said it's urgent. Apparently, someone really has been fucking around our property." Nicolas's words come out through clenched teeth, and my heart nearly stops in my chest.

"Excuse me?" That wasn't in the email.

Nicolas's frown deepens as he stares at me a moment, as if he's trying to read me. "Said they'd tell you on the phone." His eyes narrow. "But they told me that Elijah's guard is dead."

My mind races, but I don't break eye contact with Nicolas. "Who?" I ask carefully. For someone to get to one of their guards...*not fucking good because it wasn't me.*

I know the 6. I know how they are about goddamn secrets and security. It's how I was kept in their fucking basement for *years*, and no one knew.

Well, *they* knew.

My sisters.

And Sid Rain's *husband.*

Elijah's son, too.

I grit my teeth, trying very, very hard not to think about any of that.

"Didn't say, so when they call," he glances at my secure line, "better answer it."

I stare at him a long moment, decide to let his bullshit go. "If all of that is true, why would Lucifer fucking Malikov drive north to Virginia, knowing Sid is here, *with me?*" I take more pleasure in saying those last two words than maybe I should but fuck it. I've followed her for over a decade. I've earned the right to say whatever the fuck I want.

"Someone has been fucking around with Julie's house,"

Nicolas says, and I'm not sure how it's possible, but his glare deepens, and he looks pissed *at me.*

I don't like that at all, but I don't move, just keep watching him.

"Go back," I demand Nicolas, cocking my head, steepling my fingers, elbows resting on the arms of my chair. "How do they know someone has been fucking around here? And how do we know *it wasn't them?*"

Nicolas's jaw clenches. "That's what the call is for."

Before I can say anything else, the phone rings between us, startling me. "They're early," I mutter under my breath, and I stare at the black phone as it rings again, my stomach twisting into knots.

Thinking of what happened to me.

What they let happen.

*What they were going to do to my sister.*

But they'll pay for that soon enough. For now, my desire to know what the fuck is going on outweighs the demons of my past.

I snatch the phone up from the receiver, lean back in my chair, my eyes on Nicolas as I hold the phone to my ear.

"Rain," I answer with.

There's a pause on the line, and I clench my jaw.

Finally, Elijah Van Damme speaks. "Did Nicolas get you up to speed?"

I ball my left hand into a fist on my thigh. "Tell me what the fuck you're doing around *my* property before you start asking me questions, *Elijah.*" Fuck their titles. Fuck him. My pulse pounds in my head, knowing he's on the other line. Knowing he knows something about me and her that I don't know.

He laughs, a deep rumble, and I dig my nails into my palms as I stare past Nicolas, keeping those memories from the cage back. "My understanding is you are *obsessed* with Sid Malikov—"

"That's not her name," I warn him.

He laughs again. "Court records would prove otherwise." I grit my teeth, but don't say anything, think instead of all the ways I can mark my sister to prove to her—*to me*—that she's mine. "Regardless, this isn't a pissing match. I informed Nicolas someone has been on your property because whoever murdered my guard," his voice takes on an edge of anger with those words, "left photos of Sid running in a forest?" That's a question, but I know he knows about the forest surrounding this house. *"Alone."* He flings that word out as an accusation. "Someone is watching her."

My blood runs cold and I try to breathe normally. "Where?" I ask. "Where did your fucking guard die?"

"Behind the governor's mansion," Elijah answers evenly, but I hear that edge of anger in his words. "Now, you would be my prime suspect, save for the photos. But maybe you're fucking with me." He laughs, no humor in it. "Trust me, Rain, you don't want to do that."

*The fucking governor's mansion.* Phil Cooper. I should've known. I know the 6 do a lot of business with the governor. I know how security works there. Heavy in the public eye, lax where it counts. No doubt the fucking guard was likely parked *behind* the mansion.

Dumb fucks.

I guess they've got to keep their own dirty deeds hidden from view somehow.

But pictures of my sister? No fucking way. I've watched her run. Nicolas has watched her. We've *been there.* I wouldn't have let her otherwise.

I would've seen...not to mention the property is fenced in. Guarded.

"Whoever it is," I force myself to say, "is sending a warning to you. Not to me." I rap my knuckles on the table as I sit up straighter. I'm glad we're leaving today. We'll stay in the mountains longer than I intended to get away from here and I'll bring in more guards to monitor my property. "Your dirty little secret might get out, Elijah." My voice drops, barely more than a whisper as I think of the things that happened to us. The shit he allowed to happen. "But this sounds like a *you* problem. Not me."

A pause, and I bite the inside of my cheek to keep from snapping. Finally, he speaks again. "I know you have many men crawling in this city, Rain." His tone is deceptively soft. "But it only takes one of mine to kill her. Put you both down. It would make my life *so much easier.*"

My blood boils and I stand, the cord of the phone flexing as I do. "We both know I'm coming for you, Elijah." My mouth feels dry, thinking of all the ways they fucked us, but I keep talking. "We both know I'm going to pay you back for everything you did to me." I smile at the truth in those words. "To her. To everyone you thought was disposable, every child you thought you could break apart." I laugh, biting my lip as I close my eyes, imagining their blood. "But children grow up, Elijah. And when they do, they don't forget. And that poison you put in our veins? That rage you grew? *You're going to wish you didn't forget that the child that survives always becomes the adult that will fucking rip you apart.*"

I slam the phone against the cradle, cursing under my breath as I turn away from Nicolas, staring at the ceiling, trying to calm my pulse. My mind.

For a long moment, he doesn't speak.

I reach into my pocket, finger the bobby pin in there, holding onto that.

Then Nicolas speaks, and I'm pissed all over again. "What do you want to do about Ria?"

*I don't have time for this shit.* But I know why he's asking. He's thinking of her as a child, too. Or someone to protect.

He forgets I don't have fucking morals. That pain to Elijah? That's from me. From my sister. I'm not trying to save anyone else.

I'm trying to *pay them back for what they took from me.*

"What do you think I should do?" I counter as I turn to face him.

He's in the red leather chair across from my desk, his elbows on his knees, hands dangling between his lap as he looks down at the polished hardwood. I glance at those cigarette burns.

I wonder what it would be like if that's all we had to endure.

A momentary blip of pain, gone when he ran from his piece of shit mother.

Me and Sid didn't even get to run. I was eight and she was five when they took us. When they took her from me.

She was screaming my name.

She'd always craved freedom.

I'd always craved her.

But that day, the day we got pulled apart...she was desperate for me, scratching at the face of the man who pushed her back into the child service's building.

Funny how we always want what was right in front of us that moment it's too late to fucking have it.

But me? I knew I always wanted her. I'd tried to run to her too, but they bound my hands. Covered my mouth.

Shoved me in that fucking car.

I close my eyes tight with that memory, let it pass before I open them again.

I wish I could obliterate all of those things from my mind. Scrub them free of my memory, like I scrub myself raw in the shower.

But I can't.

I've learned to deal. Learned to let that poison seep into my fucking veins. Discovered how to live with the disease of anger. Hatred. Venom.

"We can't keep her locked away for the rest of her life," Nicolas says, and I disagree, but I don't speak, letting him talk this shit out. I think he's fucking Ria. I think that's why he's suddenly so concerned with what happens to her.

He's bought into that great lie. If you love something, set it free.

Bullshit.

If you love something, put it in a fucking cage to protect it. If it tries to escape, build a better cage. I think about Sid again, her messy brown hair, wide silver eyes.

She's interesting, in the way she's petite, slender. As if she wouldn't put up a fight.

But she's tough.

She's been to hell and back, and she came out alive, burning with that fire.

I've done exactly the same.

We were made for each other in so many ways.

"We could place a protection detail on her until she graduates—"

"It's April," I cut off Nicolas, still harping about Ria. Trying to manipulate me. My emotions. He should know better. *I'm better at this game than he is.* "She's missed four months of the spring semester."

"Her last semester," he presses, clenching his jaw as he brings his gaze back to me, clasping his hands together. "She's got…she's got her whole life ahead of her, J, we can't just—"

"You know who else had their entire fucking life ahead of them?" I arch a brow, leaning against my desk chair as I wait for him to answer me, a glower on his face.

He darts his gaze to the door, then back to me. After a tense moment, he blows out a breath and runs his hand over his short blond hair, his muscles flexing with the movement. "Look," he glances at the phone, "you can't punish the entire world because of what happened to someone you love—"

"That's where you're wrong." I brush my thumb over my bottom lip, hearing Sid's whimpers when she sleeps in my head. I've watched her every night. Heard her cries.

I wonder what she dreams about.

Is it them?

Is it...*him*?

I grind my teeth, my pulse picking up speed. "I can punish the world." I smooth down my dress shirt, unbutton my cuffs, roll them back. "And I fucking will." I meet his gaze again. "Is everything packed?"

I step around him, headed to the door.

When I reach it, I stop. Without looking back, I say, "If that heart of yours keeps fucking growing, we'll have to get rid of Ria sooner, rather than later." Without another word, I walk out, steeling myself to break Sid Rain's heart.

# CHAPTER
Eleven

SID

THE WIND BLOWS through my hair from the warm morning, as me and Jeremiah sit at a red light. He came to get me from the backyard where I sat by the pool, my feet in the water as the sun tracked upward across the sky.

We skipped training this morning, and he said he wanted to take me on a trip. Behind us, following in his Mercedes SUV, is Nicolas, with Ria in his passenger seat. Jeremiah seemed surprised they were coming. A little hostile about it. But Ria was excited, no doubt craving time away from the fucking mansion.

I see the sadness in her eyes though, no matter what she might have found with Nicolas. She wants her family.

At least she's got one worth wanting.

I glance over at Jeremiah, see the fit of his charcoal gray dress shirt complimenting his tan skin. I take in his sharp jawline, clean shaven and…

*No.*

I force those thoughts from my mind.

He refuses to tell me where we're going, but these drives seem to be the only time we're able to be around each other without our anger and sexual tension ruining the fucking moments.

But with Jeremiah's hand on the gear shift, one clenched tight around the steering wheel, his veins visible beneath his black watch, shirtsleeves rolled up to his forearms, I'm starting to rethink that sexual tension thing.

I like sex.

I always have.

Maybe that's a result of my past. Perhaps I'm a product of men like Reverend Wilson. Men who touched me and licked me and fucked me before I was able to say yes or no or scream or cry.

It doesn't matter.

I've long accepted that sex is a balm for me. A way to disappear. To tamper down on all those pesky fucking emotions that I want to avoid.

Since Jeremiah had me against the wall at that club, telling me a truth he'd kept from me for far too long, I haven't been able to stop thinking about it. About him. *Like that.* Him and Lucifer are the sexiest men I've ever seen in my life.

*Nothing has changed about that.*

Still, I force myself to look straight ahead. To stare at the blazing sun as Jeremiah turns right, onto the highway, Nicolas following us.

Jeremiah looks distracted. He's barely glanced at me once, and as *Comedown* by Bush plays in the AMG, he's mouthing the words without actually singing.

Jeremiah does everything deliberately.

But this seems…like an absentminded type of thing.

"Are you okay?" I ask him, trying to keep it casual as he switches lanes, over to the fast lane, of course.

He stops singing under his breath, glances over at me, his pale green eyes meeting mine for a second, but then his eyes are back on the road.

We trail to a slow crawl, traffic jammed up from the morning commute I guess.

"Good talk," I mutter when it becomes clear he isn't going to answer me. I pick at a thread on my distressed jeans, a few sizes too big to accommodate my bump, my index finger running over the denim, then my skin. I'm still pale, but I've gained some color back in the four weeks I've been away from the fucking cult.

In the four weeks I've been with this moody boy behind the wheel. Moody, but I'm pretty sure he'd do anything in the world for me, so I try not to hold it against him.

"Smart ass," he snarls back without looking at me as we coast along in traffic, red taillights as far as we can see. But his lips are pulling into a reluctant smile and I try to bite back my own, my hand turning into a fist on my thigh.

"You take me out to sit in traffic? This our trip? Very romantic," I tell him, still looking dead ahead.

A beat of silence, then he yanks the wheel.

I grab onto the handrail, my other arm darting out to his.

"Hold on tight, baby," he says softly, shifting gears.

"What are you—" I stop abruptly as I realize exactly what the fuck he's doing. He's driving on the cement median, edged between a concrete divider and the line of fucking cars to my right.

My mouth falls open as I watch the angry expressions of the people sitting in their own cars that we fly by. Traffic is moving freely opposite the divider, and I keep waiting for blue lights to flash in the mirror or ahead of us, but Jeremiah doesn't seem to share my fucking concern.

I look dead ahead, see a truck swerving out to look at what's causing the traffic jam. I open my mouth to scream, my heart flying in my chest as Jeremiah makes no move to slow the fuck down.

We're going to hit that truck.

We're going to hit that truck and, in this car, *we're going to be the ones hurt.*

Jeremiah curses under his breath in a language I don't know, still refusing to slow down, but at the last minute, the truck must see us coming and he jerks back into line with the other cars, laying on the horn as we fly past.

My nails are digging into Jeremiah's skin, my heart pounding painfully in my chest. But there's something else, too, under the fear. An adrenaline rush, heady and intoxicating.

"The fuck is wrong with you?" I ask anyway, my mouth hanging open as I turn to stare at him.

"You tellin' me you didn't like that?" he asks without looking at me as he keeps racing down the median, past the stopped traffic, his eyes darting to the line of cars every so often, I assume to ensure we don't almost smash into another fucking truck.

I'm breathing hard, my hand still clenched tight around the handle above the door.

"I don't know," I admit, a little breathless. Then my eyes widen as I see the source of the slowdown. "There's a cop!" I screech out.

Jeremiah just laughs under his breath, but this time, he slows down, downshifting as we see three cop cars and an ambulance blocking one lane. The one we're closest too.

There's a smashed van, a smaller car flipped upside down.

My breath catches in my throat as Jeremiah slides effortlessly in front of a yellow Mustang, cutting it close, having to brake hard to stop us from slamming into the Honda in front of us.

But he does it.

He stops.

No cops come our way. I sit up straighter, trying to look over the tops of the vehicles in front of us, but if a police officer saw what we did, they don't seem to care. They're too busy tending to the wreck.

Jeremiah laughs, and that sound is fucking delicious. "You can get your nails out of my arm now," he purrs.

I realize I'm still gripping him tight enough to draw blood.

I let go, releasing the handle, too.

But just as I do, his hand leaves the gearshift and yanks mine over to his thigh, the rich fabric of his black tailored pants beneath my palm.

I swallow down the lump in my throat, his hand dwarfing mine.

"You like that?" he asks me again, quietly.

I look up, meeting his gaze as we wait in traffic, much closer now to freedom. To the two lanes on this side of the highway that open up beyond the accident.

"I think so," I manage to whisper, knowing that's a lie. *I loved it.* It was a thrill, like running. It was...fun.

He dips his chin, looking down at me through his long lashes. "Yeah?"

I nod, biting my lip.

He slides my hand up higher on his pants. My blood is on fire, my ribcage feeling tight, like I can't quite draw enough air in.

"Yeah?" he checks again, holding my gaze as we idle.

"Yes," I whisper. He moves my hand up higher, and I feel his cock, hard and *big* beneath my fingers.

My breath catches as he glides my hand up and down the long length of him.

*Fuck.*

*Fuck.*

Fuck.

It's not that I didn't think Jeremiah had a big dick. I've felt it against me many times before, and in the club. It's just now, with my fingers curled around him, and barely at that...

"You like this?" he asks, arching a brow as I hold his gaze.

The traffic still isn't moving, and the warm air is stagnant through the cracked windows.

I'm sweaty and gross, feeling like I might combust in my black shirt, black jeans, combat boots. But the way Jeremiah is looking at me right now, like he wants to fucking eat me alive, I feel anything *but* gross.

"I think I—"

He bites his tongue, his mouth open, something in his expression making me falter. "You *think*, baby?" He keeps gliding my hand up and down his erection, and I suddenly hate that we're in this car. I hate that we have seatbelts on, and we're stuck in traffic and— "Or you know?"

My chest is heaving, and he doesn't have to guide my hand anymore. It's moving all on its own, up and down him, and I want to unbuckle his belt, undo his pants, and I want to lean across the console and put my mouth on him. This man that loves me and cares for me in the most wicked ways.

But then I see him.

Demon blue eyes. His pale face, sharp jaw. Curly black hair. I see his hands on my throat, feel his breath on my mouth.

*"Hate me, love me, fuck me, run from me. I don't care. You're stuck with me."*

My husband.

I yank my hand back from Jeremiah, stare at the scar on my palm, the X. *Coagula.*

I feel Jeremiah's eyes boring into the side of my head as I try to think. To catch my breath.

To remind myself I left him. It doesn't matter. I had to go. I can't stay. We can never work unless he does the one thing he won't ever do. *Leave them.*

Fear crawls down my spine, the hairs on the back of my neck lifting as it does.

*No.*

He's my husband by law, we're bound by this scar, but I can't go back to him. Not now. Not ever.

I thought this would be temporary, but I know he can't leave them. He can't break away from the 6. And they would've killed me. They would've killed me, or made him do it.

This is...beyond me.

It is beyond this world.

I can't. I shouldn't feel guilty, because *I. Can't.*

*Especially* if I keep this child.

The car lurches forward, the engine revving and I drop my hand to my lap, looking over at Jeremiah. His jaw is clenched as we pass the wreck, a muscle ticking and feathering down into his neck.

He shifts gears, following behind the Honda.

I glance at the wreckage. There are no bodies visible, but there's shattered glass and warped aluminum from the vehicles strewn across the lane that's blocked off.

I catch the eye of one of the policemen, and he's watching us. I swear he tips his head to Jeremiah in a nod, then turns around, letting him go.

*Do they know each other? Who doesn't he know?*

I hold my breath, waiting for Jeremiah's anger. For it to come out all over me like a purge. That's how he deals with it, with me. He holds it in until he can't, and when he lets go, he doesn't hold any of it back.

I think of when he fired a gun at my head.

When he missed.

I wonder if he regrets that, even now.

He switches over to the left lane, one quick glance in his side view mirror before he does. Then he utters a curse under his breath, another language I don't know.

I know he knows German. Latin. I've heard what I think is Spanish coming from his office too.

I decide to ask an innocent question, try to deflect from

the hardon he's still got, evident by the huge bulge in his pants.

"How many languages do you speak?"

He glares at me, shifting gears without taking his eyes off of mine. "A lot," he says, his eyes narrowed. "But apparently Sid fucking Rain isn't one of them." He holds my gaze even though we're going over one hundred miles per hour on the fucking highway.

"Jeremiah, I'm sorry, I—"

"You *what?*" he growls, still holding my gaze.

My stomach churns. I glance out the windshield. There's not another car for a while, but even still, he could go off the side of the road, veer into another lane.

He doesn't, though.

His hand is steady on the gear shift.

I glance to the one on the wheel.

It's not as steady.

I know he sees me looking, but he doesn't move it. "What happened?" I ask, my voice hoarse as I meet his gaze again.

Surprising me, the corners of his mouth pull up into a smile. "Same thing that's gonna happen to you, if you don't stop fucking with me." Without another word, he turns from me, staring straight ahead, that haunting smirk still lingering on his handsome face.

# CHAPTER Twelve

## LUCIFER

I WAKE up to the smell of bacon.

My stomach rumbles before I even open my fucking eyes, and my mouth is so dry, I think I taste blood on my tongue.

Groaning, I stuff a pillow over my face, rolling onto my back.

Inhaling, I catch the scent of something…unfamiliar.

Fabric softener, or some other fucking laundry detergent that isn't what my wife uses. It's strong, nearly choking me and I sit up, flinging the pillow off the bed as I blink my eyes open, scrubbing a hand over my face.

Another breath in, and the bacon scent hits me again.

My wife doesn't fucking cook bacon, and Ella only likes to bake.

My wife also uses unscented detergent. Something about the chemicals killing our brain cells. Running the edge of my hand under my nose, snorting, I think about the coke I've done and all the brain cells I've lost.

But then I take the room in.

Its sheer curtains do nothing to block the sun streaming in through the window to my right.

Pale wooden floors. A small dresser against the wall opposite me.

White sheets.

*Sid and I hate white sheets. Blood stains too easily.*

I dart my eyes to the closed white door, hear something
from beyond it. People talking. Frying bacon.

It takes me a second, then my pulse picks up speed as I see
my black backpack by the door, skeleton bandana laid over it.

*Fuck.*

Julie. Finn. *Ophelia.*

They're all in this goddamn house.

I remember the drive from Alexandria, North Carolina to
Acid City, Virginia. Ophelia leaned across the console of the
M5 and...

*Fuckkkk.*

I bury my head in my hands, elbows on my knees as I
realize I'm in boxer briefs, no shirt on.

I let Ophelia suck my dick.

*I let her suck my fucking dick.*

I think about last night. Julie greeted me warmly. O, not so
much. Finn was sleeping. Ophelia brushed her teeth, probably
getting the taste of my cum out of her mouth. Sid loved that
shit. She wouldn't have brushed her goddamn teeth.

I asked Julie about the kitten's head.

She'd thrown it in the garbage out back.

Said the alarm from one window had gone off the other
night. She seemed spooked, but also pissed O was in her
house. Gave me no other good information. Isn't Finley,
because he's stayed far the fuck away, in another state, wanting
nothing to do with his fucking son.

Julie had offered me a drink.

The three of us had too much.

Ophelia wanted to sleep in this room, but there're four
bedrooms in this airy house, and I stumbled up to bed by
myself, letting the girls deal with their shit.

I pick my head up, glance at the nightstand.

There's a line there, a snipped off straw, what I prepared in the night.

My phone is face down beside it, and I take a breath, run my hand over my nose again, taste blood in the back of my throat. Blood and whiskey and the bitter taste of coke, like crushed up aspirin.

I swing my legs, see my boxers riding up and giving me a view of the Unsaint's tattoo on my thigh, taking up nearly the entire fucking thing.

So many scars.

But I know Sid's.

I run my finger over it, deeper than the rest. Longer, too.

My chest clenches, my throat tightening.

She won't forgive me for that. Ophelia. *She won't fucking forgive me, even though I'm here because of her.*

I need to know if I can find anything here. Someone is after us. *Her.*

And he isn't watching her like he should, if those photos are any indication.

*He's giving her the fucking freedom she wants.*

I slam my fist on the dresser, snatch up the straw, rail the fucking line and drop the straw, closing my eyes, swallowing down the bitter taste of coke as my pulse picks up speed.

There's a soft knock on the door and I flinch.

Clearing my throat, I manage to call out, "Yeah?"

"Morning," Julie says, her voice quiet. "Breakfast is ready, if you're hungry."

*I'm fucking not.* "Thanks," I call out. "I'll be down soon."

I hear a baby cooing, making some kind of blubbering sound, and that tightness in my chest knots heavier.

"Okay. No rush," Julie offers, then I hear her walk away, the creak of the stairs as she heads down.

She's a lot more mellow than she used to be, and I can't

help but wonder if that's because she thinks this visit may be something more than it is.

I didn't tell her about Sid.

About the marriage.

About any of it.

*Because it's not her fucking business.* The more people mad at my wife, the more I worry. I just let it go. Kept another secret for her.

It didn't matter.

It does now, I guess.

Swearing under my breath, I run my hand through my hair, then drop it to my knee, palm up.

That fucking X.

Sid's X.

*My wife's fucking brand.*

I stand, swearing again, then walk to my bag, tie the bandana around my throat and pull out my clothes and get dressed, wondering what the fuck I'm supposed to find here when Julie doesn't know shit.

I should've stayed at the other house last night. Shouldn't have stayed in this one, with both of these girls I've fucked here, but it doesn't matter.

O and I will be on the road later today, headed out.

I'll call Mav, see if there's anything specific he wants me to look into. Otherwise, I need to get back to North Carolina.

Even if she doesn't want me right now, I have to be closer to my wife, and I know the fucking little compound he's keeping her at.

When I'm brushing my teeth in the guest bathroom, I glance at my reflection, right above my dark blue eyes, blood-shot and dry.

There's no scar on my pale skin.

But there's one on hers, and I can't stop thinking about it.

*That night I know she decided to leave.*

It takes everything I have not to drive my fucking fist into the mirror. Everything not to open up the medicine cabinet and fucking swallowing everything in it.

I fucked her up.

I promised to look after her, to protect her. I promised no one would hurt her again, then I went and did *just fucking that.*

# CHAPTER Thirteen

## SID

WHEN WE CROSS the border into Virginia, I feel sick. The last time I came north, this far north anyway, was with Nicolas. When we went to Julie's house, then Lucifer had his hand wrapped over my mouth.

Later, at another house not too far from it, I learned the truth.

That Jeremiah, my *brother*, had assaulted me on Halloween night. Not Lucifer.

But I don't say anything about any of that as Jeremiah and I ride in silence, his last words lingering in my head. *"Same thing that's gonna happen to you if you keep fucking playing with me."*

I glance at his left hand on the wheel, but I don't see any sign of that tremor.

Swallowing down the sour taste in my mouth, the feel of my panic, I look back out the window at the mountains looming on either side of the highway, the bright, clear sky. It's beautiful out, and the windows are still down, my hair blowing around my eyes, but it feels so good, I just don't care.

I glance in the rear view and see Nicolas and Ria have caught up from Jeremiah's fucking reckless driving bullshit hours ago.

"Where are we going?" I ask for what feels like the hundredth time without looking at Jeremiah.

There's a moment of silence, and I think he just isn't going to answer me. Typical. But then he says, "We're almost there. I thought we could go hiking?" He phrases it like a question and my stomach flips.

Placing a hand on my belly, wondering when I can feel this baby kick, I turn to stare at him. "Really?"

I love hiking. Being outside, in nature.

But J never wants me to get too far, and sometimes, I can't even blame him. When we split up as kids, the worst imaginable became of us. He won't even talk about all of his trauma.

It makes me feel sick just trying to imagine it.

"Yeah," he says, glancing at me, almost nervously, his fingers tightening on the wheel. "Really." He shrugs. "I thought you'd like a getaway. We're staying in a cabin." I watch him swallow, his eyes on the road.

I frown. "Cabin?" Jeremiah is not the type to stay in a fucking cabin.

"Is that a problem?"

I smile to myself, shifting in my seat, running my hands over my thighs, feeling the holes in my jeans. "Not at all. I'm just surprised that you'd stoop so low."

He laughs, and it's dark. "When you see it, you won't be surprised."


DESPITE HIS WORDS, WHEN HE SAID A "CABIN," I PICTURED something small, rustic. Charming, maybe. Nice and new, knowing him.

But what I didn't imagine was *this*.

A long, winding driveway, floodlights flicking on as we approach even in the daylight. A two-car garage, stone and brick mansion with so many windows it reminds me of the Cullen's hideaway in *Twilight*.

I dart my eyes to the thick forest that surrounds the house, the mountains looming in the distance, rising up against the bright blue sky.

Jeremiah pulls around the circular driveway, in front of the double doors, stone columns on either side. Nicolas called while we drove, and him and Ria are getting groceries.

I blink up at the house.

It almost reminds me of mine and Lucifer's house, but... *bigger*.

Thinking of my husband, my chest tightens.

The misery threatens to sweep over me, but I push it back. *Back.*

Still, I can't resist glancing in the side view mirror as Jeremiah cuts the engine, gets out of the Mercedes. I take in my reflection, knowing the scar is there, but I can't see it from here, it's that small.

I reach for it, running my index finger over the soft ridge, thinking of the night it happened.

My stomach twists into knots.

I hear Jeremiah calling my name from the trunk of the car, probably getting out the bags he packed, but I'm not paying attention.

Suddenly, I'm back *there*.


*IT'S THE TYPE OF SOUND THAT CHILLS YOUR BONES. AN INHUMAN cry followed by heavy gasps, the shift of the mattress and after that...his head buried in my shoulder, tears damp against my skin.*

*At least, that's what it had been.*

*Tonight, though, it's different.*

*He's not in bed and the wailing comes from downstairs, but I still wake up wide-eyed, my heart nearly beating right out of my chest.*

*The sheets stick to my legs even with the fan overhead and the AC on freeze and I don't know if I should sweat this much in the night, but since Sacrificium...the bodies...the cage. The knife to my throat on that altar...*

*I hear another strangled cry and I flinch, kicking the covers off as I swing my legs, bare feet hitting the cold floor. I don't bother turning on the light as I race down the stairs, his screams turning to sobs.*

*My throat tightens with that sound, and for some reason, tonight, I place a hand over my belly. Like an instinct. Still not showing, not even close, but it's the start of what could be our future.*

*If we don't rip it apart first.*

*I glide my hand down the banister, stumbling over the last step in the dark, tightening my hold along the handrail to steady myself.*

*The scream is louder down here, blood-curdling. He's in...agony.*

*Even if it isn't real.*

*I learned long ago that horrors of the mind can kill, too. A knife through the back happens once. Haunting memories get stuck and never leave and sometimes you just want to fucking die to end them all.*

*But the thought of losing him...I couldn't.*

*Releasing the rail, I sprint down the hall, toward the living room, dark enough that I couldn't see my hand in front of my face if I'd bothered holding it up.*

*But I don't.*

*Instead, my arms are churning at my sides as fast as my legs are pumping, that scream growing, the gasps for breath—for relief—tearing into my heart with every second I'm not touching him.*

*Holding him.*

*Protecting him from his own mind.*

*I feel the carpeted rug beneath my feet and instinctively dive to the left to avoid the coffee table. I've been stuck inside this house for months now; I've memorized every square inch.*

*But just as I get close to the couch, where I think the noise is coming from, something shatters.*

*I flinch at the splinter of glass, then stumble back a step, my hands held out in front of my face. My pulse skyrockets, and I strain my ears, listening.*

*Whatever it was smashed against the wall to my right, which means he could still be on the couch but right now, it's eerily silent.*

*Unnervingly quiet.*

*I can only hear my pulse thudding in my ears, feel my chest rising and falling too fast.*

*Too fucking fast as fear slides down my spine.*

*I open my mouth to call his name, but before I can, there's the scratch of a match.*

*The smell of Sulphur.*

*His face inches from mine, illuminating the pale planes of his cheek-bones. His midnight blue eyes.*

*It reminds me of Sanctum.*

*And that reminds me of...Lazar.*

*"Mors vincent omnia, pater?" His voice is a snarl. I'm not sure what he's saying, but that last word. I know that word. He taught me a few Latin basics. Pater is father. He really liked that one, and the thought has me cradling my tummy again.*

*But just as he blows the match out, the flame licking down toward his long, pale fingers, I catch the glint of the knife.*

*My blood runs cold, all thoughts of him as a dad...gone.*

*"Lucifer." His whispered name is the only thing I manage to say as I step back before his hand comes to my hair, jerking me against him, my back to his chest.*

*I cry out, hands going to my head, but he's got the knife against my temple. The sharp end of it, judging by the pinprick of pain that makes my eyes water.*

*I know how he killed his father.*

*Not because he told me.*

*Because Mayhem did.* "He drove a knife through his fucking skull."

*I'm not breathing, and I drop my hand back over my belly. He bands his forearm around my chest, and I reach for it, fingers curling around hard muscle, trying to pull him off. He drives the point of the blade in deeper and I feel the warmth of my own blood as I close my eyes tight, trying to inhale. Exhale.*

*"Lucifer," I whisper again, tears welling up behind my eyes as he holds the knife steady, his arm around my chest vise-like. "Lucifer, it's*

*me." My voice breaks on the last word and blood runs over my eye as my chest caves.*

*I can't do this anymore.*

*One night I woke up with his hand around my throat. Another with a fucking pillow over my face.*

*He refuses to see a doctor.*

*The 6 forbid him from going to a therapist.*

*Maverick suggested the official priest of the 6, Father Tomas, but he came to the house with a whip and if he had whipped my fucking husband, I'd slit his goddamn throat.*

*But I can't...I can't do this.*

*The tears mingle with my blood, warm and wet down my cheeks. A small sob escapes my mouth because he doesn't let go. Doesn't drop the knife.*

*"Lucifer," I try again, desperate now. "I'm your wife."*

*Time seems to stand still. He doesn't move. I don't even feel him breathing at my back, and I'm holding my own breath, waiting.*

*Then everything happens at once.*

*The knife falls to the floor with a clatter, Lucifer spins me around, pulls me to his chest as I shake in his arms.*

*"Oh my god," he's saying, his voice hoarse, that cruel snarl gone. "Fuck, Sid, I'm so sorry. I'm so fucking sorry." His fingers dig into my ribs as he holds me, my arms by my sides. "I'm so fucking sorry, baby girl." His voice is almost desperate.*

*Almost pleading.*

*Like he knows what I'm going to do.*

*Like he knows I've got to get away from him.*

*He kisses my head, nuzzles his nose against my neck and inhales. "I'm so fucking sorry. Please don't..." A sob tears through him. I can feel it shuddering through his chest. "Please don't go."*

*And maybe I wouldn't be thinking about it. Maybe I'd stay.*

*If this kind of thing only happened when he was sleeping...I might not be planning to run.*

. . .

"BABY, CAN YOU GIVE ME A FUCKING HAND?" JEREMIAH'S snarl brings me back to the present, and I realize he's got my door open, standing just outside of it, weighted down with bags, a suitcase in each hand.

The strap of one duffel bag cuts into his muscular chest, the dress shirt he's wearing wrinkling beneath the strap. His eyes are hard on mine, his full lips pulled into a scowl.

I glance at his forearms, the flex of hard muscle. But it's not that I'm looking at. I'm well-acquainted with just how fit my brother is. Instead, it's the way his left hand is gripped so tight around the handle of the suitcase, his knuckles are blanching, and his hand is...*trembling.*

*There it is again.*

"Sid!" he snaps, and I pick my head up, reaching to undo my seatbelt. He jerks his chin to the door. "I just need you to enter the keycode. Or maybe, I don't know, get out of the fucking car?"

I roll my eyes, glancing again at his hand.

*What happened to you?*

I get out, slam the door closed behind me as my combat boots hit the paved driveway. "This is a cabin?" I ask, trying to pull one of the matte black suitcases from his hand, but he jerks it away from me.

"Just get the door," he mutters, nodding toward the colossal entranceway.

"Yes, *sir.*" I roll my eyes and walk in front of him, toward the steps.

"Don't say that again," he warns from behind me as he follows. "You'll make my dick hard."

I swear I feel his eyes on my ever-expanding ass, but I hold up my middle finger as I bite my tongue. Memories of him, sweaty and breathing hard on top of me in the gym, spring to my mind.

My hand around his cock when we left North Carolina.

Yeah. I've felt his hard dick.

A few times.

*Don't go there.*

I can't.

Sometimes, I'm still getting used to the idea that he's not my brother. Not by blood, anyway. And my blood brother? I feel my face flame as I reach the double doors of the "cabin."

Thinking about Mayhem's belt around my throat makes my knees feel weak, and yeah, maybe I shouldn't get so fucking turned on at the memory of it, considering we share a fucking father but...the mind is a sick place.

At least, mine is.

Even still, I shove those thoughts away. It's not that relation, or even the fact that Jeremiah was my foster brother that bothers me most.

It's...my husband.

Lucifer would never forgive me for that. He's forgiven me for so much already, but that he would never get over.

And I don't have a plan. I don't know what happens after this, but I don't want him to spend the rest of his life fucking hating me. I don't want to be that person to him. He's suffered enough.

Just thinking of it...I want to run back to him.

But then I remember the scar above my brow, then Noctem, and I just...can't.

"What's the passcode?" I call out, eyeing the keypad flush against the stone. It's solid black, like the one at our house. Mine and Lucifer's.

Must be a rich thing.

"Hold your thumb up to it," Jeremiah says, and he's so close to me, his breath is against my ear.

I tense, spine rigid as I feel him behind me. His body heat is radiating into me, even though we're not touching.

Swallowing the lump in my throat, I wonder if this cabin shit was a bad idea. *Well, it wasn't fucking my idea.*

"But I've never been here, how can my thumb—"

Jeremiah presses his open mouth to my cheek, his tongue flicking along my skin.

That lump in my throat grows bigger.

I can't even breathe.

He licks his way up my jaw, and I wish Nicolas was here. Ria. But no one is here, and at some point, I have to confront these feelings. The fact that maybe I left because Lucifer is losing it, putting me in danger, but also because…I wanted to be here. With Jeremiah fucking Rain. He bites my ear, and my entire body tingles, warmth building in my low belly. "Just put your goddamn thumb up to the keypad, okay, *Sis?*"

I clear my throat, and he pulls back, letting me catch my breath. I should tell him to fuck off. Maybe turn around and punch him in the fucking face.

But I…don't.

Instead, I do as he said, and I hear an electronic beeping noise, then the unmistakable sound of a lock flicking open.

"Welcome home," he says softly, his breath fanning the back of my neck.

With a shaky hand, I reach for the lever, press it down, and scurry my ass into the house, wondering just how long my self-control will last being trapped in the mountains with my sexy, psychotic fucking brother.

▼

"Are you sure it's okay to leave her there?" I ask Jeremiah, turning to stare at him as we drive on the highway, leaving behind the cabin and the desolate, rural road it's on. I didn't see any houses along it, and he said he owns the private street.

No surprise.

But Nicolas is in the backseat of the AMG, and Ria said she was tired, fell asleep in the bedroom she's apparently sharing with Nicolas.

I'm tired, too, but I'm more hungry than tired and Jeremiah wanted to take us out to eat.

"Why? Worried she'll run?" My brother laughs, switching gears as he switches lanes, glancing in the rear-view mirror. "She's not you, baby."

Nicolas says nothing from the back and when I glance over my shoulder, he's frowning down at his phone, thumbs flying over his screen.

I turn back in my seat, looking at the sinking sun.

"Is it safe there?" I counter. "I mean you have so many people that hate you..." I shrug, trailing off, biting back my smile.

Jeremiah makes a strangled sound in the back of his throat. "A lot of people love me," he counters, and I can tell from his tone I'm not going to like his next words. "Women, especially."

I think about the dancer in his lap at Nicolas's birthday and my stomach twists into knots. I hate that.

I like to think it's just the baby, growing and shit.

"Whatever," I mutter, leaning back in the seat and letting my eyes flutter closed. "Wake me up when we get wherever the hell you're going."

Jeremiah's hand comes over my belly, making me gasp, but I bite my lip, keep my eyes closed as his fingers splay over the sheer black tank I'm wearing, a lime green bra underneath. I even changed into a leather skirt—with an elastic waist, but still. No one has to know all that.

My blood runs hot as Jeremiah brushes his thumb up and down my low belly, his other fingers gently pressing into my skin. "Watch yourself," he says softly. "You've gotten so mouthy lately."

A smile graces my lips and I wish it didn't. I wish I didn't fall for every cruel fucking word he says, but I like it.

I've always liked it. It's how we are with each other. It's like it's easier to be vicious than to admit that we…love one another.

I hated being held prisoner in my own home at that hotel. I hated that I couldn't breathe. But I loved how his overprotective nature felt like…*he cared.*

With Lucifer, it was the same. Even though I wanted more…a job, maybe, or to go back to school, or even just a car so I could do simple things like grocery shopping without him, it still felt like…he cared.

And I know he loves me, in his own way.

But his night terrors, those delusions during the day, and all the coke he can't stop doing…that was why I ran.

That, and the 6, fucking taking me. Ella. From *our. Fucking. House.*

I don't think about it. It's what I'm good at. Avoiding my problems. And right now, with my stomach growling under J's hand, the only problem I want to think about is stuffing my goddamn face.

But when I wake up, someone gently shaking me, it seems like Jeremiah Rain, as always, had other fucking plans.

I blink my eyes open, wondering how it got so dark.

It feels like I've only slept a minute, but when I glance at the clock on the center console, it's nearly nine at night.

And it *is* night.

The sun had just been setting when I closed my eyes, Jeremiah's warm hand over my belly.

Now, his hand shifted to my shoulder, nudging me softly, it's nothing but blackness surrounding his car.

I reach beside me, press the button to raise my seat as I yawn, turning my head to look at my brother, my eyes bleary with sleep as I run a fist over them.

"Where are we?" I ask, my voice groggy. I can't see shit

beyond the tinted windows, only the light from the dashboard and the electronic console illuminating Jeremiah's pale green eyes, his hand still on my shoulder, thumb stroking over my skin.

My body tingles, but I shove that feeling aside, turn to glance behind me.

See Nicolas leaned forward in the middle seat, elbows on his bent knees as his dark eyes connect with mine.

He's gripping his phone in one hand, and there's a crease between his brow.

As I stifle another yawn, I turn back to look at Jeremiah, foreboding unfurling within me. "What...what's going on?" I ask, clearing my throat.

Jeremiah swallows, glances at his hand on my shoulder.

Then he drops his hand to the gear shift, his knuckles blanching, he's gripping it so hard.

*What the fuck?*

I turn to look out the window again.

Blinking, it seems like we're pulled over on the side of the road.

I whip my head back around to face my brother. "What the fuck are we—"

"There's something you need to know, baby." Jeremiah's words are tender. Soft.

It makes my blood run cold. My heart hammer in my chest. "What's going on?" I reach for the door handle, but don't try to open it. I'm feeling closed in, though. Anxious. I fall asleep as we're on our way to dinner, now we're pulled over on the side of the fucking road, and both Jeremiah and Nicolas are staring at me as if their best friend died.

*Died...*

My throat closes up, one hand going to it as I dig my nails into my skin. Did Lucifer...*is he...*

"Oh my god." My words come out as a rasp. I dart my gaze to Nicolas, my pulse racing. "Oh my god!" My voice grows more high-pitched. I have to get out of this car. I yank on the handle, but it doesn't open.

The doors are fucking locked.

*The doors are fucking locked.*

*I Don't Belong Here* by I Prevail is playing softly through the speakers of the car and my heart is breaking as it does.

I unbuckle my seatbelt, turn away from Jeremiah and flip the lock on the door, clawing at the handle, but before I can get the door open, Jeremiah's strong fingers curl around my bicep, hard enough to bruise as he yanks me back in.

"What, exactly, do you think is happening right now, baby?" he asks me quietly, his words edged with something cold.

My hands start to tremble, and I ball them into fists. See Jeremiah's cold gaze locked on mine.

I swallow, my mouth dry.

"Did something…did something happen to him?"

Jeremiah's grip tightens on my arm and I wince, digging my own nails into the palm of my hands.

"To *who?*" he presses me, that coldness in his voice causing a chill to slide down my spine.

"L-Lucifer," I manage to say, choking on my husband's name. I dart my gaze to Nicolas, but I can read nothing in his expression. He's still just staring at me.

Just like Jeremiah.

My heart sinks.

My stomach knots up.

I think I'm going to be sick. "What happened?" I gasp out, pleading with him. "What the fuck are we doing here? What the fuck——"

Jeremiah reaches across the center console, his hand coming to the back of my neck as he leans close to me, pressing his brow to mine.

I catch his clean scent, peppermint on his breath as he speaks, his words caressing my mouth.

"You worried about him, sis?" he asks me quietly.

I open my mouth. Close it. *What the fuck is going on? Where the fuck are we?*

He smiles, but it's cold. Does nothing except make me more nervous, a twitchy feeling in my limbs, my hands still balled into fists on my thighs.

His fingers are still around my arm, hand still around the back of my neck.

"You scared he's…dead?"

My breath catches, my lip trembling.

His own lips curve back into a smile that nearly brushes against my mouth. "That's no less than what he deserves."

Time seems to stand still. For a moment, I can't breathe. Can't think.

Then the moment passes, and I think my heart is shattering. I think I might be dying, too.

My stomach hurts, and I finally react, snap out of this spell Jeremiah Rain seems capable of placing over every and anyone he meets.

I try to jerk away from him, but he only grips me tighter.

I slap at his chest, my hands going to his throat. "What did you do to him?" The words are wild, reckless. "What the fuck did you fucking do to him?"

I'm drowning, my throat closing up, my breaths coming in shallow pants, my heart nearly bursting out of my fucking chest.

"What did you fucking—"

"Do you know where we are?" he asks calmly, speaking over my heartbreak.

Pressure builds behind my eyes, that lump growing bigger in my throat as I claw at his neck, and he doesn't even flinch. Doesn't let me fucking go. I shake my head, my forehead brushing against his even as I try to pull away. To get out of this car.

My husband…

*Did something fucking happen to my husband?*

*Did he…do it himself?*

*He wouldn't do that to me.*

He wouldn't fucking *do that to me.*

"What did you do?" I ask again, my voice hoarse. "Jeremiah." I squeeze his throat, feel him swallow beneath my palms. "Jeremiah, what did you *fucking do?*" My voice breaks on the last words, and his grip on my arm hurts, making those tears fall freely.

"I asked you a question, baby," he says softly, ignoring all of my questions. Ignoring the way my heart is breaking. My mind reeling. "I said, *do you know where we are?*"

I squeeze my eyes closed tight. *Maybe he's okay.* Maybe this is about something else. Maybe I've got it wrong. "No," I finally answer, my nostrils flaring as I try to hold back my sobs. "No. Where are we, J? Where the *fuck* are we?" I keep my voice low, try to breathe, eyes still closed.

Jeremiah releases my arm, his hand coming over my heart instead, his fingers brushing against my breast, on the outside of my shirt.

I can't breathe all over again.

"We're at Julie's house, beautiful."

My eyes fly open, my heart stopping.

"Ah, yeah." He laughs, his breath against my skin. "You remember her, don't you? And *Finn?*"

Of course I fucking do. I'd thought about her when we crossed the border. About what I learned here.

That this man, the one holding me, caressing my breast as I panic, one hand still tight around the back of my neck, assaulted me.

He assaulted me, then lied to me for a year.

He fed my anger to someone else entirely to prevent it from burning up our love.

I shouldn't forgive him for that, but I don't remember that

night. Not the parts with him hurting me. In some sick way, it's like it didn't really…happen.

"Jeremiah. What are you talking about?" I keep my eyes on his, watch as he pulls back, sliding his hand from my chest, up my throat.

Higher still, until his thumb presses against my bottom lip. His eyes dart to my mouth.

"We're here, baby."

I want to get out. I want to turn and run. I don't want to hear his next words.

"And guess who else is here?"

No. *No, no,* no.

*"He is."*

I don't move for several long moments as his thumb brushes over my bottom lip. But then my brain starts to work all over again, and I reason with myself. It doesn't matter that he's here. I've known he pays for this baby. I knew from the beginning it could've been his, then I learned it wasn't, and I learned that as scary and dickish as Lucifer Malikov is, he has a soft spot.

In the form of…*children.*

I drop my hands from Jeremiah's throat, place one on my belly. The other on the gear shift between us.

My husband is here.

I don't dare look out my window, but I know now. Where the fuck we are. *Julie's house.*

"Why did you bring me here?" I ask quietly, refusing to look away from my brother. Letting my pulse settle. My fears.

*He's okay.* My husband is okay.

Jeremiah cocks his head, tugs down my bottom lip and bites his tongue, his mouth open as he stares at my own.

Finally, his eyes flick back to mine. "This is the second night," he says softly. "And he didn't come up here alone."

My stomach flips.

I can't speak.

"Jeremiah—" Nicolas starts, his tone a warning, but Jeremiah cuts him off.

"He drove up here with Ophelia." Jeremiah digs the knife in a little deeper.

"Is Mayhem here?" I ask, the only thing I can think to say. If he's here, if Ella is, if it's not just my husband with two women he's fucked...

Jeremiah laughs softly. "No." He seems to enjoy saying that word.

Enjoy the way my heart breaks.

I try again to pull away from him, and this time he lets me.

I turn to look out the window. Blink in the darkness. I still can't see anything, can't make shit out, but I know he's telling the truth about where we are. A long driveway, trees at the end of it, and beyond that...there's a house with a baby.

A baby, and if my brother is telling the truth, my husband. Ophelia. Julie.

"Why is he here?" I croak out.

No one answers me. I press my palm to the window, shockingly cold against my skin, despite the fact that I know it's hot outside. But the windows are up, the AC flowing softly through the vents of the Mercedes.

"Why is he here?" I demand again, my voice little more than a snarl. I drop my hand, turn to face my brother and Nicolas. "How do I know you're fucking telling the truth? How do I know you're—"

Nicolas sighs as Jeremiah's eyes narrow.

Nicolas pushes his phone in front of my face, the screen so bright I have to blink to adjust to the light.

But I see it.

It's dark, and the camera is in night mode, but I see my husband's fucking car. The BMW M5, black and blacked out, parked behind the fucking house, behind a Jeep. There's a bicycle too. For a kid.

Just like there was that night.

Leaned against the little shed in the back of the house.

"Lucky for us," Jeremiah purrs as I stare at my husband's car, bugs flying in front of the camera, but otherwise, the film is perfect, "they just installed these today. Your *husband's*," J almost chokes on that word, "way of keeping her *safe.*" He snarls that last word and Nicolas pulls the phone from me, pocketing it.

My chest caves.

I try to reason with myself. I left him. Besides that, maybe something happened. Maybe he's pissed with the 6. Maybe he'll actually fucking kill all of them, and in the meantime, he wants to keep Julie and the kid safe.

But Ophelia? *Why the fuck is she here?*

I turn to look out the window, resting my head against the seat.

I'm so fucking tired and torn. Torn between demanding Jeremiah drive me far, far from here. From getting out and running up to that house. Breaking the fucking window before I break Ophelia's nose and snap Julie's neck.

But I'm exhausted.

My brother did this, because…of course he did.

Even still, it's not his fault. What's happening down that dark driveway—and I don't want to think about that too hard —isn't his fault.

"He's fucking her." It's the only thing I can think to say, and I can't stop staring out my window, even though I see nothing.

I think again about the last time I was here with Nicolas.

His hand comes to my shoulder and I flinch.

"Get the fuck off her," Jeremiah snarls, his words quiet.

Nicolas doesn't let go of me. I'm glad for his touch, because my heart is…aching. Without tearing my eyes away from the abyss of darkness that's Julie's front yard, I place my hand on Nicolas's.

"It's okay," I say quietly, hoping to calm J. I thread my

fingers through Nicolas, trying to forget I did that with my husband all the time.

He seemed to like it.

Now I'm not so sure.

Jeremiah's hand comes to my thigh, his grip firm. Meant to reassure. But his fingers seem to spark against my skin.

"I don't like anyone else touching you," he says softly, and my jaw clenches as I turn to stare at him, his green eyes eerie from the dash lights of the car.

He can't even let me have this.

He can't fucking let me have this.

He took me here for his own sinister purposes, because he's a calculating fucking psychopath, but now he can't even let me grieve what I should've known all along. My marriage is over.

I open my mouth to tell him just that when his hand shifts from my thigh to my face, his thumb pressed against my bottom lip again. "I don't like anyone else hurting you, either," he says, leaning in toward me, across the console. He drops his hand to my throat again, his touch gentle. He angles his head, brushes his mouth over my lips.

I try not to react. So, so fucking hard. Despite what Lucifer did, what he's doing, this isn't right.

This isn't fair to him.

I ran.

*I ran.*

"I'll leave him alone for now," Jeremiah says, his words like a promise, "but I'll pay him back for this too."

# CHAPTER Fourteen

## JEREMIAH

*I DIG the pen in deeper to the blank notebook, folded back to an empty page. It slices through the paper, cutting into the next sheet. I drag it down —red ink—to the very end, flexing and curling my fingers when I drop the pen, my grip shaky. I lick my finger, flip past the pages, seeing how many I ripped through.*

*Ten.*

*The pen cut through ten pages, and on the eleventh, there's a little indention, but no ink. No tears.*

*If I cut through ten layers of paper, how many layers of flesh would this pen get through. I snatch it up from the floor of my bedroom, staring at the point, glancing at my wrist as I flip my palm over, see the blue veins on my forearm.*

*Closing my eyes, I take a deep breath, stretch my legs out, brushing the notebook aside as I do.*

*I think about her.*

*Gray eyes and brown hair. Her soft voice. How she didn't speak at first when Mom brought her home. She didn't speak, and she smelled bad, and she looked tiny. Gaunt.*

*I didn't know those words then, when I was just a kid. But now I know. She looked...sick.*

*My knees were knobby, and my leg had been broken and I was skinny. Probably not much bigger than I am now in terms of that, but I push that thought aside because I'm not in the cage right now. I'm free.*

*But she...she was worse off than I was.*

*And now?*

*I dip my head, pressure building behind my eyes. If I kill myself, no one will save her. No one knows her name. No one knows how much she means to someone. To me.*

*They could be hurting her. Starving her. Beating her.*

*The creak of a floorboard outside of my door has me flinching and I drop the pen and the notebook, scurrying back against the wall beside my small bed, my knees up to my chest as I try to inhale. Exhale. Breathe.*

Breathe.

*My bladder almost loosens, and after pissing so many times in a crate, sometimes I wonder if I know how to hold it anymore, but I fucking try.*

*I try now, and when I see who it is coming into my room, it becomes a little easier. My heart slows down, just a little, and the fear isn't so bright on my tongue.*

*It's her.*

*The younger sister. She's nineteen, two years older than me, but she still lives here, and I hear him yelling at her. Her father.*

*My foster father.*

*I hear her crying in the room next to mine, and she tries to muffle it in a pillow, but I know that sound well. I do the same thing.*

*She doesn't crawl into my bed like the older sister. She doesn't grind her pussy against my leg and scream for her dad. Watch and laugh as he drags me to that cage.*

*She doesn't do any of that, and sometimes, when she can, she brings me food in that crate.*

*But they always know.*

*Because sometimes I have to...use the bathroom in there. And they seem to know when she's fed me.*

*I've watched him hit her for that.*

*Now, she folds her arms across her chest and glances over her shoulder, as if she's scared he'll find her in here.*

*Silence stretches between us. Maybe they aren't home right now. They don't talk to me.*

*She turns back to look at me, her bright blue eyes holding mine. Bright but…dead. As if she's barely there.*

*Barely holding on.*

*I know that feeling.*

*But she's dressed in fitted jeans, a black t-shirt that shows her pale skin, but she's not starving. She's got big tits, straining against her shirt, and thick thighs, touching in her denim.*

*She might not have it as good as her older sister, but she still has it better.*

*She glances at the notebook with the red pen slashed through it. At the pen itself, which rolled against the wall adjacent me.*

*Biting her lip, she looks back up at me. "Are you hungry?" she asks quietly, her voice so soft. Shy.*

*I clench my jaw, and I can feel the emptiness in my stomach. Like a pit. I just got out of the cage last night. They didn't feed me.*

*My head feels spacey, my belly like its touching my back.*

*I shake my head anyway, refusing to give her my words.*

*My hand starts to tremble, and I clamp my opposite fingers around my wrist, trying to keep it still.*

*Her eyes track the movement and I feel warmth rush over me. Embarrassment.*

*I'm so tired of being embarrassed.*

*I want her to leave.*

*"They're not here," she whispers. "For a few hours."*

*I run my dry tongue over my teeth, imagine going downstairs. Finding something in the kitchen. But the Forgues have staff, and they're not allowed to let me roam. I'm to stay in here at all times, and if I'm caught wandering, I get thrown back in the darkness. In that cage.*

*A whimper seems to claw its way up my throat and my face burns. I hate her. I hate her so fucking much.*

*"Get out," I say, the words hoarse, my voice scratchy from screaming yesterday. Begging to be free. "Get. Out."*

*She takes a step back, her eyes sad. "You're safe right now," she almost pleads with me. "Sicher, remember?"*

*The German word makes me feel fucking sick.*

*I got to choose a language, besides Latin. I got to choose something for once, and I chose German, because of her.*

*Now, it feels stupid.*

*I'm stupid.*

*I'm fucking stupid.*

*"Get out!" I scream at her, hating that my eyes are welling up with tears and I'm too tired to stand up and I'm too tired to kill myself and I just want all of this to end.*

*She backs out again, then scurries to her room. I hear her close the door. Hear her jump on her bed.*

*I hear her crying, and I hate her more for it.*

*But before I can get up to close the fucking door she left open, I hear heavier footsteps. I scramble tighter against the wall, putting my baggy shirt over my knees, as if that'll protect me.*

*As if that can save me.*

*I feel it again. My bladder loosening, and this time...I can't help it. A whimper escapes my mouth as warmth floods my pants, soaking through to the floor.*

*But when Ezra Van Damme steps through my doorway, it's rage that floods through me, the fear gone.*

*Still, I draw my knees closer, not wanting him to know what I just did. Not wanting him to see all the ways they've lessened me.*

*I don't get to see them much, the children of my parents' friends. And when I do....I close my eyes, knocking my head against the wall painfully. I see his blue eyes. His pale face. That mocking smirk, always curling up on his lips when I'm around.*

*He's the worst of them.*

*He's almost as bad as fucking Francis goddamn Forgues.*

*"What do you want?" I grind out when Ezra doesn't speak. I've heard him visit the youngest sister. Heard his deep voice rumbling from beyond the wall that separates us. He makes her laugh, and I think I hate him more for that.*

*Clearing this throat, he steps further into the room.*

*I still don't open my eyes.*

*Silence stretches on for a moment, and I'm shivering under my shirt, wishing he'd leave. Hoping he doesn't smell the stench of my urine. Wanting him gone as my face burns, my eyes sting with tears I refuse to fucking shed.*

*"This will help," he finally says, and I want to know what he's talking about, but I don't dare look at him.*

*Or ever at them.*

*I've always been beneath them, the one with demon eyes made that very fucking clear.*

*"But do me a favor?"*

*My throat closes up, and his question finally makes me pry my eyes open, mine locking on his dark hazel ones. What could I possibly fucking do for him?*

*He smooths his hand over his gray shirt, looking down for a moment and swallowing, his throat bobbing.*

*After a tense moment where I want to scream at him, to tell him to get the fuck out, he meets my eyes again and he says, "When you get out…" He rakes his hand over his head, glances at the wall that separates my room from hers. "Don't hurt her too."*

*Without another word, he walks out.*

*My heart thrums painfully in my chest, pounding even in my temples, in my hollow stomach. I shift my gaze, see something on the white notebook, just beside the red line I etched into it.*

*A bobby pin.*

*And a box of matches.*

I WAKE UP IN A COLD SWEAT, BREATHING HARD, SCRAMBLING against the headboard. Blinking open my eyes, I glance at the gun on my nightstand, but don't reach for it. I don't need to.

I'm safe here.

I'm not that same kid.

I'm not someone to hide when I hear footsteps. I don't

need fucking matches and bobby pins. A girl with blue eyes offering me breadcrumbs.

*I'm not that person anymore.*

Still, my hand comes to my ribs, and I feel the jagged scar against my hard muscles, my skin hot to the touch.

I think about how it felt, Lucifer plunging in that blade. Sinking it in deep and twisting. It was a type of pain I'd never known before, but I'd known plenty of other types, and I'm not even sure it compared.

It may have been worse than the physical pain I'd endured.

The twine around my wrists.

The hunger.

The kicking, the humiliation.

But even still, the only thing I could compare it to was that night I slit my wrists in a hotel bathtub, no one knowing where I was.

*Her not knowing where I was.*

How much I regretted what I did to her.

*How much I hated that I was a monster, to the only girl I've ever fucking loved.*

I close my eyes, try to relax against the headboard, but my fingers dig in deeper to my not-quite-healed scar, one hand fisting the sheets beside my hip.

I think about how it felt, keeping Sid safe under the covers at our mom's house. When we heard moans and fighting and screaming and crying from outside my bedroom door.

One time I tied her wrists with shoestrings, because she wanted to run.

I always pushed my dresser in front of the door too.

I held her down. Sat on top of her.

Pinned her little wrists over her head.

Then, to make her forget, to help her forgive me, I read her stories from the used books Mom gave us, some with pages missing, covers ripped off.

It didn't matter.

If the page was gone, I'd make it up.

Sid's breathing would even out, and after a few stories, she'd fall asleep in my arms, under those covers.

I'd kiss her hair.

Hold her tight.

Dread the morning, knowing she'd try to run again, and I'd have to start all over, trying to keep her with me.

*Keep her safe.*

If I only knew then what I know now, I would've run with her. Ran so fucking far, no one could find us. No one would catch us.

No one would fucking hurt us.

I swallow, hard, open my eyes and take in the well-lit, airy bedroom of the cabin. The curtains are pulled away from the balcony, sun streaming in, trees and blue sky beyond it. I hear soft murmurs downstairs, and I marvel at the fact I slept so well.

Was it tasting my sister's pain last night that did it?

Listening to her soft cries in the car ride home?

Knowing she was letting him go?

A slow smile curves my lips as I move my hand from my ribs, flip my palm and glance at the scars along my wrist.

Lucifer Malikov would never do what I did for her.

And when she's with me, I don't think about how many times I've wanted to die in my life.

Mainly because she was away from me.

Never again.

And I won't have to hurt myself again.

The thing people don't tell you about suicide attempts?

They don't tell you about the fucking flinch.

That moment when the blood is pouring from your wrists, or you're drifting into oblivion, and you *should* feel peace. You *should* feel happiness, knowing the end is coming. So close, you can taste it. Feel it. Almost sink right into it.

They don't tell you that is the exact moment you fucking regret it.

The exact moment you want to die because *you don't want to fucking die.*

You want to kill yourself because *you were so fucking stupid.*

And when I lost consciousness in that tub, in a shitty hotel room in the middle of nowhere, all I could think about was her.

About how I couldn't protect her if I was a fucking rotting corpse.

How I was *so. Fucking. Stupid.*

I flex my fingers, curl them into a fist and close my eyes, listening to those voices from downstairs again.

*God, I fucking love her.*

*I fucking love her more than anything else.*

*More than life.*

*Death.*

*And I'm never going to let her ass go. Not again.*

Still, she might know what he did. How he let her go so easily. But that doesn't mean she's going to jump into my arms.

My smile pulls wider.

I planned for that too.

# CHAPTER Fifteen

## LUCIFER

I'M RUNNING *in the woods behind my house. I haven't slept in what feels like days.*

*But it feels good to run. It hurts, too, because for the past three weeks, I've done nothing but get high, get drunk, sleep, and fucking rage.*

*This feels better. Productive. I have to focus on my breathing, pay attention to the forest floor, the trees ahead. There's no clear path out here; I like it that way.*

*It's hot for spring and sweat is dripping down my bare back. My lungs are heaving, legs aching. I need to stop smoking for good, probably lay off the coke, too, but I already know I'm not going to do either of those things.*

*Three miles, and it's time to turn around, to go the three miles back.*

*There's a thick tree dead ahead, and just as I'm about to swerve around it, because it would be impossible to miss even if I wasn't focused, I stop, coming up short, my hands braced against the rough bark of the tree.*

*My heart is pounding, my breathing labored, the sun filtering through the canopy overhead, beating down on my back.*

*But none of that matters.*

*In this moment, I don't care. Because all I see, just below my splayed fingers, is the smooth trunk of the tree, the bark peeled away in the shape of a jagged square.*

*Initials.*

*L & L.*

*Beneath that? M.*

*Circled with a fucking heart.*

*I press my brow to the tree, leaned against it, arms extended, fingers curling in the rough bark. Closing my eyes, I imagine it. A few weeks after we were married, we went for a run.*

*Like we always did. Together. Even on the worst of days, even when we'd dissolve into screams and tears and hatred in the evening, the mornings were reserved for us. We went running together, or we didn't go at all. One morning, she felt sick.*

*I stayed home.*

*Another time, I was exhausted from all the coke I didn't do.*

*She stayed home.*

*And the morning this happened, this bullshit a few inches beneath my fingers, we had fucked three times before we got out of bed. Before we got dressed, slipped on our sneakers. And a bandana.*

*I don't even have one on now, but Sid insisted. She loved it, and she loved it when we both wore one.*

*Along with the bandana, she always carried a knife, and when we got to this tree, on our run back, just like this, she stopped me, flinging out her arm, catching me mid-run. I'd stopped, watched her peel away the bark.*

*When I realized what she was doing, I helped her.*

*Then she slipped the knife from the small pocket of her jogging pants and carved this. It was so unexpected. So…strange coming from her. A girl of shadows, made of darkness and regrets. Memories of trauma she barely survived, hidden behind a black curtain in her mind to keep her somewhat sane.*

*She was never one for romantic gestures, too busy trying to hold herself the fuck together.*

*It was so fucking strange, that all I could do when she was done, slipping the knife back into her pocket, was stare at her.*

*It didn't seem real.*

*It was cold that morning.*

*After New Year's. After one of my many fuck ups.*

*But she was smiling up at me, her silver eyes full of...love.*

*I'd thrown my arms around her, spun her around as I picked her up, listened to her laugh, husky and so goddamn sexy, I wanted to fuck her right there in the woods.*

*And I did.*

*She felt so fucking good, like she always did. But that was one of the only times I fucked her and cried. Because I knew she loved me.*

MY STOMACH CHURNS NOW AS I THINK OF IT, SITTING IN THE living room, watching as Ophelia and Julie play with Finn, shooting glances my way, talking to themselves about nothing.

My heart tightens, and I think I might be sick.

Thinking of him fucking her.

Of her loving him.

Would she do something like that for him? With the fucking knife and the fucking tree? Would he love it like I did?

*Would he love it more?*

*Does he deserve her more?*

"You okay?" O asks me quietly, pulling Finn into her lap. A year and a half, he's in a corduroy jumpsuit, light blue, matching his eyes. He has small wisps of blond hair, drool pouring from his mouth, a teething ring in one chubby fist.

O glances down at him, one arm wrapped around his middle, both of them on the floor, Julie a few feet from them, her legs crossed as she glances at me, then the two of them. Julie's hair is up in a sloppy bun, and O has a long braid over one shoulder, both of them in cropped leggings, O in a red tank that shows off her cleavage, and Julie in a tight, white T-shirt.

"Yeah," I tell O, flexing and curling my fingers, leaned back on the worn couch, glancing around the tidy living room. There's a fireplace that I'm sure Julie never uses, a few photos atop it. Mainly Finn, none of me, thank fuck.

She told me she's working as a recruiter and Finn goes to daycare during the week. Her voice shook when she spoke about the kitten head. How the doorbell had rung, and she'd taken a knife when she answered it, because no one ever came here.

She doesn't have family.

Few friends.

It's why she was a good target for me.

She had screamed when she saw the white head, stained with blood. No note. No body. Nothing.

Finn had cried when she screamed.

I keep my eyes on his blue ones now, running my palms over my thighs, thinking of how shitty of a father I'll probably be.

But maybe better than mine.

That's the only thing I can hold onto. *I'll be better than mine.*

But as Julie says something that I don't pay attention to, I start to think how it doesn't matter. I might not be a fucking father at all.

Lilith might not be pregnant anymore.

My heart cracks, thinking of it. Thinking of how she told me she wasn't ready. Didn't want a kid. How we couldn't have a conversation.

How she was *right.*

I did everything fucking wrong.

*Fuck.*

I run my hands down my pants then stand, Finn's big blue eyes still on me.

*You never wanna be like me, kid.*

I need to go upstairs. Need to get to the fucking coke, because my mood is crashing and I'm not ready to drive back because I haven't discovered shit, and Mav is saying I need to *find something*, and he's pissed I haven't. Pissed that all I've done is hang up cameras, *but what the fuck else am I supposed to do?*

If I don't get out of this house with two women that keep looking at me like they'd love nothing more than to get on their knees and suck my fucking dick...

Well, they're going to do exactly that.

# CHAPTER
## Sixteen

SID

"DAMN, IT'S HOT." Ria stops, wiping her wrist over her brow, placing her hands on her knees as her chest heaves. Her muted orange shirt sticks to her body, damp with sweat. The sun is high overhead, heat blazing down on us and it's only the middle of April.

I lean against a tree on the hiking trail, adjust the backpack over my shoulders.

Jeremiah takes a drink from a water bottle, smirking at the break we need. Nicolas drifts on ahead, scoping out the path. It's crowded on the trail today, and we've bumped into a few people, but Nicolas insists there could be black bears out here and we need to keep our eyes peeled.

I think about the knife in my back pocket, but it doesn't make me feel much better. Pretty sure a big ass black bear would eat my knife for lunch.

Speaking of... "I'm hungry," I whine to Jeremiah as he pushes his water bottle in the side compartment of his backpack.

He's standing in the middle of the dirt trail, his head cocked as he looks at me, shaking his head and rolling his eyes. His shirt is stuffed in the side pocket of his black shorts, and his abs are glistening with sweat. His skin is tan, light brown almost, waves to his damp, dark brown hair.

We haven't spoken about last night.

I don't even want to think about it.

*I ran,* I keep telling myself. He can do what he wants. It won't work with Lucifer and I, and maybe that was exactly what I needed to see to remind me of it. Either way, today, I just want to…enjoy myself.

"You're such a brat," Jeremiah says as Ria straightens, headed down the path to Nicolas who is at the bottom of a steep incline. There's a waterfall just up ahead, and we brought swimsuits. They're in my bag, the lighter one.

Jeremiah slides one strap of his backpack down his shoulder, swings his bag around and opens up the smallest compartment, pulling out a granola bar. He zips his bag back up, adjusts the straps on his shoulders, then closes the space between us, standing directly in front of me, my back still against the tree, the backpack I'm wearing a cushion.

He uses his straight, white teeth to tear open the bar, pockets the crinkly wrapper, and he's so close now I have to crane my neck up to meet his gaze.

I hold out my hand for the bar, but he jerks it back, out of my reach, his eyes gleaming.

"Let me feed you."

My throat tightens with those words, my cheeks flushing pink, sweat beading along my temple, along the back of my neck.

"Jeremiah, come on," I try, "I'm starving." We had breakfast at a local place not far from the cabin and I filled up on pancakes and oatmeal but it's almost lunchtime now.

Jeremiah comes as close as he can, his hand on my belly, fingers spread wide. My black tank sticks to my skin, and I feel gross and out of breath, but the way he's looking at me, I don't think he cares about any of that. Of course, *he* somehow still smells like he just stepped out of a scalding hot shower, scrubbed clean and perfect.

"Then open that pretty little mouth, baby." His words are low, a deep rumble.

I HEAR UNFAMILIAR VOICES, A GIRL LAUGHING, A DOG'S PLAYFUL bark. Someone else is coming up along the path. I straighten from the tree, try to dodge away from him, but his fingers dig into my belly and crowds me against the trunk at my back.

"Jeremiah," I say, my hands going to his forearm, "come on, people are—"

"You think I give a fuck about *people?*" he asks me, lips tugging up into a smile. He brings the granola bar into view, running it over my lips. "Open your fucking mouth, Sid."

The voices grow louder, the dog yelping again.

Jeremiah doesn't even blink. Instead, he drags his hand over my belly, slips his fingers up my shirt.

I bite my lip, my skin growing ever hotter with his touch.

I hear Nicolas calling out our names, but of course, Jeremiah ignores him.

Deflating, my stomach growling, I finally give in, opening my mouth.

Jeremiah groans, dipping his brow to mine. He places the granola bar between my lips and just as I go to bite down, he clicks his tongue.

"Did I tell you you could eat yet?" he taunts me, his eyes on my mouth.

My blood heats, my heart pounding too fast in my chest. I suck in a breath, inhale the sweet scent of granola and chocolate. "Jeremiah," I beg him, playing into his game for once. "Please let me."

"Mmm," he says, the hand under my shirt rising higher, those voices growing louder. He pushes his thigh between my legs, and I gasp. "I like when you beg me, baby. Go ahead," he turns his head, drags his mouth over my cheek, to my ear. *"Take a bite."*

I do, clenching my teeth around the bar as his fingers come to the underside of my sports bra, then slip under that too as I gasp again, his thigh pressing harder between my legs.

I hear the voices right behind him now, laughter too, then it dies off, abrupt and I have no doubt they're looking at my brother pressing me against this tree.

I close my eyes, taste the chocolate on my tongue as I chew, swallowing down the first bite.

"What do you say?" he asks me, his breath against my ear.

My nipples tighten as he palms my breast, squeezing hard.

"Thank you," I murmur.

He nips at my ear, sparking flutters in my belly. "Who are you thanking, Sis?"

I'm panting, my fingers digging into his forearm as he moves his hand to my other breast, kneading my flesh, igniting my blood.

*I know what he wants to hear.*

"Thank you, *brother*," I whisper against his cheek.

He groans, pressing harder between my thighs, then he licks a line down my throat before his mouth comes back over mine. "Now, was that so hard?" he whispers, the granola bar by his side as I open my eyes, staring into his.

"No," I admit, feeling flush all over. "It wasn't."

He smiles, finally pulls back, dragging his hand over my tits, down my stomach, then out from under my shirt. I release his forearm and he offers me the rest of the bar.

"Eat up, baby." I take the bar and he threads his arm through my free one, dragging me back to the path and leading us toward Nicolas and Ria, my mind spinning.

# CHAPTER
*Seventeen*

## JEREMIAH

"I'M GOING IN!" Ria's voice echoes around the stream, Nicolas already at the base of the waterfall, grinning up at her.

Ria gives a running jump, then freefalls over the short drop into the pool of water, Nicolas catching her as she lands with as shriek.

That water must be freezing. It's hot outside, but it's only spring. Still, the watering hole is full of people, and I don't really like that.

I glance at Sid beside me on one of the rocks close to the edge. The waterfall rushes in the background, drowning out my words from prying ears when I ask, "Do you want to get in?"

Ria and Nicolas both wore their swimsuits under their clothes, but I know Sid didn't. I felt her sports bra under her shirt.

She's got her backpack beside her on the rock, her knees close to her chest but not pulled all the way up. The baby, I think, is getting in the way.

I wonder if she's self-conscious. She's petite, and for a while, wasn't showing at all. With her flowy tank, she isn't now, but I felt her bump beneath my fingers earlier, when I had her backed against the tree.

Just thinking of it makes me want to fuck her right here on the rocks.

Her gray eyes meet mine and she quirks a brow. "You'd swim in there?"

I smile, shaking my head. "You seem to think I don't have any fun."

Her eyes widen. "Uh yeah," she says, wrapping her arms tighter around her knees, "because you *don't.*"

I bite back my laugh, my palms splayed behind me on the warm rock, my bag still on my shoulders. "I do. When the time and place calls for it." I rake my eyes down her body. "And right now, I think I wouldn't mind having some fun."

Her cheeks flush pink and she rolls her eyes, something flitting across her features that make me feel sick. Something like pain as her brow furrows.

I wonder if she's thinking about him.

What I showed her last night.

*He's a piece of shit.*

She's resisted me all this time, and he's already fucking two women. He's disgusting.

I wonder how she'd feel if she knew what he did to me in that cave at my first Noctem.

But I don't want her to choose me because she feels bad for me. That shit just pisses me off.

"Let's get in the water," I tell her, standing and offering her my hand.

She eyes it warily, then dips her eyes down to her stomach, swallowing. "I'm fine," she insists, jerking her chin to the pool behind us. "You get in, I'll be okay."

I laugh at that, wrap my fingers around her wrist and jerk her arm from her shins. "Funny, sis. I'm not leaving you alone here." I glance around at the families around us, dogs, couples.

I've got a blade in my backpack. A gun, too. I'll have to leave them both on the bank to get in the water, but I want her ass in there.

I want her to have fun too.

Reluctantly, she lets me pull her from the rock, and I yank her to me, laughing as she catches herself on her palms against my chest.

"Come on, let's find a place for you to change."

Her eyes widen. "What about you?" she asks.

I smirk down at her. "You don't want anyone to see me naked, baby?"

She glares at me, rolling her eyes. "Shut up, Jeremiah."

I laugh, then turn from her, holding her hand as I guide her through all the people in my fucking way.

Finally, we come off the trail, behind the stone built into the mountain, deserted, the echoes and splashing from the waterfall muffled now.

Sid swings her backpack around to her front, plucks out two pieces of black fabric. A swimsuit I bought her, but now, imagining her wearing just *that* in front of all those people, jealousy threatens to work its way into my fingertips, rip that shit in half.

I fight it back.

She looks up at me through her long lashes, dropping her backpack in the grass beside her.

"Can you turn around?" she whispers as I stare at her.

"Why?" I demand, my gaze traveling over her body before I meet her eyes again. "You embarrassed?"

She crosses her arms over her chest, gritting her teeth. "I don't want to get naked in front of—"

I turn around before she finishes her sentence, standing guard, keeping an eye out on the path a few feet from us, making sure no one comes this way. "Go ahead, you little brat."

She laughs, relief in that sound.

It takes an effort not to turn around and look when I hear her changing, but I don't, and finally she says, "All done," her words kind of…sheepish, and I turn to look at her.

My breath catches in my throat, and the first thing I can think to say is, "You're not fucking wearing that."

Her face falls as I take in the swell of her perfect tits, barely hidden in that V of the black string bikini, the bottom straps high on her hips, but cut close to her thigh.

She crosses her arms over her belly, her face flushing pink as anger makes me clench my jaw.

"Why?" she falters, her feet bare, toes flexing in the grass. Her voice is soft. Weak. Not like the girl I know. "Does it look bad?"

I finally drag my gaze up to her eyes, my hands clenched into fists.

I see her looking down, like she doesn't want to face me.

"What?" I counter, shaking my head, stepping closer to her. I open my mouth to speak again but she cuts me off, bending down and snatching up her shirt, the rest of her shit half in her backpack.

She goes to force the tank top over her head, saying, "Never mind, I don't even want to go fucking swimming."

I grab her wrists, pinning them together over her head, her shirt falling to the ground.

Her eyes are narrowed on me, that flush extending down over her neck, her chest. "Let go of me," she snarls, and I see it. How she wants to cover herself. Her belly, round and growing.

I step closer, my fingers biting into her wrists as she tries to get away from me. "You feeling insecure, Sid Rain?" I ask, looking down into her eyes, her body elongated with the way I'm holding her hands over her head.

"Get off of me." She tries to jerk her wrists from my grip, but I reach my free hand to her hip, shove her back against the tree behind her.

A startled little gasp leaves her lips.

"Tell me," I demand, my body pressed against hers, my cock growing hard with her nearness, her wrists pressed against the tree over her head. "Tell me how you feel."

She swallows, averting her eyes again. "Please let go, Jeremiah."

I grab her chin, jerk her head up. *"Tell me how you feel, sis."*

She glares at me a long moment, her eyes watery as she bites her lip. I see her chest heaving, and I want to dive down, bite her tits, leave a mark on her. Show her how beautiful she is.

Even when she's pregnant with *his fucking baby.*

But I wait.

And finally, she says, "I feel..." She closes her eyes tight. "Ugly."

My chest tightens.

"I feel gross. And he..." She falters, chewing the inside of her cheek. My fingers tighten around her wrists, thinking of what he's done to her. That scar over her brow that I know she lied to me about. Where he is now. "He's already fucking someone else. Maybe he thinks I'm disgusting, too."

I tighten my hold on her chin. "Look at me."

She squeezes her eyes tighter, but after a moment, she opens them, blinking back tears. "You're fucking beautiful." I lean down close to her, lick her tears from her lower lash line. She seems to relax against that tree. Stops fighting my hold on her wrists. "And if anyone looks at you for too long when we get in that water, baby," I press a kiss to her brow, "I'll drown them."

It doesn't take long for someone to do *exactly* that.

Sid is coming out from underneath the waterfall, at the edge just a light spray of water, slicking back her wet hair, her chin tilted up, face to the sun. She's sexy as fuck, and I watch her from beside Nicolas and Ria, leaned against the grassy ledge adjacent it, the squish of the river beneath our feet.

People are crowded near her, waiting for their turns under the lighter part of the stream, but there's a few fucking college kids—judging by the AU T-shirts they peeled off before they jumped in—causing a fucking scene. One of them knocks into her, walking backward and laughing, shaking water from his hair.

He's way bigger than her, and she stumbles backward, a scowl on her face as she turns to face him, dropping her hands by her sides.

He immediately whips around, the smile leaving his face as he holds out his hands.

"Don't make a mess," Nicolas says under his breath beside me, and I clench my jaw. "He's just going to apologize and walk away."

I dig my short nails into my biceps, watching, hoping exactly that happens.

Ria laughs, and I shoot her a glare, her own hair in a sloppy, wet bun. But she doesn't look at me. Instead, she's smiling at Sid.

"Sorry," the frat boy says, but that smile is curling back up on his face as he steps closer to her, and I see his eyes rake over the half of her body out of the water. "I'm so sorry," he says again, his voice taking on a more flirtatious tone.

I bite my tongue.

"She can handle it," Nicolas says.

But I think about Cindy dancing in my lap at his party. What if she wants to pay me back for that? *Because that's what she does.*

Still, I force myself not to move, drowning out everything around us except their conversation. I'm not that far. I can reach them in seconds. But if he puts a finger on her…

She glances over at me at that moment, and her eyes connect with mine.

Then her lips pull into a smile and Ria laughs again as Nicolas says, "Oh, fuck, Sid, come on," dragging out the last word.

She turns to the fuckboy. "It's okay," I hear her breathy voice. "No worries."

He steps closer to her. "You come here by yourself?" he asks, glancing around the plunge pool before looking back at her.

She chews her lip, cocks her head.

*This little fucking brat.*

"No, I came with my friends."

Fuckboy is undeterred. "Oh yeah? Well, we've rented a cabin not far from here, if you and your friends wanna—"

"Ah, come on, leave her alone," another fucker calls from opposite the pool. "She doesn't want to hang with a bunch of idiots like us." He laughs, like it's the funniest fucking thing.

Sid smiles, tucks a lock of wet hair behind her ear. "That's okay," she says, and I feel relief flood through my veins, hear Nicolas sigh and Ria scoff. "Have fun with your friends." Then she turns to go.

And *this fucker puts his hand on her arm, pulling her back.*

I don't walk through the water. I fucking swim, getting to them in seconds, my hands going around his throat as I shove his head under the water, drag him behind the stream of the waterfall as I do so no one can see me drown this useless piece of shit.

Sid is calling my name, splashing after me, but I don't care.

The asshole's hands are scratching at mine on his head and he's kicking at the bottom of the river, trying to push himself up.

"Jeremiah," Sid warns, "let him go."

No one is back here, and I smile at her, her pale face, wide eyes. "You wanted to play with me, baby?" I ask her through gritted teeth, my body jostling as I press harder on his head, keeping him down. "You wanted to fucking *play?*"

"Let him go," she says. "He was just..." She shakes her head, smacking her hands against the water. "Dammit, just *let him go.*"

I hear Ria and Nicolas, see them slip through the stream of the waterfall, Nicolas's eyes darting from Sid to me, then down to the water where fuckboy is gonna die.

"Oh my God," Ria whispers, splashing over toward me. "Oh my God, Jeremiah, you can't—"

"Shouldn't have fucked with me, baby," I tell Sid, my eyes back on hers, "his death is going to be *your fault.*"

Ria grabs my arm, trying to haul me off of him.

"You wanna get hurt too?" I snarl at her, my eyes on hers.

She glares at me, nails digging into my biceps. "You're such a fucking hypocrite."

Her words are full of venom, and Sid is calling her name, Nicolas is on my other side, trying to grab my other arm, but my gaze is locked on Ria's. "He touched her arm, but you *assaulted* Sid!" She releases me, smacking her fist into the water, cold spray dousing my face. "You assaulted her and you drugged me! What the fuck were you thinking?" She's screaming now, and I think everyone here will be able to hear her. "What the fuck were you thinking that night? What the fuck *is wrong with you?*"

And as she screams at me, and the guy under my hands stops struggling, I'm right back there.

I'm right back there in that fucking insane asylum.

*Where I always needed to be.*

*GET THE GIRL. GET OUT. GET THE FUCKING GIRL. AND GET OUT.*

*Right now, the girl is underneath me. She's smiling, and he's tied against a fucking pole, the rope digging into his skin. There's blood on his thigh, blood on his torso, but he's not fighting anymore.*

*His head is leaned back against the beam, his eyes barely open. He's saying a name, over and over, but he's fucking insane, because I highly doubt it's this girl's fucking name.*

*"Lilith. Lilith. Lilith."*

*The girl has pale makeup on, horns on the floor of the asylum, and I guess that was her costume. And as I part her thighs, one hand on her neck as she drunkenly giggles, biting her lip, it seems fitting.*

*A demon.*

*She's a fucking demon, and with that perfect, bare pussy, I'm going to make her feel hell before I hand her off to Lazar.*

Then I'm free.

*I'm fucking free.*

*Thinking of it, of how I won't have to deal with them, their taunts, the whispers, being so close to the people that made my life a living hell, it feels fucking good.*

*I almost don't even want to fuck her.*

*But she's so damn* compliant.

*I lean down close, sucking on her neck as she arches her back. My fingers find her cunt, and she's fucking soaked for me.*

What a good girl.

*I scrape my teeth against her throat and she moans, Lucifer fucking Malikov still saying that same name, over and over and over again.*

*Fucker.*

*I should kill him too. But if I do, Lazar will never let me go. And if I got put in a cage again…my heart races, thinking about two weeks in there. How two weeks seemed like ten years.*

*How I cried until I couldn't anymore.*

*How I scooped up my own shit, because I was starving and delirious and fucking* alone.

*How I slept in my own fucking filth.*

*How I* begged.

*Never again.*

*My fingers tighten around this girl's throat.*

*I think about Kameron and feel a wave of remorse.*

*Maybe she didn't deserve that, but it felt good, to have the power for once. After nearly a decade without it...goddamn, it felt good.*

*I pull back from the girl, reaching for the waistband of my pants.*

*But then her eyes open wide, that drunken smile still on her lips.*

*And I see the color of her irises.*

No.

It can't be her.

*There's a pain in my chest, and I feel cold all over as she squirms beneath me, her full lips still turned up, her eyes fluttering closed.*

*I grab her chin. "Open your eyes, Lilith," I whisper, leaning down over her, letting go of my pants, planting my hand on the bed made just for this down here. I shake her, gently slapping her face. "Open your eyes, open your eyes." I say it over and over, shocked I can still breathe.*

No, no, no. It's not...it's not her...

*My hands were all over her. My fingers were inside of her.*

*I hurt her.*

*She doesn't know it, but I fucking hurt her.*

*"Open your eyes," I whisper again, praying in my head. It isn't true. It's not true.*

*Slowly, she blinks, resting her bleary gaze on me.*

*Silver. Like a nickel.*

*I can't breathe.*

*I can't fucking breathe.*

*I take in her brown hair, short, to her chin. Her petite frame. Upturned nose.*

No.

*Fuck.*

*I scream it out loud, sitting on my heels, her body beneath me. My dick is hard, my blood pounding, lust and anger fighting inside of me and I was going to take it all out in the only way I can. The only way I know how.*

*But not with her.*

I'd never fucking do that to her.

*I hit myself, my hand over my face, over and over and over again, tears blurring my vision, that lump growing tighter in my throat.*

*I don't stop until my face burns, until my palms sting, until her eyes are closed and she drifts off to sleep, brought under by the drink I drugged her with.*

*I bow my head, a sob tearing through my throat as I bury my head in my hands, my chest heaving.*

*I have to get out of here.*

I have to fucking save her life and *get. Us. Out of here.*

*And when she wakes up, I'll remake her.*

*She'll be reborn, just like I was. Into someone stronger, someone they can't hurt again.*

*Someone I can't hurt again.*

I HEAR THE RUSH OF THE WATER, SOMEONE CALLING MY NAME. Someone yelling, angry voices.

When I snap open my eyes, Sid's back is to me, pressing against me, and she has a knife in her hand. *She has a knife.*

The boy I held under is gasping for breath, and his friend is yelling at my sister, Nicolas and Ria on either side of her.

The other guy's finger is in her face, but his dark, angry eyes flick to mine.

"Back the fuck up," Sid is saying, holding up the knife, the blade glinting in the sun. "If you know what's good for you, you're going to—"

I wrap an arm around her chest, pulling her to me, cutting off her words. I grab the knife from her fingers, tuck the blade back in and pocket the knife.

"If you yell at her again," I interrupt the second asshole, his jaw clenched, fingers still pointed toward us, "I'll finish what I started." I glance at his friend, his eyes red, chest heaving. "*With both of you.*"

# CHAPTER
*Eighteen*

## SID

I WATCH the girl grind on my brother's dick, her fingers threaded through his as she brings them up to her tits, spilling out of her red bra. He's smiling at her as she moans, directing his fingers inside the cups of her bra, throwing her head back, her long, black hair spilling down her shoulders.

But his eyes are on me.

Pale green, framed by thick lashes, he doesn't look like Satan.

*He looks like a god.*

The dancer guides his hands around to her back, and he doesn't need her help unclasping her bra. She shifts her hands to his thighs, and even though I don't want to, I glance down, see the thin material of her thong sliding to the side, exposing her pussy as she grinds up and down the thick bulge in his tailored pants.

I swallow, hard, turn my attention to his hands, his fingers sliding down the red straps of her bra. When he gets to her wrists, her tits free, she moves her hands from his thighs, dips her chin and presses her brow to his, her black hair spilling around the both of them so I can't see his face.

Jeremiah tosses the bra behind her, on the floor of the private room we're in at Remorse, a club he owns in Virginia.

This is Cindy, the same girl that gave him a lap dance at Nicolas's party. She actually works here, came down for the party just for Jeremiah.

*His favorite dancer.* I'm gathering that, since his hands are now squeezing her round ass. Her breaths come out in labored pants, her hands on his shoulders, manicured nails digging into his black shirt. He helps guide her as she dry humps him, digging his hands into her ass so hard I know there's gonna be bruises.

I hear a groan come from his throat, and at that sound, my skin crawls.

I need to get the fuck up.

I need to get out of here.

Ria, Nicolas, Roman and some other people who work for my brother are right outside the doors, on the main dance floor of the club.

*I need to get up.*

It smells like sex and perfume and marijuana, nothing like the usual clean scent of my brother. And I know what he's doing.

Fucking testing me.

He's pissed I flirted with that guy he almost drowned.

We went to dinner, he barely spoke to me, made a few phone calls to tell his employees to meet him here.

He wanted me to have a good time, he said in my ear as we all sat in a booth together. When he spoke to the dancer in private, stepping away from the booth, then beckoned me back here, I assumed he had business to take care of and didn't want me out of his sight. Maybe money to exchange. Maybe someone to fucking murder.

But then Cindy sauntered in, locked the door, and perched herself on his lap, right beside me on the seat built into the wall of this dimly lit, small room, and I realized there was no business.

No business but pissing me the fuck off. Rubbing salt in my fucking wound, knowing Lucifer isn't far from here. Knowing he's probably doing just this with someone else.

Jeremiah has always been a fucking dick.

Nothing has changed.

I glance at his finger digging into the tan flesh of her ass, see the muscles of his arms flex. I know on the inside of his left arm are those scars. Vertical lines.

*For me.*

But here he is doing *this shit*, not too different from my fucking husband, and I wonder how it is that I got cursed with only knowing the worst men in the entire goddamn world.

But the longer I stare at his left hand, his *dominant* hand, the moans growing louder, Jeremiah's groans more frequent, I see his hand tremble again.

I don't listen to the music, the dancer's labored breaths, Jeremiah's grunts of pleasure. I don't hear any of that. Don't pay attention to his mouth coming to her nipple, biting, hard enough for her to whimper.

I push it all aside.

Focus on his hand.

*It's shaking.*

I know he's holding onto her hard enough to mark her. The veins visible on the top of his hand are evident of that, along with the red marks in her skin.

But this is something else. Something I've noticed since I've been with him this past month, and I can't help but think again, *what happened to him?*

Before I can think too much about it, the dancer is leaning back in his lap, reaching between her thighs, pulling the red satin of her thong aside, and I snap my head up, aware Jeremiah's eyes are back on me.

"You can touch me, you know that," Cindy breathes out,

and I flick my gaze up, see her chocolate brown eyes locked on my brother, as if I'm not here at all. She's acted as if I don't exist the entire time we've been here, so I'm not surprised.

Still, with her fingers holding her underwear back, her slick, pink pussy on display for him, his hands still gripping her ass, his eyes on me, something hot coils around my gut.

*Anger.*

I grind my teeth, watch her middle finger slide down her slit as she shifts her hips, pressing her against his thigh.

"It's okay, J," she nearly whines, biting her full lips, batting her lashes, "please touch me."

My mouth goes dry, hands curling into fists at my side. But this isn't my place to be angry. I'm married, and not to him. Whatever he does, it's not my business, as much as he *wants* it to be my business.

Instinctively, my hand comes to my low belly.

My husband's baby, no matter what shitty things he's doing.

With that thought, I go to stand, but Jeremiah snakes his hand out, the same one that was on the stripper's ass, and circles his fingers around my thigh, forcing me back down.

I'm in the same leather mini skirt I wore yesterday—a purchase from *him*—and his calloused fingers on my skin are electric.

I hate it.

I hate that I feel a spark of anything…sensual with his touch. But he runs his hand up my thigh, to the edge of my skirt, and I slowly turn my gaze to him, my hands on the bench, my jaw clenched.

The dancer is still rubbing her pussy, soft whimpers coming from her mouth, one hand on my brother's thigh to keep herself balanced.

"Have fun," I snarl to him, narrowing my eyes as his full lips tip up into a half-smile. "I'll go wait with Roman."

I start to get up again, but his grip tightens.

And I feel it.

*The tremor.*

I dart my eyes down between us, my lips parted to ask him about it again, but he leans in close to me, one hand gripping the dancer's hip, so he's touching both of us.

His breath fans against my ear, and I stiffen, the question about his trembling hand dying on the tip of my tongue. "No, you fucking won't," he tells me, his words low. "What? Are you jealous, beautiful?" he whispers.

I feel my face heat as I stare straight ahead, pretending he's not so close to me. His hand isn't trailing up my thigh, *under* my skirt. Pretending I'm not trembling myself.

"No," I manage to say, but I can hear the lie in that word. "But this seems like a private thing between—"

"Do you want me to touch her?" he interrupts me, leaning closer, his shoulder bumping against mine. I stare at the brick wall, see the club lights flickering purple, black, blue against it.

I try to listen to the music.

*Lollipop* by Framing Hanley. Much better than the original version, but my thighs clench together, and I'm not so sure that's the best thing for me to focus on right now.

"I don't care what you—"

The dancer moans his name, and I know he's doing it.

*He's fucking touching her* there.

I start to get up again. I'm going to find Roman fucking Torres, with his sewed-up cartilage and all and I am going to suck his goddamn dick and make sure someone films it so I can play it back for my brother.

But again, he holds me down, digging his short nails into my bare thigh, sliding up higher until his finger brushes against my crease.

"You don't care, baby?" he whispers. He runs his tongue down my jaw, stopping just at my mouth.

I feel his body moving beside me, hear the bench creaking, feel it shifting. The dancer is moaning his name over and over and over and I wonder just how good my brother is with his fingers.

"You taste like a liar," he says softly against my mouth.

I make the mistake of turning to face him, our lips brushing as my eyes connect with his.

"You know what I do to liars, baby?" he whispers, moving his hand up higher.

My body reacts to him, even as my mind is screaming alarm bells. Telling me not to be so stupid. Not to betray my husband.

*Not like this.*

Not. Like. *This.*

But there's another voice in my head, too. Telling me what I need to remember. *He already betrayed* you.

"Jeremiah," I grit out, grabbing his wrist to stop his fingers from diving into my underwear. He doesn't move his hand, but he stops trying to get closer. "Please just let me—"

"I fuck the truth out of them." He pulls back, and I blink at his absence, his clean scent going with him.

He leans back against the wall, his hands at his side, against the bench, his hooded eyes still on me.

There's something odd about the way he seems so submissive. Giving himself over to the dancer.

But I see it.

I see her undo his belt. His button. The zipper. He lifts his hips, she pulls down his pants, his boxers.

I see her curl her fingers around his dick, and my mouth almost falls open with just how big he is.

I've felt his erection against me many times before. In my hand, in the car. And I was so close to giving him head in a club myself, not that long ago, before my husband stopped me.

But no one is stopping this girl and I can't fucking look away.

"This is yours," Jeremiah says softly, as I'm rooted to the spot, unable to fucking move. Get up. Run out of here.

Slap him.

Her.

The dancer lifts her hips, her thong still shoved to the crease of her thigh as she spreads her legs wider, angling herself over his cock, her fingers still curled tight around the base of it.

I dart my gaze back to Jeremiah's eyes, see him bite his full bottom lip as he stares at me. I see a muscle jump in his jaw, the veins in his neck stark against his tan skin. I watch his biceps flex beneath his shirt, and I imagine him in the gym.

Training with me.

Helping me learn to protect myself, all over again.

I see the sweat licking down his body, over that horrible scar against his ribs.

The one my husband gave him, before he left him to die in a fucking fire.

I see Jeremiah's hand over Lucifer's, blood pooling beneath their fingers, sticky and wet against Jeremiah's shirt.

I see something else, too.

My brother in a cage. Alone. Scared. Starving. And I wonder if my husband knew. Did he ever see him in there? Did he ever try to help him?

"I'm yours," Jeremiah says, snapping me out of my thoughts, those cruel words from his mouth dripping with honey as his lips are parted, his chest rising and falling rapidly, the dancer's soft moans flooding the room, drowning out the music. "I'm yours, Sid Rain, all you have to do..."

I glance at the dancer, see her grab her tit, her slick pussy so fucking close to his cock.

So fucking close.

"All you have to do is take me."

My stomach twists up into knots.

I think I'm going to puke.

Because I don't want him to fuck her.

I want her hands off of him.

I hate him, and I hate what he's doing. I fucking hate him so much, but it's only because…*I fucking love him.*

I stand, the dancer's eyes finally on mine as she strokes my brother, drops her hand to his shoulder to keep herself steady.

He's watching me, his face a mask of seriousness.

And holding up my middle finger, I walk out.

I make a beeline straight to the booth we were at, see Roman on the outer edge, a drink in his hand. He's hardly said two words to me tonight, those stitches on his nose probably have something to do with it, but I don't really need him to talk right now.

Instead, with the music so loud I can't even think, the dim lights of the club giving me a false sense of security, of confidence, I squeeze myself into the booth, sit on Roman's lap, straddling him, my arms threaded around his neck.

I hear Nicolas choking at my back, Ria calling my name, and some guy I don't know groan.

Roman still has his drink in his hand, and he blinks down at me, but there's a smile pulling at his lips and his eyes are a little glassy.

*Perfect. He's a little drunk.*

I shift my hips, my skirt leaving little to the imagination and I can feel him growing hard beneath me as I grind on him.

"S-Sid," Roman chokes out, "I don't think you should…" But I lean in close to him, shifting my pelvis over his cock as I do and he groans, his hand coming under my skirt, to my ass.

"Don't think," I tell him, "I just need to use you for a sec—"

I hear glass shattering, then feel someone's fingers around my arm, jerking me off of Roman, out of the booth.

"You want him to fucking die, Sid?" Jeremiah snarls in my ear as Roman slides further into the booth, holding up his hands, drink still in one. I don't know whose glass Jeremiah threw to the ground, but I hear glass crunching beneath my boots. I spin around to face him, gripping his shirt in my fist.

I can smell Cindy on him, her strong perfume, sweet like candy. "Fuck off," I tell him. "You started this fucking game—"

He yanks me closer, nearly lifting me off my feet. "You think this is a *fucking game to me?*"

My eyes widen as I ball both fists in his shirt. "You were going to *fuck her* right in front of me!" I scream the words, and I know people can hear us, even past the music—*Bitter* by FLETCHER—but I don't care.

Knowing what Lucifer did, seeing what Jeremiah did, being caught up in the middle of this war and trying to protect my husband while I fall in love with the man who was supposed to be my brother, it's making me feel *insane.*

"You mad?" Jeremiah asks me, his jaw clenched. He takes a breath, glances up at the ceiling. Then turns his gaze back to me, releasing his grip on my shirt. "Fucking do something about it, baby. *Take what's yours.*" Then he grabs my arm and drags me to the door of the club without another word, me fighting him the whole way.

# CHAPTER
*Nineteen*

## JEREMIAH

"YOU'RE FUCKING INSANE." She snarls those words to me as the door closes behind us and I click the lock into place, darting my eyes around the lit, open plan living room. A habit.

Nicolas and Ria are still at the club, and I told him not to come back tonight.

I want Sid alone.

If Nicolas knew what I did in that private room, he wouldn't let me be alone with her right now. But I had to get some kind of sign that she actually cares about me.

That she doesn't just see me as her *fucking brother.*

"Watch how you talk to me, baby," I tell her quietly, tossing the keys to the Mercedes in the clay bowl on a decorative table by the door.

She storms through the living room, coming into the kitchen, running her fingers through her fucking hair without looking at me. I watch her ass move in that mini skirt, marvel at how big it's getting. Her ass, and her tits.

*Fuck.*

She yanks open the steel fridge, grabs a water bottle and slams the door closed, twisting off the cap and turning to glare at me.

"Fuck you, Jeremiah." Her voice sounds hoarse. She takes a drink of water, the plastic crinkling beneath her fingers. She screws the cap back on, and as I take a few steps toward her, she suddenly hurls the fucking water bottle at me with a loud scream.

I catch it out of midair with one hand, right before it hits me in the head.

For a moment, silence steels through the airy cabin. The staircase is to my right, and I think about dragging her ass up it, pinning her down in my fucking bed.

But I'm not so sure I can wait that long to get my fucking hands on her.

I squeeze the bottle so hard in my hand I'm worried it's going to burst, just like my heart is trying to claw its way out of my chest. Seeing her on Roman...I could've fucking killed him.

I wonder what it did to her, seeing Cindy dry fucking me.

"You're just..." She runs her hands through her hair again and pulls. "You're fucking crazy," she snarls, dropping her hands, planting them against the island that separates the kitchen from the entranceway and the living room. Her silver eyes are narrow slits as I step closer, see her face flush pink. "You fucking...you fucking take me to Lucifer last night, for what? To show me he's..." She presses her knuckles to her mouth, closing her eyes a second. "To show me he's fucking cheating?" she finally asks, her voice quieter as her eyes fly open, lined with tears. She slaps her palm against the island. "Then you do the same fucking shit—"

"Except I wasn't cheating," I correct her, closing the distance between us, the water bottle still in my hand as I place the other on top of hers on the island between us.

She snatches her hand away, her lip curling with disgust. It guts me, a knife in my fucking heart. *Is she really disgusted by me?*

I catch sight of the knife block at the end of the island, force myself to look back at her.

"No." That word is full of venom from her pretty mouth. "You're right. You weren't. Why don't you go back there?" She gestures toward the door, rolling her eyes. "Why don't you go fuck her and leave me in fucking peace?" She turns from me, walks around the counter.

Like she actually thinks I'll let her go.

I catch sight of her tank top, riding up above her skirt. See her rounded belly, so subtle, but I know her so fucking well.

I see the proof of what she is.

What she has.

Something I wish was mine.

I rub my thumb over my sternum, thinking about it. About her, carrying *his* baby. About how her body will change and morph and grow more beautiful every fucking day, but not because of me.

*Because of him.*

My brother.

I try to push thoughts of him from my mind because it hurts, and because there's something else on the counter in front of me too.

A loaded gun.

I wouldn't want tonight to get out of hand, thanks to someone that doesn't deserve the very breath he fucking breathes.

But I can't let her get away.

Maybe I should be a better person. Maybe I should have a fucking heart, let her deal with whatever is happening to hers.

But something changed in me at the Forgues.

It ripped my mind apart.

I barely got out of that cage alive. It was too much to ask that I'd get out human too. That I'd understand how to feel someone else's pain, without wanting to rip it out of their fucking heart.

And that's what I want to do.

I want to heal her.

She's not going back to him.

We both know that.

Even if she wants to, *she isn't.*

I adjust myself through my pants, thinking of tying her up. Forcing her to stay here.

But first I've got to stop her from leaving.

I close the space between us, yanking her to me.

Her breath leaves her in a rush, and I bring the cold water bottle in my hand that she threw at my fucking head to her chest.

She shivers, big gray eyes glancing down at the water, then flicking back up to me.

"Jeremiah," she says, trying to keep her voice angry, her tone harsh.

But I see her nipples pebble beneath her sheer black tank, no bra underneath it. And more than that, she doesn't walk away from me.

"Yeah, baby?" I slide the bottle down, tugging her shirt, too, exposing her growing tits.

"Let. Go. *Of me.*" Her words are a fucking snarl, and goddamn, does that shit turn me on.

It's close to midnight, darkness surrounding this cabin, thick, heavy curtains covering the windows so we can stay up as late as we want, pretend its night forever.

We both know giving in to what we *really* want is so much easier to do in the dark.

The first time I touched her like this? It wasn't that night I found her on Halloween.

I wonder if she remembers.

"Is that what you really want?" I let go of her wrist, reach for the knife block on the counter, beside the gun, taking the chef's knife.

She tenses, her mouth parted, brows arched up, but she doesn't move.

She doesn't move, because she's just as fucking sick as I am.

I slowly set the bottle beside us, grip the thin fabric of her shirt in one fist, then drag the butcher knife down the middle, easily cutting the fabric, the sharp tip of the blade against her stomach.

She gasps, then bites her lip as she looks down, watching that knife so close to her belly.

When the shirt hangs in scraps, I nudge it off of her shoulders, let it fall to the fucking floor.

Her hands are balled into fists at her sides, her pink nipples sharp little points as I hold the tip of the knife to her low, round belly, just above the waistband of her skirt.

"You want me to stop? You wanna keep pretending you hate me?" I press the blade into her belly, not cutting her, but enough that if she moves too fucking fast, it will.

My hand moves to her face, my thumb over her bottom lip as she looks up at me, panting, her dark hair falling over her shoulders.

"You wanna act like you haven't wanted me inside of you for years, baby? Like you don't fucking love it when I get crazy, *for you?*"

She's barely breathing, scared I'll cut her.

Scared I'll end what he did to her.

*Maybe I fucking will.*

"You drive me fucking insane," I tell her, my voice breaking with that truth, my thumb brushing over her mouth. I swallow down the lump in my throat, her wide eyes at my admission. *As if she didn't know.* "You drive me insane, baby, and I can't take it anymore."

"Jeremiah," she breathes, "don't hurt—"

I press the blade just a little closer. Hear her hiss. Look down and see the blood trailing from the tip of the blade, against her pale skin. She brings her trembling hands up, closes them around mine on the blade.

Almost as if she'd shove it in herself.

Almost as if she'd *let me* stab her.

"You don't want me to hurt you?" I ask her quietly, glancing down at her small hands over mine. "You really want me to just...*let you go?*"

Her lip trembles as she stares at me, her eyes glistening with unshed tears, her fingers pressing into mine on the blade.

"Or do you want me to mark you?" I glance at the knife, see her face flush pink, her teeth sinking into the pillow of her bottom lip, right beside my thumb. "Use you? *Fucking brand you, Sid? Let everyone know who you* really *belong to?*"

Her fingers tremble on mine, and even though it's my left hand around the blade...*mine fucking don't.*

Because even my body wouldn't hurt her.

Not like that.

Not unless *we both wanted it.*

My body knows better. My fucked up hand.

*I know better.*

"Tell me what you want. Tell me the goddamn truth for once in your life, baby, because I'm so tired of you pushing me. I'm so, so tired. And tonight? *I want to fucking push back.*" I press the knife in closer, gliding it up, nicking her skin.

She gasps, her eyes fluttering closed, long lashes nearly grazing her cheekbones.

I grip her jaw, fingers digging into her cheek. "Open your fucking eyes *and tell me what the fuck you want.*" My dick is aching, being this close. And I think if she walks away, I might have to turn this blade on myself to not fuck her anyway.

I'd have to slit my own fucking wrists to let her walk away.

*Don't do that to me, baby.*

A moment passes. I can't breathe. I want to hurt her. Drag this knife down her belly. Lower still.

I want to wrap my hand around her fucking throat.

It'd fit perfectly, her little neck in my hand.

I want her to scream for me.

I want to make her cry.

And when she finally opens her eyes, meets mine, and starts to speak, *I know she wants the same fucking thing.*

"I want you to hurt me," she says quietly. She steps closer, and my heart picks up speed at the knife point nearly disappearing into her belly, but she doesn't even flinch. More drops of blood well up around the shallow wound, but her fingers only tighten on mine on the knife. "I want you to own me so I can *get you out of my fucking head.*"

I can't breathe.

"Show me what I've been missing all these years, J."

*J.* Jeremiah. Jamie. *I've always been those to her, and only she'll ever get that from me.*

My blood heats with her words. Her submission. With this day finally fucking coming.

I glance down between us, at the silver of the blade. The black handle, covered by our hands.

"How wet are you right now, baby?" I breathe out, staring at the knife. "Knowing that right now, *right fucking now,* I can do anything I want to you and no one," I meet her gaze, feel her chin quivering in my hand, "no one would hear you scream for help? No one would fucking stop me?" A slow smile curves my lips as I drop my hand from her face, to her soft belly. I run my finger through her blood, bring it to my mouth and suck on it, hear her little whimper as she watches.

The iron taste of her blood makes my cock ache all the more, and goddamn, I just want it all over me. I fucking want nothing between us. No walls. No lies. No secrets. No...*skin.*

"What do you want to do?" she asks me, her words quiet, but there's not a single trace of fear in her question.

Like she trusts me.

Like she knows I'd only hurt her if it was for her own good.

Not like him. *He'd abuse her in so many different ways, and never once to make her better.*

I stare into her beautiful eyes for a long moment, just watching her.

Then I sink to my knees.

Her mouth drops open as my head is level with her belly, with the knife still held against her skin.

"Let go of the handle, baby," I whisper, placing my free hand flat on her tummy, nearly dwarfing it as I cup her.

She doesn't let go though, and I look up to see her watching me, biting her lip.

"Give in to me, Sid," I whisper, my voice hoarse. I brush my thumb over her low belly, right near the hem of her skirt. "Let your brother take care of you."

She whimpers, her fingers twitching against my hold on the blade, the knife still pressed to her beautiful skin.

But then she releases me.

Submits to me.

That's something I'd never fucking take for granted from her.

My blood heats with the moment. The control. *Owning her,* after spending so many years chasing her. Trying to keep her under my control. Never wanting her to know I wasn't her brother, because I was terrified she'd fucking leave me.

But she's here.

She came back to me.

*She came back, despite what I did to her. And there's not a day that goes by that I don't regret that night.*

I drag my palm down her belly, tugging down her skirt as I do.

It falls to her feet, a heap between her combat boots. She starts to step out of them, but I dig my fingers into her belly again, my eyes taking in her black lace underwear, her slim thighs before I stare up at her.

"No," I tell her quietly. "Let me do everything."

She bites her lip, her hands in fists by her side, but she nods slowly.

I press an open mouth kiss to her belly, closing my eyes and my lips, sucking her skin between my teeth.

Her fingers come to my hair as she whimpers, and when I open my eyes, I shift my angle on the knife, pull it away from her bleeding skin. It's not a lot of blood, but it's enough that I can lick the small trail of it, sucking her again, trying to stop the bleeding. Trying to soak up every part of her that I can.

Her fingers tug the strands of my hair, and when I lick a line from the side of her belly to the hem of her underwear, *she moans for me.*

She sounds so beautiful.

I pull away, shift the angle of the knife, and I feel her hands tense in my hair, her breath leaving her in a rush as I hold the blade at an angle, poised like I'm ready to plunge it in to her pelvis.

I'm not.

I shift on my knees, look up at her between her wrists, her fingers still in my hair. Her knees are trembling, the sweet, earthy scent of her wet pussy distracting me from focusing on her face, but I try.

I'm so fucking close.

*I'm so fucking close.*

"Trust me. You want me to show you what you've been missing? You want me to fucking mark you, worse than he has?" I glide the flat side of the blade over her belly and she trembles, biting her lip. "Then *give into me, baby.*"

"J," she whispers, "what are you going to do?" Her words are choked, like she's scared to ask. Like she doesn't really want an answer. And fuck it.

I don't want to give her one.

I'd rather *show her* what I'm going to do. Make her feel it.

"Close your eyes," I tell her, one hand still splayed over her belly, the other still gliding the knife down to the edge of the lace of her underwear.

She runs her fingers through my hair, chewing on her

cheek as she stares down at me. I can almost see the struggle in her mind. She doesn't really trust me. She might seek me out for comfort, protection, *shelter.* But this baby is in my hands now, just like she is. And the world has given her no reason to trust anyone at all.

But I'd give her the goddamn world. I think the least of what she owes me is *this.*

"I know what's best for you," I tell her softly, flipping the blade, pricking the side of it against her underwear. She shivers, fingers tightening in my hair, a soft whimper escaping her swollen lips. "And you know I'd never really hurt you."

I see her throat bob as she swallows.

Then she nods, almost as if to herself, and I feel warmth building in my chest. That feeling only grows as she says, "I trust you, J. Don't make me regret it."

And she closes her eyes.

I take a deep breath in, my chest heaving as I watch her lashes flutter against the top of her cheekbones for a moment, as if she's having trouble not looking. As if trusting me is the hardest thing she's ever done in her life.

Maybe it is.

I deserve it, though.

I fucking deserve it.

I trail my eyes down her chest, over her swollen breasts, her puckered pink nipples, down her sternum to the small, round bump beneath my hands.

Running my tongue over my top lip, I stare at her pale, flawless skin, just below her belly button. This is where the bump is. The baby.

*The one that isn't fucking mine.*

Aside from killing it—it's crossed my mind a time or two— there's nothing I can do to change that.

But I can claim her in other ways.

Far better than that fucking scar on her palm.

The butcher's knife is way too big for what I want to do,

but if I get up right now, she'll move. She won't let me this close again.

I glance at the kitchen island that she's leaned against, as if she's unsteady on her feet, her tits heaving as she takes shallow breaths, her grip in my hair so tight it's making my eyes water.

I see the knife block. The black handles.

But this one will have to do.

Besides, when I shift my hold on it, gripping it around the blade, holding it almost like an unwieldy pencil, it pricks my skin, too. I feel the sharp sting on the inside of my thumb. The warmth of my own blood.

It's a minor pain. An inconvenience, just like it'll be to her.

I would know the fucking difference.

I'm the one that got stabbed and left for dead.

Gritting my teeth, shifting on my knees, I bring the tip of the knife just below my splayed thumb on her belly, right at her womb.

She sucks in a breath, but a quick glance up, and her eyes are still closed.

*Good girl, sis.*

I press the blade to her skin, and she shivers again, but doesn't open her eyes. Doesn't move.

I know she knows what I'm doing.

But she wants it too.

*She wants me too.*

I drag a small line down her flesh, see it split, the wake of blood behind the wound. Then I curve the knife upward, a smile forming on my lips as she says my name with a little gasp.

"*J.*"

Just like the letter I carved into her flesh.

*J.*

It's bleeding, but nothing too deep. Just in case it doesn't scar, I go over it one more time, deeper, and this time, a small sob escapes her lips, her grip in my hair painful.

*But I'm not done yet.*

I drop the knife to the floor with a thud, glance at my bleeding hand, then drag it over the J carved into her low belly, three inches long.

Impossible to fucking miss.

If he ever sees her naked again—and I'll probably kill him if that happens—he'll see that *I've fucking been here.*

I see our blood smeared on her skin and my cock throbs all over again. Leaning closer, I grip her hips in my bloody hand, run my tongue over the wound. My name. Who I am to her.

*Only her.*

I've always been *only hers.*

She shakes in my arms, gasping my name again.

I run my tongue over the letter three more times, savoring the iron taste of our blood.

Then I drag my teeth down her underwear at the same time my fingers go to her boots. She plants her hands on my head to balance herself, and I pull off her shoes and socks as I drag down the lace material with my teeth until it falls between her bare feet. I throw her boots away from us.

I pull back, gripping her by her hips, looking up at her face, my mouth inches from her bare pussy.

I inhale her scent, see her eyes flutter open, dipping down to the mark I left on her. She sucks in a breath, her face going pale, but she doesn't say a word.

I lean in close, run my tongue up her slit, groaning at the clean taste of her. She moans, biting her lip. I close my mouth on her clit and she tilts her head back, her throat arched. Pulling back, I stare at her pussy, so fucking perfect.

*Just like her.*

"Get on your knees," I tell her, my fingers biting into her skin.

She swallows but she does as I ask, dropping to her knees in front of me. She has to tilt her head back now to see me, and I see it in her eyes.

The trust.

It's still there, even after what I just did to her.

It turns me on all over again.

And I can't fucking wait anymore.

I drag my hand up her body, feel the subtle dips and curves, her hard nipple beneath my palm, see her skin streaked with our blood.

I splay my fingers against her jaw, push my bloody thumb into her mouth, as far back as I can, until she fucking gags.

She reaches her hands out, slipping her fingers under my shirt, nails biting into my torso as she holds onto me, her silver eyes wide.

"I bind myself to you tonight. No matter the shift of the knife." I see her surprise, her mouth opening around my thumb. I push my index and middle finger down her throat instead, watch as she gags again, her eyes watering, but she doesn't pull back. "Through blood and bone, flesh and heart, death may come," I smile at her, one hand going to her breast as I pinch her nipple and she gasps around my fingers, *"but we shall not part."*

Yeah. She thought he was the only motherfucker she'd do Lover's Death with.

*Fuck. That. Shit.*

After that, I push her down to the kitchen floor, my fingers still in her mouth as I lean over her, pushing deeper into the back of her throat. She starts to panic, her nails scratching against my ribs as she tries to say my name around my fingers.

"I don't need to hear that, baby," I tell her, glancing down at the J carved into her skin, "I just have to look at you now to know you're fucking mine."

I kick off my shoes, slowly pull my fingers out of her

mouth, see the strings of saliva connecting us, the blood on her lips.

"J," she breathes, her knees falling to the sides beneath me. She arcs her hips up as her hands come to the button of my pants, her fingers trembling. I sit up, just enough to reach behind my back and pull my shirt off, then drop it to the floor. Leaning back over her, I plant my hands on either side of her head, let her pull down my pants and my boxers until she can't reach any further and I use my hand to push them all the way off, kicking them away from us.

Her eyes go to my cock, and she reaches between us, her fingers curled tight around it as she strokes me, lying back down, biting her lip, looking from my dick to my face.

I close my eyes, savoring the feel of her tiny fingers around me.

I never thought...all these fucking years...I never thought we'd be here.

"J," she says again, pumping me faster, "I want you."

I open my eyes, glance down at her spread legs, the muscles in her thighs straining against her skin with how open they are.

She reaches her other hand to her pussy, but I slap her hand away, grip her throat. Her strokes on my cock stop, and she freezes beneath me.

"Only I get to touch you, baby," I tell her. "You understand?"

She nods slowly, whimpering as she does.

Then, with her pulling me closer, my cock lines up with her entrance.

My chest grows tight, my blood hot.

I glance down again at my name on her skin. *Is she really mine? Is this just sex?* I know how she likes to use it.

I know so many men have been here before me.

I know this might not mean fuck to her.

This could be nothing to her. Fucking nothing. She could forget me, run away, just as fast as she did with *him*.

And thinking about him…

*Fuck him.*

I shove into her tight, wet cunt, her hands going to my back, raking her nails against me as she gasps, her back arching upward, her eyes fluttering closed.

I circle my fingers tighter around her throat, my other hand going to her arm, forcing it backward, off of me, over her head. I briefly let go of her throat, grab her other arm, then pin both wrists down on the cold kitchen floor, her body stretched out beneath me, her spine hitting the stone tile every time I thrust back into her.

She moans my name, her eyes back on me as my hand is back on her throat. She feels *so fucking good.*

Better than I could have imagined.

Tight and wet and *all for me.*

My hips slam into hers, blood from her stomach sticking to my skin too, where we meet together.

I'm gripping her wrists so tight above her head I know it has to hurt, but I'm fucking drowning in the feel of her pussy, and I just don't fucking care.

Even as her face flushes pink beneath my fingers, as I lean down close to her, my mouth just over hers as she gasps for air, *I don't fucking care.*

She doesn't need to breathe.

She just needs me.

*She's always just needed me.*

My mouth comes over hers, and her lips part for me as I keep thrusting into her, her legs wrapped tight around me. I loosen my grip on her throat, so I can feel her moaning into my mouth, feel how much she loves this.

*Loves me.*

She arches her back more, her tits brushing against my chest as her tongue clashes with mine.

"You love me?" I ask her, speaking against her mouth before I bite down on her bottom lip. I taste iron and I don't know if it's from biting her lip, or our blood together from our own Death Oath.

The only one that matters. The only one that fucking counts.

I don't give a fuck about traditions. Rituals. Secret goddamn societies.

The only thing I give a fuck about is the girl I'm fucking right at this moment.

"You love me, baby?" I ask her again, pulling back even as she tries to keep her swollen lips against mine. I'm thrusting into her, softer now, but enough that her tits are still jiggling, her body stretched out beneath me. *God she feels fucking good.* "You love your brother?"

Her lips are parted, her eyes almost glassy with lust. Pleasure?

*Love?*

"Yes," she finally says as I drive my dick in as far as I can, keep our hips melded together. Her eyes dart to my mouth, and I can't hide my smile, the way she licks her lips, blood smeared across them, like she wants my mouth back on hers so fucking bad.

"Yeah?" I ask her, feeling my chest grow full. Nearly fucking bursting as I pull out of her tight cunt, slowly push back in and feel her clench around me, her eyes fluttering closed for a second before she fixes me with that beautiful gray stare.

"Yes," she says again, not looking away from me. "I love you, J," she whispers.

I dive back down, my lips on hers. She opens for me, lets me in. "You do?" I ask her, speaking into her mouth, my grip on her wrists so fucking tight it's hurting my fingers, but I can't let go.

I can't let her go.

But I loosen my hold on her throat, run my thumb over her windpipe as she says, "Yes, I love you. I love you, J."

I pull back, onto my knees, bring one of her legs over my shoulder, one hand on her inner thigh, the other dragging across my bleeding name on her belly until my thumb is circling her pretty pink clit.

Her arms are still over her head even though I've let her go, like she wants nothing more than to submit to me.

Give everything to me.

"Don't you dare fucking leave me," I tell her, watch her heavy eyes try to hold mine as she pants while I keep circling her swollen clit. She has a perfect fucking pussy. "Don't you dare fucking leave, baby, because no one is going to love you like I do. No one is going to save you like I do."

I stare down at us, my cock driving into her. I see her stretched around me, so fucking tight.

"You see this?" I ask her, jerking my chin, gripping her thigh hard enough to leave bruises when I'm done with her.

She looks down between us, her body elongated, her tits so fucking full. "Yes," she whispers, "yes."

"This is all I've ever wanted. If I lost this, if I lost you..." I'm so close, and I think she is too, the way she's clenching so tight around me, the way her back is coming off the floor, her head tilted back, eyes closed. I keep circling her clit, keep driving my hips against her, and I'm almost there...

"If I fucking lost you," I tell her, my entire body flushed with heat. I stare down at her, lost in her own pleasure, lost in mine. I see the knife, just beside us and I let go of her thigh, my hand starting to tremble with how hard I've done every-thing with her.

I snatch up the knife, lean down close as her knee comes toward her chest, stretching her. I hold the blade to her throat as she dips her chin, her eyes wide with surprise.

But not fear.

No.

She knows I couldn't live without her.

Which is exactly what I fucking tell her as I come inside of her, emptying myself into her.

"If I fucking lost you…" My voice is hoarse, I can barely say it, but I need her to know. I press my brow to hers, the knife still at her throat as I groan her name, "fuck, Sid." When I'm done, and I know she is, too, crying out my name, her arms wrapped around my back now, the two of us coated in blood as she keeps whispering my name, over and over, like a fucking prayer. Like I'm God.

"If I lost you," I start again, my forehead still against hers, the knife still to her throat as she stares up at me with wide eyes, "I'd find you again. And I'd fucking kill you, baby, because I can't…" I pull her bottom lip between my teeth, roll it out until I let go. "I can't live without you. I could *never* live without you."

She reaches between us, her hand over the handle, fingers around mine. But she doesn't try to move the knife. She just stares at me, one hand still on my back.

"You don't have to," she whispers, her voice hoarse, but strong. "You don't have to, J."

# CHAPTER Twenty

## JEREMIAH

WE DON'T SLEEP after that.

I wish I could know what she's thinking. After the kitchen, the confession, the bleeding…she went to her bedroom. Came back down in a tank top and cotton shorts. I splashed water over my face, pulled on shorts, made a drink.

Now, she's standing in the kitchen, drinking from the water bottle she threw at my head before the…sex.

I can't stop the smile on my face as I think about it. Her underneath me. Submitting to me.

*Fucking finally.*

I feel euphoric, endorphins going haywire in my brain.

She looks over at me, still drinking, and I see water drip down her chin.

I smile wider, biting my tongue and flicking my gaze down her body. But even so, even in this perfect bubble of contentment, of knowing I laid claim to her in a way she can't scrub off…I feel this strange sense of foreboding. Like when the sun comes, reality will crash back down with it.

I'll be in that cage again and she'll be far, far away.

Out of my reach.

I fight those feelings back. It's always been next to impossible for me to enjoy happiness. But with her, I want to. I want to try everything good and new with her by my side.

The plastic crinkles beneath her fingers in the quiet of the house. I pull my phone from my pocket, drink still in one hand as I find some music to play. *How to Love* by Lil Wayne might not be the song I scream to everyone that I love, but...fuck, I do love it.

Sid huffs a small laugh as I toss my phone on the coffee table in front of me. Before I can say anything, she slowly closes the space between us, drawing up short when she's a few feet from the cream-colored couch, her little toes flexing on the wooden floors of the cabin.

I take another drink, swallowing down the vodka and feeling it burn a trail toward my stomach.

Her hands come to her hips and she cocks her head.

"I like this place," she admits, her words soft. Her voice has always been deeper than most girls, in a throaty sort of way. Husky. Sensual.

*Fucking sexy, just like it was when she was moaning my name.*

My throat feels tight as I stare at her petite frame, think of the way I want her against me again. Underneath me. All over me. I don't think I'll ever get enough of her.

I hope she meant what she said. That I don't have to live without her. Not again.

"Yeah?" I ask her.

She runs her tongue over her teeth, glancing around the room. There's not much to it. The couch I'm on, a chair across from me that could seat two, a light gray color that matches Sid's eyes. Otherwise, it's fairly empty.

Only the basics.

Except for the extras, of course, because "basic" in Jeremiah Rain means something different from most people.

There's AC pumping through the vents right now, and I see Sid's nipples pebbling beneath her tank.

The little hairs on the back of my neck stand on end, my

fingers warping the cup in my hand. I hate plastic cups, but for the cabin, they seemed...standard. Besides, Sid requested them when Ria and Nicolas had gone to the store for us.

I finish my drink, my head spinning, a little loose. The constant memories that threaten to spill into my brain like black oil across a rough sea are tucked back effortlessly now, and I reconsider this whole policy I have about never drinking too much. With Sid...I'm reconsidering every fucking thing.

But I think, too, about grabbing the backpack from my room and rolling a joint.

Because my free hand is resting on my thigh, but it seems the alcohol has made my tremor worse. I have to consciously press my palm against my thigh to keep it from shaking. Luckily, Sid's eyes haven't left mine.

She's still staring at me, a slight smile on her lips.

I think about her beneath me. How she let me cut her.

How she let me own her.

Was that a one-time thing? Can we do it again so soon?

*Does she really love me? Will she run back to him?*

I lean over, set my cup on the coffee table at her back. Her eyes trail over my body, that pale pink flush on her cheeks again. She bites her lip as I lean back, resting both hands on my thighs.

"Come here," I tell her, jerking my head toward my lap. "Come sit with your *brother.*"

That pink flush turns a deeper red and she drops her hands from her hips, her fingers flexing and curling at her sides. She's bouncing on the balls of her feet, and I know she's fighting back.

But we both know now, now that I have her, she only has me to run to. She might as well make it a habit.

She lifts up her hand, her eyes tracking over her palm.

I tense, knowing what she sees.

My throat feels dry as her eyes finally shift up to mine

again, the dim light of the living room enough to see the confusion warring in the silver pools of her gaze.

I tamp down on my rage. Refuse to look at that gun in the kitchen. At the knife on the island, still bloody.

"You thinking about him?" I demand.

Her throat bobs, but fire flashes in her eyes. "Jeremiah, don't start——"

"Where's your ring, baby?" I ask her, my voice hoarse.

Her palm is still up, but now she curls her fingers into a fist, her jaw clenched. I know what she's thinking.

She's pissed.

I enjoy it.

I sit up straighter, elbows on my knees, my eyes locked on hers. "Where's your fucking ring? You tasted his blood," my skin crawls with those words, my ribcage too tight, but I keep talking anyway, keep barreling past the pain, "he got yours." Just like I did, now, fucker. "*Where's your goddamn ring?*"

She swallows, drops her hand, her eyes narrowing. "I didn't want a ring," she whispers, her words a hiss, full of venom, but I think she's lying.

I tell her just that. "You're a fucking liar, baby. You've always been a liar. A runner too." I glance toward the door, over her shoulder. "But you're not running now. After I just ate you alive. Why is that?"

She sinks her teeth into her full bottom lip, holding my gaze as she does, wrapping her arms around herself, blocking my view of her tits.

"You wanna know what he did to me, baby?" I ask her, my voice as low as hers. As full of venom. "Before you start regretting what I just did to you," I dip my eyes to her belly, covered by her shirt, "you wanna know what he fucking did?"

She stiffens, a muscle in her jaw jumping, her eyes wide as she stares at me.

*Yeah. She hasn't wanted to think about that shit.*

Neither have I, for that matter, but with the alcohol in my veins, the way my hand is trembling noticeably against my thigh—although she's too busy making sure she only stares at my face to notice—I figure tonight is the night we go down that fucking dark and dirty road. We can't just fuck it out.

If I want this to be real—and I want that more than I've ever wanted anything in in my life—we have to deal with the dark, too.

"You know what happened to me."

She shakes her head. "Jeremiah—"

"Don't interrupt me when I'm fucking talking." It feels good to say that. To put her back in her place. I gave her the illusion of power these few weeks, and I love her to death, but she can't just treat me and talk to me however the fuck she wants. She can't just let me fuck her, then go back to pining after him.

That's not how things are going to go here.

I squeeze my fingers together, entwined through one another, trying to stop the fucking tremor. I forgot this was a side effect of alcohol. Another reason I hate to drink. I want my mind sharp, I need to know who the fuck wants to kill me at any given time, but right now, I just want my hand to stop shaking before I can get the story out myself.

She glares at me, stepping closer. I wonder if she wants to slap me. I kind of hope she does. I'd love to fucking fight her right now.

I have to look up at her, as close as she is. I can smell her, too. Lavender and sweat from when we fucked. Her arms are still crossed, and I want to fucking pin her down and fuck her again until she screams my name.

But I resist.

I want her to choose me in every way, and I want her to know why she's doing it. Because she loves me, and because Lucifer Malikov *isn't shit.*

"When I was in that cage, I only ever saw three people. Three *real* people," I clarify, because I saw dozens that only existed in my mind. Depending on how long I'd been in there, I could see twelve in a single fucking day.

I see her swallow again.

She doesn't reach for me, although she could touch me, if she wanted.

I wonder if after she hears this, she'll hate me. She'll think I'm too fucked up. Too wrong. She'll understand just how much of a sociopath I really am.

I don't care.

If she loves me even just a fraction as much as I love her, she'll accept this part of me. After all, I accept all the ways she's been a little fucking whore while I've waited for her.

"Three people, one was my foster dad." Even saying those last two words causes my ears to ring, anger coiling in my gut as I think of him. Of how he tried to erase Sid's memory from my mind, from the first day I woke up in his fucking office. Telling me I didn't have that sister anymore. "One was another *sister* of mine."

I see Sid's eyes narrow, jealousy in her gaze, in the way her jaw tightens.

I offer her a small smile. "Don't worry, baby. I didn't fuck her like I just fucked you," I add, and she shifts on her feet in front of me, clearly uncomfortable. It's kind of a lie. I did fuck her. But definitely not like what I did with Sid, although there was blood, then, too. "But you know the third person that came to see me?"

I snake an arm out this time, unable to hold back from touching her. I pull her close, my forearm against her back, my fingers digging into her waist, slipping under her shirt.

Her breath catches as she drops her arms, my head level with her navel. With my name, just under her shirt. I stare up at her, and one of her hands comes to my hair. She runs her fingers through it. It feels so good, I almost don't want to tell her.

But then I imagine all the ways she did this with him, and my fingers dig a little deeper into her skin.

"The father of your child," I tell her, glancing at her tummy.

She tenses, her fingers stilling in my hair.

"I wish it was mine," I tell her truthfully, her entire body rigid. It's the truth. I do. And one day, we'll have our own. "But another truth? I don't care that it isn't. It's you I want. *It's always been you.*"

I smile at her, dip my head, nudge her shirt up with my nose, press my mouth to her stomach, just above her belly button, my eyes going to my name in her skin, the blood dried and smeared, as if she didn't want to clean it off.

She shivers in my arms, her fingers tightening in my hair, one hand still by her side.

"But you need to know what he did."

I kiss her again, feel her stiffen.

"Yeah," I whisper against her skin, tilting my head up to look at her. "Lucifer came when I got this." I lift my free hand up, watch her eyes trail to the marks on my inner forearm, vertical lines that are white scars now. I shake my head. "No, baby. He didn't do *that.*"

My hand starts to tremble, almost imperceptible, except she's staring right at it, and I know she sees it.

She reaches out, wrapping her slender fingers around my wrist, feeling the way I'm trembling in her touch.

I feel itchy, uncomfortable, and for a second I want to push her away. Shove her off of me and forget about this. Forget peeling away the mask I wear. The ways I guard myself.

I want to keep her out, just as I've ever kept anyone I've ever known out.

Even Nicolas doesn't know this much about me. Neither does Brooklin.

*No one.*

But Sid deserves to know. She's handled me at my fucking worst, and my best isn't any better than that, but she deserves all of my truths.

I let my eyes flutter closed as her thumb runs up the inside of my wrist and her fingers start massaging my scalp again. It feels so fucking good I want to groan. I've never let anyone touch me this way.

Ever.

I dip my chin, press another kiss to her belly. Then I trail my tongue down her skin, over my name.

She sucks in a breath, and I'm sure it stings. She stops massaging my wrist and my hair, and her body tenses.

But I open my lips, press my mouth to her again, closing and sucking softly on her skin.

She shivers but keeps rubbing me.

I take a shuddering breath, rest my brow against her belly as I speak, unable to look at her when I say the words. "He came when my hands were bound," I explain, trying to distance myself from the words even as I speak them. As I lay myself open for her, knowing she might try to run again. Knowing she might...reject me. "It was thin rope. Strong enough that I couldn't seem to rip it apart, no matter how hard I tried, but small enough that it bit into my skin."

I can still feel it, now, with my head against Sid's stomach, as her thumb carefully runs against my inner wrist. I can feel it.

My mouth goes dry, but I force myself to keep talking. To keep giving her my truths, because she deserves them. I aimed a gun at her head once. I pulled the goddamn trigger. I almost raped her.

I hurt her.

I lied to her.

She deserves this truth.

"I'd tried to escape," I admit, my voice breaking. "I'd tried to escape when one of my *sisters* came to feed me. I'd grabbed her, pulled her against the wire." I remember her wide blue eyes. Her pulse beneath my fingers as I held onto her throat, the bread she'd brought me tossed into a fucking corner because I didn't want her goddamn bread.

I wanted her blood.

I wanted to be free.

I wanted the light.

"I almost killed her." And I had. I'd almost killed her right then, but her father must have noticed she'd gone missing. He came downstairs, pulled her away from me. She had tried to defend me. Tried to bullshit her way over excuses, but her father had struck her with the back of his hand, and she had gone down, onto the cement floor.

Anger had surged through me, and I didn't know why.

I didn't fucking know why because I wanted to hurt her too.

But it didn't take me long to figure out why.

When he yanked me out of that cage, pressed my face against the cement floor, his foot against my spine, my arms jerked behind me as he wrapped the rope so tight around my hands, it cut off my circulation before he even threw me back in the fucking cage, I knew why I didn't like seeing him hurt her.

Because she might've been a bitch too. A worthless fucking cunt, just like her sister and just like their mother, but her dad was worse.

He was...*he was like Lucifer.*

I tell Sid all of this, stumbling over the parts where my hands had gone numb, and it no longer felt like I had fingers at all, and I didn't think, when they finally untied me, that I actually *would* have them. My mind had conjured up images of my fingers detached from my body, black and blue.

I keep my eyes closed, wrap both arms around her, pulling her tight. She lets go of my wrist, brings both hands to my hair, still massaging my scalp, as if to keep me calm. To urge me to go on.

To tell her all the ways my own brother fucked me.

"He came down when I was bound," I tell her, voice breaking. "He came down, watching me carefully, circling my cage like he was a fucking predator." I take a shaky breath, and I can feel Sid's pulse through her tummy. I think about the baby in there.

I think about the ways I hope they're nothing like *their fucking father.*

"I begged him. I fucking begged him."

I screamed. My throat was raw, and even to my own ears, I sounded like a wild animal. I shoved my shoulders into the bars while he watched me.

My whimpers were hoarse as he stared at me, emotionless. *"Help me."* I said it over and over and over. Pleaded on my knees.

I remembered the first time I was introduced to him. To the rest of them. I was quiet, withdrawn. They were arrogant, cocky.

*Mean.*

I didn't see them all together after that. Not until I was *reborn.* Not until Ezra gave me what I needed to get free, to open the padlock.

Not until *that moment.*

Lucifer had stood there, watching me, his head cocked to the side. Even in the dark, his deep blue eyes seemed to glow.

My heart had thundered in my chest, twisting as he stared at me, because I knew he wasn't going to help.

I stopped pleading, but I couldn't stop the soft whimpers that left my mouth.

*Then he left me.* Without a fucking word, he left me.

When I made it out of there, he never spoke about it, except for that night he pissed on me.

Noctem.

He taunted me about it then. *"Your hand is shaking."* He knew then, what he had done to me. What he had let happen.

He knew.

And that day, when I needed him, he walked out. Walked up the stairs without looking back, a smirk on his face.

And I hated him ever since.

# CHAPTER
## Twenty-One

### SID

HEARING THE WORDS HURTS.

I always knew there was more. I knew they hated each other long before I became involved with Lucifer. I knew that Jeremiah's anger and wrath was aimed carefully at my husband for reasons I didn't quite understand.

Hearing them now, knowing the ways Lucifer *left him*, I feel something give inside of me. A crack, breaking me, releasing pressure.

*Giving me permission.*

Lucifer had planned to kill me that night. And I know Jeremiah messed up. I know he isn't good. He's capable of violence, and I've had it directed at me many, many times. The world has hardened him, and I think he was probably born a little off too, the ways he scared me growing up. Keeping me with him.

Locking me in his room.

But he's always tried to protect me. And he knew a side of Lucifer I hadn't quite experienced.

But I know my husband is a sociopath too, and I have no trouble believing anything Jeremiah just told me.

I remember the glass he threw at my head. The coke on

the table. His hands wrapped around my throat. *"Shut the fuck up,"* he'd told me, more than once.

He'd hurt me.

He'd hurt my brother more.

Not to mention Jeremiah's hand, trembling in my grasp.

Nerve damage.

Permanent.

Lucifer could've stopped it, but he didn't. *He fucking didn't.*

I move closer to Jeremiah, and he slowly picks his head up, his gaze wary, as if he's scared of what I'm going to do next. There are so many ways I've let him down. So many ways I've rejected him, it's a miracle he even still wants me. Even after what we did, even after how he marked me in the kitchen...I saw the fear in his eyes when I told him he wouldn't have to live without me.

*Did I mean it?*

I don't know.

But as I straddle him, knees on either side of his hips, his groin pressing between my thighs, I know that I mean it *for now.* Someone needs to heal him. He's achieved so much. He's capable of so fucking much.

But his heart needs to be taken care of.

Me and Lucifer are done. I think we've been done a long, long time.

He fucked up my family.

*His own family.*

He put coke and women and *everything else* before me. I know he needs help, too. Healing. But he refuses to get it, then he flees to Julie. Fucking Ophelia.

*Fuck. Him.*

Jeremiah's hands are on my waist as he leans back on the couch, looking up at me while I cup his handsome face, tilting my head down, my lips inches from his.

"I'm so sorry," I whisper.

He swallows, averting his gaze for a second, his fingers

digging deeper into my skin. I shift on top of him, rubbing against him and he bites his lip like he's holding back a moan as he looks back up at me.

"Don't be," he tells me, and he looks like he means it. "I was always just trying to get back to you, *sis*." He smirks at me, his eyes gleaming in the dim lights of the living room. It probably shouldn't but hearing him call me that makes me want him even more. "Always. The rest of the shit we suffered along the way? *Fuck it.*"

Without another word, he grabs my hips, picks me up and spins us around, so he's on top of me on the couch.

"God, I've wanted you for so fucking long." He brushes a lock of hair from my face and I shiver at his light touch. "Having you now..." He bites his lip. "I won't hurt you, baby," he says softly, and there's nothing sly in those words. Nothing...cruel. But then his lips tug into a smirk, his eyes flashing. "Unless you want me to again."

I swallow down the lump in my throat, don't take my eyes from his.

"I do," I whisper, my voice hoarse.

He sits up, pulling me onto his lap so I'm straddling him again. We're closer together now, and my eyes finally break with his, taking in his sculpted, tan muscles. His body is perfect, tightly wound muscle and rippling abs and...

The scar on his left side.

Raised skin, white and lumpy.

He lets go of my hands as I bite back a gasp, staring at where Lucifer stabbed him. I knew it. I've seen it. But now, in this moment, it feels different. *My fucking husband stabbed him, knowing what it would do to me to lose Jeremiah.*

He laces his fingers through mine again. When I meet his gaze, there's pain there. I look down again, see the vertical lines on his forearm.

For me.

Everything he's done...it's been for me.

"Sid," he whispers, "are you sure you want me?"

*"You deserve the world. I'd burn it down before I let you have less."* I think of those words to me, the ones he'd spoken in Nicolas's apartment.

I drop his hands, cross my arms and pull my shirt over my head, letting it fall to the floor. I see his eyes go to my breasts, down over my stomach, swollen with a baby that isn't his. Over the name he carved into my skin. *His.*

His chest heaves, nearly brushing mine, but I sit up on my knees, pull down my shorts, and when both of us are completely naked save for his black boxer briefs, I push him gently back against the arm of the couch.

I plant my hands on either side of his hips, crawling down his body, my eyes on his. Slowly, I pull off his boxers, toss them with the rest of our clothes, then wrap my fingers around his hard cock.

Glancing down, my eyes widen at just how fucking big he is, and I want him inside of me all over again.

But I want to make him feel good, first.

I part my lips as his fingers come to my hair and he groans as my mouth touches the tip of his cock, teasing him. That sound—masculine and full of want—has my stomach fluttering, and it takes effort to keep teasing him.

But he doesn't let me do it for long.

"You want me to hurt you again?" he asks me, his voice low.

I meet his gaze, my mouth just over the tip of his cock as I'm crouched over him. I nod my head, and his fingers tighten in my hair before he shoves downward.

I gag, my eyes watering at how full he is in my mouth, the back of my throat. My stomach clenches, but I don't want him to stop.

Slowly, he drags me up by my hair, brushes his thumb over my cheek. "Do you know how long I've waited for this?" he whispers, his voice strained. "How long I've waited for you?"

He guides me back down, and saliva drips from my mouth, my eyes watering all over again.

He tastes fucking divine. I bring my hands to his hips, steadying me.

"I've wanted your mouth on me for *years, Sid.*" There's venom in those words, and he forces me further down, my fingers digging into him. "Everyone else got you. *Everyone.*"

My chest tightens as I meet his gaze in the dim light.

He drags me off of him, then without warning, reaches down, hauls me onto his lap. It seems effortless for him to fucking manhandle me. I circle my fingers around his cock, stroking him as he stares at me, hands on my thighs.

I feel the heat from him against my slit, so close we're touching, but I'll have to angle myself up to get him inside of me.

I make to do just that, but he holds me down, shaking his head, his eyes hard.

"No," he says, anger in that word. "Not yet. Now *you have to fucking wait.*"

I stroke him faster, harder. "I don't want to," I tell him, biting my lip as I stare at him. I run my tongue over my bottom lip, taste blood, see his jaw tick with his self-control. We're so fucking close, and I'm so fucking wet and I...I want him again.

But his hands trail up my thighs, over the slight curve of my hips, then his palms splay against my belly, covering his name.

"We should be doing this together."

I stop stroking him, my fingers still wrapped him, but my eyes are frozen on his.

"This should be *mine.*"

My heart skips a beat in my chest.

His fingers curl slightly, light pressure against my low belly.

He angles his head. "Tell me you know that, baby. Tell me you made a mistake with him. You fucked this up." His jaw tightens as he stares at me, fingers still pressed against my skin. "You've always been mine. Tell me that."

I think of Lucifer.

His dark blue eyes on mine. The way he loved me before I could ever possibly think of loving him back.

I think of him pinning me down while the warehouse burned. Jeremiah inside. *My brother.* Whether he is or not, he's always been there, since day one, just like a brother. *But more.*

"Fucking *tell me, Sid.*" Jeremiah's grip against my belly is almost painful.

I meet his eyes, my own widening.

I think of Ophelia moaning Lucifer's name. Julie, too.

Think of how he might've killed me the first night we met, except...he thought I was pretty.

What a fucking joke.

We're toxic together. Nothing but chaos. Lilith and Lucifer were only made for hell. There's no happy ending there. No chance at goodness.

But Jeremiah?

*He's always been mine.* And me?

I hold his gaze as I say, "I think I've always been yours."

With those words, he moves so fast I don't have time to breathe when he sits up, shoving me backward, down against the couch as he moves over me.

His hand comes between us, over his cock, and I spread my thighs, my hands on his broad back, down his shoulders.

His face is inches from mine as he nudges against me, his breath like mint and vodka as he says, "I love you, baby," then he pushes all the way in, not letting me adjust to him, just like he didn't before.

He's thick, stretching me, and for a second, it burns. I rake my nails down his back as his hands come to either side of my head on the couch.

I gasp, and he smiles, then brushes his full lips over mine.

"You're fucking everything to me," he whispers, his mouth

grazing my lips with every word as he pulls out just slightly, then pushes back into me.

I can't stop the moan from my mouth, and he sweeps my hair back, smiling down at me. "Say my name," he says softly. There's no command, no anger or venom. It's a request.

A plea.

"Jer—"

He stops, fully inside of me. "No, baby." His hand trails down my face, gripping my chin. *"My name."*

I run my fingers down his triceps, flexed and hard beneath my touch. "Jamie," I whisper the word, almost as if I don't believe it. As if this isn't…him. Is it wrong I still see him as my brother? The boy I grew up with? Even with him fucking me again and his mouth not even an inch from mine, he's the one that's *always been there.*

He fucks me harder, tipping his head back as I take in the sharp line of his jaw. He groans, biting his lip.

I say it again, and he dips his chin, staring at me like he… "I love you, Sid," he says, his words hoarse.

I gasp, as he hits deeper, angling his hips. "I-I—"

His mouth finds mine, drowning my words, his tongue meeting my own. He pulls back, just slightly to take me in. "You what, baby?"

I open my mouth again to speak the words, but my pussy clenches against him as he fucks me harder, as if he doesn't want me to be able to speak.

"You what?" he teases me, leaning back, grabbing both legs, placing them over his shoulder so he's hitting deeper, harder.

I gasp his name, my eyes nearly rolling back in my head as he puts one hand on my throat, then uses the pad of his thumb to circle my clit.

I grip his hips, warmth flooding through me as he fucks me, staring at me as if I'm the only thing he gives a single fuck about in the world.

"Say it, Sid," he grinds out, and I know he's close.

I know he is, but I am, too, and I want us to come together.

The slick sounds of his thrusts as he fucks me are pushing me closer, and his fingers tightening around my throat even closer still.

I arch my back, gasping as he angles his hips again, hitting deep, my knees nearly touching my shoulders.

"Say it," he snarls, his words vicious now as he stares at me and I try to catch my breath, but it's becoming harder to breathe beneath his hand.

"I love you, J," I gasp, shortening his name for only the second time in my life. Because for me? He's always been both. My brother, Jamie, protecting me from our childhood horrors. And this man inside of me, finishing in me as he gasps my name, and I come under his hand for the second time.

Jeremiah.

*Jeremiah fucking Rain.*

I love him.

I love him, and I've spent too long trying to deny it.

But as he collapses on top of me, holding me close, both of us spent, I close my eyes, and he whispers in my ear. Words that make me remember.

I might love him.

He might love me.

But if I fucked him over, he wouldn't let me run again.

He'd fucking kill me.

He literally said just that, after the first time.

His hand comes to my belly, possessive and nearly painful as his mouth finds my ear. "Don't you dare let this make you run." He licks his way around my lobe. "We'll raise it, *together.*"

I drift off into sleep not long after, but all I can see behind my closed eyes, infecting my mind, is what Lucifer would do if Jeremiah Rain dared try to raise *his child.*

# CHAPTER
## Twenty-Two

## LUCIFER

MY MOUTH IS DRY, my nose running—the fucking irony—
when I bring the phone to my ear, my eyes still closed tight as
I roll over onto my back.

"What the fuck?" I mutter into the phone. It was Mav's
ringtone. The only one besides my fucking wife's set to ring
out loud, but when she left me to go suck her brother's dick,
of course she didn't bring a phone.

"Get up." Mav's words are cold, but there's something else
lurking underneath them, causing my pulse to speed up.

Still, my eyes feel like they're glued shut. Last night I…
*Fuck.*

I don't want to think about what I did last night. I fling my
forearm over my brow, keep my eyes closed as I try to swallow.
"What the fuck time is it?" I growl at Mav, wondering why the
hell he's calling me.

"It's four." His words are a snarl. "Now, I need you to *get.*
*The fuck. Up.*"

I yawn, not bothering to stifle it. He needs to know he just
woke my hungover ass up and even though I got fucked quite
a few times last night, by two girls at once, I'm not feeling
ready to get the fuck up.

Not at four in the morning.

Not unless—

"She's near you."

My eyes spring open and I'm staring at the dark ceiling in the guestroom. I had enough sense to fall into bed alone last night. *After* Finn was asleep, and O rode my dick while I fingerfucked Julie, coming inside a condom—which I haven't worn in a long, long time.

I'd hate to kill both of them in my fucking sleep. Actually, I'm not so sure I'd mind, but then I'd have the kid and...*no thanks.*

"What are you fucking talking about?"

"She's staying in Jeremiah's cabin. Not far from you," Maverick spells it out for me. At the sound of his name, I sit up, the room spinning as I do.

"Why the fuck—"

"Have you found anything out?" Maverick snaps.

I tug on one of my curls, yanking hard. "No, but what are you—"

"You know why?"

I blow out a breath, my temper rising with these fucking mind games. Why is my wife here? Why is she here with him and why the fuck is my brother calling me at four in the goddamn morning?

"Because whoever it is that's fucking with us, they were at one of Jeremiah Rain's clubs last night. In Virginia."

My breath catches. "But Sid is—"

"She wasn't there. But if you'd pay the fuck attention, you'd know I said she was *near. You.*" It sounds like his jaw is clenched. I flex my own, blinking away the sleep from my eyes. The heaviness. Weariness. Trying to pay attention, but I can't keep up, my head spinning with every word Mav speaks. "But one of the longest employed dancers at his club was found dead. Cindy. Her throat was slit in the dressing room at the back of the club."

My mouth drops open.

"Apparently, her and Rain sometimes fucked, on and off, according to the police reports."

Of course we've already got our hands on those. "Cameras?" I croak out. If someone is after us, and after *him too*, then they could be coming after my wife next.

Elijah's guard was nothing. Even the photos of Sid could've been a way to spook us. But another death? After the shit with the kitten here in Acid City, like a way to divert me and my brothers from focusing on Alexandria...whoever the fuck this is, they're playing the long game.

"Disabled." Maverick's voice is clipped. "All of them. Whoever this is, this isn't a spur of the fucking moment vengeance. They're after us, and with Elijah's guard, and eyes on Sid...they're after all of us."

I feel dizzy, dread coiling my stomach into knots.

"You need to get to her."

I swallow down the tightness in my throat, my fingers shaking as I grip the sheets, closing my eyes, pulling my knees to my chest and resting my brow against them as I grip the phone so hard my palm starts to sweat. "Mav," I choke out, thinking of when I woke up with the knife in my hand. My wife in my arms. How scared she was. She was never really terrified of me, not for long. Not like I secretly wanted her to be.

But after that night...she was.

"I'm not better." I hate admitting that. I hate the pressure building behind my eyes. "I'm not better, and she chose him, and—"

"And our fucking family dragged her from her house. My girl too," Mav snarls. "They took them, and you had already hurt her..." He trails off, his voice little more than a whisper. I know he isn't trying to rub it in. I know he's trying to make me understand. To see why she left.

But it doesn't matter.

It hurts all the same.

She fucking left me.

*She left me.*

And if she thinks he can protect her, then fucking let him.

"I'll give you the address. You need to get her, bring her back here, and we can figure this shit out together. But we have to have all of us in one place. And with Ignis—"

"Stop." I whisper the word. *Ignis*. Fire in Latin. When the brotherhood is formed. But with me and Sid married, Coagula between the two of us, it was her turn to be brought into the fold. It would be the first ceremony between the Unsaints where a woman was there to participate as one of us.

It was where she would become *really ours*.

The fifth day of May, not far away.

But she doesn't deserve it. She doesn't deserve to be one of us, because all she does is fucking *run*.

I fling off the covers, feet hitting the cold floor as I swing my legs off the bed and start pacing in the dark room, spots popping in front of my eyes as I feel dizzy.

"He can fucking look after her. They wanted each other so bad, let them handle it. If they end up dead, so fucking be it."

There's a long pause on the other end of the line. I slump against the wall, cold against my back as I pull the phone from my ear to see if we're still connected. We are. Gritting my teeth, I jam the phone back against my face, start to snarl something out, but Mav is already talking.

"Fine," he's saying, his voice cold. "If you want to let either Jeremiah *or* whoever the fuck this is tear her apart, carve your baby out of her, be my fucking guest. But don't you dare come crying to me when she's nothing but a fucking corpse."

I can't breathe, the thoughts of her lips, cold and blue, of our baby, gutted from her precious womb…I can't breathe.

"But if, on the other hand, you want to be a fucking man, I'll send you the address. I'll help you get her. You decide what you want to do. You decide what the fuck you can live with." Before I can say a word, he ends the call.

I jerk the phone from my ear, gritting my teeth as I fucking hurl it across the room, where it hits the opposite wall, slides to the floor.

Somewhere on this floor, Finn starts to cry.

And sinking down to my knees, forehead against the hard-wood...*so do I.*

# CHAPTER
## *Twenty-Three*

JEREMIAH

I INHALE the sweet smoke on the back porch, leaning against the railing as I stare off into the woods. The sun is just peaking its way up, glowing red and orange and pink past the line of trees. It's quiet save for birds chirping, my own cough as I exhale, pulling the joint from my mouth.

Sid is sleeping.

I smile as I think about her, scrub my hand over my face.

"*I love you, J.*" She was looking right at me, arms still around my neck, when she said it again, before we fell asleep in each other's arms.

*J.*

No one else will ever own a piece of my heart like she does. Fuck. I think she's got more than a piece. Probably the whole fucking thing.

I inhale again, holding the smoke in my lungs as long as I can, wanting the tremor to stop today. We have the rest of the week here, but Ria and Nicolas are coming back today. I almost want to call him. Tell him to leave us the fuck alone.

All I've ever wanted is more alone time with her. Those moments when I had her in my bed when we were kids, holding her close to me…they were, in their own fucked up way, *fucking heaven.*

I hear the door creak open behind me and I turn, a smile playing along my lips. She steps through the doorway, pulling it closed behind her as she crosses her arms over her chest, her eyes still bleary with sleep. Her brown hair is pulled up into a bun, and she's wearing my shirt.

*My shirt.*

It hits at her thighs and I don't know if she has on underwear, but fuck, I'm hoping not. I want to fuck her on this porch, right here in the goddamn woods.

I want to fuck her everywhere.

"You're up early," she says, her voice thick with sleep.

I pull from the joint and her eyes stop casting about the forest and settle on my mouth as I form my lips into an "O" and exhale, trying—and failing—to blow out smoke rings.

She laughs, arching a brow as she shakes her head, rubbing her hands up and down her arms. "Wow," she says, "something you *can't* do."

*Fighting words.* I grind the joint against the railing of the porch, then pinch it between my index finger and thumb as I throw it off into the woods without looking, still facing her.

"Maybe you need a little fucking reminder of all the things I *can* do." I advance toward her, and she backs up, against the door, the easy smile leaving her face.

Her hands come to either side of her against the door, like she's trying to hold herself steady.

My body is flush against hers in seconds, my hands planted on either side of her head, her breasts pressed against my chest.

"Hmm?" I ask her, angling my head as I stare into her beautiful eyes. "Is that what you need, baby?"

She bites her lip and I feel my dick swell in my pants. "Yeah," she whispers, my blood heating with her consent. "Yeah, I do."

I dive down, my mouth on hers. She parts her lips, moaning against me as I grind into her, pressing my thigh between her legs.

She starts to push herself onto me, bucking her hips up and down.

"That's right, baby, use me, too."

She smirks, and I feel it on my mouth, my eyes locked on her beautiful gray ones. "Don't be gentle with me," she pleads. "I think you know you won't break me, J."

I stare at her a second, holding my breath. My hands are itching to be all over her, to make her feel. Make her *hurt.*

But she's pregnant, and I already carved my name into her fucking skin. Held a knife to her throat.

If she wants me to hurt her…I'd hate to let her down.

"How bad? How bad do you want me to hurt you?" I ask her, my eyes locked on hers, hands still planted on either side of her head. I press my thigh further against her and her eyes flutter closed just for a second.

Then she bites her lip, meeting my gaze. "What do you want to do?" she counters, like she did last night before I carved my name into her skin.

I bring my mouth to her ear. "Hit you," I tell her honestly, thinking of how good it would feel to dominate her again. She's always challenged me, at every turn. Getting her to submit to me again would be fucking heaven in this hell.

Her breath catches in her throat. For a moment, she doesn't speak.

Then she says, *"Do it."*

My stomach flips, my heart racing.

Then I step back, and she frowns, opening her mouth no doubt to ask me what the fuck I'm doing, but I grab her throat, yanking her toward me. "Get on your fucking knees, sis."

She goes to do just as I said, her eyes narrowed but a smirk playing on her mouth. I don't let go of her, though, and she can't get on her knees because she'll fucking choke herself on my hand if she does.

"J," she whispers, but that smirk is still there, and I know in this moment, she isn't afraid of me. Not like she used to be.

*I like that.*

But I also…don't.

I move my hand from her throat, spin her around and shove her against the glass door of the cabin. She catches herself on her palms, her breath coming out in a rush. I hold her still with one hand on the back of her neck, trail my other down her back, to her thigh, then up, feeling the soft flesh of her ass.

"You're not wearing underwear," I whisper, kneading her flesh as I press closer to her, pinning her to the door.

"No," she agrees. "Because I wanted my brother to fuck me this morning." Her tone is pouty, like she's a spoiled fucking brat, *which she is.*

I laugh, reaching between her thighs, cupping her pussy with my whole hand. "Did you?" I ask her, stepping back to look at her. I shove her shirt up, holding it against the back of her neck as I keep her in place.

I see the soft curve of her spine. Think of all the times I've wanted to fucking break her, but right now? Right now, I just want to give her exactly what she wants.

"Mmhmm," she murmurs, her cheek pressed against the side of the glass.

"Show me," I taunt her. "Bend over and show me where you want your brother, sis."

She seems to stiffen, the muscles in her back shifting, but then she does as I ask. She bends over, stepping back slightly, into my hand, her head still against the glass, but now I have better access.

Now I can fucking see her.

*And fuck, she's perfect.*

My heart is pounding so hard in my chest I'm surprised

she can't hear it, but when I push my finger into her tight pussy, feel her clench around me, I imagine hers is pounding just as fast.

She moans, calling my name. *"J,"* she gasps as I step back again, my hand sliding down her spine, my chin dipped so I can see her pink, smooth lips, my finger inside of her tight hole.

"My sister has such a perfect fucking pussy," I tell her, adding another finger as she backs up into me. "It's a shame she's such a little whore too."

She tenses again, and this time, I can feel it around my fingers like a fucking vise grip. She might be a whore, but she's still so damn tight.

"I'm your whore," she whispers, her hands still on the glass, sliding down it and leaving marks. "I'm yours."

I get down on my knees, pull my fingers out of her and grip her ass. My breath fans her pussy as I ask her, "Yeah?" My tongue is so fucking close, and she smells so fucking good.

*So fucking good.*

But I want to hear it again. Before I reward her, I want to hear it.

"Yes, J," she says, a whine to her voice like she's begging.

"Are you mine or are you his?" I snarl, then I sink my teeth into the soft flesh of her ass.

She tenses, whimpering. When I pull back, I see my teeth marks, red and angry against her flesh.

She reaches between her thighs, rubbing her own clit, but I grab her wrist, yanking her hand away.

"You're going to get punished for that," I tell her, and before she can say anything smart back, I lick the length of her, savoring the earthy taste and the way she moans my name again.

But I meant what I said.

*She's going to get fucking punished for that.*

"Get on your knees for me, Sid." I stand, and she does the

same, turning and taking a tentative step toward me, her face flushed, my T-shirt having fallen back down her body.

She sinks down to her knees and I know the wooden planks are hard beneath her bones, but I don't give a fuck. I don't think she does either.

"Take your shirt off."

She offers me a tentative smile, then reaches her arms across her body and peels her shirt off, freeing her small, round tits. Exposing my name branded on her skin.

She drops the shirt, waiting up on her knees for her next direction.

I smile at her, run my thumb over her bottom lip. "Such a good girl," I tell her. "So ready to serve her brother."

Her face is red, her nipples pebbling into sharp points, her mouth open as I keep running my thumb back and forth over her pretty pink mouth.

"But you've been away from your brother for a long, long time, sis." My voice is more stern, my cock harder, and I know she can see it, tenting in my shorts. "And you've been in too many beds that weren't for you."

Before she can react, I move my hand from her face and I slap her, hard enough to make her head spin.

She lets out a soft whimper, her own hand coming to the side of her face as she flexes her jaw.

Satisfaction works its way through me, and I relish in the feel of this much power over such a spoiled fucking brat. *The girl I love.*

"Look at me," I command her, and slowly, she turns her head, her eyes angry, my handprint against her face as she drops her hand into a fist by her side. "All I've ever wanted to do was love you, baby. *Let me love you?*" I cock my head, smiling down at her.

She arches a brow, as if she wants to talk back, but being a good girl, she swallows whatever stupid shit she was going to say. Instead, she nods.

"Good girl, baby. I'm your brother, and you know brothers love *so fucking hard.*" And without a warning, I slap her again, her head snapping to the side once more.

She closes her eyes, tight, reaching for her face again, and I think I see a tear streaming down her cheek.

*Good.*

I'm not fucking playing with her.

I don't wait for her to recover this time. Instead, I reach down and grab her hand away from her cheek. She looks up at me with defiant eyes, tears streaming down her face and her lower lip trembling.

I flip her palm over as I step even closer.

"You see this?" I tell her, showing her the inside of her own hand as I run my thumb down her fucking scar.

She swallows, eyes flicking to her hand, then back up to me. She nods slowly, and I see the apprehension in her eyes.

I fucking like it.

"This doesn't mean shit to me," I tell her, digging my nail into her palm and hearing her gasp, her face blood-red from my hand. "This doesn't mean shit to me, and it doesn't mean shit to you either, you got that?"

She doesn't answer me.

I step closer, lift my knee so it brushes against her tit, her hard nipple on my skin. I think she gets my threat.

She closes her mouth but nods, her eyes wide and glistening in the rising sun.

I press against the scar with my thumb, my stomach twisting with the reminder of what it is.

*Coagula.* To bind. But we didn't need blood and a scar. *She was mine before she could fucking talk.*

"Lilith and Lucifer," I whisper, mocking her. I see her jaw clench as I circle my free hand around her throat, cocking my head to stare down at her. "Fucking *bullshit.*" I drop her hand, grab her by her throat, force her to her feet before I shove her against the glass door at her back with a thud.

Her hands come to my forearm, her breath leaving her in a rush. She still looks scared, and I like it.

I trace her lips with my thumb, smirking at her. "You know that was all bullshit, huh? You know the only thing that matters is my fucking *name* carved into *your body?*"

She swallows, hard, heavy pants leaving her full, pretty mouth.

I step closer to her, getting in her face. "You know you were never meant to be with anyone but your big brother, right, baby?" My fingers dig deeper into her skin, but she loosens her grip on my own.

Almost as if she wants me to choke her into unconsciousness. As if she fucking *wants* me to kill her.

I don't want that.

I want her to see all the ways she's fucked me. All the sins she's committed against me. All the ways she's fucking tore me apart, but I don't *really* want to hurt her.

I loosen my hold and she sucks in a breath, sliding her hands down my arms, over my shoulders, kneading me. Hanging onto me.

"Yes," she breathes, nodding. "Yes."

My heart swells, blood heating as I press my thigh between hers. She gasps again, her cheeks flushing, one still carrying the redness of my hand against her face.

"All those times you talked back to me? All those times you fucking hated me? I know you wanted me to fuck you, just like this, with my hand around your throat." I lean in close to her, cup her face with one hand. It trembles against her jaw, and anger surges through me. Anger combined with lust, especially as her eyes dart to my hand and I see pity flicker in her gaze.

"Oh, don't look at me like that, baby," I tell her, my voice deceptively tender as my mouth moves over hers, feeling her soft breaths against my lips. "It makes me want to kill you."

"J," she whispers, meeting my eyes again, "you don't want to hurt me." *But I know she wants me to do just that.*

I pull her away from the door only to shove her back again, her head banging against the glass. "I don't?" I check, because I'm pretty sure I fucking do, too. I trail my finger down her jaw, watch her shudder with my touch. Glancing down at her belly, I'm satisfied to see her eyes narrow as she looks back up at me. "What do you think, huh? You think we should end this shit, start all over? Let *me* knock you up." I step closer. She can't move. With the way my fingers squeeze around her throat, she can't fucking breathe.

I reach down under her shirt, trail my hand up her thigh, press two fingers into her wet pussy, see her eyes flutter closed.

I laugh, running my tongue over her lips. "Yeah, you want me to hurt you. You want me to make you bleed. *You want to cut ties with him for good.*"

I pull out of her, hand still around her throat as she opens her eyes.

I push down my shorts, my cock aching for her.

Without waiting for an answer, I pick her up, and her legs wrap around me as I push into her, groaning as I do, shoving her against the glass door with every fucking thrust.

Her arms are wrapped around my shoulders, her brows pressed to mine as I bounce her up and down on my cock.

"You've always wanted me, haven't you baby?" I ask her as her hands move up to cup my face, little whimpers escaping her lips.

"Yes," she whispers, her moans and her tight pussy slick against my cock making *my eyes* nearly roll back in my fucking head. "Always, J," she gasps, her breath fanning my mouth as I fuck her.

Her back collides over and over with the glass, her head, too, and I can't find it in me to care. She doesn't care, either.

She's going to be covered in bruises, but I'm not sure it's enough.

I want them around her throat, too.

I want another visual reminder of the ways I fucking own her.

I wrap my hand around her throat, knock her head back against the glass. She tilts her chin up, facing the sky, her eyes closed as I slam into her.

I'm so fucking close.

*So fucking close.*

I dig my fingers into her ass as I fuck her, her tits bouncing beneath her shirt, her mouth wide open but nothing coming out because she can't fucking breathe.

I groan, yanking her head down as I sink my teeth into her bottom lip, loosening my grip around her throat so I can hear her gasp as I taste blood in my mouth, and she clenches around me from the pain.

I finish inside of her, pissed all over again that my cum is going to waste. That I can't knock her up, ruin her body, not in the ways *he already did.*

She's breathing hard, her eyes on mine, her hands cupping my face again as I hold her against the glass.

It's okay.

I know what it's like to be raised by two people who can't fucking stand you. I won't do that to her kid.

*It'll be our kid.*

# CHAPTER
## Twenty-Four

### SID

I GLANCE at my reflection in the mirror in the bathroom of the cabin. Bruises line my throat, and I finish tying the bandana around it, although it does little to hide them. I don't necessarily want to.

Unlike all the other times my brother has bruised me, I wanted it this time. I wanted him to punish me for the hurt he's felt at all the times I've denied him. I deserve it. All the fucking pain. I deserve it, for him and for Lucifer.

I close my eyes as I think about my husband, my hands coming to the counter, curling around the tile as I bow my head.

*I wonder if he's still with Julie.*

Does he think of me? Did he fuck both of them? *Does he hate me?* Does he know why I ran?

I think of Mayhem, and hope he's told him the truth. That I loved him, Lucifer, so much. So fucking much, and that's why I had to leave.

He was going insane being around me.

And even with our stolen moments of happiness…I don't know why I am the way I am. Why I want to run when I have every reason to stay. I don't know why it's so fucking hard for me to be *happy*, content.

Maybe because I think it'll never last.

And besides that…as happy as Lucifer made me sometimes…the other times, they were fucking hell.

My hand goes to my belly, and fear floods through me all over again.

Not just from the 6. They're not here. They might find us eventually, but I know Jeremiah won't let them touch me. He won't let them, and he'll fight for me. Destroy all of them.

But he's part of the reason I'm terrified.

He said he'd raise this child as his own. I think, if it comes out looking the slightest bit like his brother, he might kill it.

Fucking him was everything I'd imagined it to be.

But I wonder if now…I could just get him out of my system?

I have a feeling he wouldn't let me do that. *Why do I always want to fuck shit up?*

I sink my teeth into my lip, tasting blood from where Jeremiah bit me this morning.

The rough skin of his name on my belly snags beneath my index finger.

For a split second, my heart drops.

If Lucifer ever saw that…

But he let me go. When I ran for him to have space to heal, he fucking *let me go* by being with Ophelia. Julie.

And he let Jeremiah suffer.

Startling me from my thoughts, I hear the door catch.

Behind my eyelids, everything seems to go dark and my eyes fly open, seeing nothing in the mirror that's vanished from view. There's no window in this guest bathroom and besides that, it's nightfall. Ria, Nicolas, and Jeremiah headed down to a little shop within walking distance to get some kindle for a bonfire.

Nicolas convinced J to go, because he didn't want to leave

me. But he was a little high, his eyes glassy, a smile permanently affixed to his handsome face.

I told him I'd be fine.

Now, a sense of unease washes over me.

"Jeremiah?" I whisper, making to turn toward the bathroom door.

But just as I start, a hand comes over mine on my belly,
threading through my fingers, touching my bare skin.

I flinch, startled, my breath hitching.

Another hand comes to my throat, fingers curling tight
around me, but not quite cutting off my air supply.

I lean into Jeremiah's touch, but as I do, I inhale.

I feel the difference in the body at my back, compared to
Jeremiah's.

Lean muscle is behind me, different than J's bulk.

And that scent…pine.

And nicotine.

My pulse races, and the hand threaded through mine
presses tighter against my low belly. The one around my
throat tightens.

Soft, warm breaths fan against my ear.

Then my husband whispers, "Miss me, baby girl?" and my
blood runs cold.

*He's come back.*

# CHAPTER
## Twenty-Five

## LUCIFER

SHE DOESN'T MOVE.

She's completely frozen against me, but I feel her pulse flying in her throat, under my hand.

I feel the slight swell of her belly, her thin fingers beneath mine. I inhale her lavender scent, nearly groaning as I do. My heart aches, my own pulse unsteady in my chest. My mouth is dry, and I feel breathless.

She's here.

In my arms.

For over a month, I've tried to live without her.

Over a month, I've tried to forget her.

She's never left my mind once. Not even last night, with someone else's lips around my dick. With another girl's pussy on my cock.

I never stopped thinking of her.

In this dark bathroom, it's like nothing ever happened at all. It's like we've gone away for the two of us, spent time alone, and now we're reunited, happy again.

But we aren't.

*She. Fucking. Left.*

"So quiet," I tell her, whispering against the shell of her

ear. A shudder runs through her small body and I smile, walking her forward so her hips are against the counter in the dark bathroom.

I hear the rumble of voices from down the hall, but luckily, I can't make out the words, so she probably can't either.

I have no idea if they've got *him* right now, but I don't give a fuck either.

"Has he touched you, baby girl?" I ask her, feel her chest heaving, her belly rising and falling under our hands.

*Over our baby.*

"Have you been a bad girl, Lilith?"

She doesn't answer me. *Of course she fucking doesn't, because if there's one thing I know about my wife, it's that* she's always bad.

"Hmm?" I prod, running my mouth over her jaw and relishing in the way she's trembling in my arms. "Did you let him fuck you, love?"

I nip at her ear and she whimpers as my fingers tighten on her throat in a warning. *Interesting.* She wasn't so fucking fragile before she left.

Unless… My stomach drops as I think about that time I found her in the woods. About the bruises around her throat.

But no.

She would only have those if she really did fuck him, and I know she knows better than that.

She wouldn't have.

*But I did.*

She still isn't answering me, and for the first time since I started to ask her, only wanting to hear her say it wasn't true, I feel a prickle of worry at what the answer might be.

I might not have been, but she's faithful.

She loves me.

*She loves me, doesn't she?* She wouldn't break my heart in that way. She wanted me to breathe. To heal. To get help.

I haven't, but she doesn't know that.

She doesn't know where I've been. What I've done.

"Baby girl," I warn her, feeling my stomach twist inside out as I think about his hands on her. His dick inside of her. His fingers around her throat when she's pregnant with *my goddamn baby.* "What did you let him do to you?"

She's not breathing anymore. Her chest isn't rising and falling like it was, and it's not because I'm holding her throat.

She's pregnant with my child.

For all of our fights, all of our hatred and disdain wrapped up in a broken package I liked to believe was love, I wouldn't *really* hurt her. Not now. Not like this.

But if she fucked him…if she *did that…*

She inhales, almost gasping as she does, her throat moving beneath my fingers.

I hear my brother's voice down the hall. I think he's calling my name.

She tenses, her hand not underneath mine going to my forearm as she holds on tight to me. Afraid.

She's afraid *for him.*

"What are you doing to—"

I release her, then thread my fingers through her hair as I spin her around, shoving her against the door, cradling her head with my hand so I don't really hurt her. The door thuds against the wall, and she's hisses under her breath, my hand planted against her chest, one still tangled in her hair.

"I've been lenient with you before, baby girl," I tell her, my body dwarfing hers as I crowd her against the door. "I've let you fuck your own fucking brother. I've given you space. Grace. *Forgiveness.*"

I jerk her hair back, so her throat is pulled taut even though I can't see her in the dark. I don't care. I don't fucking care.

I don't need to see her. In fact, right now, it's best if I don't.

Someone calls my name again, from down the hall.

Sid tries to shove me off of her, her hands wrapping around my biceps, or trying to, anyway.

But she can't move me.

She's not getting to him.

Not now.

Not fucking ever.

"Answer my question or I'll make *you* kill him." Those words leave my mouth in a growl, and her nails dig into my biceps, beneath my black T-shirt.

"Let me go, Lucifer," she snarls, but there's panic threaded through her anger. I know it's not for me.

It's for *him.*

I shove her back against the door again. "Answer me, goddammit!" I snarl at her, pulling her hair back so hard I know her eyes must be watering. She whimpers, still trying to push me off and there's another thud in the living room and I roll my eyes, unseen by her in the dark. I push my forearm against her throat, keeping her still as my body is nearly flush with hers. "If you don't answer me, *he's gonna fucking die.*"

"No," she whispers quietly in the dark, "I didn't fuck him." I let up the pressure against her throat, her hair as I stroke my fingers down her scalp. To her neck. Massaging her.

Relief runs through me like a welcome warmth.

If she didn't sleep with him, if she didn't give that part of herself to my worst fucking enemy, then I can live with this. I can deal with this.

I can fix it.

"No?" I question her, leaning down so my mouth touches hers. Her warm breath, fresh and alive and *for me*, caresses my lips, and that relief seems to explode through my veins. "You didn't, baby girl? You were all mine, all this time?" My voice almost breaks on that last question, but I don't care.

She's seen the worst of me.

The best of me.

She's seen all of me. I don't care if she hears how weak I am for her. How weak I've always been for her.

"Yes," she tells me, her soft, plush lips brushing mine. "Yes, Lucifer."

Hearing her say my name makes me hard and soft all at once. Hard for her, my dick aching to have her hands on it. Her mouth. *Her.* And soft, because I'm melting with those words.

I'm melting and drowning all at once, like fire and ice, because she's mine.

*She's still my girl.*

*My fucking wife.*

I regret everything I did with Ophelia. Ella. Julie. *Maverick.* I feel sick just thinking about it now. I hope to Satan she'll understand. When I tell her everything—because I have to, she deserves to know—I hope she'll forgive me and—

"Let me see him," she demands, cutting through my thoughts. Reminding me why I'm here.

That this isn't a reunion.

"Don't you dare hurt him." Her voice is a whisper, and her words are a plea.

My anger is back, and I regret the lines I did on the way here, at the gas station when we all stopped so I could take a piss. Mav thought I was sober.

Thought I didn't take shit when I drove here.

He's an idiot.

My pulse is thrumming in my *jaw*, and I pull Sid away from the door, yanking her hand, dragging her behind me.

"Don't tell me what the fuck to do," I mutter, glancing over my shoulder in the dark. I see the gleam of her eyes and nothing else. "You're done fucking making decisions."

# CHAPTER
## Twenty-Six

SID

THERE'S nothing in the living room except…wreckage. The couch is flipped over, the chair too. There's a bottle of vodka shattered on the floor, the sharp scent of alcohol coating the room like the fear is coating my mouth.

Did they do this because they can? *Did they hurt him?*

Lucifer holds my hand tightly, making the bones ache. I barely notice it. It's just a dull pain in the background of my panic.

It's silent now, and beyond the closed curtains I see slivers of darkness.

Lucifer yanks me toward the door and I stumble in my black sneakers, but then he turns.

I see him.

For the first time in a month, I see him.

He looks…awful.

There are dark shadows beneath his beautiful blue eyes. His cheeks are gaunt, more defined than they usually are, which is saying something. His black curls are a little longer, past his ears, messy and tousled, one flopped just above one eye. He's always been so pale, but the veins are so stark against his skin, his ropey muscles leaner than before I left him.

I can't breathe, looking at him.

At the mucus dripping down his nose that he wipes away with the back of his hand.

My stomach clenches. He's still using. And as I step closer, taking a good look at his nearly blown pupils, I feel sick.

He's not going to stop.

Another reason I can't go back. Another reason I have to save Jeremiah.

I can't do this.

I shake my head, fear clawing at me, closing up my throat. I open my mouth to tell him everything—*everything*—but then I see his eyes flick to the small scar over my brow, a frown on his face.

But he trails his gaze lower.

*To my throat.*

Murderous rage seems to pass over his features. His jaw is clenched, his full lips pressed into a line, his dark brow furrowed.

I realize he isn't wearing a bandana, only a black shirt, black pants, black Converse.

But there's no bandana, and as he reaches for mine, dragging me to him, I have a sinking feeling that I don't quite understand about that.

About the fact we don't match.

Not right now.

And the fact that I finally understand what he sees on my throat as he yanks me up, my tiptoes just barely grazing the floor. He stares at me with disgust in his eyes, like he wants to spit on me. Like he hates me.

I grab for his shoulders, but he shakes his head, his jaw clenched. "Don't fucking touch me."

"Fuck yourself," I growl at him, not letting him go, digging my nails in. "Go *fuck yourself.*" Where is he? Where the fuck is my brother? Ria? Nicolas?

Lucifer smiles. "Didn't have to, baby girl. Somebody

already beat me to it." His eyes shift to my throat as my blood runs cold. "Did he do that? Did he fucking put his hands on you?"

I already lied to him. I'll do it again and again, if I can just get. To. *My brother.*

"No," I whisper, feeling my stomach churn as I do. As I lie again. And then more. "It wasn't him. It was—"

He drags me closer, and I swallow, the bandana digging into my neck, closing around my throat as the knot slips tighter, the way he's got the end of it, ensuring it *does* choke me. "Are you lying to me?" he asks me, his voice low. More hoarse than usual. Delicious and raspy and so fucking angry.

I move my hands from his shoulders, try to yank at the bandana, to give myself room to breathe. He slaps my hands away, his nostrils flaring, more mucus dripping down his nose, over the Cupid's bow of his beautiful lips.

"No," I tell him, swallowing down my regret. My anger, so I can just find him. "No, I'm not, Lucifer. He—"

"Who touched you?" he snarls, not easing up with his grip. "Who. Fucking. Touched you?"

My mind goes wild, trying to think of someone in a split second. Someone. Anyone that isn't my brother or Nicolas. "One of his men, it was an...argument and he—"

Lucifer lets go of me. Steps back, looking down at the floor. "Are you lying to me?"

I grit my teeth, trying to swallow my anger again. But he just fucking admitted he cheated on me. I don't know why the hell I'm lying anymore. "You piece of shit." I snarl those words, stepping closer to him. "You fucking *cheat on me,* and you fucking *lie to me,* and the entire time we were together, *you fucking treated me like shit!*" I'm screaming those words now, my finger against his chest. "How fucking *dare you?* Of course it's from him!"

I see him look up, pain crossing over his face like a shadow.

"You didn't fucking wait! You were at Julie's!"

He blinks, like he's surprised that I know. My stomach twists into knots when he doesn't deny my words.

"Fuck you. He fucked me, three fucking times, and you fucking deserve it!" I slap my palm against his chest and he flinches, still staring at me. I hit him again. "*I fucking hate you. Why are you even here?*" I'm screaming the words, my hand going to his throat this time, digging my nails in as I get in his face and he walks backward, coming up against the wall.

"*Why the fuck are you here?* Why didn't you just leave me?" I let go of him, slap him, hard, but he doesn't even move, he just keeps staring at me, his nostrils flared. "Why the fuck are you here, and *where is Jeremiah?*"

Moments pass.

I drop my hand.

We're both breathing hard.

Then he slaps me.

The sound echoes in the living room. Nothing follows in its wake.

I'm frozen.

Paralyzed.

He's never...*he's never done that before.* Not when we weren't fucking.

I'm not even breathing as I stare at him, my mouth open, hands by my sides. I feel unsteady on my feet because he couldn't possibly have just done that.

His lips twist as he stares at me, his eyes narrowed. "You lied to me. You fucking *lied to me.*"

His chest rises and falls rapidly, his hands curled into fists.

I still feel where he slapped me.

And Jeremiah too, earlier today. But I wanted that. I allowed it. This...this is different.

This is a fucking line he should have never crossed, but the past few months, that seems to be just his thing.

There's no coming back from this.

And even if there were, it doesn't matter.

I bring a hand to my face. "Let me see him. Right fucking now, Lucifer, or I will *never* go back with you."

He doesn't laugh like I thought he might with my threat. Instead, his eyes flutter closed, his brows pinched together. And I feel for him.

In this moment, I feel for him. For all the ways he's missed me. But I remember what Jeremiah told me.

Lucifer knew he was in that cage.

The tremor in his hand. The ways he's insane. *Not quite there.*

Lucifer helped do that.

"Don't say that," he whispers, slicing through my thoughts. "You will. And you didn't really...you didn't really fuck him."

Despite the anger I try to hold onto, my heart aches. Even still, my eyes dart to the door, wondering where my brother is. What they've done to him. I need to get to him.

I need to see him.

"I hate myself for leaving you." The words come out in a rush, and I know Lucifer is surprised when his eyes fly open, his lips parted. *I'm* fucking surprised.

He steps closer, brings his hand up gently to my face as I drop mine. He smooths his thumb over where he slapped me.

I take a deep breath, wanting to get it all out. Wanting to find my brother. "But you know it wasn't safe for me——"

"Stop." He shakes his head, pulling back enough to take me in entirely. "I don't want your excuses for leaving. I know the reason you did."

I grit my teeth as I stare up at him, sure whatever he thinks is fucking wrong.

"The fucking nightmares? My...pain? You can't stand it," he says, his words little more than a snarl. "You can't stand that I might hurt just as bad you fucking do."

My chest tightens with those words. With the way I always

knew he was falling apart, but I couldn't help him because *so was I.*

"And more than that? You can't stand being away from *him.* He's got you on a fucking leash." His hand slides from my face to my neck, and I stiffen, holding my breath, but he doesn't apply much pressure. He glances down at his hand, at my neck, and I see that disgust in his eyes. "You're addicted to him, and he can't get enough of you."

"That's not—"

"Shut the fuck up, Sid. I'm not done talking."

I try to pull away from him, but his hand leaves my face and comes to my arm, wrapping around my bicep.

"We're not fucking done here."

"Lucifer, get your hands off of—"

"*Shut. The fuck. Up.* For once in your fucking life, you're going to listen to me, you got it?"

I glare at him, my nails digging into his chest, through his shirt. Gritting my teeth, I don't say anything. If he wants to scream at me, it'll only help me remember why I left. Why this can never be.

"He's going to hurt you, Sid. He's going to *really* hurt you. When he does, you'll wanna come running back to me. But here's the thing, baby girl." He smiles at me, and I feel light-headed, dizzy, as if I would faint without his hands on me. Even the one around my throat. There's something familiar about it.

Some kind of sick comfort.

"I don't want you anymore."

My mouth goes dry.

"I'm tired of your fucking games."

I can't think.

"I'm tired of *you.*"

I open my mouth, but he glares at me, silencing me without a word. When he's satisfied I'm not going to interrupt him, he keeps talking, digging the knife deeper into my heart.

"You can keep fucking him. Keep getting on your knees for him, knowing he only wants to own you—"

"And what the *fuck* do you want?" I scream at him, unable to keep my mouth shut any longer. I shove him, but he doesn't move, like a fucking wall. His grip on my arm, around my throat only grows tighter. "What the fuck do you think you feel toward me, Lucifer?"

He looks like he wants to kill me, that vein in his neck pulsing with his anger.

"You haven't asked how I've been. Haven't asked about your fucking child—"

"The one you *don't* want to have?" He snorts, rolling his eyes. "You're going to end this, Lilith, don't act like you're gonna go through with it. In fact, I think you kept it just for this. Just so I'd come back to you. But I'm not here to get you back. No, I'm setting you fucking free." He releases me, stepping back, and my hands fall to my sides, no longer planted against his hard chest. He lifts up his arms in a shrug. "Do you, baby girl." He smiles coldly at me. "I'm done. I came here to help you. But I don't think you fucking need it."

He takes another step backward and I want to run to him, but I don't dare. It's better this way. We were never made for each other, no matter what he wanted to believe. What I might've wanted to believe, once upon a time. We're too bad for that. We'd set the whole fucking world on fire if we ever made this work.

But we'd burn right along with it.

"Where's Jeremiah? And what about the 6?" I ask him, wondering what happens next. He can't just let me go, and we both know it, unless he's worked something out and that's why he's really here. But the way they took me from my own home, they don't really seem like the type to "work something out."

Lucifer flashes a white smile, running his palms together. "Better start running." He pulls a lighter and a cigarette from the pocket of his sweats and places the cigarette in his mouth. "You've always been fucking good at that."

He inhales, the cherry on his cigarette glowing bright in the dark room. "But watch your back, baby girl. I won't be there anymore to do that for you. And it's not just us you have to look out for now." He exhales smoke through his nose, eyes still on mine as a chill makes its way down my spine. "There's something worse coming for you."

I laugh, bitter and low. "I don't think there's anything worse than you, Lucifer."

He smiles. "Maybe not. But when you had me on your side, I could protect you from everything, just for that reason. Now," he shrugs, the cigarette dangling from his fingers, "you're on your own."

He turns to the door, yanks it open. The warm air from the night rushes in, the scent of pine.

Just like him.

*Just like him.*

He exhales smoke as he turns to look at me over his shoulder.

"Where the fuck is Sid?" I hear a familiar voice call out.

And something beyond the voice.

An engine is running. A truck?

But something else. Something that makes my stomach twist into knots.

"I'm fucking done with her, and don't you dare think about taking her with us." Lucifer is staring at me as he speaks, his eyes narrowed. "She's let him all over her." Those words are just for me, but I hear footsteps. See the headlights of what *must* be a vehicle, but I can't see them.

Just the light, blinding through the forest directly in front of the cabin.

The footsteps get closer.

Maverick comes into view.

My brother.

My stomach flips as his eyes land on Lucifer, but then slide to me.

He stills, one hand on the railing of the little porch, the other clenched into a fist. He has a skeleton bandana around his throat, and he's wearing black, ripped jeans. A black tank that shows off his tattooed arms, lean like Lucifer's. But Mav has a golden tan, golden hair.

And that tattoo on his face, an inverted cross, would be sinister any other day, but right now, it feels like home.

*Relief.*

That's what it feels like.

Because he wouldn't let that sound I heard...he wouldn't let that happen.

But I hear it again.

Clanking. Like metal on metal.

"Angel," Mav whispers, and a growl escapes Lucifer's mouth as he steps up into his brother's face. His back is to me, that cigarette dangling from his long, lean fingers.

"I told you, she's not fucking coming back with us." He pushes Mav, hand flat on his chest. "We don't need her to figure this shit out anyway."

Maverick's baby blue eyes narrow as he glares down at Lucifer. He grabs his wrist, shoves him aside.

Lucifer stumbles back, and Mayhem comes up the steps, toward me.

I don't know why, but I take a step back.

I'm against the siding of the house, and I hear that sound again.

Metal on metal.

"Maverick," I whisper in the dark as he stares down at me, leather and marijuana enveloping me. His hand comes to my face, the side where Lucifer slapped me. His jaw tightens, and he doesn't look away from when he speaks, but I know he's not asking me.

"Did you hurt her?"

Lucifer scoffs. "Let's go."

I see Maverick swallow, watch the ink along his throat shift as he does. He brushes his thumb along my lower lip. I wince and forget why.

Then I remember.

That was Jeremiah.

But Maverick's nostrils flare. "Do you want me to kill you, Luce?" he asks, and there's no humor in his words.

"That's my fucking wife, so why don't you let me deal with her and you get your fucking hands off—"

A scream.

A fucking scream pierces the air.

Not just a scream.

*My name.*

My. Name.

I make to dart around my brother, but he grabs my wrist, slamming me back against the house, stepping close to me and forcing me against the stone, shaking his head, his eyes full of...grief?

"No, Angel. You can't help him."

I shove my palms against Mav's chest, hard muscle beneath my fingers. "Let me get to him," I say, moving to the side, trying to see around the cabin. Trying to see the source of the fucking headlights.

The source of that noise.

Metal. Against metal.

*Like chains.*

*A cage.*

"Let me get to him," I say again, my voice panicked.

Mav doesn't move away from me. He grabs my upper arms, forcing me back again, my breath leaving me in a rush as my spine jars against the stone of the house.

"Let me get to him!" I scream those words, panic ripping through me. The clanking gets louder, like someone banging against...something. Rattling a...*cage.*

"No," I tell Mav, holding his gaze, his eyes narrowed on me. "No, please, don't—"

"You see how she fucking begs for him?" Lucifer snarls, and Maverick holds my gaze as Lucifer adds, "Why don't we put *her* in that fucking cage too?"

My heart sinks, even as it's beating so fast it nearly bursts out of my chest. "Mav, no, please don't leave him in there." I try to push away from the siding again, try to dart around him, but he's faster, grabbing my arm and hauling me back, slamming me again, my head hitting the stone of the house.

I whimper, bringing my hand instinctively to the back of my head.

"Maverick," Lucifer snarls at the sound of my whimper, but Mav ignores him.

"Nah, Angel. That's not how this is gonna work. Because I think he's done some bad things, and we need to know who the fuck he's working with."

Another clanking. Another whimper.

Lucifer laughs, and I. Fucking. Hate. Him.

But I remember something, too, with that sound. My mind seems to settle for half a second. Just that, but as Maverick loosens his grip on my upper arms, his eyes searching mine, as if he's trying to get me to be reasonable, to *let him hurt J*, I remember what I have.

What I haven't gone without since that first Unsaints Night. Since I met the boy from hell.

"Okay," I tell Mav, playing along as I chew my lip, trying to appear uncertain. Scared. Trying to hide how I really feel.

He arches a brow, clearly concerned that I'm going to try to run again. But he shouldn't be. Because I'm not.

Because when he lets go of me, takes a small step back, turns his head to Lucifer, I reach for the knife in the pocket of my shorts.

And by the time he turns back to me, I've thumbed the blade free, and I'm angling it at his chest.

His eyes widen as he takes another step back, but there's a smirk on his lips because he's not scared of me.

*Not yet.*

"Oh, this is good," Lucifer says, an edge to his words. I dart my eyes between the two of them as Lucifer comes to stand shoulder to shoulder with his brother, the cigarette to his lips. He inhales, the cherry glowing red.

I try to remember what Jeremiah taught me. The different ways to attack head-on. Only enough to get away.

Just to get away, then *run.*

I'm good at that, even though I'm not running *away* this time.

I'm still fucking *stellar* at running.

And when I hear the clank of the chains, I know what I'm going for.

Lucifer exhales through his nose, looking like he just arrived from hell itself, then he holds up the cigarette, making my mind pause as I even out my stance, ready to lunge, the knife still angled down in my hand, easier to sink into their fucking flesh.

"Come here, baby girl," Lucifer says, jerking his head, his blue eyes full of amusement, the light from the porch reflected in his big black pupils. "Let's see how rough you really like it."

The tip of his cigarette is still glowing bright in the dark, and my mouth goes dry as he takes a step forward.

"I've always wanted to fucking brand you where no one can miss it." His eyes go to my throat, my hand, then my face. *But not my belly, where the real brand is.* "It's a fucking shame we're done now, but I can still make sure you're not good enough for anyone else to fuck."

Mav's eyes shift to Lucifer, his tattooed hands curled into fists.

I catch sight of the top of one, some of the adrenaline in my blood slipping from Lucifer's words.

There's a new tattoo, in fresh black ink scrawled over the top of Mav's hand.

My stomach drops as I realize what it is.

*My name.*

My fucking name.

My mouth falls open, and just as I look up, to ask him when, and *why,* Lucifer moves.

He's in my face, hand back around my throat, the cigarette an inch from my cheek.

But I move too, and he has the upper hand because I was distracted, but I have the tip of the knife pressing against the soft flesh of his neck, just to the side, right above his shoulder.

It's a wicked sharp blade, digging into the fabric of his black shirt, but I see him scowl and I know he feels it.

His fingers flex around my throat. I can feel the heat of the cigarette on my face.

His eyes lock with mine.

I hear the chains rattle again.

My name.

Muffled this time.

Softer.

*They drugged him.*

"Let me go, Lucifer," I snarl. Maverick hasn't moved, but I know he's watching us. I know, and I don't care.

I'll let him watch his brother die, because of what he's doing to mine.

"I'm going to hurt you, baby girl." Those words are soft. Twisted. Haunting. His big blue eyes don't leave mine, and I see how bloodshot the whites of them are. I see his long lashes, too, the deep circles, the signs of his exhaustion.

Maybe he missed me.

Maybe he's just been coked up the entire time I've been gone, like he was while I was *there.*

"You can try," I agree, "but if you don't let him go, I'm going to *kill* you, Lucifer."

He snorts, a dimple flashing in his pale skin as he brings the cigarette closer. "Let's play a game. See who shoots first."

"Lucifer." Maverick's voice is a warning.

I hear the cage rattle again.

My stomach twists into knots. It's such a faint sound this time, like he's fading. *He's fading away in there.*

He's terrified.

I know he is, and I hate my husband for putting him there.

"Why do you have him?" I ask, my voice hoarse as Lucifer's fingers flex against my throat. "What are you going to do with him?"

Lucifer's lips pull up into a sneer. "I'm going to torture him," he whispers softly, bringing the cigarette so close I flinch. "I'm going to torture him, and I'm going to make him watch me fuck you, *whether you want it or not.*" His smile becomes more twisted and I feel the cherry against my face.

So fucking close to burning me.

*He's going to burn me.*

I drive the knife in closer to his neck. He doesn't even blink.

"And when I'm done," he snarls, backing me up, still holding the cigarette close to my face, warmth heating my cheek, "when I'm done, I'm going to gut that child out of you because you know what, *baby girl?* I'm not so sure it's fucking *mine.*"

I dig the knife into his shirt, through his skin, and he hisses but before I can plunge it all the way into his neck, he's jerked away from me.

The cigarette falls through the wooden slats in the porch.

I don't wait to see what Maverick is going to do to my husband. How much damage I caused. I run.

My bare feet skim across the porch, into the soft grass of the forest floor, and I see it. A truck. All my mind registers is black paint, dark windows, then I'm racing toward it, the bed of the truck.

There's a tarp of some sort over something big and square.

My gut churns as I hear Maverick yelling at Lucifer, and Lucifer snarling back. I still have the knife clenched tight in my hand, but I have to drop it to the ground as I open the bed of the truck, place my palms on the interior and haul myself up, my heart beating too fast in my chest.

I hear it again.

My name.

A soft, broken murmur.

Clanking, like metal on metal. Fear runs over my body in a hot wave as I grab for the tarp, yank it off of the...*crate*.

A wire crate.

Like for a dog.

Jeremiah is inside, his knees to his chest, hands bound in metal cuffs in front of him, his back hunched as he's curled into a tight ball.

And there's a black skeleton bandana over his mouth, his eyes half closed as he tries to focus on me. His face is swollen, blood under his eye. Seeing me, he knocks his wrists against the wire of the cage.

That clanking sound again.

He's barely conscious, his movements lethargic, slow.

But he's trying to hold on. I feel sick, the forest spinning around me, but I have to move. I have to move, but my knife is gone, and I don't hear Lucifer and Mayhem arguing anymore and I know they're coming. The truck is only a few feet from the house. Still, I crouch down to my knees, my fingers skimming over the metal bars of the crate, searching for the latch in the dark.

"It's okay," I tell my brother, my voice shaky. "It's okay, I'll get you out, J, it's okay." I can barely hear myself, and I don't know if, in his lethargic state, he can hear me or understand me, but I have to get him out.

*I have to get him out.*

I have to fucking get. Him. Out.

*Where is Ria? Where the fuck is Nicolas?*

My fingers are shaky, adrenaline still surging through me as my fingers finally catch on the latch.

My pulse spikes, and I pull up, my eyes on Jeremiah's pale green ones, glowing in the darkness as he tries to keep them open.

But I already know it's fucking hopeless.

I feel the bed of the truck shift, someone jumping on top of it.

I hear footfalls as I try to yank the door of the crate up.

It's not big enough for him. He's crouched into a ball, and he's already been through this. He's already fucking done this, and he can't again.

We can't do this again.

We can't be bait for a cult, we can't be killed for powerful men that seem fucking untouchable, who've used us our entire lives for their advantage.

And what has anyone done about it?

My chest heaves and I realize I can't lift up the latch, like it's stuck, caught on something, or locked closed, but in the darkness of the forest I can't see what, and when arms band around my chest, a sob tearing through my throat, I know I'm fucked.

I was never going to get him free.

This was always going to end with both of us dead.

Still, I don't let go, my fingers straining against the latch, the metal biting into my skin.

"Let it go, Angel," Maverick whispers in my ear, his scent enveloping me. He's crouched down behind me, arms wrapped tight around me, his hot breath fanning my skin. "You can't save him."

I swallow down the lump in my throat, watch Jeremiah's eyes flutter closed.

We just got to the good part. We just worked our shit out,

and I just started to understand him. I don't want to let him go.

*Not like this.*

"Maverick," I whisper, closing my eyes tight, slamming my palms into the cage. The sound rings out in the forest, but Jeremiah's head is against the wires now, and he's not here. I know he isn't dead, or they wouldn't have bothered to bind him, but even still…he always ends up fucked.

*We* always end up fucked.

I'm sick of it.

"Maverick, what are you going to do?"

Mav's hand comes to my mouth, running across my swollen lip, silencing me with a gentle touch.

"We just need to ask him some questions," he whispers.

Goosebumps run down my arms, the little hairs on the back of my neck standing on end. "About?" I ask, keeping my eyes closed, my fingers clenched tight around the metal bars.

"Someone has been hunting down the 6," Maverick confesses, and my eyes fly open, staring at Jeremiah's motion-less body. Mav pulls me tighter against his hard chest. "You, too."

I shake my head. "He wouldn't work with anyone that would hurt me—"

"I don't think there's anything in the world Jeremiah Rain wouldn't do. Not if he got you in the end, Angel."

# CHAPTER
## Twenty-Seven

## LUCIFER

THE SILENCE in the truck is deafening, even though it isn't actually fucking silent. My pulse throbs in my head, the windows are cracked and *Send The Pain Below* by Chevelle is playing way too loud as Mav drives, one hand on the wheel, the other on the gear shift even though there's no fucking shifting gears in this thing. I hate trucks, and we had to borrow this one from the 6's fleet of them for the fucking garbage we have in the bed of it.

And Sid is in here.

My wife is mute behind me, making this feel like what it isn't. *Silent.*

I have a cigarette between my fingers, unlit, and I'm flicking the lighter with my other hand, staring straight ahead at the desolate highway, the darkness seeming to cave in on both sides of me.

We've got about an hour before we get back to Alexandria and I'm itching to get the fuck out of this truck. Cain is driving my car back, and I should've just gone with him.

I don't want to smell her.

I don't want to see her.

I don't want to fucking think about what she did.

But there's going to be a surprise back at my house, where she's staying whether she likes it or not, and that thought brings a smile to my face.

"Cut that shit out," Mav growls, glancing at the lighter in my hands.

My jaw is throbbing from where he hit me, and I think I've got a fucking split lip too, not to mention the cut where Sid knifed me.

Mav's protective big brother bullshit makes me want to break his spine. "I'm sorry, is the flame distracting, Mav?" I keep thumbing the dented ridge of the lighter, and he slams his hand on the wheel, the truck veering to the median for half a second before he straightens it.

"Yes," he grits out. "Now cut it out."

I laugh, shaking my head, but I slip the lighter into the pocket of my pants, running my hand over my thigh, digging my fingers into my skin. I need to get out of this truck.

I need to get away from my fucking wife or I'm going to hurt her. I already did.

But what she said to me…*she's lying.* She has to be fucking lying.

"Where are we going?"

Her voice makes me tense, my entire body going rigid in my seat as I lean my head back against it, closing my eyes. Trying not to lose my goddamn mind.

She's so close.

So fucking far away.

*I can't stand her.*

I would've left her, just like I told her I would. I would've left her, let the 6 find her. I don't need her. We need her piece of shit foster brother to tell us what the fuck is happening to everyone around us, who the fuck he's pissed off, but we don't need her.

The 6's greatest fear is she'd go public with what my father did to her. What Maddox did. But no one would believe her. She's nothing in this world.

She's nothing to anyone except Jeremiah Rain, and he's currently where he belongs—in a goddamn dog crate—so she's nothing at all.

Fucking. Nothing.

*Even if she's everything to me, and I hate that.*

Mav turns down the music with the control on the steering wheel and I grit my teeth, annoyed that he's indulging her.

"To my house."

My eyes fly open. "The fuck we are," I cut in, turning my head to face him. He doesn't even look at me, but I see his jaw tighten. "We're going to my fucking—"

"No." That word is harsh. Cold.

But it doesn't mean shit to me. I straighten in my seat, twist around to face him. "Yes, we are. She's my fucking wife—"

"I'm not letting you be alone with her," Maverick says, flicking his gaze to me. "And I know what you'll have at your house."

My mouth goes dry as I think about Lilith behind me, listening to these words. I don't know why it matters. I *want* her to hurt. I *want* to break her fucking heart.

But I know that when I do, it'll break mine, too.

My fingers tighten around the cigarette and it breaks in half. I slam my fist into the door, toss the broken thing out the window.

"I don't care what you know," I keep going with Mav, because no way in hell is she staying at his house. I think of what we did. With Ella. I think, too, about the fact that Mav has *already* fucked my wife, and that shit is not happening again. "She's coming home with—"

"Shut the fuck up, Lucifer. I don't want to listen to your bullshit right now." Then he turns the music up so loud that I can't even hear myself think and as I stare at his hand clenched around the steering wheel, see my wife's name in the lights of the dashboard, tattooed diagonally across his goddamn hand, I think about killing us all.

I could jerk the wheel, drive us all off the fucking road. Get rid of the four of us, just. Like. *That.*

I've contemplated my own death many, many times. And since now I know shit is never going to work with me and Sid, seems like a good time to go.

But just as I think about really doing it—really going for the steering wheel—Sid speaks again and Mav hurries to turn down the music so he can hear her.

"What's happened?" she asks, and her voice isn't hesitant. It's angry.

I see Mav glance in the rearview mirror, no doubt meeting her gaze, and that pisses me off even more. I ball my hands into fists, my pulse racing, the desire to get the fuck out of this truck growing ever stronger.

Mav's eyes are back on the road when he answers her. "Someone has been targeting the 6. Elijah's guard is dead. A dancer at Jeremiah's club too. And there's been photographs…" He blows out a breath. "Of you."

There's a lengthy silence and my lips pull into smile as I imagine Sid taking this in, because I know she's going to say something fucking snarky when she finally responds.

And I'm not disappointed.

"If someone killed a dancer at Jeremiah's club, *why the fuck would you think he had anything to do with this?*" But I know she isn't done. She takes a breath, then mutters, "And everyone in the 6 deserves to die."

Her words ring out in the cab of the truck, and I can't hold back my fucking smile. That's my girl. Angry and bitter and out for blood.

But as much as she makes me proud in some sick, twisted way, she doesn't really get this shit.

Even though she's lived it, she was a product of it, and I

found her *because of it*, she doesn't understand how much of the workings of the world depend on the 6 and the shadowy organizations that operate within them. The world isn't built upon elections. No. It's constructed from cults and dark magic and things that are beyond the average person's comprehension, which is exactly why most people never know we exist. But without us, life as we know it would vanish.

Turmoil. Chaos. Anarchy is too light of a word.

Institutions would burn to the ground, and while people think they want it, they think they need a revolution, need to upturn everything that knits the world together, they'd really be fucking lost, starving, and begging for our return if that ever happened.

Mav glances at me, and I know he doesn't know what to say. But he can deal with her big fucking mouth. I'm done with her.

He sighs, looking back at the empty highway as we pass a green exit sign, a chain on the blue sign before it indicating a fast food spot that Sid loves because she's obsessed with their veggie burgers.

I close my eyes again, pushing away the guilt. Trying to shove away thoughts about when the last time she ate was. How she's been taking care of herself. Has she seen a doctor? Had an ultrasound? She barely looks pregnant, but her tummy was round under my hand in that dark bathroom.

*She didn't get an abortion, like she wanted.*

"Angel, I know you don't understand what's—"

"No, Mav, I think *you* don't fucking understand." Her words are a low growl from behind me, and just like that, I'm smiling all over again.

So. Fucking. Feisty.

"What do you plan to do with him? With us?" She whispers the last question, and I wonder if she's thinking of what I said to her.

If I really meant it.

*I fucking did.*

I'm not living my life like this. I refuse. I tried to make a wild animal a pet, but it's impossible. And when an undomesticated girl starts wreaking havoc? You put her the fuck down.

I don't think I have the heart to do it myself. I can admit that.

But the 6 won't have that problem. Maddox himself is probably itching for her blood, because of all the trouble she's caused him, displacing his position within the 6.

*And because she shot him.*

I'm smiling again and I hate it, but I can't stop.

"I'm going to take care of you," Mav says, a scowl forming on my face as he does, the smile long gone.

"And him?" Sid asks, her words vicious, as if she doesn't want anyone to take care of her, let alone one of us. But her question sends rage lighting through my veins all over again.

I wipe the back of my hand over my running nose, and twist around to glare at her behind me.

"If you fucking mention him again, Sid, I'm going to—"

She leans close to me, the seatbelt straining against her chest as her beautiful eyes lock onto mine. "You're gonna what?" she snarls.

I grit my teeth, one hand fisted on my lap, the other on the center console.

Maverick says nothing, but I can practically feel the tension radiating off of him in hot, angry waves.

"Behave yourself, baby girl. Don't fucking push me."

In the interior lights of the truck, I see the corners of her pretty little mouth pull up into a smile.

*Bitch.*

Her hands are by her sides, and I catch sight of that pale white scar above her brow.

*I did that.*

My mouth goes dry, my heart sinking. I hurt her, and she

was scared of me. I thought I liked her fear. But in that way? *No.* No wonder she didn't stay with me.

I was never her shelter.

*He always was.*

"You wanna know how much I missed you?" she asks, surprising me, shaking me out of those dangerous thoughts.

I stiffen, my nails digging into my palm as I take a breath in through my nose. Out. I think about turning around, because I'm close enough to touch her. To hurt her. I'm close enough to do some permanent fucking damage if she breaks my heart again.

"Angel," Mav says softly, but there's a warning threaded in his tone.

She ignores him, instead flashing me her white smile at the sound of his voice. Because she knows she can hurt me.

She knows it, and she's not going to hold back. "When he was fucking me," she leans closer as my vision seems to blur, an edgy, twitchy feel to my fingers, still balled into fists. "I didn't think about you once," she continues, her voice deceptive. Dripping with honey. "I never wished he was you. When he was coming inside of me," she continues, inching even closer. So close her lavender scent nearly chokes me, because I know he's smelled it too. He's tasted her, and her, him. "I wished he'd done it all the times before, too."

I try to let it roll off of me in the silence that follows her words. I try to take them for what they are—my wife being a selfish fucking bitch. That's what she is, and that's probably all she's ever been. She might've had a hard life, and she might've gotten fucked over more times than anyone ever deserves, but I did what I could for her.

I killed for her. I bled for her. I would have protected her from every bad thing in the world. But now?

*Now, I just want to fucking kill her.*

I undo my seatbelt in a blink, before she has time to react, and I'm reaching into the back of the truck, twisted around and half out of my seat as my fingers find her hair, yanking hard.

"The fuck did you just say to me?" I snarl at her. The coke I did before our trip is long gone, and I'm craving it all over again, but the worst part of the comedown is the fucking *rage*. And that, combined with what my wife just said? I'm ready to hurt her all over again. Tear her to fucking pieces. "What the *fuck* did you—"

"Lucifer." Maverick's voice is low. I notice he's slowed the truck, but I don't care. He's not going to haul me back into my seat. Not after this. He heard what she said.

He knows what that does to me, because he knows exactly how much she fucking means to me.

And her chest heaving and her teeth bared as she glares up at me, I want to break her apart to show her just how I've felt without her this past fucking month.

I try to swallow down the rage though as the truck slows and Mav switches lanes. He hasn't said anything else, but he's going to stop the car, and that's not going to go well for any of us because then we'll really be able to fight it out.

I inhale. Exhale. Maverick keeps driving, but I know one wrong move and he'll stop.

My eyes search Sid's, and I'm not holding her tight enough to stop her from breathing, but I kind of wish I was.

"Do you know how much I've missed you?" I finally whisper, my mouth inches from hers.

Her brows pull together.

Mav keeps driving.

Neither of them expected that truth.

"I missed you so fucking much, baby girl." I smooth down her hair, cup her chin. "But you know what Sid?" I lean closer still, press a soft kiss to her mouth, her own rigid beneath mine. "I don't think I do anymore."

She's perfectly still in my hands.

"You're not who I thought you were," I tell her, and I want

the words angry. Harsh. *Painful.* But instead, they just come out broken. Snot drips down my nose, to my mouth, and I pull back, darting my tongue over my lip.

She notices, her eyes flicking to my mouth.

I feel my face heat as she sees all the ways I haven't changed since she left me.

"You're not who I thought you were either, Lucifer," she finally says, her voice less angry. More...sad.

My heart cracks with those words.

I feel her throat move beneath my hand as she swallows.

"Who did you think I was, baby girl?" I ask her, wanting a real answer. Wanting to know where the fuck I went wrong. Why she can't love me like I love her. Why she will never stop running, and why she'd rather be with him than me.

She looks down, at my hand on her throat, the other cupping her face. For the first time since we've been reunited, she looks sad. Genuinely anguished.

Heartbroken.

As if she's realizing for the first time what I've realized.

*That this will never work between us.*

We're too volatile. Too broken. And we hate just as hard as we love.

We're not meant to be. Not forever.

But the time we had together? I already know now, even if I live for a hundred more fucking years, I'll never forget it.

Or her.

Her eyes meet mine after a long moment and she takes a shaky breath as I stroke her cheek, trying to ignore the pale white scar above her eye that I put there.

"I'm not sure," she answers me softly, her voice hoarse. Broken.

My heart hurts, and I have to resist the desire to run my thumb over my sternum, trying to keep it together. Trying not to break down right here, right fucking now.

"I just thought..." she trails off, her shoulders narrowing

as she seems to shrink into herself a little more, but she doesn't look away from me. "I just thought it was me and you forever." She laughs, as if the idea is insane. "But I think we'd kill each other before we even got through a year."

I bite the inside of my cheek, feel pressure building behind my eyes.

Because she's right.

I searched for her for a year. For this past month, I did the same. But the thing I've realized about me and Lilith?

The hunt between us? That's the best part.

Because everything after that? The catch?

That only leads to the kill.

# CHAPTER
## Twenty-Eight

SID

PULLING onto the street I was taken from makes my hands shake. A knot twists in my gut, and I place my palm over my belly, try not to think about what's under my shirt. The letter carved into my skin.

I wish I was wearing something more. A hoodie. A blanket. A fucking bulletproof vest, because now that Lucifer knows this will never work between us, now that I've dropped my goddamn knife, I think the only protection I have is with Mayhem.

And even that won't last long.

He'll choose Lucifer over me every time, and I don't blame him.

I'll do the same for J.

Mav pulls up Lucifer's driveway—*my* driveway—and I wait with bated breath, twisting my head to look out the window at that cage, the tarp pinned down to it. I have to get him out of there, and I can only hope that he's still unconscious. That, just like me, he won't remember his trauma.

*Which dancer was killed? Was it Cindy? Did it happen while I was there?* I should ask, but part of me doesn't want to know. And I should feel worse about it, but…I fucking don't. Still, the fact someone killed a person working for J, took photos of me… and Elijah's dead guard…

I push it from my mind. First, I have to get J out of that fucking crate.

The garage door is closed, Lucifer's M5 presumably behind it, and I think about what it would be like to have my own car. To be able to go wherever I wanted, whenever I wanted, not a target. Not a possession. Not a dirty little secret that needs to be constantly threatened with death to keep me in line. Not that it works, of course. But still.

It must be nice to have it. *Freedom.*

Lucifer opens up the door of the truck, the interior lights flooding through the cab. He stands in the driveway, ducking his head to look at me, behind his seat. He reaches for the control to lean the seat forward, but I don't move.

And I don't need to say anything because Maverick speaks first. "She's going back with me. Shut the door."

Lucifer smiles, a dimple flashing in his pale face. "No." His eyes stay on mine. "This is her house." He has one hand on the top of the truck, the other flicking the switch as the front seat folds forward, allowing me room to step out and down, into the warm spring night.

But I still don't move.

My hands are on my knees, and I shake my head, unwilling to budge. "I'm going to——"

"Get out of the fucking truck, Lilith."

"If you don't shut the goddamn door, Luce, I'm going to fuck you up." Maverick's words are irritated. Impatient.

Lucifer's blue eyes narrow, his lean jaw clenched. He blows out a breath, but I know he isn't going to give this up. Before he can say anything though, we hear shouting.

From down the street.

Angry. Loud. Someone calling their names.

Lucifer's head darts up as he looks toward the source of the noise.

"The fuck?" Maverick hisses, glancing in the side view mirror.

"It's from Ezra's house," Lucifer says in his raspy voice, sounding concerned.

"Goddammit." That curse is a snarl and Maverick applies the emergency brake, shuts the truck off and hops out, slamming the door shut behind him.

Leaving me with Lucifer.

Lucifer's eyes find mine, as if he's thinking exactly that, the corners of his mouth tugging up into a wicked little smile. "Gotcha, baby girl." Then he reaches into the back of the truck, undoes my seatbelt, and grabs my wrist, yanking me out, pushing me against the side of the truck as my bare feet stumble on the cement of the driveway.

He closes the door, the screaming getting louder. More people joining in with the shouting.

Silence from the bed of the truck.

From Jeremiah.

Lucifer's hand is planted against my chest, but he drags it down, his fingers skimming my belly, then coming to rest on my low tummy, over my shirt, one hand planted against the side of the truck, beside my head as he stares down at me.

I try not to wince with his fingers digging into the spot Jeremiah carved his initial into me. I don't want to deal with that shit.

"What's going on?" I ask, wanting to know even as I want my brother free. If no one is paying attention to him, they'll leave him alone.

Let him sleep.

And when he wakes up, I promise myself he'll wake up free. *Whatever it takes to get him there.*

"I don't know," Lucifer purrs, tilting his head. "Let's go inside."

A warm breeze blows through the night, lifting the hairs

on the back of my neck as I think about being alone with Lucifer. In our house.

A house of fucking nightmares, the last few weeks I was there.

And on our couch, Maddox had—

"Lucifer, get your ass over here!" Maverick's words are harsh, and Lucifer jerks his head up, looking in the direction of Atlas's house.

Lucifer groans, rolling his eyes.

"Now!" The word is a bellow, and urgent.

My heart races as Lucifer steps away from me, dropping his hand. He glances at the bed of the truck.

"Don't bother trying to get him out. There's a lock on the latch. I'll be back, baby girl. We're not done here." Then he takes off down the driveway at a jog, and I think about all the mornings we ran with each other.

Never one without the other.

Ever.

I lean back against the truck, closing my eyes as I tilt my head up toward the night sky. I try to breathe, try not to think about whatever the hell is going on at Ezra's. Instead, I'm thinking of how to get J out of this.

I'm thinking of tearing that cage apart with my bare hands, but I know I can't.

Then I realize I can just fucking go inside my house—my thumbprint unlocks it, or at least, it did before I left—and I can find something. A crowbar, a gun. There are plenty of both of those.

I'm getting him out.

I open my eyes, step away from the truck and don't look back, knowing my heart will break if I lay eyes on that tarp again. I hear hushed voices carrying down the street, and see the porch light on at Ezra's house, three down from Lucifer's. They all live on a private street together, probably for this reason. So they can't keep secrets, even from each other. But I don't bother waiting to hear what's going on.

Instead, I run to the front door, skipping my way up the stone steps.

There's a light on, I see through the stained glass, but everything is distorted, morphed with the pattern of the glass. There are no guards outside of the door, but we passed the guardhouse on the way in through the iron fence that shields this street from the rest of the world.

Whatever is going on at Ezra's house can't be that serious; the guards would've seen anything strange or unusual.

I press my thumb to the handle, hear it beep. I push the door open, walking into the cold house.

*My house.*

A shudder runs down my spine as I close the door behind me, leaning back against it, taking a deep breath. I think of Maddox. His mask. Hands on me. The threats he whispered.

The way he drugged me. Ella.

Shaking my head, I pull myself together, step away from the door, turning toward the stairs. The light is coming from the kitchen, and I assume Lucifer left it on because when you don't worry about money, you do wasteful, asshole shit like that.

Did he leave it on before he went to Julie's?

Where the fuck is Ophelia? Where did he drop her off at?

I push all that shit aside, just like the dancer's death. Photos of me. Elijah's guard being murdered.

I see the coffee table shadowed in the living room, but from this far away, and with no light on in the room, I can't tell if there's coke on it like there always seemed to be before I ran.

I take a step up on the stairs, one hand curled around the bannister, the other going for the light switch along the wall.

But then I hear something.

A creak of a floorboard.

I freeze, holding my breath, my hand falling away from the light switch. I don't want whoever it is to see me until I see them.

My mind starts racing as I hear another creak.

Definitely coming from upstairs.

The door was locked when I walked up, so whoever is in here has to be someone Lucifer let in.

But...*was* the door locked?

I didn't check.

I only placed my thumb over the lever. Some kind of rich prick shit that I didn't even know existed until I got involved in this fucked up world.

*Who the fuck is inside my house?*

I don't move, frozen at the bottom of the stairs, one foot on the step above me. My palm grows sweaty against the railing as I hear another creak, then steady steps, coming down the hall. My eyes dart up and I have this sinking feeling in my gut.

Because those steps are coming from my bedroom.

*Our bedroom.*

Who the fuck is that?

A sour taste coats the inside of my mouth and just when I think about charging up these damn stairs to confront whoever the fuck it is, I hear a voice.

Calling my husband's name.

"Lucifer?" A feminine voice, uncertain and cautious. The steps grow closer, and as I tilt my head back, looking up, I see her.

My stomach churns as she says his name again, because she hasn't seen me. She's running a hand through her long blond hair, wearing nothing but short shorts and a hot pink bra, barely containing her tits.

I feel sick.

"Lucifer? I've been waiting for—" She stops short as she

flicks on the light at the top of the stairs, and her eyes find mine.

I clench my fingers around the railing of the stairs.

Her blue eyes are wide, her lips parted, and I take in the curves of her body, full and round and *better than mine.*

I see her bare feet, golden skin, her nipples hard beneath the thin fabric of her bra.

Her shorts are more like underwear.

And she came from the direction of my bedroom.

I take a step back, letting go of the bannister.

It was one thing for him to check on Julie with her. To ride in a car with her. *But here? At my fucking house?*

I'm still in my bare feet, and the cold floor is the only thing I really feel as I take another step backward, toward the door. I need to go.

I have to run.

I'm going to vomit.

I can get in the truck. Maybe Maverick left the keys. I can drive me and J out of here, but I don't want to stay in this house a second longer. I already didn't want to. I didn't want to think about why I left. What happened after Lucifer went with his brothers to Noctem.

I didn't want to think about the danger our baby is in, even now.

But at this moment, there are more visceral things I don't want to think about. Like Ophelia fucking my husband. In my house. *Our bed.*

Her hand is on the bannister at the top as she glares down at me, her expression morphing from surprise to anger, as if she has a right to be angry. As if she fucking has a right to be here at all.

I imagine what it would be like to kill her. Slit her fucking throat and spill her blood down these stairs.

She's fucking my husband *in my house.*

Her eyes dart to my throat, and at first, I don't know why,

until she opens her mouth and hisses, "I see you didn't waste any time."

Anger and shame both wash over me in an uncomfortable wave, and I want nothing more than to run up these stairs two at a fucking time and bash her head against the wall of my house, but before I can move an inch, the door opens at my back, the security alarm chiming someone's entrance as it does.

Ophelia's eyes dart past me, but I don't dare turn around even as I hear multiple people crowding at my back.

The door closes softly.

Someone mutters, "Not this shit," and I tense. That's Ezra's deep rumble.

I still don't look. I just keep staring at Ophelia, who's staring at the people behind me. The Unsaints, I'm sure.

After a tense moment of silence, my husband finally breaks it. "Welcome home, baby girl," he says, and I can hear the smile in his words.

# CHAPTER
## Twenty-Nine

### LUCIFER

SHE TURNS TO RUN, because that's what she fucking does. Whipping around in a blur, she's shooting straight for the door, but there are five of us and my wife is tiny.

She's not fucking going anywhere.

Maverick gets to her first.

It's like watching a wild animal caught in a net, the way she twists and kicks and tries to hit him. She might be small, but she's full of rage.

I glance up at Ophelia, see her watching me with a scowl. *Whatever.* Cain obviously beat us here.

He was at Ezra's when I jogged down there.

I turn back to Mav, watch him grab Lilith from behind, pin her arms down to her sides. Her chest is heaving beneath his arms and I don't like it. I don't like what she's wearing—a skintight top and short shorts—and that she's flush against him, but I don't move.

Her eyes are wide, but it's like she's not seeing. She's still twisting in his grip, trying to kick her foot back, trying to hit his groin. But he puts a leg around hers, squeezes her so tight I see her eyes widen as he does, and she stills in his arms.

"Calm down, Angel," he whispers.

I shove my way toward them, coming to stand in front of them both. I hear Ezra's deep laugh, bitter and low, and resist the urge to break his fucking nose. He's got bigger problems to worry about, so he should shut the fuck up.

Cain strolls down the hall without looking back, letting everyone else handle the mess that is my life. Atlas scrubs a hand over his face, eyes full of exhaustion.

Things aren't going well with him and Natalie, and although I kind of feel for him at the moment, things are going *fucking godawful* for me and my wife, so I also can't find it in me to care too much.

"Let's get a drink," Ezra says, placing his hand on Atlas's shoulder, his words calm, as if we didn't just find out through a video call that his mother is *missing*.

Atlas looks to me, adjusting the backward cap on his head. It's as if he's asking for permission to leave us.

I don't need his help dealing with my wife for the simple fact that it is *impossible* for anyone to deal with my fucking wife.

I nod, and him and Ezra walk off after Cain, into the kitchen. It's a testament to the fucked up world of the 6 that Ezra isn't more upset about this shit.

I am, though.

Because it means whoever it is that's targeting us likely *isn't* linked to Jeremiah, unless this is some fucked up mind game that he's trying to play. To get back at us. At me.

Sid's eyes are closed, and I slide my hands into my pockets, staring at her.

Mav's eyes are on me, his arms still around Sid's small body, but I don't look at him. Or Ophelia, who hasn't moved from the stairs.

"I want to get out of this house," Sid says through clenched teeth. Her brow is furrowed, her small tits rising and falling just below Mav's arm, which is over her stomach, one hand on her hip, above her shorts.

I want his hands off of her right fucking now.

"You're not leaving," I snarl, getting in her face.

Her eyes fly open, connecting with mine. "Mayhem," she whispers, staring right at me, "get me the fuck out of here and get me to Jeremiah."

I grit my teeth, lift my hand like I might hurt her—and fuck, I want to but I'm not going to—and Mav pulls her back, away from me.

Then he spins her around, his hands on her upper arms.

I dart a glance at her ass, small but round in those black shorts, and I think about how good it would feel to hate fuck her, but I don't want to give her the fucking satisfaction. And besides that? After *he's* been inside of her?

I don't fucking want her.

"Let's go," Mav says, and he wraps his tattooed arm around her shoulder, glaring at me as he reaches for the door.

"I don't fucking think —" I start to say.

"Yeah, that's your problem," he snarls at me, still holding my gaze as he pulls the door open and a chime rings out in the house.

I want to smash that goddamn alarm and everyone in here's bones.

I clench my hands into fists and open my mouth to retort, but Mav's eyes dart past me, up at Ophelia, still silent at my back.

"Get her out of this house or I'll get her out in fucking *pieces*," he snarls.

"You know they might come after her too," I say in a rush, not referring to O. I know he's going to leave, I know I can't stop him, and I kind of don't want to.

But still. The thought of her, in someone else's arms again…it hurts.

Mav doesn't say anything in response to my warning. Instead, he pushes Sid through the door and slams it closed.

"Lucifer—"

I spin around, cutting off whatever the fuck Ophelia was going to say to me as I stare up at her.

I should send her home. My wife obviously fucked Jeremiah, and that thought is like a punch to the gut. It makes me want to hurl.

I feel like the room is fucking spinning.

*But I did the same thing to her.*

Even still, knowing that she let *him* touch her like I touched her? If it had been anyone else, if she'd fucked his guard, or fucking London goddamn Hamilton or *anyone at all…*

*Fuck.*

"Go to my room," I tell O, raking a hand through my hair, thinking about the coke I've got in my dresser. "I'll be there soon."

She wraps her arms around her chest, rocks back and forth on the step. I imagine her slipping and falling. Breaking her fucking neck, and I imagine the satisfaction I might feel if it happened.

She's been a good friend, one of my earliest. But I don't want her. I don't think I've ever wanted anyone but my wife, but she's only ever wanted her fucking brother, and right now she's off with her real brother, whom she. *Also. Fucked.*

"Why don't you—"

I don't let O finish that question. A guttural roar leaves my mouth as I turn from her, slamming my fist into the wall hard enough to leave a fucking dent and crack my goddamn knuckles.

It feels good.

Without the blow, I can feel how it hurts. I shake my hand out, flexing my fingers.

Then I curl them into a fist and hit the wall again, breaking through the drywall.

I have a feeling I'll be doing a lot of that before this is all over.

# CHAPTER Thirty

## SID

THE SOUND of someone calling my name wakes me. My mouth is dry, and I taste iron in the back of my throat. My eyes feel heavy, and it takes an effort to blink them open. When I do, I'm not quite sure what I'm looking at.

Ink on skin.

A name.

*Ella.*

Leading down into the waistband of blue shorts and—

"Angel, get up."

My arms are slid under a pillow, my head feels…heavy. I swallow, and the taste of blood is bright on my tongue.

Blinking again, my eyes trail up the ink, the six pack, a broad chest, and…Mayhem's baby blue eyes are on mine, his brows pulled together, his expression, *ominous.* The inverted cross beside his eyes tugs down, his lean jaw clenched.

"What—"

"I need you to get up in about two seconds, or your husband is going to come burn my fucking house down." He sighs, scrubbing his tattooed hand over his face. I see my name, and my stomach flips.

He drops his hand, cocks his head as I try to muster up enough strength to push myself up.

*Why am I here? What the fuck happened...*

With a gasp, it all comes back to me.

Jeremiah.

*Where is Jeremiah?*

I must ask it out loud as I push myself up, the room spinning, because Mayhem steps closer to the bed I'm in, reaching a hand out to me, but I jerk out of his touch, scrambling back against the bed, the sheets clenched tight in my fists.

"Where is he?" I ask again, taking in the room. Dark floors, dark walls, dark curtains just parted, letting in a stream of sunlight. How long has it been since Mayhem led me out of Lucifer's house? Since I saw fucking Ophelia walking from our bedroom? How long has it been since Jeremiah has been in that—

Mayhem's hand is around my arm, jerking me to the edge of the bed. I snap my head up, my legs dangling off the mattress, and he steps between them, bringing his other hand to my chin, tipping my head up to meet his gaze.

I've still got my hands fisted in the sheets, my jaw clenched so tight it hurts, my mind spinning, chest aching.

*Is he still in that fucking cage?*

*Is he still there?*

"I need you to get up, get dressed," Mav jerks his head toward the door, "Ella has some shit you can borrow. Speaking of, she made breakfast, and she's going to be very fucking upset if you don't eat it, okay?"

"Where the *fuck* is Jeremiah?" I ask, bringing my hands to Mav's hard torso, shoving at his core.

His muscles flex beneath my fingers but he doesn't even take a step back. His grip around my arm only tightens, and it isn't until he says, a sly smirk on his face, "Careful, Angel, I saw what he did to you," that I realize what I'm wearing.

I look down, Mayhem holding my face too tight for me to

dip my chin, but I see my bare legs. The oversized black T-shirt I'm wearing that must be his.

I see the scar on my thigh, from my husband.

But that's not what he's talking about.

He's talking about…Jeremiah's initial carved into my skin.

He saw me naked. Changed my clothes.

"Yeah," he bites out, and that smirk is gone as I look back up at him. "Did you want to start World War fucking Three?" His light blue eyes dip down to my lips before he looks back up at me.

My stomach flips all over again, and I clench my thighs together, around his legs.

He still doesn't smile. Instead, he jerks me even closer, so my head is nearly level with his abs. "Please tell me he forced that shit on you," he grits out.

"Where. Is. *He?*" My pulse is racing, thinking of him in there, of him suffering all over again.

We can't catch a fucking break.

*We can't catch a goddamn break.*

Tears burn behind my eyes and I see Mayhem's face soften, but his grip on my chin, around my arm, that doesn't.

But before he can say anything there's a pounding from downstairs, and it sounds like someone is going to tear down the door.

Then Ella's voice floats up to us. "Mavy, I think he's—"

Maverick groans, turns over his shoulder and shouts, cutting off her words, "Just leave it alone. I'll deal with his ass."

He turns back to me.

Releases me and steps back.

I can breathe again.

"He ran," he finally says, shoving his hands into the pockets of his shorts, looking down at the floor a second, before he looks back up at me.

"What?" I gasp out, sliding off the bed, my feet hitting the cold hardwood. I tug down my shirt, but it hits mid-thigh anyway, and besides that, Mav's eyes are on my face. "What do you—"

The pounding on what I assume is the front door grows louder, and I think I hear someone yelling. My blood runs cold, my hands in fists at my side. Mav rolls his eyes, shaking his head.

"I had to..." He smiles softly, meeting my gaze again. "Drug you, because you almost took my eye out last night, trying to get to him." His jaw clenches again as he stares at me. "By the time I carried you home and came back, Cain holding Lucifer inside his own house to stop him from getting to *you*, Jeremiah was gone. You guys are like fucking children."

"He got himself out of the crate?" Anger burns through me all over again, hearing Mav tell me about it. About Lucifer. And they did it again. They fucked us again. I step toward Mayhem, the pounding on the door making the whole fucking house shake.

I shove Mav backward, and this time, he stumbles, keeping his hands in his pockets as he stares at me.

"You fucking put him in a dog crate, Mav!" I scream at him, my fists coming to his chest. But it's not enough. I shove him again, and again, and he goes backward each time, until he's up against the wall beside the open door, hands still in his pockets.

His expression is unreadable, his eyes locked on mine.

"Why would you do that? Why would you fucking..." I slam my fist against the wall beside his shoulder, stepping closer to him, getting in his face. "You know he didn't have anything to do with the fucking guard and last night, with Elijah's fucking wife, he was in the back of your goddamn truck!" My finger is in his face, my fist still planted on the wall. It throbs with that hit, and I punch the wall again, my heart racing, blood boiling.

"Where did he fucking go? Where is he? He wouldn't

have left me! He wouldn't have fucking left me with you crazy fucking *assholes!*" I'm screaming so loud I can't even hear myself think. I can't hear my pulse pounding its way throughout my body. "Did you hurt him?" I scream again, dropping my fist from the wall, hitting Mav's chest. "Did you fucking hurt him? What have you done? What the fuck have you done to us?" My voice breaks on that last word, my hands coming to my hair, pulling at the strands until my eyes water and my shoulders shake, a sob tearing through me.

My chest is so tight, and there's a stabbing pain in my stomach and all I can picture is Jeremiah, eight years old, trapped in a fucking cage. Thinking about *me.* He's always thinking about me.

And we didn't ask for this shit.

We did nothing but be born at the wrong place at the wrong fucking time.

And in this moment, I hate my husband so much. He wasn't my flinch. He was my fucking nightmare, sent to extend this curse on my stupid fucking life.

I hear pounding footsteps. People yelling.

I don't realize I'm screaming until someone's arms come around me, tugging me back against them, my eyes screwed up tight shut.

But when I open them, still pulling my hair, still screaming, I see Maverick. Standing against the wall, looking defeated, his eyes sad, and there's Ella, stepping into the room, her long, red hair down her back as she looks from me to Mav, then throws her arms around him, and he slings one around her back, pulls her close to him and kisses her head.

And it's my husband voice that's whispering in my ear.

"It's okay, baby girl. You're okay, Lilith." His strong arms flex as he pulls me closer, dragging us both back to the bed. He sits down, forces me into his lap, my back still to his chest, his mouth still against my ear.

I'm not screaming anymore, but my lungs are burning, and my eyes are blurred, my shoulders still shaking.

And Lucifer's hands are over my belly, over my T-shirt as he holds me tighter, and I close my eyes to cry, hands over my face. I tell him what I was thinking. I tell him he was never my flinch. *Always my nightmare.*

He ignores me. Holds me tighter, as if he can squeeze those words away.

"I love you, baby girl," he whispers in my ear. "I love you so fucking much." And as I let the tears fall, let myself be weak in his arms, I realize I don't think I've ever heard such a beautiful, beautiful lie.

# CHAPTER
## Thirty-One

LUCIFER

"SHE'S GONNA RUN AGAIN." I inhale from my cigarette, looking up at the night sky. No moon, no stars. Fucking darkness.

It's haunting.

Beautiful.

I snap the cigarette in half, drop it to the pavement, grind it out with my shoe.

"No, she's not. A guard is at the front door. The back fucking door. Ella is there—"

I laugh, cold and low as I turn my gaze to Mav. "It's like you don't know her at all." I turn to face Ezra as I lean against my car, folding my arms over my chest. Ezra is across from me, Atlas's Range at his back, Atlas and Cain already inside of Sanctum for Council.

It's taking me a little longer to cool down enough to go in there without fucking murdering all of them.

Maddox Astor is in the meeting room.

The idea of stringing his intestines across those sconces and inhaling the scent of his burning flesh is a little hard to resist right now.

"You think someone really took your mom?" I ask Ezra, jerking my chin toward him.

His dark hazel eyes are locked on mine, a scowl on his face. He runs his tongue over his teeth, glances past me, at the expansive lawn of Sanctum. Shifting on his feet, he slides his hands into the pockets of his gray joggers. He's sober, and I guess Brooklin Astor has a golden fucking pussy keeping him that way.

Then again, Jeremiah's dick was in that shit. Probably not so golden.

My stomach aches, thinking of who else Jeremiah put his dick in.

"She's not your wife," Ezra says, gaze coming back to mine, his low voice cold. "She didn't run."

I arch a brow, my pulse picking up speed, my nose running, but I don't bother doing shit about it. The coke is still bitter in the back of my throat, and Mav already busted my balls about that shit when I got out of the car and apparently, he knew I'd railed a few lines.

I couldn't sleep last night or the night before.

It's been two days since Lilith broke down in my arms, crying for Jeremiah fucking Rain, and I haven't seen her since. Mav kicked me out when we started screaming at each other.

Ophelia went home the night Lilith came over. I'd wanted to fuck the shit out of her, to get the image of those bruises around my wife's throat out of my head, but I couldn't. Not because I wasn't hard. Not because I didn't *want to.*

Because the hallucinations were worse that night.

The eight ball and the vodka probably didn't help. Probably why I woke up to my curtains ripped from the rods.

*Whatever.*

My life is a fucking shit show.

Why fix it now?

Besides, soon enough, Lilith is coming up to the house in

the woods for Ignis. Since she likes the mountains so goddamn much, *this should be fucking fun.*

"Then where the fuck is she? Who would want her, to kill your dad's guard, *and* murder one of Jeremiah *goddamn Rain's* dancers?" I challenge Ezra, stepping closer to him, my face inches from his.

"And don't forget the kitten," Mav adds. I swing my gaze to him. He shrugs. "It's important."

I want to scream at the top of my lungs and punch him in the face all at once, but instead I try to think.

It seems Jeremiah didn't do it, unless he's playing us all.

But why run? And why run without her, unless he's running from *something?*

I can think of one thing.

One connection between Ezra and Jeremiah. One that he's tried to deny over the years, but now that I think about it, him attacking Jeremiah first that night Lilith found out who really hurt her...I can think of why that might all make fucking sense.

"Step back, Luce," Mav says softly, shifting closer to both of us.

I ignore him, getting in Ezra's face. His nostrils flare, the green flecks of his eyes visible in the light from the lampposts around the parking lot of Sanctum.

"Is this your bullshit?" I accuse him. "You were fucking that Forgues girl, weren't you. And we never did find her body—"

"Shut the fuck up. If you could stop your wife from sucking her brother's dick, maybe none of this—"

My fist connects with his face before I can even draw a breath. I grip his shirt tight in my fist, slam his ass back against the fucking Range.

His hand is over his nose, blood pouring down his fingers, and I lift my fist to hit him again but someone shoulder checks me, hard, and I stumble away from him, his shirt slipping through my fingers.

When I round on Mav, he backs me up against my car, his hands planted on the roof of it, on either side of me. We're the same height, and we're nose-to-fucking-nose, my hands going to his arms, trying to throw them out from around me as Ezra swears under his breath at Mav's back.

"Watch yourself," Mav says quietly, his mouth close to mine. "You're not doing yourself any fucking favors in her eyes—"

I step closer to him, my hands still around his arms. I feel his muscles flex, coiled with tension. "I don't want to do myself any fucking favors!" I shout at him. "I don't give a fuck what she thinks about me. I don't give a fuck about her. I'm fucking done with her. She fucking..." I close my eyes, my grip on Mav's arms loosening.

I stumble back against my car, dropping my head, eyes still closed.

"She fucking ran to him, Mav, she...she left me." My voice breaks, a lump in my throat. "She left me and she..." I pick my head up, drop my arms, run one hand over my face as I stare at my brother. "She fucking let him...touch her and use her and—"

"And what did you do?" Mav's voice is low, soft, but his words...he might as well have punched me in the face. "What did you do, Luce? You try to get yourself straight, bro?" He cocks his head, his hands coming to my shoulders, his touch not gentle. "You stayed away from women, too? Don't you think Jeremiah Rain has been keeping tabs on us, just like we've done with him?"

I blink at him, shaking my head, confused, but before I can say anything, he keeps talking. And as he does, I remember Sid's words. About Julie. I didn't listen to her then. I wasn't paying attention.

I was so fucking hurt, I didn't bother to see the pain beneath her own anger.

"You think she didn't know you were at Julie's? Maybe she even knew O was with your ass." His eyes narrow. I hear Ezra muttering something under his breath, but I can't see him, and I'm locked on to Mav's words, my heart sinking.

"You could've killed her, Luce." Maverick swallows, drops his arms from the car and steps back, running a hand over his blond hair as he chews on his bottom lip. "You could've killed her," he says again, then turns to look at me. "Your dad might be dead," he shakes his head as my mouth goes dry, "but he's still haunting you. Just like he did when you were alive."

He bites his tongue, looking at the pavement.

"We need to go in," Ezra grits out, and without another word, his hand still over his nose, he turns from us, swaggering up to the heavy black door of Sanctum.

I watch him go, that familiar anger under my skin, hearing his words in my head about my fucking wife.

But he wasn't wrong.

Whoever is after us, after Jeremiah, maybe Sid was a catalyst. Maybe by dividing herself from us, she started this fucking war.

*Fuck her.*

I start to follow Ezra inside, ready to get this shit over with, but Mav wraps his hand around the back of my neck, yanking me back.

I spin around to face him, my hands fisted by my sides. I'll fucking deck him, too, if he doesn't get out of my face.

I don't want to think about my father.

I don't want to think about the fact he was *Jeremiah's* fucking father, too.

I don't want to think about the Forgues.

That fucking...cage.

The things I did to him.

In the end, he deserved them...didn't he?

"Did you mean what you said to her?" Mav asks me.

I don't know what the fuck he's talking about and I start to tell him exactly that, his hand still on the back of my neck, but he interrupts me.

"Did you mean you love her? *Do you love her?*"

Cold floods my core, my skin tingling. I think about my words to her, before we started fighting again, when she was crying in my lap.

*"I love you, baby girl."*

My throat closes up, that ache in my chest back. She's not with him anymore. She's on my street. With Ella. Being watched.

*She's back with me, but why does it feel like we're further apart than we ever were?*

Mav's fingers dig into my skin. "Did you mean it?" he snarls.

I uncurl my hand, glance at the X on my palm.

*It means something to me, even if it doesn't to her. That shit means something to me.*

"Yes," I tell him without looking at him. "Yes. I love her. I fucking love her. And I hate it, you know?" I lift my gaze, dropping my hand by my side as I meet my brother's gaze. "I hate that I think...I think I'd even..." I swallow down that lump in my goddamn throat, trying to hold it together. Keep myself sane. "Sometimes, Mav, I think I'd even *let her* go with him, if it made her happy."

I hate myself for saying that.

I want to hit myself.

Hurt myself.

I want to be stronger. To keep her with me always.

And for now, I will. She's in danger while someone is after all of us. Until we find out where Elijah's wife is, who killed the guard, who took Sid's pictures, who seems to want to get to all of us, I can't let her go.

But after this? If there's a way I could *let her* be with him, and ensure she was safe?

I'd probably take my own life, because I never really had much to live for anyway.

But I'd let her go. Be happy.

"Yeah?" Mav asks, snapping me out of my misery. "You'd let him raise your kid, too?"

My lips curl up in a sneer with that question. I shrug out of his grip, and he lets me go. Stepping back, toward the cathedral, I shrug. "I don't know, Mav. Not so sure its fucking mine. You know how my wife is."

With that, I turn my back on my brother and walk into the church that I love to hate.

# CHAPTER

## Thirty-Two

JEREMIAH

I ADJUST my grip on the bar, trying to breathe as my shoulders ache, my muscles throbbing. Staring at myself in the mirror, my body stretched taut, that scar from my piece of shit half-brother a visual reminder of just how much I hate him, I pull up one more time. My chin clears the bar, sweat beading down my back, my entire body trembling as I slowly let myself lower down.

I count to ten, closing my eyes, forcing myself not to clench my jaw. Not to grit my teeth. To think of nothing but the pain in my body, the feel of myself growing stronger.

At ten, I let go, dropping down to the floor of the gym in the basement.

My hands are on my knees as I breathe, eyes open now, chest heaving.

But something in the reflection of the mirror that stretches from one wall to the other in the gym catches my eye.

Slowly, I straighten, then turn, feel my blood catching fire as I do.

On one of the weight benches, there's a black piece of fabric, folded over into a triangle.

I bite the inside of my cheek, inhale through my nose, exhale.

A black fucking bandana, the ends hanging over the seat of the bench.

I know Sid must have left it in here. How I didn't notice, I have no idea. Just looking at it makes my skin crawl, my stomach twist into knots. I'm wanting to dive my hand into the pocket of my shorts to curl my fingers around the bobby pin.

The one that saved my life again.

But I don't dare, trying to fight back on that weakness. Trying to push all of those triggers to the back of my mind, as if they don't exist. As if I'm stronger than that. Than *them*.

"Roman is here." Nicolas's voice interrupts my thoughts and I snap my eyes to the bottom of the basement stairs where he's jogging down two at a time, rounding the corner, his eyes on mine.

But he must see something in my expression because he stops, frozen, his brows high on his head.

"Are you okay?" he asks slowly, hands fisted at his sides.

I glance at the bandana again.

His eyes follow my gaze.

"Oh," he says on an exhale, slipping his hands into the pockets of his jeans. He clears his throat. "I can get rid of it if you—"

"I'm not fucking scared of it," I say through clenched teeth, bringing my eyes to his. I wipe the back of my hand over my brow, stopping the sweat from dripping into my eyes. And I'm not scared.

*I'm not.*

I'm not that boy anymore.

I'm not a boy at all.

But I feel my body bent inside that cage, the fight leaving me. I hear the chains clanking against the crate, feel the pressure against my wrists.

Hear Sid running for me.

See her hopping up on the bed of that truck, telling me it'll be okay.

I can see Maverick, too, touching her. Holding her.

It takes an effort not to grab a free weight from the rack and throw it against the mirror behind me. An effort not to break something. Tear shit to pieces.

I can feel her loss like a severed limb. She was beside me. With me. *She was mine.* Of course, they had to take that from me.

But it's okay.

I'm coming for them.

"Remind me why you're waiting for Ignis again?" Nicolas asks, clearing his throat.

I swallow, running my hand over my abs and scratching at that scar. "They'll all be in one place," I answer simply. But I know what he's really asking. *How* can I wait for Ignis? How can I let them keep her? I glide my hand over my torso, rub my palm over my thigh, on my shorts. "With Elijah's guard dead, they're going to be more cautious. Probably go into hiding while their sons are *bonding.*" I smirk at Nicolas. "It actually makes them so much easier to catch, dividing and conquering them like that."

Nicolas nods once, arching a brow. "True," he says. "And Lazarus is good. Got what we needed."

I force myself not to roll my eyes at the nickname. "Yeah, but this whole anonymity shit is grating on my nerves." I walk across the room, past Nicolas, who swivels to face me. I grab a white hand towel from the pile of them, folded neatly and stacked on the cabinet beside the water cooler. I wipe the towel over my face, around the back of my neck. "If they want to keep working for us, we need to meet in person."

Nicolas bounces on the balls of his toes, folding his arms across his chest. "I've checked into them. Their reputation is stellar."

I sling the towel over my shoulder. "Maybe," I concede, "but their fees are a little fucking excessive." Draining my bank account slowly just for *information*. It can be currency, but I'm still having to do all the fucking work.

"Everything you do is excessive, J," Nicolas says mildly, and I dip my chin, arching a brow, my hand clenched tight around the towel over my shoulder. "But Roman has news for you," he adds quickly, almost nervously. "And by news I mean…"

I smile at Nicolas, relaxing. "Pedo Phil?" I run my tongue over my teeth, glance at those free weights again. "You know, I've always wanted to bash the governor's skull in with a dumbbell."

# CHAPTER
## Thirty-Three

### SID

"ARE YOU HUNGRY?" Ella asks for about the hundredth time.

I look over my shoulder, see her hovering by the door to the screened-in porch. Her expression is wary, as if she doesn't quite know what to do with me.

The feeling is very, very mutual.

I twist my fingers in my lap, try not to think about Jeremiah's question. *"Where's your goddamn ring?"*

Rings don't matter to boys like Lucifer. Fuck, *marriage* doesn't matter to girls like me. But all I can hear is Jeremiah's words ringing in my head, and if it weren't for the guards surrounding Mav's house, for his insistence that he's keeping his eyes out for J, I'd have already run again.

I haven't seen Lucifer since I broke down in his arms, three days ago.

I don't want to fucking see him, but apparently, Mav is taking us to Liber next week. I think he's lost his fucking mind, but he says they need a break. Ezra needs an escape, and turning to drugs and alcohol seems to be the Unsaint's MO.

I'll hide in my room all night. Lock Lucifer out. Fuck them all.

*Why did you leave me, J?* But even though I've repeated that question over and over in my head for the past few days, I know the answer. I would have done the same damn thing. Besides that, if he had fought back...they would've hurt him more.

*Don't leave me for good.* My stomach twists into knots, thinking of what he might be planning. Thinking of where he is. I know how easy it can be to run from this street, despite the guards.

I went through the backyard once. Got picked up by Nicolas. As controlling and rich as my husband is, *he actually* isn't *God.*

I offer Ella a fake smile. "I'm okay," I tell her, lying through my teeth. I don't think I've been okay in a long, long time. Maybe never.

I turn back to gaze out at the dark forest beyond the house. The guard is in front of the door the leads off to the backyard, to the oasis of trees and a garden that I'm sure Ella tends to.

Ella isn't even Mav's wife, but she's the perfect housewife all the fucking same.

I wonder what she does all day while he works. I wonder what she wants to be doing. If she ever thinks of running, or if that's just me.

I shift in the rocking chair I'm in, leaning my head back against it and closing my eyes. I hear the screen door close to the house and I think Ella has gone back inside, but then the creak of wood is beside me and my eyes fly open, connecting with her green ones. She's in the chair beside me. Off to her right, a little stone fountain provides the only break in the heavy silence between us on the hot spring night.

"Do you know what's going on?" she asks me quietly.

I stare at her a moment, trying to gauge her angle. The only person who has always been on my side has been Jeremiah, and even he lied to me about the biggest things. I wonder if Ella is trying to pry. To report back to Mav. Lucifer.

But her eyes are wide and innocent, her red hair in a messy bun, a few strands framing her freckled face. She's wearing a red skirt, her feet bare, red coating her toenails. Her fingers are drumming against the arms of the chair, and I see her breasts straining against the white T-shirt she's wearing, tied just over her hip. Her belly is soft, spilling over the top of her skirt, her skin flawless.

I think about Lucifer taunting me about O's curves. Julie's.

I feel sick and dig my nails into the top of my hands. "No," I finally answer her, because I don't know what the fuck is going on.

She nods, as if she expected that answer, and then she turns to gaze out at the guard, at her backyard. She looks so young from this angle, her lips plump, her face, too. She's nineteen, Mav had told us. Nineteen, and she's already thrown her life away by entangling herself in something as sinister as the 6. The fucking Unsaints.

The brotherhood from hell.

"Someone had photos of you," Ella says quietly, still staring straight ahead, telling me something I already know. "You were…" she shakes her head, her brow furrowing, but she still doesn't look at me. "You were running. The pictures were delivered like a message. On Elijah's guard's lap, in the car they shot him in."

She turns my way, her eyes searching mine.

I keep my head tilted back, against the rocking chair, listening. I knew about the photos. But I didn't know about all of this shit. Seems I wasn't crazy after all. Someone was watching me.

"Then the night you came back, Elijah's wife never came home from her private Pilates class." She shrugs. "And the night before that, a dancer was killed in Jeremiah's club." She stumbles over his name, like it's a curse.

I kind of hate her for that.

I hate how everyone hates him.

I think about Cindy grinding against Jeremiah, wonder again if it was her. How long was she alive after that?

"That's why Lucifer finally came for me?" I spit at her. "Because someone is after them, and he's getting scared?" I sit up straighter, twisting in the seat. "That's it? Let me guess, the entire time I was fucking gone...he didn't get help? Go to rehab? Have someone come to him to get clean?" Imagining any of the Unsaints in rehab is hilarious, but I know they have means. Someone could've fucking helped.

There has to be some mental health professional he could see that isn't Father goddamn Tomas.

"He was fucking Ophelia, all this time?" I press, my blood pressure rising. "Julie, too?"

"He went to Julie's because someone left a..." She clears her throat, glancing down at her lap as she smooths her hands over her thick thighs. "Someone left a cat's head," she finally finishes.

I blink, my mouth going dry.

"On her doorstep. He wanted to see if anyone was connected to that, and what's happening here." She meets my gaze again. "He's in love with you, Sid."

I roll my eyes. "You don't fucking know him." But I think about the cat's head. About why Lucifer really went to Julie's.

But even still. "Why'd he take Ophelia there?" I press Ella, wishing I didn't fucking care. "Why'd she have to fucking go for that?"

Ella glances down at her lap again, and she doesn't look at me when she answers, her voice low. "He doesn't like to be alone."

Something about that answer causes my stomach to twist into knots. That answer, and the way her cheeks flush pink.

I dig my nails deeper into the tops of my hands, deep

enough to draw blood. I don't fucking care anymore. *I don't care.*

But I still can't stop from snarling, "Seems you'd know all about that, huh? My husband not wanting to be alone?"

I'm bluffing, because she wouldn't have touched him. Mav wouldn't have let her.

But then I think about Maverick fucking me at that house in Raven Park. He didn't hesitate. Didn't hesitate to run and tell Lucifer right after either. If he'd be okay with his girl fucking anyone, it would be Lucifer.

I feel sick.

Ella's blush deepens, and she doesn't look up at me.

"You didn't." I stand, taking a step back, away from her and she finally picks her head up. "You didn't actually fuck my husband too, did you?" I want more venom in my words, but instead, there's just a harsh whisper. A broken sound.

Her eyes flick to my belly, then back up to me, and for some reason, that pisses me off more.

"Yeah," I snarl, anger heating my blood, "I guess you didn't think about his *pregnant fucking wife* while you were *fucking him?*" I shriek the last words, and all I can think about is Ophelia in my house. Coming from *my. Fucking. Bedroom.*

All I can think about is Julie.

*Ella.*

I'm going to vomit.

My stomach heaves, and I clamp a hand over my mouth.

Ella stands on shaky legs, taking a step toward me.

I throw up my free hand. "No," I mutter beneath the hand over my mouth as my stomach heaves again. "Don't touch me. Don't you fucking—"

"Ella?" The screen door opens, and Maverick steps through, a smile on his face, but as he looks between the two of us, his light eyes gleaming in the dim overhead lights of the porch, his smile slips.

And on his heels is my husband.

His nose is red, his eyes, too, demon blue and zeroed in on me.

He looks from Ella, to the hand over my mouth, the one held out in front of me.

Maverick curses under his breath, and I know he knows. He knows what the fuck we were talking about.

*He fucking knows.*

"You *let her?*" I ask him, dropping both hands by my sides. Ignoring my husband's stare. Ignoring the fact he has blood on his knuckles. Ignoring his black T-shirt, clinging to his hard, lean frame. His black pants, hugging his thighs. "You fucking *let her?*" I ask Maverick again, taking another step back, until I'm up against the screen that wraps around this porch.

I see the guard shift on his feet beyond the door, dressed all in black with a gun on his hip, but he doesn't dare look at me.

"Look, Angel, you left—"

"You fucking *let her fuck my husband?*" My mouth drops open as I finally turn to Lucifer. I can feel my pulse thudding in my ears. My skin itches, uncomfortable. I want to be sick. I want to fucking vomit, but for once, my stomach seems made of lead. Unshakeable.

Instead, it's just my mind that's all fucked up.

"Who *didn't you* fuck?" I ask my husband, his deep blue eyes on mine. He doesn't smile. Doesn't scowl. Doesn't do a fucking except stare at me. I take in the circles under his eyes. His long, thick lashes. His pale face, ashen under these lights. "Who didn't you put your dick in, you stupid fucking asshole!" I scream the last words, running my hands over my face. I feel like I'm losing my mind. I feel like I'd rather be dead than deal with this. "Why didn't you let me stay with him?" I finally ask. "You went to Julie's with fucking *Ophelia?*" I spit her name out like a curse. "Why'd you come after me at all?"

He still says nothing. Maverick moves to Ella's side, wraps

his arm around her shoulder and spins her around, toward the door.

"Fucking coward," I mutter to Mav.

He stills, the muscles in his back flexing under his white T-shirt. Then he turns to look at me over his shoulder. "Says the girl who's always fucking running. Don't be a bitch about shit *you do, too, Angel.*" Then he yanks open the door and pushes Ella inside, slamming the door closed, the screen door following afterward.

I don't want to be out here with Lucifer. And I know the guard is listening.

*I don't want to be here.*

"Fuck this shit," I mutter, wanting to dart behind him, into that house, disappear into the guest room I've been staying in. Disappear into my own head. Lose my mind in peace.

I take a step toward him, but he moves to block the door.

I knew he wouldn't make this easy. He never does.

"Lucifer," I whisper, "I don't want to talk to you."

He crosses one arm over his body, hand on his elbow, his fingers under his chin. "When's the last time you ate, baby girl?" he asks me quietly, as if I didn't just find out he fucked a *third* girl.

I gape at him, words escaping me at his stupidity.

A slow smile curves his beautiful mouth. "I know you're shit at cooking, but I assume Ella has been making enough to feed a small army, so—"

"You really fucked her." It's not a question. The three of them basically confirmed it. What surprises me most, I think, isn't even that they did it. They're sick fucks.

What surprises me is that...it hurts.

Ella. Julie. Ophelia. It fucking...hurts.

He still doesn't say anything. Doesn't make to move toward me. To comfort me. Not that I'd want his filthy hands on me.

"Aren't you worried you'll have more kids not to give a shit about?" I snarl, placing a hand on my low belly and forcing myself not to think about the still-healing wound Jeremiah carved into my skin.

Lucifer's eyes dip down to my tummy, and my chest tightens as his face softens, losing some of the hard edge.

He drops his hands, takes a step toward me.

I'm rooted to the spot. I can't move.

I can't even fucking…breathe.

"I wouldn't…" He trails off, swearing under his breath and running his hand over his nose. He drops his hand, meets my gaze again. "Believe it or not, I know how to use a condom. And I did."

I hate that that makes me feel marginally better.

"But since I got there first," his eyes dip to my belly again, "I assume *he fucking didn't?*"

I laugh out loud at that, shaking my head. "Oh no. You don't get to do that." I grind my teeth as his eyes narrow into brilliant blue slits. I see that blue vein in his neck throbbing and, still fucking pissed as hell at him, he has the ability to make me think about fucking his brains out all the same. "You don't get to do that after you…" My throat closes up, thinking of him with Julie. Ophelia.

I close my eyes. "You didn't, did you?" I ask him, the words hoarse. I already know the answer, but just like before I ran, I want to forget it. I want to…I just want to forget all of this shit sometimes.

I want to forget I was born wrong.

I was made a gift to grown men wanting to touch little girls.

I want to forget my brother was made a prisoner, to be reborn into a perfect and holy son that no one really wanted for a cult that cares more about having soulless men than it does what it takes to get them that way.

Silence greets my question.

I keep my eyes closed.

"Did you fuck her, Lucifer? Ophelia? How many times?"

"Three," he answers me, stealing the breath from my lungs, my eyes screwing up tight to keep the tears back. "Twice from behind, so I could think of you as I stared at her ass. And once? Once, I fucked her against the wall, my hand around her throat. You know, your thing, baby girl."

My stomach drops, my heart cracking in two, even as his words are so venomous, I know he's trying to hurt me for Jeremiah.

I know, but still, it's like another reminder. Another reminder that we could never be. That the boy who ran from the fucking dog crate…*that's the boy for me.*

I turn away from my husband, finally opening my eyes. "Where is he?" I ask quietly.

Of course he doesn't answer me because he's an asshole, but I hear him step closer.

Sense him at my back.

Inhaling, I catch his scent. Nicotine and pine. I became addicted to that scent. He always smoked outside, and never when I was in the car, but sometimes I'd sit out there with him, my arm threaded through his, my head on his shoulder, just to breathe him in.

"Is this really over, Lilith?" he asks me quietly from behind, not touching me, but his presence is palpable. I can feel his body heat through the oversized white shirt I'm wearing. A borrowed one from Ella, like her black leggings.

At his question, I feel cold even in the warm night.

I glance to the door, notice the guard has walked off. As if even he knows this is ending, and he wants to give us our grief.

I think about my bad cards in life.

Lucifer's.

His stepmom.

I imagine her screams. Her blood. How good it felt to fucking kill her for the man standing at my back right now.

How I wanted to protect him from everything after that.

Every hurt, every nightmare. I wanted to be there. But he made it impossible.

Then the 6...

"You know they took us." I whisper the words in the dark, arms folded over my chest as I stare at the woods.

He's silent behind me, but I know he's waiting. I know I didn't get to tell him this story. Didn't get to tell him that yeah, Maverick and Jeremiah may have exchanged letters because Mav knew my husband was having some kind of psychotic break, but I didn't make up my mind to run until that day.

Noctem.

"They took me and Ella. They had on...masks."

Lucifer steps closer, one hand coming to my neck, brushing my hair aside with his fingers, then holding me, kneading my muscles, urging me in his own way to continue.

"They had us bound. Gagged. Said we were to teach you all a lesson." I close my eyes, thinking of that night.

Of the last time I saw my husband before I left.

*ELLA IS LAUGHING AT SOMETHING IN THE LIVING ROOM, A STUPID fucking romcom playing loudly through the mounted speakers.*

*I wrap my arms around myself as Maverick walks outside, having kissed his girl goodbye. I don't know what's going on with them—him and Ella—but I like her. I think she's too good for even him. Not really him... but...this life.*

*It's...draining. Constricting.*

*Terrifying.*

*My husband walks in at night covered in blood more times than I'd like to count. Sometimes I hear him whispering words in Latin from his office. Words that I don't know the meaning of but send chills down my spine all the same.*

*I use that office. It's got two desks, big bay windows. Books on the dead, Satanism... Magic.*

*It's intriguing, but some of those books are covered in blood, too. I've seen it as I turn through the pages. I've never asked. I'm too caught up in the secret workings of the 6 that I don't think I want to know more. If I did, it might break me.*

*What they do, what they've done...*

*I think of Reverend Wilson and my body goes cold.*

*Lucifer's hands come to my face. "You look so nervous, baby girl," he says softly, and I can see it, in his eyes. He's sober today.*

*He's sober for the first time in a long, long time. He still has night-mares. Just last night, he held a knife to my head.*

*He thought I was his father.*

*Even being sober, the hallucinations haven't left. The night terrors.*

*He needs help. I don't know what to do.*

*"I'll be okay, I promise. It's three days. No one will hurt you. The guards are right outside the door. You know I'd never leave you unpro-tected, right, Lilith?"*

*I offer him a weak smile. I do know. I know he loves me, and I know he would never want anyone else to hurt me. Even if he has. Even if our fights have gotten...worse.*

*He's trying.*

*I know he's trying.*

*But he thinks I don't want him. That I don't want this life. And there are some parts of it I hate. The control he wields over me because he's paranoid that someone will get to me again. The fact that I don't do anything without him; that I can't, because he won't allow it. I know it's wrong, and toxic, and it's driving me up the fucking wall, but I love him.*

*I fucking love him.*

*He just can't see it. And his love? It's suffocating, stealing my breath, my choices, trying to stifle my pain. It only lets me discuss what he wants to hear.*

*Jeremiah? Those wounds? He doesn't want to hear it, even though it's ripping me apart. How do I explain that I need to know that my brother is okay, because he was always the one making sure I was okay? That he was the only one I ever had to love me, before Lucifer. And just because I chose him, just because I never want to leave my husband, that doesn't mean I don't still love the boy I always believed to be my brother.*

*But Lucifer doesn't want to discuss it. So, I swallow it down. Just like I do waking up with his hand around my throat, the sheer terror that comes with thinking your own husband is going to kill you because he's fighting against ghosts.*

*Even though I accept the fucked-up parts of him that are stupid and foolish and piss me off, he doesn't want all of me.*

*He brushes my hair from my face. "I love you, baby girl." He tilts his head, his lips over mine. "So fucking much."*

But do you really, *I want to ask? Do you love me, or do you just love the idea of me? A broken soul as fucked as yours, is it just the shared pain we have, from your family, that you love?*

*He's a good man.*

*I know it.*

*Even though he's an asshole and controlling and a dick, he's so good. With Julie and the baby, and the fucked-up shit, at his heart, he's good. He'll be a good dad. He'll love me in this wicked way, too, and he won't let anyone hurt us.*

*But even as I think it, there's that sense of foreboding. That this cere-mony—Noctem—is going to break us apart.*

*I try to shake it off. Maybe it's the hormones. The knife wound above my brow.*

*"I love you too," I tell him. And with that, he kisses me, passionate and raw and full of just what he professed. Love.*

*His hands tangle in my hair, then one slips down to my ass as he squeezes me. I laugh against his mouth, feel him growing hard between us.*

*I feel how much I want him, too, but with Ella here, and Maverick and the rest of his brothers waiting outside, I know we can't fuck again. Besides, we did half a dozen times today.*

*I swear, the one good thing about our relationship is the fucking sex.*

*"I'll be back soon, baby girl, I promise you." He kisses me again, grabs my ass, and pulls me to him, groaning.*

*Finally, he breaks away, and I try to catch my breath as he adjusts the skeleton bandana around his neck, pulling it over his mouth.*

*He winks at me, one deep blue eye glinting under the lights of the foyer.*

*Then he's gone.*

*I DON'T LISTEN AS ELLA GUSHES ABOUT THE HOT GUY IN THE movie they're watching. She's started talking a lot more now that she's with Mav, but the guy she's gushing about looks bland to me; blond and boring. There's no devil in his brown eyes. No anger beneath the surface of his flawless face. Nothing to draw me in. Nothing to scare me away. Mesmerize me.*

*He's nothing like my husband.*

*I pull my knees to my chest, tugging the black velvet blanket up to my chin as I let my eyes flutter closed. It's late, and I want some cereal. Lucifer keeps an endless supply of it in our cupboard, but I'm too tired to walk in there and get it.*

*I wish they didn't leave so late.*

*I wish he didn't do these fucking rituals.*

*But I know it's important. I know that whatever most sane people think holds the world together…they're wrong.*

*It's not the presidents or prime ministers. It's not the governments at all. Governments have to follow laws.*

*The 6 and organizations like them? Not so much.*

*He's told me about some of the shadowy things that occur in his world, the one he tries to keep from me because we both know how much I despise it. I know there are things he doesn't like either, but he swallows it down like poison with sugar, taking the good with the bad.*

*All he cares about is me.*

*The rest of the girls caught up in the bullshit the 6 do? I don't think he minds so much. Part of me hates that.*

*Part of me never wants to think about it again, so I say nothing. Do nothing. What power do I really wield here, anyway?*

*Yawning, my eyes flutter closed. I'm safe and warm under these blankets, and he's right. It's just three days.*

*Three days, and he'll be back. We'll make this work.*

*I fall asleep.*

*And I don't dream, for the first time in a long time.*

*But when I wake up, I swear I've stepped into a fucking nightmare. I swear this must be what he sees when he closes his beautiful eyes.*

*Ella is bound and gagged, men all in black with masks over their faces—skeleton masks, but not bandanas, obscuring everything but their eyes—are in my house.*

*They're in my fucking house.*

*I start to move, anger flashing through me as two men drag Ella down the hall.*

*She isn't moving. I don't think she's...conscious.*

*The man closest to me has familiar eyes.*

*He reaches for me, but I scramble back on the couch, shuffling out of his way.*

*"Don't make this harder than it has to be, Sid Rain," he snarls, and I recognize that voice.*

*I recognize the voice, and the eyes, and my skin crawls as the recognition renders me motionless.*

*Still.*

*Letting him touch me.*

*And not just my arms.*

*His hands, his body, he's...all over me.*

*All over me, and he's...*

*"M-Maddox." The word comes out strangled as he climbs over me. I smell the warm scent of his cologne, and I marvel over the fact that he's Maverick's father.*

*That he's...my father.*

*He leans down close, clamping his gloved hand over my mouth. "I'm not going to hurt you, baby." He laughs against my skin, and despite his words, his free hand goes to my throat, curling around me, stealing the breath from my lungs. "But we both know you can't live. Lucifer would be better off without you, and I can't let this secret out." He laughs again, fear coiling my muscles tight as his hand trails down from my throat, over my chest, to my stomach. "It's a shame." His words are distinct, even with the plastic of the mask against my cheek. "I think I was really ready to be a grandfather. But there are other things this baby will be good for. A sacrifice."*

*His hand shifts from my mouth, to his pocket, then a cloth is pressed over my nose, rough and putrid.*

*I start to fight back, inhaling beneath his hand to take air while I still can.*

*But he starts to laugh as he lifts up, staring down at me.*

*That was the wrong thing to do—the inhale. Because everything seems fuzzy, my tongue thick in my mouth. My limbs are heavy, and I can't think...*

*Nothing.*

*There's nothing but a voice in my head that tells me as soon as I open my eyes, I have to do it. I have to do what my husband fears most.*

*I have to run.*

"Did she not tell you?" I ask Lucifer, his silence unnerving. The only way I knew he was listening is his fingers digging deeper into my skin, his body brushing against mine. "Did Ella not—"

"She didn't remember anything," he finally says through gritted teeth. "She said she fell asleep on the couch, woke up underground. *With Maddox.*"

"I shot him," I whisper, closing my eyes, relaxing into my husband's touch for the first time in a long, long time. "I fucking shot him, but is he—"

"Alive. He's alive." Lucifer's words are a snarl. His mouth comes to my ear and I stiffen, waiting. "But you know what, baby girl?" He presses his mouth just below my ear, on my neck. "He won't be for long."

I swallow the lump in my throat as his arms come around me, pulling me back into him. "You didn't know?" I ask him. "About..."

"I knew they brought you there. Picked up Ria too, as punishment for Mav. I thought it was part of Noctem. I didn't know about the threats," he bites out. "I thought..."

I chew the inside of my cheek, the fear from that night

momentarily pushing past my anger with Lucifer. My grief. "You thought I left because you held a knife to my head?" I laugh, that anger coming back.

I step out of his arms and lets me go as I spin to face him.

His eyes go to the scar above my brow.

"I did," I tell him honestly. "That. Your fucking...drugs." I step back again, needing more space between us so I can think. He's always made it so hard for me to do that. "The fact that you won't deal with this shit. That—"

"And how do I do that, baby girl?" he snaps back, stepping toward me, one hand coming flat to his chest. "How the fuck do I deal, huh? Do I see a fucking therapist and get shot in the head on my way to their office?" A vein in his temple is pulsing against his pale skin, his blue eyes full of feeling. Anger. Frustration. "Someone else is after us now, after *you*."

"Someone is always after me," I mutter, but I don't look away from him, his hand still on his chest.

"I can't think about anything but you. No matter what I'm doing." He steps even closer. "No matter who I'm fucking."

I clench my jaw hard enough to hurt, but I don't say anything.

"You being gone, you fucking hurt me, Lilith."

My skin crawls with that admission.

He slaps his hand against his chest. "You were supposed to be the one to *stay with me.* Don't look away, remember? You weren't supposed to do that to me. You should've fucking told me—"

"I just told you now, and what?" I ask him, watch as he drops his hand, his full lips pressed into a line. "You're gonna kill him, too? Why not disband the entire fucking thing? How are you okay with *any of it* happening? You think they stopped with me? You think I'm the only little girl that got hurt? Raped? You think I'm the only one an old man got their hands on because of your fucking *family?*"

He laughs, so bitter as he shakes his head, running his

tongue over his bottom lip. "That's fucking funny, Lilith, coming from you." He steps close, and I step back, a dance we've been doing since the night we met. "From the girl who ran right into the arms of the man who assaulted her and *made me fucking watch.*"

He narrows his eyes into slits. Then he lifts up his middle finger, steps back from me. "Fuck you, Lilith. *Fuck you.*"

Without another word, he turns and walks inside, slamming the door so hard the whole fucking house shakes.

I hear something outside the porch, see the guard step back up to the door.

I flip him off, just like my husband did me. "Fuck yourself," I snarl at the guard, then I head into the house, too, hear Lucifer and Maverick yelling.

I don't fucking care.

I go to my room, slam the door closed and lock it, burying my head under a fucking pillow as the tears fall.

# CHAPTER
## Thirty-Four

**JEREMIAH**

"WE NEED to know who took those photos of—"

"Stop talking, Nicolas." I don't look up from the papers on my desk. My hand is shaking worse than ever, in my lap, clenched into a fist. The nightmares are worse. It's been a week since they came to us. A few days since I put Governor Phil Cooper in the hospital.

He's lucky he's alive, but I needed him that way. Less chaos when he can go back to his post.

Besides, without a dick, he's not gonna touch another kid again, and with all the child porn I have evidence of from his computer, thanks to Lazarus, he isn't going to talk.

Still, it's been a week since we've been separated, *again*. Since fucking Nicolas and Ria drove off down to the gas station while I hauled the kindling back to the cabin. We needed a lighter, or matches, or fucking something to make a goddamn fire.

I kept a bobby pin in my pocket all these years. Should've added fucking matches, too.

A week since Lucifer Malikov and fucking Maverick Astor jumped me like a couple of fucking pussies.

A week since I used the bobby pin to get out of that fucking crate.

*She was inside his house.*

*I heard her dragged back to Maverick's.*

Saw the guards too.

The longer I wait, the longer it plays in my head. The worse it hurts, not having her here.

But if I had gone after her then, unarmed…

I slam my fist on the desk when Nicolas opens his fucking mouth to speak again. He wasn't there when I needed him. He wasn't there when *she* needed him.

"Did you hear me?" I ask him, tossing down my pen. My handwriting marking through the numbers on the expenses on my desk is garbage, but I have to use my right fucking hand because my left one isn't *working*.

Nicolas's dark eyes are narrowed, his jaw clenched, palms splayed on my desk. If he doesn't back up in about three seconds, I'm going to break his fingers.

"Lazarus didn't take those photos. Didn't kill Elijah's guard. Cindy," he says, working at keeping his tone even. "He might've helped with the kitten, and the hacking, but he didn't do those things. She could still be in danger, because it's not just your mercenary fucking shit up. And right now, she's with him again." He takes a deep breath in. "I don't want to wait, J. I don't like this. You know what he did to her."

I arch a brow, tilting my head as I cross my arms and lean back in my chair. I can hear her, screaming for me as I screamed for her. I can hear them fighting.

I can see her running to the truck, hauling herself up. Over and over again in my mind.

"I don't know what he did to her. She never got a chance to fucking—"

"That scar on her brow?" Nicolas asks, his voice deadly.

My blood runs cold and I swallow down the tightness in my throat.

"He gave it to her. He's having hallucinations."

I flex my jaw, try not to feel it. The hurt. I *know* he's having hallucinations. I've known that before even Maverick told me he was behaving erratically. It's how Lazarus started working for me, giving me valuable information. But I didn't know about the scar, even though I assumed Sid lied to me. "And how do you know this?" She let me brand my name on her skin, because she fucking belongs to me, but she didn't feel comfortable enough telling me that?

"I asked her," Nicolas says back, in a tone that suggests I should have done the same.

I stand, my fingers grazing the top of my desk as my chair rolls back behind me. "So. Did. *I.*"

Nicolas arches a brow, looking up at me as he straightens, sliding his hands off my desk. "And you just listened to the bullshit she gave you, right off the bat?"

She said she ran into something. I knew it probably wasn't true, but I let it go.

"Yeah." Nicolas laughs, but there's no humor in it as he takes a step back from my desk. "You wanna own her, huh?"

I curl my fingers into fists, ignore the tremble in my left one. Ignore the sounds of her screams in my ears.

Ignore the thoughts of what they're doing to her right now.

"But do you want to go through the work it takes to *love* her?"

"I do love her." I would have thought that would be obvious by now.

"So, what's your plan?" he asks again, shrugging, tucking his hands into his pockets. "Why are you waiting? You don't need them in one place. You can pick them off one by one, but instead, in the meantime, you gonna go over all the millions you make?" He nods his head to the paperwork I'd been pouring over. "The bodies you're gonna fucking drop? Why are you waiting to get the girl you *love* back?"

At that, I can only stare at him. Is he really that stupid? Does he really think I *don't* have a plan?

He exhales, rolling his neck. "You know, I was fine with Ignis before, but I'm not anymore. Not with all the shit going on that we can't account for."

"It's probably one of their own, trying to set a fire from the inside to distract from other hideous shit they're doing, Nicolas."

"Someone stalked Sid through the woods, and you don't give a fuck? Someone sent a message with her photos on the lap of a fucking corpse," he counters.

Thinking about it makes my blood boil. About Elijah's call, his threats to kill her. But that's exactly why I think it could even be *him*. He just wants to start a war. Wants me to overreact, blow my shot. So instead of answering, I just stare at Nicolas, waiting for him to say something that isn't a waste of my fucking time.

"You're unbelievable." He shakes his head, and I wish those words didn't affect me, but considering Nicolas is the only person in my life aside from Sid that's something like a friend, they kind of do. "Someone slit Cindy's throat. Doesn't that bother you?"

*No, it doesn't.* A lot of people that work for me wind up dead. It's just the way it is. "What do you want me to do, Nicolas? Interrogate everyone in the club? Burst through Elijah's security, risk getting shot in the back, so I can ask if he was tiptoeing around the forest to snap pictures? She's not even here. The fuck does it matter who was in the woods?" I bite the inside of my cheek, shake my head. "You said you were on top of the club shit anyway."

"They claim they didn't see anything, but someone disabled our cameras. Someone knows what the fuck they're doing. Someone had pictures of *Sid.*"

As if I don't remember.

"And someone has abducted Elijah Van Damme's wife."

I arch a brow, this being news to me, but I'm not quite surprised. "When did you find that out?" It's pretty bold. Go straight for the fucking Dominus. I hate their bullshit. Their Latin. I fucking hate all of it. All of them. Anything and anyone connected to them. But this…this is news.

"Yesterday," Nicolas admits. "Police reports. Sealed, of course, since they're stonewalling us now that they've got what they want." I know he means the 6, and the fucking Unsainted. Not the police. The police wouldn't stand a fucking chance trying to keep us out of their business. I'd set their entire precinct on fire and dance in the fucking flames if they tried to do that.

"Any leads?"

Nicolas's brows raise high on his head. "No, but it doesn't take an idiot to figure out it's probably the same person fucking with all of us."

"There is no 'us', Nicolas," I say sharply, my skin crawling with thoughts of it. "And trust me, I'm concerned. But one fucking thing at a time. Great things come to those who come in like a sledgehammer and destroy everything in sight before anyone sees them coming."

Nicolas is staring at me, confusion etched on his face. "Can you explain what the fuck you just said?"

I roll my eyes, go to work on rolling back my shirtsleeves. "No. Now, I need you to get eyes on Elizabeth and Maddox Astor, and *keep them there*. I don't want them to leave that house for a fucking grocery store run without us knowing about it."

"Don't you think we should work on getting Sid—"

I finish my sleeves, drop my hands, slip them into my pockets. *"I am."*


THAT NIGHT, WITH HER NOT SLEEPING DOWN THE HALL FROM me, as I toss and turn and hope to Satan I'm doing the right fucking thing, I dream about someone else entirely.

. . .

*I'VE COME TO LOVE THE DARKNESS.*

*It means they aren't here for me.*

*I'm alone, and I'm cold, and I'm hungry, but…they can't hurt me in the dark.*

*It's when the light spills down the stairs from the basement door that I can't breathe. That I seize up with fear, curled into a ball, my aching back pressed against the steel bars of the cage. Too small for me to stand. Too small to lie down completely.*

*I've been coming here for years now, for days at a time. Sometimes only hours. If I'm really lucky, if I say all the right things, if I get the Latin words and the kneeling positions and the promises to Satan that I'll be better, if I get all of that right, it's only minutes.*

*If I get it wrong…*

*I'm here longer.*

*I think this is the longest. It feels like an eternity.*

*And lately, with my seventeenth birthday coming up, I've been thrown in here more frequently.*

*I'm the holy one.*

*Chosen.*

*No longer Jamie, the name I was born with. Since the Forgues became my* parents—*that word leaves a bad taste in my dry, cracked mouth—I've been reborn.*

*Jeremiah.*

*They don't speak my last name. They don't join my first with theirs. And I know why.*

*It's because I don't belong here.*

*They all ensure I know exactly that.*

*All of them except the younger sister.*

*Sometimes I think I hate her more for it.*

*She's quieter. Doesn't often look at me. Doesn't often speak to me, save for that one word. That lie.*

"Sicher."

*Even when I try to believe it, even when she tiptoes down in the dark and offers me scraps of food that I snatch from her with shaky hands, I despise her for that word. For the fact I took up learning German because of her. Because of that. Her deep blue eyes are haunted, I've seen when I'm free—although am I ever really that?*

*But her eyes are full of her own demons, and she isn't doted on like her older sister. It makes my skin crawl for the way she might taste my pain. Sometimes I want to hurt her for her visits. For her kindness.*

*It makes me hurt all the more, knowing she pities me.*

*My foster mother acts as if I don't exist.*

*I've never known tenderness from her, but I've seen her kiss the oldest sister. I've seen my foster father wrap his arm around her lovingly, joy in his eyes as he watches her play piano or kick a ball.*

*I've never gotten that.*

*A ball. A piano.*

*The affection.*

*The only thing I get to enjoy is languages.*

*Now, I'm shivering, the urine beneath me long cooled. I don't know how long I've been in here this time. I haven't eaten in what seems like days. I can feel my ribs. Feel the constant ache in my belly.*

*No one has offered me anything, let alone scraps.*

*It'll be over soon, they promised me.*

*I'll be eighteen soon, and I'll be* one *with them.*

*I close my eyes tight, the ache in my hand causing my fingers to tremble more violently than the rest of my naked body.*

*I try to sleep.*

*It's the only thing I can do.*

*I clutch the bobby pin in my hand, but I couldn't get it to open the padlock. I don't know what I'm doing. Next time I'm out, I'll have to use a computer and watch a video. Or try again when I can see, when the light spills in from the door for those stolen moments of time.*

*At first, locked up like this, you try to keep track. You want to know how many days have passed.*

*But then, after a while, when the voices in your head are screaming and crying and sometimes laughing, turning into real people—lovers.*

*Friends. Parents that want to protect you—when that happens, you…lose it.*

*I push it all away, try to find the numbness. The darkness inside my head. The wires of the cage dig into my spine, the hard floor leaving bruises along my bottom half, and extending my legs is agony instead of refreshing.*

*So, I stay in the ball.*

*And I try to disappear into myself.*

*For a moment, it works.*

*I'm gone.*

*Not here.*

*Not here.*

Not. Here.

*But then I hear it.*

*The door creaking open at the top of the stairs. I jump, my eyes flying open, chin quivering. Light spills down the stairs. Heavy footsteps, the smell of something sweet wafting in from the open door.*

Do they bake?

Do they cook?

Do they have meals without me, knowing I'm…starving?

*I see black shoes. Polished. Tailored pants. But I don't look beyond that.*

*I don't look, and when I hear his voice say, "You've done so well, Jeremiah. I think one more day, and you'll have served out your punishment for what you did to my daughter, hmm?" all I can do is plead.*

*I promised I wouldn't.*

*I told myself I was stronger than that.*

*That I would never want my beautiful sister, Sid, to do this. To beg. To kneel. To give.* In.

*But I can't stop it, the word that leaves my dry throat. "No. No." I didn't touch his daughter, the eldest. She lied.*

*She lied, because she's fucking insane.*

*Another whimper. Snot bubbles from my nose, tears well up behind my eyes, and I'm amazed, as I scream the last word, that I have enough liquid in my body to cry at all.*

*"NO!"*

*But he doesn't listen. He never does. He turns away, and I think, as he walks up the stairs…I think he laughs.*

*But I scramble upright, the bobby pin shaking as I use the light to find the keyhole in the padlock.*

*I die a little more, my chest caving in, that plea still flowing from my cracked lips. My broken heart, even as I dig the pin in.*

How did I get here?

And why me?

*I turn the bobby pin, my hands trembling. Just as he closes the door, the padlock falls to the floor, and for a moment, I can't even breathe.*

I'm fucking free.

# CHAPTER
## Thirty-Five

SID

"WHERE IS HE?"

Maverick inhales from his vape, looking like he wants to kill me, his brows knitted together, eyes full of anger. I don't care.

I haven't been able to leave this house.

*Just like old times.*

Tonight, in just a few hours, we're leaving. But Mav wanted to talk. *Fucker.*

Ella is on Maverick's lap as we sit in their living room. I try to ignore the fact she's here, that she *lives here*, but it's a little difficult, considering her current fucking position.

Mav has his hand on her ass as she leans back against him in the big leather chair, her head resting on his shoulder. She's in sweatpants, just like he is. But unlike him, she's got a shirt on.

Her green eyes are locked on mine, and she says, quietly to the room as Mav tosses the vape on the table, "I'm going to make cookies. Is that okay, Lilith?"

I wish everyone would stop fucking calling me that. That was his name for me. But I'm not for him anymore.

I force a smile anyway, even though that's the last thing I

feel like doing. Nearly a week has passed since our fight on the porch, since I cried in that pillow. I haven't seen Lucifer since. I've played cards with Maverick, watched movies alone. Ella has done a lot of fucking cooking, and Mav had a doctor come over to "check me". Baby is fine. I'm growing fine. The doctor said he'd come again in a month.

I'm not planning to be here in a month, but sure, he can knock himself out thinking I will.

I've heard nothing more about who is stalking the Unsaints and the Order of Rain. Elijah's wife is still missing, and apparently, he's trying to tear apart the world to find her. I heard Mav speaking in a low voice on the phone the other night. Elijah has been to Moscow, Berlin, down to Mexico, and to D.C. looking for his wife.

At least someone cares about that kind of shit.

Ella smiles back at me and turns to kiss Maverick on the head.

He slaps her ass as she gets up and her freckled face flushes pink, but she bounces out of the living room to the kitchen.

My legs are stretched out on the coffee table as I sit on the couch opposite Maverick. The overhead light is dimmed down, blackout curtains pulled closed. There's a TV beside Mav, and behind me is the door to the back porch. I think about walking outside. Maybe going upstairs.

I'm tired. Or maybe I'm just fucking depressed. All seems the same these days.

I'd be in my room right now except for the fact that my brother said he wanted to talk to me about something, and that we're leaving soon, so here I fucking am.

I hear Ella pull a pan out from under the stove, the sound probably louder than it needs to be. Mayhem looks over at her, flashing a smile, and she giggles.

I feel sick being so near their happiness.

Why can't my relationships be easy like that? Why can't *anything* be fucking easy like that?

"Lucifer told me. What my dad said to you." Mav clears his throat as I go rigid on the couch, my hands balled into fists on my borrowed sweats from Ella. "*Our* dad," he amends.

I hold his gaze, warmth flushing to my face, but I say nothing.

His eyes go to my left hand. I know what he's thinking about. The fucking X. Coagula.

To bind.

*"This doesn't mean shit to me. And it doesn't mean shit to you, either."* Jeremiah's words echo in my head. I think about repeating them for my brother but decide to keep my mouth closed.

He runs a hand over his face and closes his eyes a second. The inverted cross on his face is pulled down as he frowns, drumming his fingers on his sweats, the muscles on his chest flexing, his abs too. He's covered in tattoos.

I can't help thinking about Lucifer's. Just the one, on his thigh. The skull with smoke coming through one eye, a 'U' through the other.

Lucifer asked me to get one, too. He said after Ignis, I could do it.

*Like I couldn't before. Like these rules actually fucking mean something.*

Mayhem drops his hand and meets my gaze. "I didn't know. Ella didn't know."

I stare at him, unspeaking. I hear another clattering of pans in the kitchen and wonder if Ella just plans to tear the entire cabinet apart to pretend she isn't listening.

She has a scar too.

I've seen it.

And my brother's, although his hand is currently balled into a fist right now, only my name visible, over the top of it.

He didn't even marry her. But Lucifer did.

*He married me.*

Made sure I was his, in every fucking way. I force myself not to think about the baby. About how my world will be a little more fucked when it comes.

"She doesn't remember any of that night, Sid." His voice is hoarse.

I don't give a fuck about this, but saving me from saying anything at all, Ella drops another fucking pan. I swear to God if she doesn't—

"Pretty girl," Mayhem says softly, but his words aren't kind. There's a command in them. I recognize it well. Lucifer's used that tone with me many, many times.

"Yes, baby?" Ella replies.

Yeah. I never responded like that to any of his commands unless we were both naked. I roll my eyes, slide down on the couch and swing my legs around, so I'm on my side, hands tucked under the throw pillow.

"Could you be a little fucking quieter?" Mayhem asks in that same falsely sweet tone.

A moment of silence and I can't see Ella from this angle, but my eyes are on my brother's. I see a smirk pulling on his lips, and when Ella snarls back, "Do you want to bake your own fucking cookies?" I almost laugh.

That's exactly what I would've said too.

Except I never tried to bake Lucifer cookies. I tried to cook though. And failed. Many, many times.

He never seemed to care. I feel something uncomfortable twisting in my chest. Something like grief.

Mayhem bites his lip, his eyes flashing. "Keep talking to me like that and I'm going to come fuck you in—"

I cough, loudly, and my brother's eyes dart to me, then back to his girl.

"Go ahead, pretty girl," he says, waving his hand before his attention is back on me. "I'm going to deal with my father." It sounds like a promise, the way he says it to me.

I stare at him a second, not blinking. Trying to imagine what he's thinking. What he feels for me. Protectiveness? Guilt? I sit up all at once. Anger makes me clench my jaw as I stare at him, my eyes narrow, both hands back in fists. *"Deal with him?"* I echo, my words quiet.

He grips the edge of the leather chair he's in, the veins in his forearms stark against his golden skin. "You think I'd let him do that to you and get away with it?" he asks me in that same deadly voice he used on Ella.

I feel pressure build behind my eyes, and I'm so sick of fucking crying. "You let him get away with it for a long, long time." My words are shaky, but I can't stop talking anyway. "Since Sacrificium."

"I didn't know what he knew then, Angel. But I believe you. About Noctem."

I glance at the coffee table between us. Think about fucking flipping it over. "That's nice," I tell him, not looking at him. He should've fucking killed him before, but now because he *believes* me, he wants to do something about it? As if what Maddox did to me wasn't enough? What Lazar did to J?

"Don't fucking act like a bitch with me, okay, I'm just trying to—"

I count to three in my head.

*One.*

*Two.*

*Three.*

But I'm not any fucking calmer.

I stand, flipping the fucking table.

I'm jumping over it before I can stop myself, launching toward my brother, shoving him over the side of the chair which flips behind us.

His head hits the hardwood, my hands around his throat as his dig into my shoulders.

"You don't want to start some shit you can't finish, Angel," he growls, then flips me to my back.

I don't hear any more fucking pans rattling around, but Ella doesn't come over, either. Good thing, or I'd rip her apart too. Fuck them both. Fuck him for not believing our father was a piece of shit as soon as he found out what he did to me. Fuck Ella for fucking my husband.

"You should've murdered him that night," I snarl at him as he pins my arms to my side, his fingers curled around my wrists, my muscles shaking as I try to fight him back. "This is your fault. This is all your fucking fault."

He stops fighting for a second and I gain the advantage, my hands going to his throat as he frowns down at me. He grips my forearms again, straddling me, his knees on either side of my hips.

"Angel, I didn't—"

"Why did you let him live?" I drop my hands by my sides, to the floor, closing my eyes. I feel my chin quivering.

Mayhem's leaning over me, his fingers still around my forearms as he leans closer, his bare chest heaving.

"Why did you let him live?" I ask him again, my voice hoarse.

"I didn't know. I wanted to think..." I hear him swallow. "I wanted to think he could be better."

My stomach clenches with those words.

"And I'm sorry, Angel. I'm fucking sorry, and I know why you ran, and I know what Lucifer did." That grief in my chest curls into a tighter knot. I still don't open my eyes. As if, maybe, if I keep them closed, none of this will be real.

I spent a long, long time burying the worst experiences of my life.

Maybe I could do the same with my husband. Maybe I could forget he exists. Maybe I could run away and never look back this time. Break away from all of it. All of them.

"But fuck, Angel, he loves you. *He fucking loves you.*"

I still keep my eyes closed.

Silence rings out in the house. Silence as Maverick stays on top of me, his fingers around my forearms.

He leans down closer, his mouth inches from mine. I can feel his breath against my lips.

I hear footsteps.

I think about him. Ella. *My husband.*

How I wrecked them. How they put each other back together. If only for a moment.

I open my eyes.

Ella crouches down beside me as Maverick leans back, but he doesn't get up and doesn't let go.

Ella's hand is on Maverick's back, but another is on my brow, pushing my hair out of my face. Her green eyes are wide on mine as I stare up at both of them, my heart racing in my chest.

Are they going to try to fix me, too?

Ella is on her knees, and she leans close, presses her lips to my brow.

I flinch with her mouth on me, but I don't move away. I try to understand, instead. I know sex can heal.

I know Lucifer needed healing.

And for the first time, I regret what I did. I regret running, even with the knife to my head. The words Maddox whispered in the dark. Even dragging me to Noctem.

I shouldn't have run.

Maybe I could have helped Lucifer heal by staying. Maybe we were both so busy drowning in our own grief, we couldn't keep each other afloat.

But I could've tried.

*I could've fucking tried.*

But then I think about Lucifer leaving Jeremiah in that cage, and I don't know what to feel anymore. What to think.

*What to do.*

Maverick's fingers dig in deeper against my forearm as Ella's lips linger on my brow, but he doesn't say anything, and when she leans back up, her hand still pushing back my hair, his grip loosens.

"I'm going to take care of my father," he says, his voice full of barely contained anger as he stares at me. "But first, we need to talk about Ignis."

"I don't want to—"

His hips grind against my pelvis as he leans closer, gently placing his hand over my mouth. The hand with my name on it.

I try to feel nothing at his dick against me.

Try, and fucking fail.

*What the fuck is wrong with me?*

He doesn't smile at me, doesn't give any indication he knows what I'm feeling, even though it's impossible to miss and I'm sure he and Ella both know that.

"Unfortunately, Angel, I don't care what you want." He drags his hand down my lips, to my throat, running his thumb over the hollow of it. "You're going to be there, because it's *for you.*"

I arch a brow, my pulse pounding too fast, and I know, underneath his hand, he can feel it.

I avoid looking at Ella as his cock grinds against the seam of my sweats.

His movement is subtle, and I think he's just shifting his hips but *fuck.*

"An initiation. And as Lucifer's wife," he glances at my hand by my side, "more than that, you've got to be there." He looks at Ella, but I keep staring at him.

"Don't worry, pretty girl. Next year's is for you." He smiles at her, and I'm sure she returns it, but I don't look away from my brother.

He turns his head, gaze back on mine, hand still around my throat. "We'll have extra guards here, on the lookout for... anything unusual. And I know you're worried about Jeremiah." He leans down close to me, his mouth against my cheek as he says his next words. "When Ignis is through, I'll make sure we find him, too. So you can give him a proper fucking goodbye."

I open my mouth to protest, but his hand is back over it, drowning out my words.

"For now, he can look after himself. He's a big boy." Mav presses his lips to my cheek, drags his mouth to my ear. "Lucifer, though? Not so much. *He needs you.*"

# CHAPTER

Thirty-Six

## SID

"WHY DON'T YOU GO UPSTAIRS?" Atlas's voice startles me out of my thoughts.

I flinch, turning to look over my shoulder at the back door of Liber. I'm on the steps leading out to the parking lot, no one out here but guards, all six of them keeping an eye on me of course.

I can hear music thudding from the stone mansion at my back and I pick at another blade of grass, turning away from Atlas.

He's got on a backwards cap, and I briefly wonder where Natalie is. I haven't seen her at all tonight. Then again, as soon as Mav, Ella, and I parked here, I made off to disappear. First to the bathroom, then when I was sure Lucifer was getting fucked up somewhere without me, I came out here.

"I'm good here," I tell Atlas dismissively as I stare back out at the parking lot.

I hear nothing but the heavy bass for a moment, then Atlas's steps as he approaches and my stomach sinks. Atlas is nice. The nicest one of them all, but I don't really want to talk.

He sits down beside me with a sigh, and I catch the scent of his cologne. Something aquatic.

He's got his elbows on his knees, hands dangling between them as he stares out into the night.

"You okay?" he asks softly.

I roll my eyes, unseen by him. "Obviously not."

He laughs, and it's a nice sound. Unlike Lucifer's cruel rasp. "I didn't think so."

I let the silence stretch between us, ignore the guards darting glances our way as I stare up at the moon. "Why are you out here? Where's your girlfriend?"

He seems to tense beside me, his spine going rigid as he sits up straighter. I can see it out of the corner of my eye, and I marvel at the fact every Unsaint has fucking relationship problems. I guess it should be no surprise, but Atlas is kind. He deserves something good.

"She's not my girlfriend anymore," he says, and his words are low and angry. Almost…evil. Like there's something lurking beneath that smile he always wears.

"Oh?" I ask quietly, not wanting to press too hard, but it would be nice to think about someone else's pain for a moment instead of being consumed with all the thoughts of my own.

He blows out a breath, adjusts his hat, drops his hand back to his thigh. "Don't change the subject, Sid," he says quietly. "Why don't you go find your man? He needs you, you know?"

Just before I can cuss him out, he turns his head, his dark eyes locking on mine as I keep ripping apart a blade of grass with my fingers.

"We all need someone, and I know you two have fucked each other over a thousand times." His jaw clenches as he glances down at the space between us a moment, and I wonder in what ways Natalie fucked him over. Was it the drugs? Like my husband?

His eyes meet mine again after a moment. "But he's

having a fucking psychotic break, and he doesn't want to hurt you. He wants you to...help him."

I stand, taking a step back, dropping the blades of grass. "I'm not a psychiatrist, if you didn't know that, Atlas—"

He stands, too, towering over me, a skull T-shirt stretched tight over his chest. "I *did* know that, thank you very much. I'm not as dumb as you seem to think I look." He glares at me, his jaw ticking. "But he can't see a fucking psychiatrist, and I don't think either of you are looking for a *healthy* relationship." He cocks his head, glaring down at me. His face is boyishly handsome, but right now, he looks a little scary. "You don't want that. You don't want someone that doesn't fight for you." He steps closer. "Someone that doesn't hurt you. *You want to be roughed up, Sid."* Another step and that aquatic cologne seems to consume me as I stare into his dark eyes. They're not nearly black, like Cain's. No, they're some sort of brown-blue mix, and the shards of blue seem to glint in the lights around the parking lot. "And he *wants* to rough you up, but he doesn't want you to *fucking run all the goddamn time.* Grow some balls and stay."

For a moment, we just stare at each other, our chests heaving, anger between us, and it's not even towards each other. His is no doubt to Natalie, and mine to Lucifer. He's just taking his pain out on the wrong person.

I get that.

Even so, he needs to back the fuck off.

After a moment, I step away from him, toward the back door. "You must be just as dumb as you fucking look," I tell him with a shrug, "because I don't have balls, shithead." Then I turn around and head inside.


I STOP OUTSIDE OF OUR ROOM, AND I DON'T HEAR ANYTHING. Even the music is drowned out up here, on the hallway with all the boys' bedrooms. I snuck in through the back stairwell, successfully avoided seeing anyone.

Now, with the silence beyond the door, relief spreads through me. I can go inside and fucking sleep. I'm sure he knows I'll be in here and leave me the fuck alone. Or maybe he'll be so fucked up, he won't be able to find his way up the stairs at all.

Either way, I reach for the door, find it unlocked. Good thing, because I don't have the damn key. My copy is somewhere at our house, which I've avoided like the plague since I saw Ophelia in there.

Fucking Ophelia.

My stomach twists into knots.

I push thoughts of her aside and step into the dark room, taking a deep breath as I close the door at my back.

But immediately, I know something is wrong.

The lights are off in the room, but down the hall, the blinds are open, from the balcony, and the dim light casts a glow on two people.

One is laid out on the table. The one Lucifer and I had breakfast at in the mornings that week we came here after we got married. He smoked out there, too, careful to blow the smoke away from me, unlike that first time we met at the intersection. He drank too, mimosas in the morning, but no fucking blow.

Not yet.

Not then.

Maybe he was stronger then. Maybe the nightmares hadn't started. Maybe our fights hadn't been so fucking vicious.

I don't see any coke now, either, but I see plastic cups. A bottle of vodka about to teeter off the edge of the table, dangerously close with every thrust my husband makes into Ophelia.

She's stretched out over the table, her arms over her head

which is tilted back, her mouth open in ecstasy. Her big tits are bouncing as my husband pounds into her, slapping one of her tits as I watch him, one hand on her upper thigh, pulling her closer to him.

I see his core muscles flex, his pants around his ankles, and Ophelia's bikini top tied around her throat where he must have been choking her, because after he slaps her tit, he grabs the string and pulls, hard.

She gags, the moans that were coming from her mouth—faint, because the sliding glass door is closed—dying off.

His head is tilted back, the long, pale column of his throat exposed. I see the Unsaints tattoo on his thigh. The scars down the middle of it.

So many.

So many that aren't mine.

I think I must be in shock, because for a long, long moment, I just hold up my hand and stare at it even though I can't see it in the dark. But I know it's there.

*Coagula.*

I curl my fingers into a fist, think of when he carved that knife across me. When he put my blood in his mouth.

Left Jeremiah to burn in that building at our back.

The hole in my heart gets bigger. I drop my hand to my low belly and watch them, wondering if she's on birth control, because my husband probably doesn't know what the fuck a condom is, despite what he said.

Like seeing a car wreck, I can't look away, numbness flowing through me, and I take a step further into the room. I see the bed is made, and I don't know why I feel some small amount of relief at the fact that he didn't fuck her in there.

The same place he held me down. Promised to never leave me.

I step closer to the balcony door, and I can see my own shadow reflected from the light outside. I look small, like a kid.

Ophelia, with her curvy hips, big tits, and the meat on her

thighs that Lucifer grabs now, still holding that bikini top tight around her throat—her face is red and she's tugging at it, trying to pull it off—looks like a woman.

I take another step, bile rising up the back of my throat.

*But I'm pregnant with his fucking child.*

Another step.

With a trembling hand, I reach for the door and I think for a split second of locking it. Locking them out of on this balcony to look out at the woods beyond Liber all night until someone checks on them, and I assume that'd be a fucking while.

But I can't do it.

I don't want to.

I don't want him out here with her.

Instead, I pull open the door. I feel as if I'm walking underwater, everything in slow motion. I can't *think*, and I can't *feel*.

For a moment after I open that door, nothing happens. Or rather, Lucifer just keeps fucking her, biting his bottom lip, his eyes closed.

Ophelia is still clawing at the bikini string, and my husband is totally oblivious to the fact that she might pass out if he doesn't let go.

A warm spring breeze fans over me as I stand there, in the doorway, neither of them noticing me.

Lucifer groans, finally bowing his head, and just as he does, the vodka bottle topples off of the table and shatters on the concrete floor of the balcony.

Neither of them seem to react, but I flinch, wrapping my arms around myself, my mouth so dry, I don't think I could speak even if I knew what to say.

And I don't.

Lucifer releases the string of the bikini, his hand going to her breast as he grabs her, hard enough to leave a bruise, that groan guttural and from his core. She's panting, her breaths loud and nervous, chest rising and falling.

I see Lucifer's fingers digging into her flesh, her nipple peeking beneath his splayed fingers.

And I think they still don't see me.

As my stomach churns, my own fingers dig into my upper arms. I think I'm going to vomit as my husband releases into her, grabbing her breast still like it's his fucking lifeline, the veins in his forearms straining against his skin.

But when I look up, another groan, softer this time, escaping his mouth, he's staring right at me.

"Hey, baby girl," he says softly, his bare chest heaving, the muscles of his six-pack flexing, the scars a reminder of all he's done for me.

The position he's in a reminder of all the ways we've fucked each other over.

"I was wondering where you were." Then he pulls out, and Ophelia scrambles up and off the table, covering herself with her hands.

I shift my gaze from Lucifer to his "childhood friend", and my fists clench.

"What the fuck are you doing?" she screams at me, her legs crossed, arms too.

I step through the door, my boots crunching on the glass all over the cement floor.

Lucifer rolls off a condom, pulls his pants up at my side, watching us.

"What are you doing here? You fucking whore!" Ophelia's voice is high-pitched. Grating on my last goddamn nerve.

And when I reach down to pick up the handle of the vodka bottle, spiked glass at the ends of it from where it shattered because my husband was fucking this cunt, I know I lost my last nerve a long, long time ago.

And all this rage? This fear?

I want to take it out on someone I can make fucking bleed.

# CHAPTER
## Thirty-Seven

**LUCIFER**

I TOSS the condom to the ground, with the shattered glass. But I don't know if Sid saw it. She's got that bottle in her hand, and she's advancing on Ophelia like she's going to slit her fucking throat.

I prop my elbow in one hand, my fingers over my lips as I watch her, my chest tight. I know I should feel bad, and maybe I would if my head wasn't spinning and I wasn't having trouble standing from everything I drank tonight, but at the same time…she fucked Jeremiah.

She didn't want to see me.

She's cried over him.

*She'd rather be with him.*

*We're on a fucking break.*

Still, seeing my wife backing a woman against the balcony railing, a weapon in hand…it's all I've ever wanted from her.

For her to want me like I want her. Love me like I love her. Be fucking obsessed with me *like I am with her.*

Ophelia is still screaming, her hands over her chest, and I bite back my smile as Lilith clenches her jaw.

And this is Lilith.

My wife from hell, coming back to me, where she fucking belongs.

"Shut the fuck up," she snarls, whipping that glass up to O's throat.

Ophelia's scream dies from her lips. She darts her eyes over to me, but I just shrug, cocking a brow at her. She knew I was married. She can deal with the consequences.

"You fucked my husband." Those words are a low, husky growl, and my dick gets hard all over again hearing it.

"You fucking left him!" Ophelia shrieks, trying to back up further, but the railing is digging into her shoulders, and there's nowhere for her to go.

Sid glances at me. I know those words got to her, because they're true.

I say nothing, staring right back at her.

She did leave me. Left me in fucking pieces. I don't even know why she was looking for me now. I thought she'd jump on London's dick, and I don't know what we do after this, but I want to see what she'll do. I want to see how she'll claim me.

She turns away from me and Ophelia lifts one hand to push her.

I clench my teeth, my fingers closing into fists. I'll push that bitch over the balcony if she hurts my wife.

But Sid slaps her hand down, brings the shards of the vodka bottle to O's chest, digging in deep enough to make her bleed.

I see it, the blood welling as O looks down, her mouth open, her eyes wide, chest heaving, which brings the glass further into her skin.

Sid smiles, her eyes flicking up to O's, but she doesn't drag the glass down. She just rests it there and O looks up, horrified, one hand down by her side, the other still covering her tits.

"You're going to get your shit, and get out of here," Sid

says quietly, not moving the glass, even as blood trails in rivulets down O's chest and she can barely breathe.

"He wanted—"

Sid throws the glass to the side where it shatters all over again, but this time her hand shoots out to O's throat, fingers tight around her. She grabs her long hair, yanking down hard, pulling O to her level.

*Yeah. Get mad baby girl. Fight for me like I fought for you.*

*I fucking killed for her. I'd do anything for her.*

*All I ever wanted was her to do something once for me.*

"I don't care what he fucking wanted. *Get. The fuck.* Out." She releases O, then shoves her back into the railing. She brings her hand up and slaps the fuck out of her, and O shrieks, her hand raising to the side of her face as she does.

*If she hits my wife back, I'll kill her.*

But before she gets a chance, Sid turns on her heel, struts across the fucking glass, her hands fisted at her sides.

*I just want to chase after her ass.*

"Aren't you going to do something about that?" Ophelia shrieks, swiping at the blood on her chest, pulling on her bikini, shaking out the glass as she does. She pulls up her bottoms, then adjusts the top on her chest. "Aren't you going to—"

"Get out, O." I gesture toward the door Sid just walked in through. "That wasn't even her mad." I flash Ophelia a smile. "Trust me, you don't wanna see that. It gets fucking ugly."

I watch as she stares up at me, blood streaked across her chest, tears down her eyes.

*I think I should feel something.*

*I fucking don't.*

*My wife is in there.*

Ophelia finally breaks off into a sob, then stomps into the room, racing down the hall toward the door. I don't know where Sid is, I'm just glad she doesn't stop O from flinging the door open, slamming it back and running down the hall, sobbing.

"Lilith?" I finally whisper in the silence as I stand in the room, closing the sliding glass door at my back.

I cast my eyes around the darkness, but everything seems to spin around me, and I have to grip the handle of the door to hold myself steady. I don't hear anything, and for a second, I'm worried she's left me.

Again.

I'm worried she's gone, and her anger was for seeing someone play with something she thought was hers, not because she wanted to come back.

Not because she wanted *me*.

But then I hear her soft voice and all she says is, "I'm going to fucking kill you."

# CHAPTER
## Thirty-Eight

SID

HE FLIPS on the light in the bedroom, sees me sitting on the chair across from the bed. My hands are shaking, which makes me think of my brother, but I try to push that thought aside.

And it's easy enough to do, because all I can see in my head, playing on repeat, is Lucifer fucking Ophelia on that goddamn table.

I stare up at him.

I notice his eyes are bleary, and he's unsteady on his feet, like he has to hold onto the door to keep himself from collapsing onto the bed.

I ball my hands into fists in my lap.

"How do you want me to die?" he asks me quietly, his voice a rasp. There's no smile on his face, though, and his words don't sound condescending. I don't know why I hold onto that. Why I take the scraps he gives me, but maybe it's because I've torn him apart, too.

Maybe it's because I know I don't deserve anything more than what I walked in on.

"She feel good?" I throw the question out with indifference, even though the pain is eating me alive.

His eyes narrow into beautiful blue slits and he leans back

against the door, his palms flat against the glass behind him. "You really wanna know?" He jerks his chin, to the door of our bedroom. "Where were *you*? Who were *you* fucking, baby girl?" His eyes flit to my throat, then back to my face, and I see that beautiful vein in his neck pulsing.

I shake my head. "Answer my fucking question."

He scoffs, knocking his head back against the glass as he looks up at the ceiling. "You think I'm going to let you walk away again?"

I bite the inside of my cheek hard enough to taste blood. "I didn't ask for your goddamn permission. I asked if it felt good. Fucking her?"

He dips his chin, his gaze leveling mine, a dimple in his pale face flashing as he smiles at me. "All pussy feels good."

I roll my eyes, standing and cocking my head, trying to calm my racing pulse. There're a few feet between us, but if we get any closer, this will turn dangerous. "All dick does too." I shrug. "Especially Jeremiah's. I think he's about the same size as you, maybe a little thicker." I throw up my hands, turn to go as his expression turns murderous.

For a beat, he lets me walk away. Three steps, and I think I'll have to do it because he's waiting to call my bluff. Three steps, and I'm passing our bed, my mind spinning. I guess I'll go to Mav's room. Maybe I'll find Ophelia and actually fucking kill her.

"Lilith," he finally calls, his voice hoarse. Broken.

I still, my back to him, my chest rising and falling rapidly. *Don't turn around.*

"Come back," he finally whispers, and my chest cracks with those words. "Come back and fix me. Fix us. *Fix this.*"

*Now he wants to fix shit.*

I bite my lip, pressure building again behind my eyes. I hate crying, and I've cried so much for this boy. For the future I didn't ask for. A legacy I never wanted to be a part of.

I swallow down all of that, because all I can think about is him fucking O, his veiny hand wrapped around her breast.

Jealousy claws at me, and I try to reason with myself. I try to tell myself that I deserve it. That I've done worse.

That I obliterated his trust when I left, and I made it worse by sleeping with the one man he may never forgive me for.

I can't reason with myself. The thing about logic is that it's hard to find in the face of strong emotions, especially when you're drowning in them. And right now, I'm well under water.

I spin around, and before I can think through it, I'm running at him, my palms held out as they collide with his chest, knocking him back against the glass door, his head hitting it with a thud.

I'm hitting him, every inch I can find, all along his torso, his chest, his fucking face. "How long did you fucking wait?" I scream at him. "How long did you fucking wait, Lucifer?" My chest is heaving, my palms burning as I slap him, and I curl my fingers into fists, punching him instead. Along his stomach, his arms.

He just stands there, his hands by his side, taking it.

"Did you fuck her as soon as I left? When I was trying to save *your baby's* fucking life?" My voice breaks, tears streaming down my cheeks, and I don't even know where I'm hitting him anymore. All I know is it feels good for my fist to collide with his flesh. It feels good to take out all of this pain on someone who deserves it.

It's not Ophelia.

She's not the fucking problem.

It's him.

*It's us.*

My hands are shaky and I'm breathing hard. I take a small step back, catching my breath, seeing the red marks on his pale skin.

But I'm not done.

He opens his mouth to speak and I lift my hand, slap him across the face. His head spins, and for a moment, he just stares at the wall, away from me.

I still have my hand raised, I'm still panting, rage pushing through me in hot waves. Rage, jealousy, grief.

I want to curl up into a ball and fall apart.

But I don't want to give him that.

After a moment, he flexes his jaw, turns his head to stare at me.

I drop my hand but curl it into a fist.

"How long did *you* fucking wait?" he asks me quietly, his voice full of venom. "Huh? Did you let him fuck you in the car? Suck his dick while he was driving, baby girl? How many times did he bruise you?" His words are little more than a whisper, but they're so fucking cold. "You *left me* when things got hard. You fucking *left me when I needed you*—"

"They took me from our house!" I scream at him, my fingers coming to my hair as I step closer to him, going up on my tiptoes. "They took me from my goddamn house!"

His jaw ticks. "They took Ella, too," he snarls. "Guess where she is? Here, with *your fucking brother, where she belongs.*"

My mouth goes dry, my tongue, too. How can he not see he's hurting me? How can he be so fucking self-righteous after what I walked in on? *Did he ever actually love me?*

I don't know what he sees on my face, but he steps closer. So close we're nearly touching.

I tense, wanting to run again. To fucking bolt.

"Did you ever care?" I ask him instead. "Did you ever care I was gone? What the fuck is wrong with you? Do you just want to own me? How could you fucking *fuck her* again?"

His face is expressionless. I don't know what he's thinking. What he's feeling. He's so hard to read, and I swear, most of the time, he really does hate me.

I feel like I'm going to break again.

I feel like this has to end.

*This has to fucking end.*

But he still doesn't say a goddamn word.

"I fucking hate you," I tell him, my words breaking. "I hate you. I can't stand the fucking sight of you. You have done *nothing* but ruin my fucking life. You should've let me die, Lucifer."

His expression changes. His eyes are big and sad, and he takes another step closer.

"You should've let me die, if you were just going to…" I bring my hands back to my hair, pulling at it and closing my eyes. "If you were just going to fuck me up and fuck me over, you should've just *let. Me. Die.*" My voice is hoarse, and I can't get the last words out before a sob rips through me, and his arms are around me.

He smells like vodka, and *her*, and I hate him all the more for it, but I'm too tired.

So, fucking tired.

I just want things to be okay, one way or another.

*I just want shit to be okay. I just want this to end.*

"I'm sorry," he whispers, my head against his chest, his head resting on mine. "I'm fucking sorry. I didn't think you cared. I just thought…"

His own body shudders, but I can't hold him.

I can't.

Not now.

"I thought you never loved me, when you left." His arms are tighter around me, and there's a lump in my throat that I can't break through even as I cry in his arms. "I thought you'd never come back. And I'm scared, Lilith. I'm fucking terrified I'm never going to be okay again. *I see him.*" His words are so broken, and he pulls back from me, leaving me disoriented.

He slides down against the glass door, coming to the floor, his fists against his temple as he bows his head. "I fucking see *him*, every time I close my eyes. And I see *Jeremiah* fucking you.

*Raping you.* And I see...*everyone* that hurt you. Everyone I fucking burned for you."

I stare down at him, torn between going to him, and leaving him. Between thinking he deserves this shit and thinking I should've been better.

*I should've been better.*

"But what does it do for you?" I ask him, biting my lip as I take a step back, his head still in his hands, his shoulders shaking. I don't want his pain to vanquish mine. He can't do that to me. He can't fucking manipulate me with that. "What does it do for you to fuck her? *Are you in love with her?*"

He picks his head up, his eyes bleary, those shadows so thick beneath them. I don't know if he's sleeping at all. Has he been fucking her in our bed?

I think I'm going to ask it, it's on the tip of my tongue, but his red rimmed eyes connect with mine and he says, "I'm in love with *you*. I've only *ever* been in love with you, Lilith." His hands are on his knees, and he's so fucking tall and so strong but sitting on the hardwood floor, crying at my feet, he looks like a child.

"But it...makes everything stop. The sex makes it all...*stop.*"

"That's your excuse?" I counter, shaking my head. "Your excuse for fucking her while I've been holed away with Mav—"

"I haven't," he cuts me off, his eyes narrowing, jaw clenching. "I haven't fucked her since you've been back. Not until tonight."

"Why?" I ask, wanting to scream. Wanting to hit him again. To shake him. "Why would you do that to me? To *us?*"

"I wanted to know if it hurt you, as much as it hurt me, thinking of him *fucking inside of you.*" He stands, comes toward me. His hands come to my face, and he pulls me close as I stay rigid in his arms. "I wanted to know if you ever gave a fuck at all—"

"Get off of me."

He blinks at me, surprised. So, fucking shocked, because since we've met, he's been calling the shots. Controlling me. Dominating me. Belittling me.

I know he's going through some shit, but what he did…

"Get the fuck off of me."

Shocking me, he drops his hands.

Steps back.

Then he groans, a low, throaty sound just before he turns to the television against the wall, opposite the bed, and yanks it off the mount.

He throws it to the floor, the cord unhooking from the outlet, and the sound of it shattering on the hardwood makes me flinch. My limbs feel shaky, and I'm holding my breath, watching him.

He's not done.

There's a desk in the corner of the room, a spare laptop plugged into charge. He stalks to the desk, grabs the computer and throws it against the sliding glass door.

My mouth drops open, my pulse pounding in my ears.

He upturns the desk, smashes it into the wall, two of the legs snapping.

"What do you want from me?" he screams, turning to face me, his bare chest heaving. "You fucking run one minute, you cut a girl over me the next? What the fuck do you *want, Lilith?*"

He brings his hand to his pocket, pulls out a knife, one like I have. One that *is mine.* He thumbs the blade, brings the tip to his inner forearm, and before I can breathe, he drags it down, hard, blood oozing in the wake of the blade.

"You want me to die for you? *You want me to fucking die for you, too?*" He keeps dragging it up his arm, another long line of blood dripping, his already pale complexion even more ashen.

My throat closes up, but I cross the room and grab his arms. He tries to fight me, keeping the knife to his skin, but I say his name, over and over and over again, clutching the handle with shaky fingers, and in the struggle, my fingers are coated with his warm blood.

The knife finally falls to the floor between us and I stare in horror at the line he drew. It's not deep enough to kill him, but crimson contrasts with his pale skin in a way that makes me feel sick.

"What are you doing?" I scream at him, yanking his arms down.

He stares at me through red, bleary eyes, dropping his arms, blood dripping down his fingers, onto the floor.

"What the fuck are you doing?" I scream again, my chest heaving, my mind splintering.

"I just want you," he says, his voice broken, his shoulders sagging. "I just fucking want you. I've always wanted you. It's always been me and you since I saw you at that intersection, Lilith. But you..." He shakes his head, biting his tongue as he stares at the floor, at the blood.

I think I should grab a towel or a shirt, but I'm rooted to the spot, watching all that blood. All that pain.

After a moment, he lifts his head up. "You want him."

I can't breathe as I stare at his grief, meeting his gaze.

"After everything I did for you, all the ways he hurt you...*you still want him.*"

I don't know what to say. I don't know how to feel. I know that I love him. That I want him to be okay. That I think I might die if something bad ever happened to him. That if he'd killed himself right here in front of me, I'd probably go right after him.

But I love J, too.

And I don't know how to stop.

### SID

"HE'S REALLY MISSED YOU." Ella's words at my back make me flinch. I didn't hear her come down the stairs, down to the basement my brother held Ria in.

I hope Ria is still okay.

Mav said because Elijah's wife, Edith, is missing, the 6 haven't bothered discussing her at Council again. And now it's like Mayhem has wanted to destroy any sign of her time down here. The space is well lit, full of sparkling new gym equipment, a place for yoga mats surrounded by mirrors which is where I am now, in downward fucking dog.

I slowly lower to my knees, a hand on my belly.

It's hard to believe I'm only just over halfway through with this pregnancy.

I tuck a strand of hair behind my ear, the rest secured in a messy bun. One day until Ignis and I don't see the point.

After Liber last week, with Lucifer…he walked out.

Mav said he crashed in his room. My brother bandaged his arm, but he didn't tell him anything. Didn't talk about Ophelia, about our fight.

I decided not to tell him about it, either.

I haven't seen Lucifer since, and I've asked Mav to check

on him, which he has every day. But I don't know how to help him. I don't know how to help myself.

And I don't want to hear about my husband from Ella now.

I already can't get the image of him fucking O out of my goddamn head. The memory of that knife sinking into his forearm.

I feel sick. There was so much blood.

"Yeah? He tell you that while he was fucking you? Or maybe when he was railing a line?" I stretch my legs out, flex my bare toes, see my feet look a little swollen. I reach for the water bottle off the side of my black mat, unscrew the cap as Ella watches me.

She's got her arms crossed, her long red hair loose around her face. She's in cut-off denim shorts, a dark green tank that shows her belly and dips down low to show off her cleavage too.

I try not to think about my husband touching her.

I try to tell myself it doesn't matter anyway.

"Ignis will help him," she says quietly, glancing down at her bare feet, flexing her toes. They're painted in the color of a fucking rainbow.

I swallow down the water, plastic crinkling beneath my fingers. Then I screw the cap back on, smack the bottle against my opposite hand, over my useless scar. I don't say anything, because I don't have anything fucking nice to say.

"*You* could help him." Her voice is stronger now, like she's just grown some fucking balls or something while she picks her head up and looks me in the eye.

I arch a brow, feeling white-hot rage course through me. "How's that? Because one of the last nights I spent with my husband, he held a knife to my face." *Seems to be his thing.* "And maybe he's having some kind of delusions. Maybe he's hurting. But the eight ball he did before bed that night probably didn't help either, right?" Everyone feels sorry for him.

I do too.

But no one seems to get that *I did not ask for any of this.*

I take a deep breath in, glance at my reflection in the mirror at my side. My cheeks are flushed from my workout, but I see something else, too. The bump in my belly, straining against my black tank. More prominent now. Still, if someone didn't know me, they might think I'd had a huge meal, but the irony in that is no one ever saw me that didn't know me.

Dates? Hanging out outside of our house? Spending time together that wasn't running or screaming and yelling inside the walls of our home?

That didn't exist between Lucifer and me.

"He messed up," Ella whispers, and I stare at myself in the mirror taking in my gray eyes. The scar over my brow. My hollow cheekbones. I haven't eaten much of Ella's food on principle.

*She fucked my husband.*

"But he's...he's really hurting. With his dad, and you know, you leaving, and—"

"You don't fucking know him." I stand, too fast, the room spinning as I close my eyes, bring the side of the cold water bottle up to my brow, waiting a moment to steady myself. Trying not to see him destroying our room in my head. Him cutting himself, for me.

"Are you okay—"

"You don't fucking know him," I say again, lowering the bottle by my side and glaring across the gym floor at Ella. "And you don't know me. Don't try to play some type of armchair fucking psychiatrist, okay, Ella? You have *no idea* what we've been through—"

"But you've been through something, haven't you?" Her question is quiet, but her tone is strong. She lifts her chin, takes a few steps toward me until we're only a couple of feet apart.

I grit my teeth, try to breathe evenly so I don't attack her like I did Mayhem. She's a lot taller than me, a lot sturdier. But I've been training, and I don't know where Mayhem met her, but she's seemed to be happy here locked away in this castle.

I've got a lot of anger at having my freedom taken from me.

I think anger can beat size any day.

"You've been through it, together," she keeps talking, holding my gaze. "And when you weren't together..." She runs her tongue over her teeth, glancing down, then back up. "He's been falling apart without you, Sid. And I know I don't know you. Or him, really. But it's easy to see when someone is hurting. And it's easy to see when it's from a loss. And when he lost you, he couldn't feel anything but that pain."

I don't know if she's trying to guilt trip me, but I think of Jeremiah. Of how he was falling apart without me. All those years. All those *fucking* years.

But before I can say anything, Ella keeps talking.

"I'm not trying to make you feel bad. And I don't know what Jeremiah Rain feels for you." She stumbles over his name like he's a god that she doesn't want to summon to this house. I think about his mouth on her, then Lucifer's dick inside of her.

*Which one hurt worse?*

"I'm sure he loves you too. But..." She trails off, chewing on her bottom lip. I realize I'm hanging onto her words.

That maybe I don't have this right.

That maybe I did the wrong thing. That maybe my husband has problems, like I do, like J does, and when I ran to J for shelter, I took away Lucifer's.

My throat feels tight as I wait for Ella to finish. I hate her for fucking my husband, but I think, if I feel this way about him with *her*...how does Lucifer feel? About me, willingly sleeping with the man he watched hurt me?

If Ella had hurt my husband, *then* he fucked her...

My stomach twists up into knots.

I don't know what to do.

*I don't know what the fuck I'm supposed to do.*

"Fucking say something!" I scream at Ella, throwing the bottle to the ground.

She doesn't even flinch. She just meets my gaze, steels her spine.

Then she says, "Would he let you go?"

That knot grows tighter.

"Jeremiah?" She whispers his name. Takes another step toward me. My knees are trembling. I think about Lucifer telling me he was done with me at the cabin. "Would he let you go, if he knew that's what you really wanted?"

"Lucifer didn't exactly—"

"He came for you because he thought you were in danger. Because he thought you would be physically safer *here.*" Ella smiles small at me, tilting her head. "But where is he now? He hasn't come by, because he knows you want the space. And it's killing him." Her voice goes hoarse with those words.

My throat feels raw, and I think about Noctem. When I ran to Jeremiah. What I said to Maverick. Sometimes we run to save people from ourselves.

But maybe I didn't do that.

Maybe to save him, I needed to *be there.*

"It's killing him that you're so close, and you don't want him here."

I think about Ophelia, but for some reason, I don't want to tell Ella. I just don't want to relive it. Instead I say, "But he's dragging me to Ignis—"

"This date has been planned since he made you one of them. The 6 took us, Sid, and if he doesn't do things the way they want, by the stupid book," she shrugs, shaking her head, "it's another excuse for them to take you."

"But Maddox—"

"Maddox is going to die." Those words sound haunting

coming from Ella's pretty mouth. But they sound like something else too. Something they might not have sounded like from my brother or my husband, because they both like to talk a lot of shit. Coming from Ella, those words sound like truth.

And I know it'll hurt Mayhem. Just like...

"Just like Lucifer's dad," Ella continues. "He killed Lazar for you." She wasn't around then. She doesn't know about that. I want to tell her that. I want to argue with her. Tell her to fuck off, but I don't. Because she's coming at me with the painful truths, and for once, I can't run from them. "He's hurting because of it. He might've hated his dad, but...he was the only family he had."

"No," I tell her, unable to hold my tongue again. "He has Jeremiah—"

"And I think that's why...he hates him all the more. For what he did to you. For what they went through, growing up." She drops her gaze, and I wonder what she knows. I wonder if Lucifer ever told Mayhem about leaving J in that fucking cage.

Why? Why did he fucking do it?

Could I forgive him for that?

"He needs you, Sid." Ella steps back, like she's going to go, and for one wild moment, I don't want her to. I want her to stay. I want her to tell me I'm not crazy. Tell me how to fix this. Fix him. *Fix us.* "And I think you wanted to heal things with Jeremiah. But you haven't tried to run again."

I start to say something about the guards, but she keeps talking.

"And from what I know of you," she smiles softly, "I don't think you'd let a few guards that wouldn't dare lay a hand on you stop you from going."

Then she turns and heads back up the stairs, the hole in my chest growing a little bigger as she walks away, leaving those uncomfortable truths to fester inside me.

# CHAPTER Forty

## SID

I SHOVE some leggings and a few tanks into my black back-pack, nervously darting a glance toward my open bedroom door. Mayhem brought me here, said Lucifer was *out*.

I wonder if he's fucking Ophelia again. I swear to God, it's like I can *smell her* in this house. My stomach flips thinking about it, and with that sensation, I'm thinking about the steady, strong heartbeat whooshing through the doppler when the doctor came to check in on me at Mayhem's house.

Lucifer has never heard that sound.

Never heard what our baby sounds like in my belly.

A pang of guilt stabs through me, but I zip up my bag, throwing it over my shoulder, tucking a strand of hair behind my ear.

I think about Jeremiah.

Wonder where the fuck he is.

If he had anything to do with Edith's disappearance. He might have been in that crate—my skin crawls thinking about it—but he controls an empire.

Lucifer was going to meet with Elijah at Sanctum before we left for Ignis. I don't really know Ezra, but I remember how he held me that night I found out that Jeremiah had been the one to...hurt me.

I feel queasy, my mouth going dry.

Glancing at our made bed, the empty vodka bottles on Lucifer's nightstand, a bright blue coke straw, I grit my teeth and turn my back on it all, heading to the door.

The house is quiet, Mayhem is waiting outside with Ella. They promised to keep Lucifer busy if he pulled up. I'm just not quite ready...not quite ready to feel. To talk. I don't know what he has planned with me for Ignis, but I have a feeling I won't be ready for that either.

I take some small comfort in knowing that Ella is coming too, even though it's not really *her* initiation.

Blowing out a breath, gripping the strap of my bag slung across my chest, I'm walking out of my bedroom when I collide with a hard body that nearly knocks me on my ass.

Stumbling back a step, I snap my head up, my pulse picking up speed. I didn't hear a thing, but I fully expect to see my brother standing in front of me.

Of course, it isn't.

*It's my husband.*

My face flushes hot, my knees feeling weak beneath me as my mouth opens, closes, opens again.

But I can't think of anything to say.

He doesn't move from where he is, just leans against the door, his shirt off, and I think the M5 must've been in the garage. He must've fucking been here the entire time, and Mayhem probably knew it.

Still, despite my anger, my eyes rake over his lean, strong body, the scars on his torso, the deep V leading down into his low-slung, fitted sweats.

He crosses his arms over his chest, and I see his biceps flex with the motion. A bandage still wrapped around his arm.

Suddenly, I'm back in our room at Liber. I'm watching him hurt himself. I'm watching him fuck Ophelia.

I'm wondering *where the fuck we go from here.*

I push it all back, swallow down the lump in my throat, meet his blue gaze. I expect to see a smirk on his full lips, but I don't. That dimple in his pale face isn't visible. He isn't smiling, not even a little. He's just staring at me.

For a moment, we stand like that, facing off, and so many emotions are warring within me, I don't know which one to grab. Usually, it'd be anger. So I could run. Leave him standing right here. Push past him and fly out of this house.

But I'm tired, and Ella's words from yesterday...they're still bouncing around my head. Reminding me that I'm not innocent. That he isn't either. That we have unfinished business.

I glance at his nose, see it running, a little red, and that anger threatens to flare hot again, but I push it back.

*He needs help.*

*"He needs you,"* Ella had said.

"Are you ready?" he asks me quietly, his hoarse voice sending chills down my spine. I've always loved his voice. Rough and raw, dirty and sexy even when he talks about mundane things. Like his favorite cereal. He liked fruity cereals best. I told him he was fucking crazy. Chocolatey ones are superior.

He'd laughed so hard at that, and I'd been in his lap, sharing a bowl of both with him, after one of our runs.

That was a few weeks before I left.

He'd wrapped his arms around me and kissed a trail down my neck. Spoon fed me and forced me to tell him fruity was best before he gave me another bite.

A small smile plays on my lips and I know he sees it when he asks, "What are you thinking about?" leaving his first unanswered question behind.

I clench my fingers tighter around the strap of my bag. "Nothing," I lie.

He looks sad with that answer, the corners of his mouth pulling down. I'm so used to him looking angry or sexy that this look feels new, just like it did at Liber, and it hurts.

He never wanted me to see his grief before.

I never really wanted him to see mine, either. We both ran from that. It's so much easier to be angry. You can pretend nothing hurts that way.

Fuck the world, and everything in it. Don't bother mentioning while you're holding up that middle finger that the world is eating you alive.

He glances at my bag, and I watch his throat bob as he swallows. "Did you bring bug spray? It's a place in the woods—"

"I don't want to go into a forest with you," I tell him, and it's not really a joke, but it feels like that. I think about when he knocked me to the ground in the forest that first night we met. Took that gun from me. The one that was supposed to end this all.

His eyes flash, and he steps closer to me. I stumble back until I'm against the wall, and his cold blue eyes are livid. Just like that, he's reached for the anger. His hand comes over my mouth.

"You don't have a fucking choice, Lilith. Because I can't keep an eye on you without you always running, and I won't give them a reason to come for you again. Always trying to save your fucking life, baby girl, and I'm not about to stop now." He glances down at my belly. "I'm not going to let them hurt my wife, *or my fucking child.*"

I grab his wrist to pull his hand from my mouth. He lets me, threading his fingers through mine, but his eyes are still narrowed, his full lips pressed into a line as he glares down at me.

"We can forget this," I tell him, my words quiet. "Don't take me in there. I don't want to be a part of this. I don't want anything to do with the 6 and their bullshit, Lucifer." My voice is still low, but it's only truth I'm speaking. Can I take him without all of that shit? Can he separate himself from the cult?

He grips my hand tighter, his blue eyes gleaming from the sun streaming in through the curtains at our back.

I know I shouldn't say it, but I do it anyway. Because his anger feeds mine. His hatred makes mine swell. And I do it because I don't know where J is, and I think about what he said Lucifer did.

Heard his screams. Saw him in that crate.

And he did nothing.

"At least Jeremiah had a plan. At least he was going to fucking kill them. You're just going to let them bide their time. Let them get their hands on—"

He slams his fist beside my head, and I flinch. "If I knew where Maddox was, he'd be dead, baby girl." His tone is soft, but his words are venomous. He brings a hand to my face, brushes his thumb over my lips. "But he's gone. When I find him though, he won't last long." He wraps his arm around my back, fingers still grazing my lips as he pulls me flush against him.

For a moment, I shove aside all the shit that's happened the past few days. For a moment, I just let us be what we are. Married. Together. Close to having a fucking family.

My own hands come to his back, holding him to me because I know he means what he's saying. I know he'd kill for me. He already has.

But hearing Jeremiah in that cage...his screams. Lucifer's laugh...

Maybe it could be different. Maybe they could work their shit out.

"He's your brother, you know that, baby? Whether you hate him or love him, he's still your—"

"And my dad was still my dad, and you saw exactly what the fuck I did to him."

He releases me all at once and turns away, stalking through our room to the door. "Mav is waiting for your ass," he mutters, "since you can't seem to stand being in the same fucking room as me."

# CHAPTER Forty-One

### SID

"LILITH, GET IN HERE, BABY GIRL!"

I drop my empty journal, the pen still in my mouth as I hear the rest of them laughing, then Ella snapping at my husband to, "Leave her alone."

Maverick cracks up, his boyish laugh easily distinguishable from the group of them. "She's gotta be in here. It's almost midnight."

The fourth of May giving way to the fifth.

*5/5.*

Of course these psychopaths do everything with numbers in mind.

I tap my pen against my journal, my knees to my chest in our king bed. Even in a cabin in the woods—decadent as it is —he'd have a fucking king-sized bed. If he only knew how alike him and Jeremiah really are.

I close my eyes and lean back against the headboard, thinking of J. Where he is. How he got out of a cage in the back of a truck and ran without anyone noticing.

Without coming back to...*fight for me.*

A lump forms in my throat and I toss my journal and pen

aside, eyes still closed as I hear the thump of music from downstairs.

I grit my teeth, anger running through me that I'm here. That I feel like Lucifer's child instead of the fucking mother of one. This place isn't so different than the cabin in Virginia, just a little more creepy, and slightly bigger. We pulled up at night, a few hours ago, and it looks like something out of the Blair Witch Project with menacing trees too close to the big, dark house. Even this spacious room is dimly lit, only the lamp beside my bed on, because there's no overhead light. There aren't any curtains on the expansive window beside the bed, so I've got a great view of the scary forest, just outside of Alexandria.

The smell of incense reaches my nose and I'm surprised. Once, in the middle of a breakdown, Lucifer told me how much he hated it.

It reminds him of his stepmom.

A surge of rage mingled with empathy twists through me and I want to be with him.

But then the moment passes, and it's replaced with dread.

I have no idea what happens tonight.

*Is this like a gang initiation?*

"Lilith!" Lucifer calls again, and he doesn't sound so nice this time. His voice is a snarl when he commands me to, "Get the fuck down here, *mama!*"

Amazing, how he can pretend we can't fucking stand each other.

Even still, my face heats with that last word and I splay my fingers against my belly, swollen beneath my tight, white tank. It's not the first time he's said something like that, but it is the first time since I...ran.

I ignore him again, keep my eyes closed. I need to get up and lock the door before he decides to yank me down those stairs.

Not even seconds later, I hear someone coming up them,

and my eyes fly open as I leap off the bed, my bare feet skidding on the floor as I race to the door.

I don't want to be here.

I can't do any drugs and I don't want to be around my husband. No one will tell me a thing about what goes down tonight even though I pestered Mav in the Audi from the backseat on the way here. He just kept saying, "You'll see," which are, coincidentally, my husband's favorite words, too.

Just as I go to slam the door to our room, Ella appears in the doorway, her long red hair up in a high ponytail, not a stitch of makeup on her pale face.

She smiles shyly at me, her arms crossed over her chest. She's wearing a cropped black top, stretchy pink shorts, and I see her thick thighs and think of what my husband said.

About Ophelia. The girl with Ezra. Julie.

My stomach churns and I grip the door tighter.

"Hi," Ella finally says, and I nod toward her, gritting my teeth instead of answering her. She glances past me, and I think of the journal on my bed. Slowly, her green eyes shift back to mine. "I was going to make some cookies." She shrugs, looking down at her pink, fuzzy socks. "Do you want to help?"

I bristle at her question because the last fucking thing I want to do is make food for the assholes in this house.

*Fuck. Them.*

But before I can say just that, the boys' laughter echoing from down the stairs and pissing me off more, she says, "He really wants you down there."

I narrow my eyes. "Why, when he's got *you?*"

She averts her gaze, picking at the hem of her cut-off shirt. I see her belly, love handles over the side of her shorts, and those words from Lucifer that night after I killed Pammie *for him* come back to me.

"How'd he feel?" I ask her, unable to stop digging the

wound into my heart a little deeper. "He's got a big dick, huh?"

She takes a small step back, and I almost go for her throat.

"You guys all fucking Ophelia, too?" I don't even recognize my own voice, but I'm very familiar with what I'm feeling. That anger to disguise my pain. "The four of you fucking—"

"No," she breathes out, shaking her head, her eyes almost pleading with mine. Fuck her pleas. Fuck her. Fuck him.

"It wasn't like that, it was—"

"I don't want to hear it. I don't want to fucking hear what it was like."

I can't stand still after that. I knock my shoulder into her arm as I push past her, my chest tightening when I round the staircase. I don't know why I want to confront him now, about Ella, but I feel high. Manic. Fucking insane. And since Mayhem helped, too, since he was fucking part of it, now seems like the exact right time.

I hear Ezra mutter, "Uh oh," and Maverick's wild laugh because he thinks everything is a game.

My husband is silent, and when I wrap my hands around his throat, he's going to stay that way.

I jump the last step, anger pumping through my veins as I catch sight of the five of them sitting on the floor of the empty living room, something that looks like a weird pipe in my husband's hands, a baggie of what resembles sand beside his knee. There are red candles, unlit, in a corner of the room. An incense burner curling up pale gray smoke toward the ceiling, dim lights on overhead.

Otherwise, there's nothing but them, and my eyes narrow on *him.*

His legs are stretched out, one ankle crossed over the other, and I notice they all have their stupid skeleton bandanas on.

Good thing because I'm about to fucking choke them with 'em.

Everyone seems to stop talking as I advance toward them, seeing nightfall beyond the windows.

I hear Ella creeping down the stairs at my back and my hands ball into fists as I come to stand beside my husband, Maverick sitting on the floor behind me.

Lucifer holds the pipe in one hand and offers his scarred one up to me, and I see the bandages on his arm. "Come sit with me, baby girl," he says, his raspy voice grating on my fucking nerves. He must be drunk or already high if he thinks I came down here to *sit with him.*

I glare at his hand, my chest heaving. I think about tackling him to the floor, but I don't. Instead, I take a step back, try to take a steadying breath.

I hear my brother call my name behind me, but I ignore him, trying to think. Breathe.

"You fucked Ella too." I bite those words out, almost choking on them.

There's only silence from the circle, save for my brother calling my name again.

*Fuck him too.*

Lucifer's blue eyes widen, and I see his already-pale knuckles blanch around the pipe in his hand as he drops the one he offered me, fingers splaying on the wooden floor.

I gesture toward the pipe. "You got high every day, fucked your best friend's girlfriend, Ophelia, Julie, and who the fuck knows else while I did what I had to do to protect our baby, but you want me to believe you gave a fuck I was gone?"

"Sid, I—"

"I'm not done," I snarl, taking another step back. Someone's hand clamps around my ankle and I know it's Mayhem, but I don't care. "You wanted me down here, you fucking listen to me."

He narrows his eyes, but I keep going.

"You know what Jeremiah did while I was with him? You know what he fucking did?"

My brother's fingers tighten around my ankle and I hear Cain's voice say, *"Sid,"* his tone a warning, but he can go fuck himself too.

"He cared for me. Taught me self-defense. He was there when I had nightmares. He fucking cooked for me and he cared for me and the only time he touched any drug was when he was trying to stop the pain that *you* fucking caused him!" I realize I'm screaming now, leaning down close to him, my finger pointed in his face.

Maverick's grip is painful against my ankle, but I don't move away from my husband.

He stares up at me with narrowed eyes, that glass pipe probably close to bursting in his hand. His fingers are digging into the wooden floor and his jaw is clenched tight.

My chest is heaving, and I want to grab the bandana around his throat and twist it. I want to hurt him. See him bleed all over again.

I don't know what we're doing here. I don't know why we're all pretending *I'm not going to leave as soon as I can.*

I glance at the edges of the Unsaints tattoo just visible because his black shorts have ridden up, the way he's twisted toward me. There are so many scars there, mine just one of many.

I hate him all over again for that.

For dragging me into something he should've left me alone for.

I should be dead now.

I shouldn't have to deal with this. With raising a baby in *this* world—*his world*— with running from what seems an inevitable early death.

I drop my hand, rake it through my hair as I step back, away from him.

My brother's thumb strokes the inside of my ankle and

finally, Lucifer speaks as I deflate, wanting nothing more than to curl up in a ball and cry. The anger is slipping away, becoming impossible to hold onto. It's so fucking heavy, sometimes I just want to drop all of it.

"Lilith," Lucifer says, rough and gravely like his throat is tight. "It wasn't...it wasn't what you think it—"

"You *didn't* fuck them? Because I saw you with her, in case you forgot," I bite back, but the conviction is gone from my voice. I don't even care anymore. I'm so fucking tired. So, so tired of this shit.

Maverick pulls gently on my leg and I turn to look at him for the first time since my tirade.

"Angel," he says softly, his eyes kind, hand still gripped around me, "I was there."

I know he's talking about with Ella, and I already knew that, but still, tears blur my eyes and I take a shuddering breath, waiting for him to say something to make this better.

"It wasn't...what you think. Come here," he offers, letting me go and holding up his arms, muscles flexing beneath the ink coating his skin.

I bite my lip and shake my head, but he cocks his head, his eyes rounded, and Atlas says, "Come on, Sid, look at that pout," and I hear Ella laugh at my back. For some reason, the sound of it doesn't make my skin crawl.

*I'm just so tired.*

Reluctantly, I reach for Mav's hands and he hauls me down to his lap, spinning me so I'm facing my husband, but his arms are banded around me.

A shiver slides down my spine as his breath caresses my ear. I see Lucifer's jaw tighten, his eyes on Mav's hands, linked together against my chest. I think about the fact my name is tattooed on one of his hands. "He needs to say he's sorry, doesn't he, Angel?"

I smell marijuana and I know my brother is probably high. I'm aware his girl is watching us, my husband, and all of the

Unsaints. Maybe that's why I lean back against his hard chest.
I can feel his soft laughter rumble against my back.

"Yeah," I say as Lucifer's angry eyes find mine. "He does."

Maverick shifts his hands, slides them down my arms, then
back up, over and over, his grip firm, almost like a massage.
He goes up to my upper arms, kneading my shoulders, then
down to my fingers, his thumbs pressed hard on my palm. My
body feels loose and limber, relaxed with his sure touch, some
of the tension leaving me.

The fight, too.

"You heard her, bro." Maverick's voice sounds deeper.
Hoarse. "Why don't you tell my sister you're sorry?"

Lucifer's pale face is a granite mask of anger, and I see the
muscles in his forearms flex as he brings his arms around his
knees, pulled close to his chest.

"Get your fucking hands off of her," he snarls.

Maverick laughs again, pausing his massage at the top of
my shoulders, then moving his hands toward my chest, his
fingers grazing my collarbone, exposed from my tank top.
"Nah. Not until you say you're sorry."

"*Maverick,*" Lucifer counters through clenched teeth.
"Watch your goddamn hands."

I smile at Lucifer, tilting my head back against Maverick's
chest as he trails his fingers higher, circling my throat gently.
An involuntary moan escapes my lips and he whispers in my
ear, "I wonder if he's hard right now." Before I can respond,
Mav's hands come over my mouth. I part my lips and he pulls
one down with his thumb, and with the opposite hand he puts
his index finger in my mouth. "Suck it and let's see what he
does."

I know I shouldn't. I know I should go back upstairs.
Forget this shit. But it feels too good, doing this in front of
Lucifer. Letting him feel some of the pain I do.

I circle my mouth around Mayhem's finger, taste sweet
earth, marijuana lingering on his skin. I look down as his

other hand slides down my throat again, and I can't see it from this angle, but I know that's the hand with my name on it.

I push further back against him and feel him growing hard behind me.

I deep throat his finger, my eyes back on my husband's. Mav's fingers dance along my collarbone and he groans in my ear.

Lucifer's eyes are on my mouth, then Mav's hand.

"Spread your legs," my brother whispers in my ear.

I don't hesitate. I part my knees, my feet flat on the floor. I'm wearing cotton shorts, nothing beneath, and Lucifer's jaw jumps.

"I'm going to fucking kill you." But he doesn't move. He just watches, his hands clenched into fists, knuckles blanching. "If you keep touching her, I'm going to—"

"Yeah?" Mav cuts him off, his hand coming to my upper thigh, clamping down around me, his mouth running over my cheek. "It's almost midnight. We're all going to be inside of her soon. But go ahead," the hairs on the back of my neck stand on end, "kill me, Luce," he taunts him against my lips.

*"That's enough, Mavy."* At that voice, Ella's voice—polite but cold—Maverick freezes. His lips are still hovering over mine, hand around my thigh, other fastened around my throat.

But after a moment, he pulls his finger from my mouth, straightens so his lips aren't near mine.

"I don't know, Ella," he says, trailing his hand up my thigh. "Doesn't seem fair, pretty girl. Lucifer got to fuck you and I think we're all just getting started with my sister. This is Ignis, after all."

Someone sighs, then Cain's voice echoes around the living room. "I'm tired of being teased." Lucifer's eyes snap to his, but I don't look. I just watch my husband, and Maverick squeezes my inner thigh, his other hand back around my chest, keeping me still. "I'm tired of you two acting like you aren't fucking obsessed with each other," Cain continues in a bored voice. "We all know it doesn't matter if either of you fucked the entire world; you belong together."

My mouth falls open and I hear Mav's low rumble of laughter at my back, his thumb brushing against my inner thigh, goosebumps trailing in its wake.

"Now show us she's yours, Lucifer," Cain continues.

"I'm not sharing her like she's a goddamn—"

"Whore?" I whisper.

Lucifer's eyes dart to mine. I hold his gaze, feel pressure building behind my own, and I don't even know why. He's never judged me for the people I've slept with. Never judged me for the people who touched me even when I was too young to allow them. I know he's been angry, and said hurtful things, but I know, too, that he's never held that over my head.

"You're not a whore," he says quietly. For some reason, the gentleness in his voice, it feels painful.

Cain yawns, loudly, making a show of it. "We know she's not a whore. But we know, too, this is *Ignis.* You want her to be one of us?" There's a pause, Lucifer's jaw ticking, but his eyes still on mine. "Let us *initiate her.*"

My blood heats with his words.

There are five men in this room, my husband just one of them. My brother another. And Ella is here, too.

Could we...would Lucifer let us all...*do this?*

Ezra is hurting, his mom still missing, and I'm surprised he's here at all. Surprised he didn't stay home with Brooklin, who got a job down at the coast and has been away the past few days.

I've heard from Mav and Ella's whispered conversations in their house that Atlas and Natalie aren't speaking at all.

Cain is constantly fucking girls, getting into fights.

Mav is wrestling with the guilt over things he can't control, and no doubt, the guilt of what he plans to do to his dad.

And my husband...my husband's demons haunt him so

deeply, I'm surprised I still see anything human when I look into his beautiful eyes.

Ella is learning all about a world that she's probably scared to death of, but she won't leave my brother.

And I...I'm torn between two brothers that would tear each other apart before they'd agree to let me have them both.

This room is full of pain.

*Sex can heal.*

And even if it can't, *it fucking feels good trying.*

Before I can think too much about it, Maverick's fingers are at the edge of my tank top, warm against my smooth skin.

But I freeze, the second I think to lift my arms over my head.

*The scar.*

*The fucking J.*

"Aw, don't be shy, Angel. I know how you really are," Mav whispers in my ear. I hear footsteps, light and hesitant, and I think it's Ella, but Mav is still trying to pull my tank top over my head, while Lucifer's eyes seem to be burning a hole in his fingers just under my shirt.

"Why you so scared, Angel?" Mav asks me quietly, but then he stills behind me, his body radiating tension.

Because he knows too. He changed me that first night.

Saw me naked.

He clears his throat, doesn't let go of my shirt, but he starts to speak, and I know he's talking to Lucifer. "Why don't you hit that DMT?" he asks quietly. "Might make this more fun for you."

I tense but Lucifer has his fingers around that pipe, and he glances down at it in his hand, then back up to me. "No."

Mav laughs. It's carefree. He's convincing. "Come on, bro. We have to set everything up anyway, and I need to ask my wifey for permission before I can *play.*"

Cain's dark rumble comes from behind us. "Sorry, Ella. Doesn't matter what you say. *Ignis is for the fire.*"

Lucifer ignores Cain, but his eyes dart up, just past me, and I know he's looking at Ella. That familiar feeling of anger starts to swell within me. He didn't bother asking *my* fucking permission. But I push the anger down. I don't want him to see J's initial.

After a moment, Lucifer sighs, brushing his hand over his curls, then picking up the little baggie. He jerks his head. "She doesn't need to see this."

I hear someone laugh. I think it's Cain, and before I can twist in Mav's arms, music starts to play.

Kid Cudi. *The Mood.*

Mav's fingers trail up my arms, goosebumps forming in the wake of his touch, and he says to me, "Let's get you some water," then pulls me to my feet after he stands, too. I glance back at my husband, see him watching me as Atlas comes to sit beside him, a hand on his knee.

His eyes don't leave me until Mav, Ella, and I are in the kitchen.

# CHAPTER Forty-Two

SID

THE SAME SONG is still playing.

I smell something like burnt plastic, but Mav assures me it's the DMT. *As if that's an assurance.*

The lights are off, and it takes me a second to even find Lucifer.

But I see him, because those red candles are in silver holders in a circle in the center of the floor, enough room for someone to lie down inside with space left over. The flames flicker and dance along the walls, over the pale planes of my husband's face

His back is against the wall, outside of the circle. He's near the front door, the pipe beside him, his shirt off, legs to his chest and his wrists on his knees. Atlas is still beside him, and the rest of the boys filter in behind me, Ella, and Mav.

No one is touching me.

I didn't talk to anyone since I left this room, but Mav and Ella had a whispered conversation, I assume about this *initiation.*

I know what DMT is. I assume Lucifer has done it before, because he used to talk to me all the time about psychedelics. How they could change the world. Heal people. I always found it ironic, because of all the times he'd done them, he hadn't seemed healed.

But when I mentioned that to him before, lightly, he told me, in all seriousness, that drugs couldn't heal him.

*Only I could do that.*

Now, as I stand in front of him in the darkness of the cabin, very aware of that scar on my belly, aware that while he's probably still feeling the effects of the DMT—even though the height of it is ten minutes or less—he isn't in the middle of his trip, and he'll see it.

But Mav doesn't seem to care anymore.

Because as Lucifer's demon blue eyes lock on mine, his expression unreadable, Atlas staring up at me, too, the music too loud for me to think, Mav's fingers come to my waist, slipping under my shirt.

"You ready, Angel?" he asks me softly, his hard chest against my back. I can feel his cock, too, and I assume that Ella gave him permission to touch me.

*What else did she give him permission to do?*

I bite my lip, but nod my head, not speaking.

"Si vis vitam, para mortem," Mav says in my ear, the Latin sounding like a language that's very much alive when he speaks it. "*If you want to enjoy life,* prepare for your death." With that, he pulls my shirt up.

I think of another Latin phrase, along the same vein. *Memento mori.* The Unsaints love that one.

*Remember you will die.*

How could I forget, when lately, that's all I've wanted to do?

Pushing it all aside, I lift my arms, holding Lucifer's gaze. Hoping he doesn't look down.

*Don't look down.*

I resist the urge to do it myself as Mav drops my tank on the floor.

Lucifer's eyes stay on mine.

Mav's fingers come to the waistband of my loose shorts, and I feel his mouth against my shoulder, sucking my skin.

A whimper comes from my lips, the music so loud, I feel it in my fucking soul.

My shorts fall to the floor, and I close my eyes, unable to hold my husband's gaze, knowing J's initial is there. In my fucking skin.

It's hard to see anything in here with the lights off, only candle flame.

But I have this feeling Lucifer knows every inch of me, dark or light. And if he's discovered I'm blemished...would he forgive me for that?

Before I can think any more about it, someone is in front of me, Mayhem brushing my hair off of my neck, his fingers trailing down my spine, causing me to shiver.

I open my eyes, my gaze connecting with Ella's.

She smiles at me, her hands coming to my hips, and I'm grateful for her in the moment, because Lucifer can't see.

As if she knows what I'm thinking, Ella's fingers brush against the still-healing wound on my low belly.

I suck in a breath as Mav kisses my neck.

Then he steps back from me, cold rushing in where he was.

I start to panic, whipping my head around to search for him, but I see Cain take his place behind me.

His coal-black gaze is heavy on mine and I can smell the dark scent of his cologne as he steps closer, but he doesn't touch me. Instead, he arches a brow, and I think he's...asking for permission.

Such a strange, strange thing in my world.

I nod my head once as Ella's fingers skim up my torso, then she's squeezing my growing breasts. I groan as Cain shrugs out of his shirt and I see his rippling abs, then his cut thighs as he pushes down his sweats, his boxers, too.

His hand comes to his cock and my mouth falls open.

*Good fucking God.*

But then his hand comes over my eyes, and he's dragging me backward, Ella's fingers drifting away from my body.

My back is flush with Cain's chest, and he bands an arm around my waist, covering J's name, like he knows it's there too.

"Are you ready to be one of us?" Cain whispers in my ear.

My throat feels tight, my pulse thrumming all over my body. My chest, my wrists, my temple.

"I-I don't—"

Abruptly, Cain picks me up, my feet off the floor as he steps carefully backward, and I think we're in the circle of candles. Just as quickly, my feet touch the hardwood, and he says, "Are you here of your own free will, Sid Malikov?"

My mouth is dry, and I have a strange urge to laugh.

*No.* It's my automatic response, but I bite it back for some reason as Cain's teeth find my shoulder, biting me.

I gasp, but before I can say anything, Lucifer's voice rings out over the music.

"Ella." That word is a growl. "I want to see my fucking wife and you're in the way."

Cain's hand is still over my eyes, and all of my other senses seem heightened. The heady scent of incense and the music playing, *Going to the Ceremony* by Kid Cudi, surround me. Infecting me.

And with Lucifer's words, it seems like no one is breathing.

Then I hear the creak of the floor.

Lucifer's groan, like he…wants something. *Is it me?*

Cain's question is in my ear again, his hand coming up my belly, over my breasts, cupping me, his thumb smoothing over my nipple. "Did anyone *force you* to come here, Sid?" His breath fans over my ear, and it's like he's breathing for me, because I can't.

I swallow down my nerves, shiver in his arms.

"What is this?" I ask him quietly.

Before he can answer, Lucifer does. "You're my wife, baby girl," he says softly, but his voice carries. "This is all for *you.*"

I bite my lip, Cain's hand slides over to my other breast, palming me as he presses his cock against my back.

"I don't want to ask you again," he says softly, his nose grazing my neck.

"I'm here of my...own free will," I finally manage to say, stumbling over the words.

He bites my neck, the hairs all over my body standing on end. "Are you worthy, Sid Malikov?" His words are a low rumble, and desire unfurls in my belly.

"Yes," Lucifer bites out for me. "She's *always been worthy.*"

There's a pause, a moment of silence save for the music, then Cain moves his hand from my eyes, picks me up with one arm under my knees, the other around my back. A startled breath leaves my mouth as I blink in the darkness, and before I can think, he's setting me down gently on the floor, in the circle of the candles, the hardwood cold against my back.

I'm shivering, naked, my arms over my chest as Cain kneels beside me, inside the flames.

My eyes are on his and he has a smirk pulling at his lips, but before I can think to ask anything, say anything, the rest of them come into the circle, too, all on their knees.

Maverick is opposite Cain, on my side.

I feel the floor shift above me, and I lift my chin, craning my neck back. Atlas is at my head, staring down at me.

Ezra comes beside Maverick, closer to my hips.

Then a flame flickers, going out, the smoke unfurling toward the ceiling as Lucifer's fingers circle around a candle at my feet. He crawls *over* my body, the candle in his hand, dripping red wax over my belly, my chest, my throat.

He has one hand planted beside my head, the other holding the candle which he poises over my temple. I feel the warm wax drop above my brow, *where that scar is.*

Lucifer dips his chin, his eyes on mine.

"Are you nervous, baby girl?"

Before I can answer him, Cain's fingers are circling one wrist, Maverick's the other, pulling my arms away from my chest, pinning them down to the floor.

My chest heaves, panic and lust consuming me.

"L-Lucifer, what are—"

"Submit to me, Lilith," he whispers, dropping his mouth just above my own. "Submit to *us.*"

My legs start to tremble, my arms too, but Cain and Maverick keep them pinned down.

Atlas's fingers come to my hair, massaging my scalp, and I feel like I'm drowning in sensation.

Lucifer twists his body and I see his muscles flex, his shorts still on as he hands the candle to Ezra, who sets it down.

Then Lucifer's blue eyes are on mine as he sits back on his heels, between my legs. His fingers find the bandage along his arm and he pulls it off, tossing it out of the circle.

I see dried blood against his skin, see the index finger of his opposite hand snag against the crusted laceration, splitting open the wound.

I gasp, try to sit up, but Ezra's hand comes to my thigh, Atlas keeps my head down and Cain and Maverick don't let up their grip on my arms.

"Open your mouth, Lilith," Lucifer says quietly, crawling back up my body. He swipes one finger over his bleeding arm, coating it in crimson.

I dart my gaze from his finger to his face, and a furrow creases his brow.

"Baby girl," he chides me, "you drink my blood, you get their cum, and I know they're tired of waiting *to fuck you.*"

My eyes widen as I try to look to Maverick, holding my arm, but Lucifer's hand comes to my face, gripping my chin.

"Don't look at them," he says quietly. "*You look at me. Right now,* I'm your master."

My mouth falls open and before I can speak, he lets go of

my face, pushes his finger down my throat just like he did that night at the asylum.

I taste iron, and on instinct, I suck his finger as he pushes further back, making me gag.

He smiles down at me. "Such a good girl, baby." He licks my cheek, over my eye as I close it, his finger still in my mouth. *"My fucking girl."*

He pulls his finger out of my mouth, wraps his hand gently around my throat as my chest heaves, the taste of him lingering on my tongue.

"Are you ready to be one of ours?" He pushes down his shorts, his boxers, and all around me, everyone is moving. Shifting. *Getting undressed.*

My thighs clench as I hold my husband's gaze while he throws his clothes out of the circle.

"Y-yes," I whisper. "Yes."

He smiles, but there's something like pain in his eyes.

Then he looks up, at Atlas.

Atlas's fingers leave my hair.

Lucifer stands, walking around the circle, taking Atlas's spot, but he lifts my head, lowering it back down to his lap, his hands gripping my skull.

I tilt my head up and meet his gaze.

Then someone's heavy, hot body is on top of me and I flinch, seeing Cain's black gaze on mine as he reaches between us.

I bite my lip, my arms still pinned down by Maverick, and now Atlas, taking Cain's place.

Ezra's fingers are still on my thigh.

Cain's calloused ones come to my low hip, then he's pushing into me without a word, staring right at me.

I moan, feeling him stretch me, fill me.

His hand leaves my hip, comes to my hair, tangling in my strands, as he yanks my head back, further into Lucifer's hand.

He moves slowly at first, leaning down over me, angling his head as he holds eye contact.

Then he's faster, and as I whimper, jerking my hands against Maverick and Atlas's hold on me, Cain drops his head and swallows down my sounds, his tongue twirling around mine.

Lucifer's fingers press harder against my skull, almost painful.

"You like that, Angel?" Maverick whispers, and I moan again in Cain's mouth as he moves inside of me, jarring my spine against the floor. "You always wanted all of us, didn't you, baby?"

I'm panting against Cain's mouth as he fucks me, his fingers still jerking my hair. But he pulls back and Lucifer dips his head down over my face.

His eyes are blue slits. "You want Ella to suck me off, Lilith?" he asks softly as Cain rolls his hips so he's hitting deep inside of me, fingers digging into my skin, just over the brand of J's name.

"N-no," I manage to say, holding my husband's gaze, the sensation of Cain filling me up overwhelming, the sounds of our hips colliding causing my core to tighten.

"No?" Lucifer teases me.

He leans closer, one hand going to my throat, wrapping his fingers gently around my neck. His lips are over mine as Cain keeps fucking me, my legs spread wide, my arms still pinned to the floor.

"No," I say again, fiercer this time.

Lucifer smiles. Then he gets to his knees, my head gently connecting with the floor.

He wraps his fingers around his cock and my stomach flutters as I arch my neck, open my mouth wide for my husband.

"Are you okay, baby girl?" he asks quietly as he stares at me, his hand stroking the length of him, my body jolting with every thrust of Cain's, my pussy clenching tight around him, the taste of my husband's blood in my mouth.

"Yes," I tell him, and it comes out as a breathless moan.

He grins at me, then he pushes his dick into my mouth, all the way to the back of my throat with no mercy.

He groans, his head dropping back as Cain keeps fucking me.

Then someone let's go of my arm.

Someone's hand is on my breast, grabbing me, pinching me, bruising me.

Ezra forces my knee to bend as he plants my foot on the floor, then spreads my thigh wider.

"Your wife feels so fucking good," Cain groans.

"Yeah?" Lucifer whispers, dipping his chin to stare at me. "Then *use her,*" he tells his brothers, eyes still locked on mine. "*She's our offering tonight.*" His hand comes over my throat, there's another hand on my other breast, hands all over me as Cain fucks me harder, getting closer, low moans leaving his lips.

"You're so beautiful, Angel," comes Maverick's low voice, and I think his hands are on me. I think he's clawing at my breast, gripping me so tight my eyes water. "*Unus ex nobis,*" he whispers, and I feel his mouth against my skin. "*One of us.*"

Cain groans, melding his hips with mine, and he releases into me as Lucifer pushes his cock far back into my throat, stealing my breath, almost like he's punishing me.

Cain pulls out slowly, pushing against my thigh with his hand, Ezra and him both keeping my legs wide.

"Look at that," Cain says, his voice cocky. His fingers come to my lips, peeling me apart as Ezra's hand comes to my low belly, pressing gently. "Look at how good she fucking looks covered *in me.*"

My husband makes a sound like a low growl deep in his throat as Cain's thumb strokes my clit, his fingers still pulling me apart, watching him drip out of me.

"It's my turn," Ezra says, his voice a rumble.

He starts to move as Lucifer pulls out of my mouth, kneeling down to bring his lips to mine, kissing me for the first time in over a month, his hand still wrapped around my throat.

Then I feel something hot and warm along my slit, and I moan into my husband's mouth as someone's tongue licks along the length of me.

"That feel good, baby girl?" Lucifer asks, pulling back just enough to let me breathe, his eyes on mine. I bite my lip and nod.

Lucifer's grip around my throat tightens. "You like my brothers fucking you, love?"

I take a breath and nod again.

Gently, he slaps the side of my face. Not enough to hurt, but enough for me to gasp. "That's the wrong fucking answer, baby girl." Abruptly, he pulls away, grabs my arm and pulls me up, so I'm sitting.

"Get on your hands and knees," he says, and I do, facing him, my ass to Ezra as I catch a glimpse of him sitting at my feet.

*It was his tongue on me.*

I glance at Maverick beside me, and his hand comes to my low back. "Arch your back," he says softly.

I do, then someone is pushing against my ass.

I tense as I stare at my husband, still on his knees, towering over me, his hand around his dick.

Once more, he pushes himself back into me, and I choke on him, the biggest dick I think I've ever seen in my life. My eyes water, and I feel something warm against my ass, realize Ezra spit on me.

I open my eyes as Lucifer thrusts his hips, sending his cock to the back of my throat. My stomach convulses as I gag, his fingers in my hair tightening as he stares down at me, his expression unreadable.

I try to pull back, to tell him I don't want Ezra to fuck me in the ass, but it's like he's reading my mind.

Like we're...*connected.*

"Ezra," he grits out, his eyes still on me as he pulls his hips back, then pushes them forward, one hand on my throat so he can feel how I gag every time he fucks my mouth, "don't you fucking dare."

Ezra laughs, slapping my ass.

Lucifer's grip on my throat tightens as he stares at Ezra, and I make a choking sound around his cock. He tastes so fucking clean, so fucking *good*, and when Ezra pushes his cock into my pussy, I moan around my husband's dick.

Lucifer's fingers release my hair, stroking it back from my brow instead as he stares down at me. I see his hard edges soften, even his demon eyes. His grip on my throat turns gentle, and as every thrust from Ezra sends Lucifer's cock deeper into my mouth, I can't stop staring up at him.

Drinking him in. Literally, and...not.

And while I stare at him, making him feel good for once, even as someone else is behind me, I forget everyone else around us. Maverick's hand on my back. Atlas palming my breasts.

Cain. Ella.

I forget it all until Ezra is moving faster and I really can't breathe. Lucifer's eyes narrow, his gaze on Ezra, but I guess whatever he sees makes him feel better because he doesn't say anything. A second later, Ezra's palm is flat against my spine, beside Maverick's, and he slows his movements, groaning, "Fuck, Sid," as he does.

He's finishing.

Inside of me.

Drool pools at the corner of my mouth, and Lucifer drags me off of his dick by my hair, painful but not as painful as it usually is with him. Either way, I can breathe again as Ezra leans over me, his hands gripping my hips.

He presses his brow to my back, slowly pulling out of me with another groan.

Then, before I can catch my breath, he's flipping me on my back. Lucifer lets go of my hair, but he doesn't say anything, and suddenly I'm staring up at the high ceilings of the cabin, and Ezra is crawling over me.

He smiles down at me, those dark eyes gleaming in the darkness.

"You thought we were done, *Sid?*" he says, dipping his head and trailing his hot tongue down my throat.

I crane my neck back, look at my husband upside down.

He's watching us, his hand around his cock, but there's a scowl on his face, his jaw clenched.

"Get off her," he says, his voice quiet and cold.

Ezra laughs against my throat, sliding his tongue lower, dipping over my collarbone, then between my breasts, before he pulls my nipple into his mouth, biting.

My nails find his broad back and I dig them in, gasping.

"Get the fuck off of her," Lucifer says, stepping closer.

Ezra lifts his head, then presses his mouth to mine for one brief second before he does as Lucifer says, getting off and, before I can think to say anything, Lucifer takes his place, his hands planted on either side of my head.

He pushes into me before I can breathe. I've never been this wet before. Never been so full of cum.

As I gasp, I catch sight of Maverick and Atlas both kneeling over me, by my head.

Lucifer grips my jaw, tilts my head up.

"Stick out your tongue, baby girl, you're not done."

My eyes connect with Maverick's, then Atlas's, and I realize they're both pumping themselves, and I do as my husband said, sticking out my tongue as Lucifer fucks me, heat rushing between my thighs, pleasure building at being used by them.

*All of them.*

My tits heave as Lucifer drives into me, hard and fast like he wants to fuck Ezra and Cain out of me. Like he wants to make sure he undoes everything they did to me.

His hand leaves my jaw, trails down my chest, over my belly.

I suck in a breath, turn my head to look up at him, my tongue still out, Maverick and Atlas still staring at me.

Lucifer's thumb is so close to that wound. Jeremiah's initial.

But he doesn't seem to be thinking about that. His face is full of...something else. Something like...marvel, even as sweat beads over his temple, the way he's fucking me so damn hard.

But he slows, rolling his hips as I moan. Atlas grabs my hand and forces my arm over my head and my fingers around his cock.

He uses my hand to stroke him, but my other hand is on my husband's shoulders as I stare at him. Consumed by him, my legs spread for *him*.

He slows his pace, burying himself inside of me, then not moving at all.

"This mine?" he asks me quietly, stroking his thumb even closer to the cut on my low belly.

A shiver crawls over my body, a lump forms in my throat at Atlas uses my hand and I hear Mav groan as he says, "My sister is fucking beautiful, isn't she pretty girl?" But I focus on my husband's eyes.

His tired, beautiful eyes.

"Yes," I whisper, knowing it's true. The timing for when Maverick and I fucked is off, and besides that, he pulled out. Not always fool proof, but Mayhem seems to have some...experience.

"Yeah?" I hear the crack in that word. The emotion behind it. His fingers tremble on my belly.

I suddenly hate what I let Jeremiah do, in this moment.

*Fuck.*

"Yes," I confirm, giving my husband at least that.

Maverick groans again, and I feel Atlas's cock swelling beneath my fingers.

Lucifer bites back a smile but that dimple flashes in his pale face and my heart melts. He shifts his hand to around my throat, forcing my head back as he picks up the pace, pulling out, driving back in.

"Let them use you, baby girl," he says, "open your mouth for your brothers. *You're ours now.*"

I do as he asks, closing my eyes, and a second later, I taste them both. Salty and warm along my tongue as they both groan. The tip of someone's cock is on my tongue, dragging down it as whoever it is releases into me.

I don't want to look.

I don't want to know.

Besides, I have both of them in my mouth.

And after a moment, Lucifer jerks my head up, and I close my mouth as I stare into his eyes.

"Swallow them," he commands me, his eyes narrowed as he fucks me harder, his grip tightening. "My beautiful, beautiful girl," he bites his lip, moaning my name as he closes his eyes a second. Then they're back on me. *"I don't want the taste of them in your mouth when I come inside of you, baby girl."*

I swallow, hard, and he must feel it, because his face changes from anger to something like adoration as he moans, "Goddamn, Sid," then he's finishing inside of me, swiping his finger through his bleeding wound on his arm again as he does, pushing into my mouth, as if to get the taste of everyone else off of my tongue.

I suck his finger as he comes inside of me, panting as he gags me, my stomach convulsing.

When he's finished and I clench around him, making him moan all over again, he pulls back, his eyes on mine, hands planted on either side of my head.

Slowly, he pulls out of me, and a whimper escapes my lips. *I'm fucking spent.*

"You're so beautiful," he whispers, and I realize I don't know where anyone else is. Most of the candles have gone out, only one flickering beside my head. "You're so goddamn beautiful and you're so fucking mine."

He trails his hand down my chest, my belly, lower still.

And I know the second he feels it.

The rough skin of my healing wound.

I see his brows knit together, that dimple slowly fading as a frown forms on his perfect lips.

The breath leaves my lungs.

I can do nothing but lie underneath him as he shifts on his heels, dragging his hand over my skin as he does.

I see his jaw clench. See his eyes take in the letter.

Then his thumb.

He traces it, gently. Almost reverently.

Goosebumps form over my flesh as I cover my breasts with my hands, and I don't even know why. I've never been shy in front of him. But suddenly I'm wishing for clothing. Armor, maybe.

I don't hear Mav, Atlas, Cain, Ezra or Ella. Don't sense them in this room.

It's just me and my husband.

And his growing cloud of...confusion. Aside from his clenched jaw, a muscle thrumming along the side of it, he doesn't *look* angry.

He just looks...confused.

His eyes flick to mine, and my skin feels too hot. Uncomfortable, his thumb still over the carved initial on my belly, his other hand resting on my thigh. I see the muscles of his arms flex as he's half-leaned over me.

I see his Unsaint's tattoo, littered with scars.

I'm watching all of that, avoiding his eyes, that when he

finally says, "Fuck, I must be tripping," and forces a laugh, I don't understand what he means.

Not at first.

He moves his hand from my thigh, rakes it through his curls as he shakes his head, laughing again. "I thought..." His thumb traces over the J, and his eyes dip down again, then back up to me. "I thought that this was real." A manic smile forms on his face, and I feel like I'm going to throw up.

My stomach convulses, but his eyes are on mine, still running his thumb over the letter. Three inches long, a perfect J.

Jeremiah, it seems, is good with a knife.

"But that's not...that's not really there, is it, baby girl?" He smiles down at me, his sleepy eyes crinkling as he does. He doesn't look like a demon right now. Doesn't look like a man who wants to eat me alive at all costs.

He just looks...hopeful. Exhausted.

*A little nervous.*

I bite my cheek. Glance behind my husband as I hear movement. Mav and Ella are getting dressed, Mav pulling his shirt down over his abs as he flicks his gaze to me, and it's so subtle I almost don't notice it, but I know that he just shook his head.

*No.*

A warning? A plea?

I take a shaky breath in, using my abs to lean myself up as I meet Lucifer's gaze, still searching mine, just like his thumb is still tracing that scar.

"No," I tell him, "I don't know what you're talking about, baby." My voice breaks as my heart cracks.

But he doesn't seem to notice.

Or maybe he just really needs to believe this lie.

His mouth pulls up into a smile, and he glances down at the initial carved into my extended low belly, but only for a second. Then his hands are sliding up my body, and he's pulling me to him, onto his lap.

I wrap my arms around his back as he holds me, breathing me in.

"I love you, Lilith."

I close my eyes tight, holding back the tears. I think of Ophelia. Julie. Ella. Jeremiah. *All of the Unsaints.*

I think of all of our damage.

I know he's only saying this now because he's coming down from the DMT. I know none of this is behind us. But exhaustion weighs heavy on my eyelids and I just sigh against him, inhaling his pine and nicotine scent.

I know he's got too many demons.

His dad. Coke. His stepmom.

I just wish I wasn't one of them too.

I hold him tighter. "I love you too, baby," I tell him, and feel a hot tear streak down my nose.

# CHAPTER Forty-Three

## JEREMIAH

I SEE THEM FUCKING.

Curling my fingers around the hilt of the knife, I smile to myself, listening to her fake moans, seeing his hand gripping the gilded headboard of their bed.

A safe house tucked away at the coast, they don't even have guards here.

*Shame.* Would've been fun to put a few more pedophiles down before I drag the Astor corpses out of this goddamn house.

But before I do all of that…

I drag the blade down the door, listen as the wood splinters beneath it, a horrible, screeching sound. For a fleeting second, I'm in that fucking cage again, scratching my own nails against the floor of it. I broke all of them, and they had gotten long in there. I broke them all, and there was blood oozing from my fingers. Without anything but my own urine to drink, I sucked off the blood until the tips of my fingers were raw.

Aching.

Burning.

I hear her scream first, dragging me out of my thoughts

but I'm still watching that knife drag through the white wood of the door.

But it's not until I hear *his* voice that I turn to face them again.

Sid's father.

The man who gave up his own daughter to be abused and fucking assaulted.

I might come for Brooklin too. Do what I did to Kameron to her.

Make Maddox watch like I did with Francis Forgues.

But staring at him now, at those blue eyes so like fucking Maverick's, I don't think he's going to last that long.

Shit, he might not even last until we get to the goddamn cabin.

*Fucking shame.*

He pulls out of his wife, yanking the sheet up to his chin, blocking my view of both of them. As if *that's* what I fucking came for.

I lean against the doorway, arms crossed, glancing at the sharp, curved blade in my hand.

*"Hello, fuckers."* My voice is muffled beneath the black bandana. I couldn't resist the irony.

Elizabeth Astor goes pale, her bright red lipstick the boldest thing about her as she pushes back against the headboard like a fucking little bitch.

She's as guilty as he is.

She knew.

*She fucking knew.*

"J-Jeremiah," Maddox chokes out. "What are you—"

"Did you kill one of my dancers?" I ask him, knowing he didn't, because now I know who did. But I watch with satisfaction as the surprise shadows over his face and he glances at his cell phone on the nightstand.

*Yeah, too far away now, bitch.*

And besides that, who the fuck is he gonna call? We both

own the cops. They're not going to arrest us. And his guards? They're back in Alexandria. I'd know. I've had Nicolas watching them.

"W-what?" he asks, and I see his lips tremble. Notice they're the same shape as Sid's.

I want to puke.

"N-no, why would you—"

"You know about Edith Van Damme going missing?" I press. I know that wasn't him either. Neither were the photographs of Sid. The fucking kitten—that idea was all mine.

The other shit? None of that was him.

And I don't give a fuck about any of that, because *I know who it was.*

But I want to torture him a little more before I gut Elizabeth and drag Maddox to Ignis.

And slit Lucifer fucking Malikov's goddamn throat for putting me in a cage again and kidnapping my fucking girl.

*Sid Rain is mine.*

I've been repeating it over and over to myself for the past week to stop from setting fire to Maverick's house and dragging her out.

But Maverick saved me *for her.*

I can only hope that he's treating her well.

That Ignis won't cause her too much damage, and that my name carved into her skin will keep Lucifer off of her.

And if he hurts her because of it, I'll draw out his fucking death while I carve out his heart.

Maddox's face turns green as he stares at the knife. "I didn't have anything to—"

"You take pictures of *Sid?*" I sneer. "Your fucking *daughter?*"

I hear Elizabeth Astor scoff, and after that, I can't really think.

I just...*react.*

The knife is to her throat before Maddox has time to

move. I've already crossed the room before he could breathe, and as I drive the blade into her windpipe, watch her eyes fucking roll back in her head, no time for her to scream, all I can think to say is, "You are a fucking *cunt.*"

I KNOW THE HOUSE, EVEN THOUGH I WAS NEVER INITIATED. All the bruises they left on me, all the taunts, Lucifer's goddamn *piss,* I should've been.

Doesn't matter, I tell myself, glancing up at the headliner of my car, gritting my teeth.

Looking up.

I was always looking up in that cage too, at the darkness through the wire. The ceiling was never visible. It looked like infinite space above my head. A place I could float away too. It was calming, in a world where the only thing I could control was myself, or at the very least, my emotions. Sometimes my physical releases were...too much. But my mind...it's the only thing I occasionally had a hold on.

Grinding my steering wheel in my bad hand, I glance in the rearview mirror.

Maddox Astor's naked body is contorted in the backseat, his eyes closed, a busted lip, broken nose, blood dripping into his parted lips. He's knocked out, but I see him stir, and I know he won't be for long.

Smiling to myself in the darkness of the car, the bandana flecked with blood back down around my neck, I have to bite back my laugh.

I'm parked about half a mile from the Ignis house, and I already watched Atlas's white Range Rover flying down the private gravel road.

*Thanks, Nicolas.*

Some bullshit about finding Edith and everyone is ready to abandon their posts.

*My sister is in the hands of some dumb motherfuckers.*

Not for long.

I wait a little longer, leaned back in my seat as I roll up a joint, papers and weed in the center console. I toss the lighter back in there when I'm done and inhale the sweet smoke and close my eyes, waiting for it to course through my system. I never really smoke enough to get high.

Just enough to get my tremor under control.

And the thought of seeing *him* with *her*...well, the anger makes it more difficult to control.

But it's okay.

He'll be dead soon.

And if he's fucking hurt her while I've waited to get her, *again*, it'll be a slow death. I'd hate for her to have to see that. Hate the ways it might scar her, but she knows who he really is. *What* he really is.

I'm nothing compared to his darkness.

But that'll all be over before the sun comes up.

I exhale smoke from my nose, think of what we'll do after that. Go on a trip. Greece. Spain. Fuck, we can head back to California and keep it in the country. Just so long as she's by my side, I don't care.

I'll need to get a nursery set up.

Crib, fucking change table, rocking chair. All the shit I looked up springs to my mind and I almost don't hear the soft whimper behind me.

*Almost.*

I take one last inhale, toss the joint out the cracked window, and snatch up the twine in the passenger seat as I turn to face Maddox, blinking his swollen eyes open, drool down his mouth.

It takes him a minute for his gaze to meet mine, and when he does, he moves fast. He bolts upright, but that was clearly the wrong thing to do, because his complexion turns green and he's clutching his bare stomach, still hard and fit because when you're a fucking perverted bastard, you seem to have all the time in the goddamn world to take care of yourself while you let everyone else burn.

Epstein comes to mind.

Maddox leans his head back against the seat as I watch his abs convulse.

"You puke in my car and you'll be licking it up before you get out of here, Maddox." I keep my tone quiet, enjoying his suffering.

"Why are we..." He gags, one hand clamping over his mouth as his eyes, lined with silver, meet mine.

"I'm warning you," I tell him with a little laugh. "I don't make empty promises."

He closes his eyes tight, bows his head as he tries to breathe. Get himself together. I avoid looking at his dick, because it'll just be too tempting to cut the fucking thing off.

Later.

"Why are we here? What are you going to do to my son?" he demands, his eyes still closed, hand on his lap, one still over his belly. His neck is bent, a crease lining his brow. Botox must be wearing off.

"Your son?" I whisper in the darkness of the car, the only lights from the dashboard and center console system.

He shakes his head, shoulders slumping. "What are you—"

"Your fucking *son?*" I repeat my question quietly, my hand shaking all over again as I curl my fingers around the thin twine. Thin, but strong enough that he's not fucking getting out of it.

He slowly picks his head up, and the confusion on his face makes the anger burst through the surface of my brain. I tried to keep it down, but the fact that he doesn't even think of her, that he doesn't even *see her as someone to protect...*

I leap through the fucking seats, and there's not much room in the back of my car, but I don't give a *fuck.*

I wrap the spool of twine around his throat, crossing my

hands as I cross it around his neck. His own hands come to my arms, trying to force me back. He doesn't stand a chance with my weight crushing him against the leather seats.

"You remember you've got two fucking daughters?" I whisper, pressing my brow to his, smelling iron and rot from his mouth.

"Jeremiah, I didn't mean—"

I pull the twine tighter and he can't breathe, his face turning red.

Fuck, I want to kill him now.

After everything he did to her, everything he let happen to me. My hands are both shaking now, and not from nerve damage.

From fucking rage.

He doesn't deserve to breath another second, but I want Lucifer to watch him die.

I want *Sid* to get to see his death.

That gunshot wound to his shoulder was a fucking graze.

But thinking of it, I pick my head up, let go of one end of the twine, then dig my finger into the still-healing wound, pink and nearly closed up.

*But not fucking quite.*

He screams, and I clamp my hand over his disgusting mouth.

"I'm not going to kill you yet, because that would be too easy. Because when you let grown fucking men make my sister cry, you were living your best life." I dig my nail into his wound, and his own dig into my arms, beneath the sleeves of the black shirt, I'm wearing, but I don't give a fuck. I can barely feel that pain, because I'm thinking about her pain.

I'm thinking about *my past pain.*

"When you let them throw me in that..." I swallow down the word, see his eyes connect with mine, and I don't like the look in them.

Something like regret.

Something like he actually feels something about it.

But I know he's good at manipulation. *Just like I am.*

"You were sleeping like a goddamn baby at night, weren't you, Maddox?"

He shakes his head, his nostrils flaring as he tries to speak beneath my hand clamped over his face.

"Shut the fuck up. It was a rhetorical question."

He swallows, silent as he breathes through his nose, staring up at me.

I lean back, half-sitting on the console behind me, but I've got to nearly fold myself in half to do it.

"Put your hands together," I tell him, sliding the twine from his neck.

He releases his hold on me, but his hands are shaking as he brings them between us.

I watch that tremor—from fear—and see the veins beneath his skin, light blue, stark against his sinewy arms.

Yeah. Won't take long to cut off that circulation, fucker.

I wrap the twine around him, as tight as I can. He tries to cradle his hands to his chest, but I don't think. I just hit him in the side of the face and he groans, his head snapping to the side. I don't look up. I just keep digging in the plastic twine deeper into the skin of his wrists, and it's already leaving imprints in his flesh, something that causes joy to swell in my chest.

He's crying in earnest now, apologizing too, as if I give a fuck about an apology.

I reach behind me, in the passenger seat, snatch up the switchblade and thumb the latch. After I knot the rope, I cut it off, toss the spool in the front floorboard.

My neck is cramping, my back, too, being folded at this angle in my car, but I can't resist.

I bring the sharp blade to his inner thigh, refusing to look at his fucking cock. Refusing to think about where it's been. Who he's hurt. If he ever touched her that way, maybe before she was sold. Fuck, maybe even after. Maybe they passed her around.

Maybe he was her first.

My fingers tremble as I hold his gaze and the knife slips, cutting him.

I know, because he hisses, glancing down with wide eyes.

"Jeremiah, I never meant to—"

"Stop talking or I'll cut your fucking balls off and feed them to you."

He stops talking, his eyes full of tears as he stares at me.

"You're a weak fuck. Your wife is—*was*—a weak bitch." And after I killed her, he tried to run.

Fucking dick.

"You two deserved each other, and you deserve everything I'm going to do to you when I get back."

He glances at the door of the car, and I know what he's thinking. He's thinking I'm going to leave him just like this, let him run off.

He's thinking I'm not so fucking smart.

He's obviously thinking wrong.

I rotate my neck, the blade still against his thigh. Then I cock my fist back on my right hand and hit him in the side of the head.

His neck seems to snap back as he grunts, his eyes rolling back in his head, but I'm pretty sure that wasn't enough to keep him out for as long as I need him for.

So I hit him again.

And again.

*And again*, until blood stains my knuckles and the side of his head, and he isn't crying anymore because he's not doing much of anything anymore.

I have to check his pulse when I'm done, my breathing ragged, heart racing.

He's still alive, which is, in this case, a blessing.

I need her to know.

I need her to know what I did to him. I need to let her have a chance to fuck him up, too.

When I'm out of the car, the knife with me, the keys, too, and the doors locked, I lean against the driver's side door, bowing my head.

I hate the feel of his blood on my hand, but I don't dare try to clean it off.

I feel pressure building behind my eyes.

The taste of freedom on the tip of my fucking tongue out in this dark forest.

*We're going to be free.*

We're going to leave this fucking place behind.

I'll build an empire somewhere else, with her by my side.

And these fuckers will never hurt us again.

*Fuck them all.*

# CHAPTER
## Forty-Four

## LUCIFER

WHEN I WAKE up in the night, the first thing I remember is my brothers inside of my wife.

The second thing, though...the second thing is much worse.

I feel like I'm going to puke, and I roll over in the bed, my arm dangling off the side as I kick the sheet off of me, trying to be careful not to disturb her.

But...*fuck that.*

My stomach convulses, and my head is spinning, mouth dry. I blink in the darkness. Think about Cain and the others leaving us here.

Because Edith...apparently, they found her?

Everything is a blur in my mind.

I close my eyes, clench one hand in the sheets as I hold my breath, hoping *that* memory is wrong. Hoping I'm just having a fucking nightmare.

Hoping there's something to hold onto with us.

That this isn't over. She didn't really let him *carve his fucking name into her belly.*

I stumble off the bed, spinning around, casting my eyes about the darkness, only a sliver of moonlight through the expanse of windows to see by. But I do see her, curled up into a ball on her side, covers pulled up to her chin.

She's still asleep.

For so long in our house, she didn't fucking sleep.

Neither did I, because I dreamed of my father. I dreamed of that knife in his brain. His screams.

But I think this dream, this image in my head...I think this is worse than that shit.

My stomach twists into knots as I walk around the bed, feet against the bare floor. My head feels heavy, lingering effects from the trip I think, but on the plus side, it's been two days since I had any coke.

I walk around to Lilith's side of the bed, see the slice of moonlight illuminating her mouth.

*God, she's fucking perfect.*

That's why she wouldn't do that to me. She fucked me over, and I fucked her over, but she wouldn't have done that.

She just wouldn't.

She's not wearing anything, and I'm only in boxer briefs. We didn't have sex again last night, but she let me hold her for the first time in far too long. We didn't talk, and we'll have to.

We'll probably have to scream at each other. I'll have to kill Maddox. We have a lot of fighting to do, but as long as that was just a dream, I'll make her work through it.

I can't live without her by my side.

For a long time, I didn't want to live at all.

Then she wrecked my entire world with that gun on her hip, those devil horns around her head like a twisted little halo.

*My girl.*

She's my fucking girl, and I knew it that night we met. Knew I was hers too. Always.

That's how I know she wouldn't have let him brand her like that.

I clench my hand into a fist, thinking about it. Coagula.

About how I wanted to get her a ring, but she didn't seem like the type of girl to want something like that. Black diamonds, maybe, but even still…she never wears jewelry.

I thought we could get matching tattoos instead, rings on our skin.

But there was never really a good time to bring it up.

Not with the fighting and my delusions and…

My mouth goes dry as I sink to my knees, my hands coming to the sheet tucked around her chin.

She's breathing softly, deep in sleep, and I almost don't want to wake her for this. I'll see her soft, round belly and it'll be free of his name, and I'll feel bad for disturbing her sleep.

But I can't resist. Because as much as I know she wouldn't…well, *I also know her.*

Softly, carefully, I pull the covers back, exposing her arms tucked under her pillow, the curve of her beautiful spine. The slight swell of her hips.

I let the sheet flutter down just below her hips and I take a breath, her arms tucked close to her chest, her breasts bigger than usual from the baby and fuck, I want to lick a line down them, but she's still sleeping and maybe I can just look and see and get back in bed and hold her close again.

But when my eyes trail down past her sternum, to her soft belly, just above her hip…my blood runs cold.

I try to swallow, but I feel like I'm choking instead.

My palms are against the edge of the bed, a sour taste in my mouth as I stare at it, not really believing it. Thinking it's some kind of…some kind of…trick of the moonlight or maybe I'm still fucked up from last night because it can't be.

That can't be a jagged, red name.

That can't be a fucking goddamn *J* branded into her skin, just above her fucking pelvis, probably put there right before he fucking…

I stand with a scream, swinging my arm, knocking the lamp on the nightstand to the floor with a loud clatter.

She bolts upright, scrambling against the headboard as her wide eyes dart around the room. I take a step back from the bed, my hands clenched into fists. Because if I get too fucking close to her…if I fucking come near her…

It feels like my skin is crawling when she looks at me with that fear, leaning across the bed to flick on the lamp on my side, casting a dim white light around our bedroom.

When she turns back to me, I see concern in her eyes, the way her brows are pulled together, her hands fisted in the sheets, pooled down around her waist, her breasts exposed.

But I'm staring at her fucking face.

"How could you do that?" I manage to get out, feeling like I'm choking as I ask it. Like I'm fucking…drowning.

My chest caves in as she stares at me blankly, confused.

"Baby," she whispers, and I used to love when she called me that. She didn't do it nearly often enough, but when she did, my heart fucking burned for her, brighter than it usually did, because I've *always* burned for her. Since the moment I fucking met her at that intersection.

She was it for me.

*She was fucking it.*

But as my chest heaves, my heart fucking breaking, I realize she could be the one for me, but me? *I might not be it for her.*

Apparently, soul mates don't exist and I am a dumb motherfucker.

I bring my knuckles to my mouth, stumbling back against the wall as she makes to get off the bed.

"Don't," I rasp out, shaking my head.

She freezes, one leg swung over the side of the bed, dangling above the floor. "Lucifer, did you have a bad dream—"

"You," I tell her, choking up all over again as I lower my fist to my side. "You're the bad dream, baby girl." Tears pool in my eyes, not yet spilling over, and god, I want them to stay. I don't want to cry over her. Not anymore. Not again. I'm so fucking sick of hurting over this beautiful fucking nightmare. *"You're* the bad dream. I can't believe you. I can't believe you would…" I throw my hand out toward her and she's still so fucking confused.

I want to shake her.

I want to carve her flesh away, carve his name off of her beautiful body.

Finally, as I drop my hand, raking my fingers through my hair, she looks down, and I hear her rush of breath as she sees the top of the fucking J, and she yanks the covers up, snapping her head back up to meet my gaze.

"Lucifer," she whispers, "it's…" She trails off, staring at me with an unreadable expression on her face. She doesn't look nearly as broken apart as I feel.

*She doesn't look broken apart at all.*

Instead, I watch as her pretty pink lips turn down into a frown, a small crease forming between her dark brows.

She flings the covers off, swings her legs over the side of the bed and glances down at the wooden floors, snatching up my black T-shirt, a pair of cotton shorts and pulling it all on.

I watch her, holding my breath, those tears still welling up behind my eyes. *What the fuck is she doing?*

"You don't get to do this," she finally says, tugging down the oversized shirt, as if it'll help erase the memory of seeing his fucking name. She steps toward me, her finger pointed in my direction. "You don't get to fucking do this. Stop fucking cry!" she snaps, dropping her hand and closing her eyes a second. "You fucking—You fucking cheated on me. *Multiple times, with multiple women."* Her voice is little more than a whisper, but her words are broken.

Cutting me open all over again as I lean against the wall.

"You refused to get help! You fucking refused to open up to me, to let *me,*" she slaps her hand against her chest, "open up to *you."* She keeps her hand there, curling her fingers into a fist. "You told me all about the fucking bitches you wanted to fuck, Lucifer, *fuck you.*" She takes another step closer, her fist still over her heart. "You don't deserve me. *You don't fucking deserve me.*"

She turns away, but I grab her arm, pulling her back.

She tries to get out of my grip, but I grab her other arm, too, holding her in front of me.

"Let go of me," she hisses, her silver eyes full of so much rage, it physically hurts to look at. "Let fucking go of me. Fuck you. I hate what you've done to me. To my fucking...*life.*" Her voice breaks, her shoulders slumping as she goes nearly limp, stops trying to get away from me. "Sometimes, Lucifer, *I hate you, too.*" It sounds like a confession, those words that drive into my heart so deep I can't even breathe.

I hold her tighter and there's space between us, but I can't let her go.

"Do you love him?" I ask her, my voice so quiet, I'm not even sure she's heard me.

But when her eyes meet mine, I know she has. She's angry all over again. "This isn't about *him!*" she snarls, throwing up her hands, trying to get away again. I yank her closer, her hands planting against my bare chest as she tilts her head up to look at me. "This isn't fucking about him. It's about you, and your family, and what they did to me. *What they fucking did to me.*" She's breaking apart in my arms, for the first time. I've never seen her like this.

Never seen her cry, not like this. Even at Maverick's, it wasn't like this.

It's a full body sob that rips through her, her shoulders shaking as she beats her head against my chest, over and over, hurting me. Her.

"They fucking ruined me, Lucifer, they *fucking ruined me!*" Her nails dig into my skin and she buries her face in my chest, her hot tears trailing down my chest. "They fucking ruined me. My body," she convulses against me, a scream tearing through her throat. "My fucking *mind.* They ruined me for you. *For anyone."*

I still can't breathe. I can't speak.

I wrap my arms around her back as she falls apart.

"They took everything from me. They took it all." Her nails are digging deeper into my skin, those tears flowing freer. "They took it from him too," she whimpers. Then she picks her head up, looking at me with watery and red eyes. "You did too," she chokes out even as I hold her closer, our bodies flush together. "You let him rot there. How could you do that to him? How could you..." She closes her eyes tight, her lips pressed together as she tries to breathe.

I don't know what to do.

How to feel.

What to say.

I imagine him in that cage.

She opens her eyes. "How could you let that happen? I thought you were...I thought you were my fucking devil, come to light the way to hell. I thought it was...*us.* Against the fucking world. But you don't play fair with me. You're not *beside me.* Is it because I'm...broken? Is it because you hate me? Is it because you think I'm disgusting and—"

I grip her chin in my hand, jerk her head up as I bow my head over her, our lips brushing. "I don't think that. I've never fucking thought that."

"How could you let those things happen to him? When all that shit was happening to me, you were *letting it happen to him!"* She slaps her hand against my chest, crying all over again.

But I think about it. About Pammie. About her touching me. Grinding against me. Her mouth on me, her words.

I think about how *she* went through that. Lilith. When she was far younger than I was, and for years afterward. Different men, different families. Different people that were supposed to care for her and love her and protect her and all they did was break her. Hurt her. Abuse her.

How many times did she want to die?

How many times did she hate herself?

How deep did that self-loathing go, infecting her veins? Poisoning her mind? Her fucking soul?

And him...

I want to hate her for loving him. For bringing him up.

*My half-brother.*

I want to hate her so much.

"Tell me why you did it. Why you left him there. How could you fucking do that to him?"

"*SIT DOWN.*"

*My father's cold words send a chill down my spine, but I haven't done anything wrong in a long, long time—I can still feel his fist against my face from the last time I did—so I sit down with ease, running my palms over my sweats.*

*His blue eyes lock on mine as he twists the 6 ring around his finger. "Ophelia's father had some interesting things to ask me about this afternoon."*

*I tense, shifting in my seat, trying not to squirm too much under his gaze. "I haven't seen O all day," I tell him truthfully. "And Cain wants us all to meet him at the strip, so—"*

*"Don't interrupt me."*

*I close my mouth, clench my jaw, but I try not to show any outward sign of anger.*

*My father sighs, leaning back in the leather chair behind his desk. It's dark at Sanctum, as it always is, smelling like the incense that Pammie loves so much, and my stomach churns thinking about it.*

*"Her father wanted to know why we didn't open up this* facility"— *he snarls that word—"for the* community." *Another snarl.*

*My throat feels tight, but I keep staring at him, waiting for my chance to speak. Fucking Ophelia. I told her about Sanctum when she kept bugging me about where the fuck I go on Sundays. I fucked her right after that, and I thought it would make her forget. Apparently not.*

*"Her father shouldn't even* know *about this place, Lucifer. Do you understand that?"*

*I do my best to keep the sarcasm out of my voice, my legs bouncing as I fist my hands on my thighs. "Dad, come on, it's a big church. There's a steeple and everything." I force a laugh, but he doesn't look amused in the slightest. I shrug. "I didn't tell her anything——"*

*"But you did," he cuts me off coldly. "You clearly* did, *Lucifer."*

*I chew the inside of my cheek, thinking. How can I make this better? I think about the tabs in the car. About skipping the strip altogether and losing my mind in my bedroom when I get home. At least it's night now. Pammie will keep to herself.*

*I can get lost alone.*

*My dad sighs, glancing down at his long, pale fingers drumming atop his desk. "Tomorrow afternoon, you're to go to the Forgues house."*

*My blood runs cold.*

*I've heard screams from inside that house.*

*I know there're three kids there. I've met them, briefly. Two girls. A scared boy.*

*I think Ezra is fucking one of the sisters, but he won't talk to us about it. He goes over there to visit them, though. He must be getting his dick wet somehow.*

*"W-why?" My voice shakes, and I hate that, but I can't stop it.*

*My father's lips curve into a cruel smile. "You'll see." Then he waves his hand dismissively, picking up a pen on his desk, glancing at papers stacked neatly in front of him. "Get out, Lucifer. Go home. Think about keeping your fucking mouth shut from now on, even to girls you're involved with. She doesn't need to hear you speak for you to fuck her."*


WHEN I GET HOME, PAMMIE IS STILL UP.

*I smell the incense drifting from her room, just down the hall from mine, but I duck behind my door, close it tight.*

*Before I can flip the lock, though, she's knocking softly.*

*There's a lump in my throat, but I can't ignore her. She knows I'm in here. And if my dad hears I didn't let her in, he might accuse me of more shit.*

*I open the door.*

*She's wearing a red, silk robe, and nothing else.*

*I see the swells of her tits, her plump lips pulling into a smile.*

*My stomach plummets.*

*Later, when she's riding my dick and I'm staring at the ceiling, I think about the Forgues. What happens there? What are they doing?*

*When Pammie kisses my forehead, tying her robe and telling me good-night, I'm thinking about what I'm going to find.*

*When she flips off my light, and closes my door softly behind her, I wonder what it would be like to kill myself.*

*I tried before, but it was a false alarm.*

*A flinch.*

*I wonder if all women are this fucking depraved. Ophelia seems to care about me, but she ran her fucking mouth to her dad and now…*

Fuck.

"THERE'S SOMEONE WAITING FOR YOU DOWNSTAIRS," MR. *Forgues says. Francis is his name, but my dad insists I call all of the 6 by more "respectful" titles. I'd like to fucking break* Mr. Forgues *neck the way he's looking at me right now, fucking gloating, but I clench the keys to my BMW in my fist and only nod.*

*"Okay," I tell him, glancing into his big ass house. Bigger even than mine, even though we live on the same private street.*

*I marvel at the fact Ophelia's family can live here and not know what the fuck is going on.*

*Ignorance truly is bliss.*

*"When you get down there, Lucifer," Francis's hand clamps down on my shoulder and I nearly stagger under the weight of it. He's not a small man. I'm taller than he is, but I'm skinny too. Something Pammie likes to tease me about.*

*I swallow down the bile rising up the back of my throat.*

*"Look, but don't touch. If you do," he leans down close to me and I*

*want to fucking rip his throat out, "you'll switch places with my son."*

*My blood runs cold, and I hear my shoes echo on the polished tile floor as Francis releases me and I head through the entranceway, to the first door on the right.*

*I turn toward it, see a keypad beside the door, but Francis says, "Go on, it's unlocked," and I twist the knob, darkness greeting me.*

*Silence as well, and the smell of something foul.*

*Gritting my teeth, I head down the stairs.*

*Only the light from the doorway at the top spills down the steps, and I can't make out much of anything.*

*But then I hear something that's like a whimper.*

*A word.*

*"No. N-no."*

*My skin crawls. It sounds like it's coming from a wild animal, the voice hoarse and the word almost unintelligible. I keep going, glancing over my shoulder, seeing Francis looming in the doorway now, a strange smile on his face.*

*The foul smell—like urine—hits me harder in the coldness of the basement.*

*I reach the bottom step.*

*That plea grows louder.*

*Fear coats my tongue, infecting my mind.* What the fuck is this shit?

*I keep walking, making a right, because the noise is coming from there, and although I don't want to see it, I can't seem to stop moving toward it.*

*A crate.*

*From the light at the top of the stairs, what Francis isn't blocking, I see a...crate. Like...for a dog.*

*But there's a boy in it, vaguely familiar, and I realize it's a...cage.*

There's a boy locked in his basement.

*My heart thumps so hard in my chest, I can't even breathe. I'm frozen for a moment as he stares at me with livid green eyes. The greenest I've ever fucking seen on anyone, ever. He's so...skinny, too. Skinnier than I am.*

*And…naked.*

*My stomach churns.*

*I make myself keep moving. Stalk around that cage.* Crate. *Fuck if I know the difference anymore.*

*His arms are bound behind his back and his hands look…blue. They look fucking blue, like the circulation is…*

*Oh my god.*

*He's begging me, I realize.*

*He's fucking…asking for help.*

*I stop moving, stop circling around that crate. There's piss in it, and my chest heaves, stomach turning into knots.*

*He's* pissed *in here.*

*How long has he been in here?*

*I open my mouth, but nothing comes out as he stares at me, and I realize he's pleading. He's…begging me to get him out.*

*Oh my god.*

*Oh my fucking god.*

*I'm going to be sick.*

*I'm going to be fucking sick.*

*I think about it. Opening up that crate.*

*I think about it for a second, but I hear Francis clear his throat, and the only thing I can do is fucking run.*

"THAT'S WHAT HAPPENS WHEN WE NEED TO KEEP SECRETS, *Lucifer, do you understand?" my father's cold voice asks from across his desk that night.*

*No. No I don't fucking understand. Why is that boy in there? Jeremiah? Why is he…in a crate?*

*"And he's the biggest secret of all. I trusted you with that," my dad continues, and I'm only half-listening. I'm staring at a letter opener on his desk and imagining plunging it into his brain. "I trust that you'll keep it, and if you don't…" He blows out a breath. "We can arrange a cage for you too."*

# CHAPTER
## Forty-Five

**SID**

"THAT WAS TOUCHING." A cold voice pierces the room as I flinch, my fingers still cradling my husband's face as tears streak down the bridge of his nose. My blood runs cold as his blue eyes leave my gaze and he's right back to being the demon I know him so well as.

"That was *so fucking touching*," Jeremiah says at my back, the hairs on my arms standing on end. "You deserve a goddamn round of applause for that one, *Lucifer.*" The way he speaks my husband's name makes me feel sick, and so does Lucifer's fingers digging into my hips as his chest heaves, his eyes narrowed, and his lip curled up in a snarl.

I slip my fingers from his face and spin in his arms, shocked he lets me, but relieved he doesn't fight me on this.

"Jeremiah," I whisper, seeing his green eyes flick from Lucifer—whose hands are still on my hips—to me.

He's dressed in a black shirt that hugs his broad shoulders, tailored gray pants, black boots. His hands are in his pockets, and he cocks his head, staring at me.

There's a black bandana around his neck.

One I left at his house.

"You fucked him already, baby?" he asks me, his words deceptively sweet.

"She's not your fucking *baby.*" Lucifer's tone is venomous behind me.

I keep my hands by my sides, try to breathe. Try to digest everything Lucifer just told me. Why he left J in that fucking cage.

And he heard.

*Jeremiah heard too.*

"Didn't you see?" Jeremiah taunts him. "Didn't you see how I fucking *owned her?* Or have you not gotten to fuck her yet? Because I think she really, really likes how I do it. My hand against her face, a knife in her skin? I think she likes that a lot more than whatever bullshit you do, Lucifer."

Lucifer's grip is painful, hard enough to bruise, but I speak first, feel the anger radiating off of him at my back.

"Jeremiah," I whisper, "where have you been—"

He laughs coldly, cutting off my words as he steps into the room, glancing at the unmade bed, coming closer to me. To Lucifer. "Where have *I* been, baby?" he purrs, locking eyes with me. "Where the fuck have *you* been? They put me in that goddamn crate, and you didn't even try to run? Isn't that one of the only things you're fucking good at?"

I don't have time to think before Lucifer moves. He pushes me to the side, closes the space between him and Jeremiah and grabs his throat, shoving him against the wall opposite the bed.

His head cracks against it and for a moment, J doesn't fight back. He just laughs. Him and Lucifer are roughly the same height, but where my husband is long, lean muscle, J is bulkier. Fucking ripped.

As he laughs, my stomach drops, and I take a step toward them as Lucifer cocks back his fist.

"Don't you dare talk about my wife like—"

But Jeremiah grabs Lucifer's throat, knocks his fist down, and spins them, so Lucifer is shoved against the wall.

I realize in a moment of startling clarity that Jeremiah has never fought Lucifer back before. *I realize that was for me.*

J has one hand still on his throat, and with the other he pulls a knife from his hip and thumbs the blade free, holding it just over those scars on Lucifer's bare torso.

Fear has me frozen to the spot, staring as Lucifer's hands still by his side.

"Don't call her that," J says, his voice quiet, sending chills down my spine as my hands come to my mouth. "She's not yours at all. She's nothing to you. You're nothing to her." He trails the flat side of the blade against Lucifer's stomach, and I see my husband's nostrils flare, his hands balled into fists. "But you know what she is to me?"

"Jeremiah—" I try to speak.

"She's fucking *everything* to me."

Lucifer's eyes dart to me, then back to J.

The silence blanketing the room is chilling.

No one moves.

It seems like no one fucking breathes.

"She's everything to me, and you don't fucking deserve her. You were going to kill her—"

Lucifer steps closer to Jeremiah, choking himself, the flat side of the knife digging into his abs. "You raped her." He spits those words out, like they make him feel physically sick. "You fucking raped her. *You hurt her.*" His voice almost breaks.

Jeremiah's triceps are flexed as he holds tight to Lucifer's throat, but some of the tension seems to leave his body as Lucifer speaks.

"You fucking hurt her, and *you made me watch.*" Lucifer's voice breaks, but he doesn't look away from Jeremiah. Not for a second. "You're a fucking piece of—"

Jeremiah knocks Lucifer's head back against the wall with

a thud, then he angles the knife so the sharp side grazes my husband's skin.

I force myself to move then, to close the distance between us as I stand to the side of them, staring at Jeremiah.

His eyes don't leave Lucifer's.

"Please don't," I beg him, my fingers going to his arm, feeling his hot skin beneath my own. "Please don't—"

"He doesn't deserve you," Jeremiah repeats his earlier words without looking at me. "I fucking do, baby." He finally turns his head, his green gaze on mine, his brows creased. "I fucking do, Sid," he's pleading with me, his voice cracking. "I deserve you. I've done *everything* for you. Fucking everything. I fucking…I love you, and he's done nothing but fuck you over." He glances at the scar on my brow, his jaw clenching. He turns away from me. "You hurt her, too. You did that, didn't you—"

A growl leaves Lucifer's throat, and all he says is, "Stop fucking touching him, baby girl," before he grabs the blade against his ribs and yanks it from Jeremiah's grip, tossing it to the floor with a clatter. With his bleeding hand, he curls his fingers into a fist and launches it into Jeremiah's face.

Jeremiah barely reacts except to laugh again, then shoves Lucifer back against the wall, and he swings before I can even breathe.

I hear something crack.

See blood pouring from Lucifer's nose, down over his lips as he holds his hands up to his face on instinct.

"You fucking coke head, piece of shit," Jeremiah growls, cocking his fist back again. "You left me in that fucking cage. You fucking *left me. Fuck. You.*"

But before he can hit him again, I come between them, holding up my hands.

Jeremiah stops launching his fist toward my face at the last second, his bloody knuckles grazing my cheekbone, but not hurting me.

"Get out of my way, Sid," he growls, and Lucifer's hands come to my shoulders, trying to shove me away.

I back up against my husband, feel his warmth behind me. His surprise.

His hands are still on my shoulders, but he doesn't try to move me.

"Don't hurt him," I tell Jeremiah, forced to crane my neck back to meet his gaze. His fist is still raised, my husband's blood over it. His jaw is clenched, and his eyes go to Lucifer's fingers against my shoulders. "Don't fucking hurt him."

"Baby girl, I don't need you to—"

"Shut the fuck up," I snarl to Lucifer at my back without looking at him.

His fingers dig in a little more against my skin, but I don't give a fuck.

Jeremiah glances up at the ceiling, looking as if he's begging for patience. I take the opportunity to plant my hands against his chest and shove.

But he's like a fucking wall and he doesn't move.

Instead, his bloody hand goes to my throat.

Lucifer's hand darts out to Jeremiah's wrist, trying to yank him off. "Get your fucking hands off of her," he snarls, and I'm caught between them as Jeremiah steps closer.

J laughs, and he's not holding me hard enough to hurt, but he bites his lip as he steps even closer, then says, "Why would I do that? That's the exact opposite of what I want to do to her."

The look in his eyes as he stares down at me makes my thighs clench, and I want to hate it. I want to hate him. Both of them.

But I don't.

I just fucking don't.

I love them.

*I love them both.*

"J," I whisper, my voice rough, my hands still planted on

his chest. I open my mouth to speak again, but I don't know what to say.

*How did we get here?*

*How did this happen to us?*

*Why did the world fuck us so. Goddamn. Hard?*

His eyes hold mine. "Baby," he whispers.

Lucifer's fingers dig a little deeper against my shoulder, and he still hasn't let go of J's hand at my throat.

"I need you to come back with me, Sid," Jeremiah whispers.

I tense, waiting for Lucifer to say something. Waiting for him to shove me away.

But there's silence.

There's just fucking silence, and even Jeremiah is surprised. I see it in the way he looks past me, just for half a second, at my husband behind me.

The silence almost feels…worse.

Like he's letting me decide. Like Lucifer is *letting* me run.

I can't breathe.

"I…" I can't speak, either. I don't know what to say. What to do.

I glance at both of their hands so close to my throat. They've always been at my fucking throat, since the days we met. They've been at each other's too, for reasons neither of them could help. Neither of them chose.

I feel my blood heat, seeing Lucifer's pale fingers wrapped around Jeremiah's tan wrist, his own fingers against my throat, feeling my pulse pick up speed.

*Why am I like this?*

It's like I told Lucifer. *They fucking broke me.*

But the thing about being broken is no one expects you to be wholesome. You're already in pieces. *You can fuck everything up, and it's all anyone will ever expect.*

So when I look up through my lashes at Jeremiah, and his eyes dart to my mouth, and when I feel Lucifer tug me back, his hand leaving my shoulder to go to my hip, and I feel his cock digging into my spine, I don't care.

*I get to do this, because I'm dirty. I'm wrong. I can do anything I fucking want, and no one will think any less of me than they already do.*

*Fuck 'em.*

"Lilith." My name from my husband's mouth sounds like a warning.

*I don't care.*

"We can either do this together, *or not at all.*" I can't live without them both. I just fucking can't.

Lucifer doesn't say anything.

There's just silence.

Nothing.

Then…Jeremiah's hands cup my face as his tongue flicks against the seam of my lips. Lucifer reaches for the waistband of my shorts, pushing them to the floor.

Jeremiah breaks away from our kiss with a groan, crossing his arms and pulling his shirt over his head. I inhale his clean scent and place my hand on his bare chest.

Lucifer moves from behind me, pushing me against the wall as he stands in front of me, but he cradles my head with his hand so I don't bang it against the wall, then his hand pulls at my shorts.

I have one hand on J's bare chest, the other gripping Lucifer's veiny forearm. He tugs down my shorts until they hit the floor.

Using them both for balance, I step out of my shorts, kicking them to the side. Jeremiah slides one hand down my face, over my throat, a possessive snarl vibrating against my mouth as his fingers shove my underwear aside, the pad of his thumb circling my clit.

I moan into his lips, but Lucifer's hand is around my throat, thumb on my chin as he turns my head toward him, pulling me away from J.

His deep blue eyes are boring into mine, thumb running

over my swollen bottom lip. "You're beautiful, baby girl," he says as Jeremiah's fingers part my lips, then he pushes two into me, his free hand splayed against my stomach, beneath my shirt.

I moan, clenching around J, and Lucifer's eyes flash, that vein in his throat pulsing as his fingers curl tighter around my throat, thumb slipping past my lips.

"Even like this," he says, his voice hoarse as J keeps fingering me, his hand sliding up my shirt, over my breasts, pinching one nipple and then the other, causing me to gasp against Lucifer's finger in my mouth. "Even when you let him use you, too." He leans closer, his brow to mine.

Jeremiah pinches me tighter, adds another finger to the two inside of me.

I gasp, my lips brushing Lucifer's, his thumb on my tongue between our mouths. "You're still so fucking beautiful. You deserve this. Enjoy it, baby girl." There's something sad in his words. Something I should think more about.

*But I don't.*

Instead, I moan around his thumb as Jeremiah brings his tongue over my jawline.

Closing my eyes a second, I do just as Lucifer said.

*I fucking enjoy them devouring me.*

Lucifer shoves down his boxers, but Jeremiah suddenly yanks me away from the wall by my hair, away from my husband.

He wraps an arm around my chest, and I'm staring at Lucifer, my pulse racing.

"What the fuck are you—" Lucifer starts to speak.

"Get on your knees, Sid," Jeremiah says in my ear, interrupting my husband, who looks like he wants to kill us both, his brow furrowed, jaw clenched.

My mouth goes dry, but Jeremiah doesn't release me.

Instead, he pulls my shirt up, releases me enough to pull it over my head, drop it to the floor.

His thumb comes to his name.

Lucifer's eyes narrow, but he doesn't speak.

"On your knees, baby," J says, his breath against my neck. "Show him how well you've taken care of your brother."

I lock eyes with Lucifer, my mind spinning, my body hot.

I'm trying to ask him for permission, even though I don't know if I need it. He fucked Ophelia in front of me, and this is for both of us.

Slowly, I slide to my knees, Jeremiah releasing me.

I hear him moving at my back, see Lucifer's jaw clench.

"Turn to me," J commands me.

Lucifer watches, quiet, and I slowly turn, tilt my head back, and look up at J. His hand is wrapped around his cock, and he's only wearing that fucking bandana.

My eyes linger on his handsome face before trailing down over his shoulders, his bulky muscle, the scar over his ribs.

His cock, inches from my face.

His lips pull up into a smile. "Open your mouth, Sis."

I hear Lucifer make a noise that sounds like a growl, deep in his throat. Jeremiah's smile widens.

My hands come to his thighs. My heart is racing, my skin tingling. Craving to be...touched.

I open my mouth, blinking up at J.

He steps closer to me, slaps his cock against my tongue.

*Why do they both always taste so good?*

"Stick your tongue out," he says, his voice lower.

I do, and he glides the head of his cock over it, up and down.

My nipples harden into sharp little points, and Jeremiah groans as he threads his fingers through my hair.

"She's so good at this."

My face flushes, knowing Lucifer is listening. Watching. Knowing those words are for me.

"So fucking good," J says again. He grips my hair tighter,

yanking back my head. "Now show him just how good you are, baby."

He pushes his cock into my mouth and my lips close around him, taking him in the back of my throat as I stare into his green eyes, my own watering, my nails digging into his thighs, feeling the flex of muscle beneath.

"Good girl," he whispers, and he sounds like he means it. It's not a taunt, even as he uses my hair to guide my head, pushing and pulling as I suck him. "You're so beautiful with my cock in your mouth, baby."

I'm still staring at him, and he's not as rough as he's been. In some ways, he's gentle.

My heart swells.

I hear the floor creak behind me.

J doesn't take his eyes off of me.

"Don't you dare fucking hurt her," Lucifer whispers, and I hear the pain in his words.

He doesn't like this.

*And I kind of like it all the more.*

Jeremiah smiles. "Do you want me to hit you, baby?" he asks me as I take him down my throat, drool pooling at the corner of my mouth, his grip more painful in my hair.

Lucifer is behind me, his hand around the back of my neck.

"Don't hit her," he says as I gasp when J pulls his cock out of my mouth, letting me breathe.

"Look at me, baby," Jeremiah coaxes. He grabs my arm, pulls me to my feet. Then he's kneading my breasts with one hand, the other wrapped tight around my throat.

I can feel Lucifer behind me, but he's no longer touching me.

I hold J's gaze.

He arches a brow. "You want it?"

Before I can answer, Lucifer grabs my arm, forces me against the wall, out of J's grip. He reaches between my thighs, pushes two fingers into me and I stare at him, the breath rushing out of my lungs. He still has blood all over his face, down his nose, one hand planted against the wall beside my head.

"She doesn't want it," he says in a low voice as Jeremiah steps closer, almost shoulder-to-shoulder with my husband.

His hand comes back to my throat.

I stare at Lucifer as he stares back at me, fingering me and using his thumb to circle my clit. Keeping my eyes on my husband, I answer J's question.

"I want it."

Lucifer's face falls as he bites his full lip, shaking his head, but I grip his arm, still staring at him. "It's okay," I whisper, knowing this will only happen once.

Might as well make it the best there is.

"I want it."

Lucifer's jaw flexes, but Jeremiah is already gripping my own, turning my head to him. "Yeah?" he confirms.

I stare into his beautiful green eyes as he caresses my tits. "Yeah," I tell him. "I trust you."

Jeremiah's eyes soften. He leans in close, angles his head, and kisses me.

It's a kiss that steals my breath, and Lucifer works his fingers faster, harder inside of me, his hand still clamped around my hip as Jeremiah's tongue collides with mine and I taste all of him.

All of his pain.

His anger.

His desire.

Then he pulls back and before I can catch my breath, he drags his hand down to my collarbone and lifts his other hand, slapping me hard enough to hurt, to make my head snap to the side.

"You fucking dick," Lucifer mutters, but he doesn't stop fingering me. And when I spin my head back around, I connect with his eyes first. "You okay, baby girl?" he whispers, and I still see the pain in his eyes.

I see how this hurts him.

"Yeah," I breathe out, a smile pulling at the corners of my mouth.

"Good," J clips out, "but I'm not done." He grabs my throat, pulls me away from Lucifer whose fingers rip out from inside of me. J throws me back on the bed. I scrambled backward, so I'm not half-off, and I try to catch my breath, but J doesn't give me a chance.

He's yanking me up, lying down, pulling me on top of him. He shoves me down on his cock before I can think, and I gasp with the sudden fullness of him.

His hand is back around my throat as he yanks me down close to him, thrusting his hips. "You want us to use you?"

I stare into his eyes, his thumb coming over my bottom lip.

"*Use me,*" I tell him softly, moaning and dropping my head to his brow as he thrusts harder into me, one hand gripping my ass.

"Use me," I whimper against his lips. "Fucking use me, J."

And that's what I want.

I want them both to use me. Fuck me. Hit me. Hurt me. When we're done, I don't want to feel anything when *he* walks away. Because I know he will.

The way he's so quiet now, letting this happen. Giving me up.

This will end with him walking out.

But for now, I want him. I want them both.

I feel the bed dip, and I arch my neck back, J's hand still on my throat.

I see Lucifer behind me. The pain in his eyes.

"Fuck, Lucifer," I gasp, and Jeremiah releases his grip on my ass, slaps my breast. I flinch, dropping my head, see the anger in his eyes.

"Look at me," he commands me, "don't you fucking look

at him." He brings his hand over my brand, his thumb tracing the J. "You belong to me, baby, you get that?" He thrusts his hips, working me harder. "*Not him.*" Then he wraps a hand around the back of my neck and pulls me down, kissing me so hard my moans are drowned in his mouth.

A moment later, I feel Lucifer behind me. At my back.

I feel his fingers thread through my hair as he jerks my head back and I'm looking at the ceiling. J digs his short nails into my hip, over his name.

I gasp as Lucifer's warm spit drips down my ass, and without waiting, he pushes his cock against me.

His fingers tighten in my hair, Jeremiah's tighten around my hips as I try to ride him while Lucifer pushes into me.

My eyes water with the pain in my scalp, the pain from my husband, and I realize I'm holding my breath when Jeremiah lets up on pressing my wound. "You okay, baby?" he asks me, and the way his voice is so soft, so fucking...*tender*...my eyes are watering for a different reason entirely.

I chew my lip, my head still yanked back from Lucifer's fingers in my hair.

But he slows, pushing into me.

He's...gentle.

I can't see him, but the feel of him, circling the head of his cock against the tight ring of muscle instead of forcing himself in, it's soft. Much softer than we usually fuck.

And when he finally gets the head in and I whimper, the sound lodged in my throat, he changes his grip on my hair. He threads his fingers through the strands, almost cradling my head as he leans forward, his chest against my back.

The pressure makes my thighs shake, the feel of him pushing into me, Jeremiah lodged inside of me.

But when my husband's hand come to my throat, it's reassuring. Comforting as his mouth comes to my ear. "Does it hurt, baby girl?"

I swallow down the emotion lodged in my throat. Swallow

down knowing what happens when we're done. He's going to leave me.

*He's going to leave me.*

I close my eyes tight as Jeremiah's fingers caress my hips and I roll them, moving slowly on his cock, but the pain—emotions—it's too much. I almost can't move. Can't breathe. Can't....do anything but feel.

"Yes," I tell Lucifer as he presses his lips just under my ear and my body trembles. "Yes," I say again, opening my eyes and glancing down at J.

He's staring up at me in...something like wonder.

Something like...anguish.

I don't know how we ended up here.

How they agreed to share me, but I know that we need it. And we've needed it for a long time.

Lucifer kisses me again, pushing further into me as he does until they're both deep inside of me and the feeling of fullness is...*everything.*

They're both spreading me apart, keeping me together.

And as Lucifer pulls out, pushes back into me, and Jeremiah guides my hips, still staring at me, at Lucifer's hand wrapped around my throat, I've never felt anything more perfect.

Painful, fulfilling. *Heartachingly good.*

They both pick up speed, becoming rougher, harder. Lucifer's fingers are squeezing my throat so tight, my breaths are just shallow gasps.

But I don't care.

*I don't care.*

I stare down at Jeremiah.

He's still watching me, biting his lip as he glances down between us, watches me ride him, his thumb still over his initial.

And when all three of us are sweaty, fucking spent, when I feel like I can't take any more of them, when I want to collapse onto Jeremiah's chest, he groans, saying my name, and behind me, Lucifer's teeth sink into my shoulder as a deep moan comes from his throat.

I feel myself cresting, everything clenching around them.

All of us are moaning, a loud sound, drowning out everything else.

Lucifer's grip on my neck tightens and I think he's bitten me hard enough to draw blood as Jeremiah says my name, and Lucifer isn't far behind, his words against my skin.

Heat rushes through me, and when Jeremiah grabs my tit, gripping hard enough to bruise, I'm coming too, all over the both of them as they finish inside of me.

I call both of their names, like a chant, over and over, and Lucifer runs his tongue down my throat, sucking my skin between his teeth.

J shifts his hold on my breast to my belly, cradling me.

And when I'm done, pleasure coursing through my veins, I can't stay upright any longer.

I collapse against J's chest, him still inside of me, but Lucifer slowly pulls out, then his chest is against my back, his arms wrapped around me, grazing Jeremiah's body.

For a long, long moment, the only sound is the three us catching our breath. My eyes are closed as I listen to Jeremiah's fast pulse beneath my ear, feel Lucifer's chest heaving at my back.

I don't open my eyes.

I don't want to move.

I don't want to get up.

I don't want to leave this sanctuary between the two of them.

The three of us have run our entire lives, to different things. Different highs. Different demons.

But we can never run far enough, never quite get away.

*You can't hide from your own mind.*

And as the minutes tick past, my belly growing uncomfortable against J, but I'm too exhausted to move, I wonder if we could live this way. The three of us. I wonder if I could have them both. It makes me selfish, but I've always known I was that. We all are, which is why I know it won't work.

I've always known.

But just for now I hold onto that thought a little longer, because the idea of Lucifer walking out for good…it fucking guts me.

And before I can feel it, the pain of losing one of them, there's a knock on the door downstairs. Loud, demanding, nearly rattling the fucking thing off its frame.

All three of us tense, and Lucifer reluctantly lets me go, gets off the bed, starts getting dressed without looking at me as I slowly pull off of Jeremiah, his hands still on my hips.

When Lucifer is yanking his shirt over his head, I hear a voice, taunting from outside of that door.

My heart races in my chest as Jeremiah sits up, every muscle flexing with tension as he turns toward the bedroom door, listening too.

It's Maddox out there.

*My fucking dad.*

# CHAPTER Forty-Six

## SID

I'M RUNNING down the stairs.

Jeremiah is shouting my name, trying to snatch the back of my shirt. We both got dressed quickly, me in the tank top I was wearing, the cotton shorts. But Jeremiah is yelling for me, and I don't care.

*I don't care.*

Because I picked up that knife he'd threatened Lucifer with, and I have it in my hand now. My other hand is sliding along the banister of the stairs, and this feels like racing to my husband in the night. Trying to get to him before the nightmares ate his fucking mind.

This feels exactly like that, except I know he won't try to kill me tonight.

No, the only person murdering anyone will be *me.*

And unlike he did that night, I won't stop.

I hear loud shouts from the door as I hit the stairs, Jeremiah still clambering after me, yelling my name.

I ignore him, tearing down the hall, through the living room.

"What the *fuck* are you doing here?" Lucifer is shouting, his voice full of barely restrained fury.

My bare feet skid on the floor but I keep going, my palms growing sweaty as I see the doorway.

Maddox fucking Astor standing in front of the door, completely naked.

My breath catches in my throat, but I see he's got a gun in his hand, and he's aiming at Lucifer.

My mouth drops open.

Jeremiah runs into me, sending me forward, toward the foyer, through the threshold of the living room. He wraps his arms around me and pulls me back into his chest. Then he seems to see what I see.

Maddox. Fucking. Astor. Naked. With a goddamn gun.

His biceps are flexed as he keeps the gun trained on my husband, who is glaring at Maddox, his head cocked to the side, hands by his sides, as if he isn't being threatened with a weapon two feet from his head.

Maddox's wrists are red, his hands a strange, purple color.

His jaw is clenched, and I think he's staring at me. I grip the knife tighter in my hand, but I can't move, because Jeremiah is holding me firmly to him. Until he lets go of me, steps around me, blocking my view.

Blocking Maddox's view of me.

And I realize, though, that Maddox isn't looking at me.

His lips curl up into a smile, his pale blue eyes—just like his son's—are glaring at Jeremiah as I angle my head to see him.

Jeremiah says nothing.

I see Lucifer's eyes dart to me, his lips pressed together into a line. But then he's staring back at Maddox, and for a moment, no one speaks.

Until Maddox finally breaks the silence.

As he does, I see the bullet wound in his shoulder, and I force myself not to look any lower than that. Not to think about what he's done with the rest of his body. Wonder if he tasted me, just once.

How did it feel for him to let me go? To let his own daughter into the hands of Lazar Malikov's darkness? Whether he knew where I was going or not—and I have no doubt he did—I can't help wondering how he felt.

Did he ever regret it? Over the past twenty-one years, did it ever keep him up at night? Even once?

But I remember what he said to me when he took me from my own fucking house. I remember how he said he'd sacrifice my baby.

*My* baby.

*Lucifer's baby.*

I place a hand on it now and see Lucifer's eyes dart my way again, trailing up my body, locking his gaze with mine.

We don't speak.

I'm not even breathing.

But for a few moments, we hold each other's gaze, and for the first time since I knew he'd leave, it's this moment I want to beg him not to.

My hand over what will be his child, my eyes on his, he holds me in the palm of his fucking hand. What he let me do, what he did *with me...* He loves me.

And I know, as my heart skips a beat in my too-tight chest, I know he loves me enough to let me go. Set me free.

I want to tell him not to do anything stupid for me right now. I want to tell him to live his life, because he deserves it.

He deserves happiness.

Even if it isn't with me.

*It's okay, Lucifer. You can let me go.*

I keep thinking it, as if maybe our connection is more than scar deep. Maybe it runs further than the marks on our palms. The rushed, angry wedding vows at the courthouse. The nights we spent together as a married couple. Even last night. *Ignis.* Maybe we really do love each other and maybe we really are soulmates. Maybe all this shit about doing everything to save my life was an undercurrent, not the wave.

Maybe he loves me, too.

And if we weren't so fucked in the head, we'd probably build a future together. A good one. He'd be the perfect dad. *He's the perfect man.*

But I don't deserve him.

*Let me go.*

Live a life you can be happy with.

I'm not that person for you.

*I'm not it.*

"I've waited a long, long time to fix my mistake." Maddox's voice slices through my thoughts like a knife, and I grip the one in my hand ever-tighter, aware that because I'm behind Jeremiah's body, Maddox might not see it.

Lucifer turns from me, a look of anguish on his face as he bites his lip, his brow creasing. But when he's staring at Maddox, that anguish is gone. Replaced instead with a cold, calm fury.

"Put the gun down, Maddox," he says quietly, his voice full of that that raspy edge that still makes my stomach flutter. "You're fucking embarrassing yourself."

Maddox's jaw clenches as he turns to Lucifer, stepping closer to him.

My stomach drops.

*No.*

I make to move around Jeremiah, but he senses it, shifting with me, holding his arms out to stop me from going around him.

Maddox and Lucifer are having a standoff, but that gun is too close to my husband's fucking head.

Then Lucifer moves, standing directly in front of me and Jeremiah.

*Shielding both of us.*

Maddox laughs. "You're a little shit, you know that?" he asks Lucifer coldly, his brows creased, but a manic smile on his face, full of hard edges just like my brother's. "A disrespectful shit. Your perceived power has gone to your head, Lucifer," he steps even closer, and Lucifer doesn't back down.

The gun is *inches* from his head, and my stomach churns, but it's like I'm frozen. Behind Jeremiah, knife in hand, I can't move.

"But you don't run things. *We do.*" Maddox's words pick up at the end, like he's…happy about finally putting Lucifer in his place. *Fucking happy.* "And you?" He smiles, takes another step, the muscles in his shoulders flexing as he brings his other hand up to help him aim, but he doesn't need to aim.

The barrel of the gun is against Lucifer's head.

I don't think.

I try to dodge around Jeremiah, but he spins around, gripping my arms as his green eyes connect with mine.

*I don't care.*

I bring the knife up, angle it over his bare arm, just beneath the black sleeve of his T-shirt. "Let me go."

He smiles at me, his fingers curling tighter around my arms. He glances at the knife against his skin. "You'd choose him *over me?*" he asks coldly, his voice low.

"You killed my best friend," Maddox is saying. "You killed *your own father, Lucifer.*" Gone is the manic high of his words. Now he's pissed, choking on grief for a man who sold me to be used as a child. Sold Jeremiah to be trapped inside a crate, locked away in a basement like a dirty, unwanted secret.

I try to shrug out of Jeremiah's grip, but it's impossible.

"The day you were born, I was there."

I stop trying to fight Jeremiah, instead, go limp in his arms as I turn to look at Maddox.

At Lucifer's fists by his sides, his jaw clenched as he stares at Maddox.

"I was there with your father, right outside of the delivery room. Your mother didn't want any drugs. She wanted to *feel* you ruin her."

My stomach convulses and Jeremiah's grip loosens as he

turns too, letting go of one arm, standing beside me while he holds the other.

"But we couldn't be in there for that, of course." Maddox looks repulsed by the idea. I think of him on top of me on that couch, the cloth over my face. I think of his words in my ear. How Lucifer never could have had me. He wrinkles his nose, his brow furrowing, too. "Your father didn't want to watch his wife's pussy get torn apart by a fucking *baby.*"

Lucifer's nostrils flare, and I can hear my pulse pounding in my head. I'm gripping the knife so tightly my fingers *ache.*

"He'd pushed for an elective C-section. But your mom…" Maddox rolls his eyes, but then he glares at me behind Lucifer's back.

My spine stiffens at his cold blue eyes on mine, staring at me with disgust. *My fucking father.* "Your mom was a lot like *her,*" he drawls, and my mouth goes dry, Jeremiah's fingers digging into my arm.

"Maddox," he says, his voice little more than a growl, "why don't you shut the fuck up?"

But he doesn't.

He keeps talking, his eyes still on me, the gun still to my husband's temple.

I feel sick.

My stomach hurts.

*It feels like a cramp.*

"Stubborn, disrespectful. A complete fucking *bitch.*" He spits that word out as he stares at me. "You're no daughter of mine," he finally addresses me. "Any daughter of mine would learn how to be fucking *obedient—*"

"Yeah?" I ask him quietly.

Lucifer turns his head to look at me over his shoulder, and I see, beneath the overhead light of the cabin, that his eyes are gleaming with unshed tears.

I ignore him, holding my father's gaze.

"Is that why *neither* of your daughters can fucking stand

you? Forget me. I can be the little slut you never wanted." I swallow down the lump in my throat, thinking of the names they called me. The men *my father* sold me too.

Jeremiah steps closer to my side but doesn't say a word.

"But what about Brooklin? You think she ever wants to see you again? And what about Maverick?" I take a step forward, and Jeremiah moves with me, not dropping my arm.

My palm is sweaty, but I grip the knife tighter. It feels like the past two decades of rage are bubbling up under my skin, and now I can see the man I can take it all out on. He's right in front of me. He's threatening my fucking husband.

I want to kill him.

"Maverick fucking hates you," I tell him, digging a little deeper, because I know the 6 only give a fuck about their sons. "He can't stand you. Your wife can't stand you. Who are you, Maddox? Who the fuck are you, beneath all that anger?" I finally let my eyes rake over his body, everything.

When I bring my gaze back up, he arches a brow.

"You like what you see?" His voice is a whisper. "You're used to getting on your knees for your fucking relatives," his jaw twitches, "why don't you come over here and do the only fucking thing you could possibly be good for—"

Lucifer's growl makes me flinch, pushes past my anger, and before I can even look at him, he's grabbing the gun, yanking down Maddox's arm and pulling away from him.

A shot rings out in the room and I flinch, the sound ringing in my ears as I somehow manage to get out of Jeremiah's grip, charging at Maddox.

"Sid, no!" Lucifer's voice is full of panic, but it's too late.

I collide with Maddox, one hand on his arm, the other angling the knife and sinking it down into his chest. It takes effort, his skin and muscle resisting, but they give way as he stumbles back against the front door, reaching for me, one hand digging into my side as we sink to the floor.

I vaguely register that means he could still have the gun in his other hand, but I can't think about anything but how good it fucking feels to do this. To get rid of one more demon that broke apart my world. My husband's world. Jeremiah's. My brother's.

I make to pull the knife out, blinking as I register the blood, the fact that my body is pressed against his naked one and I want to puke, but just as I go to yank it out, I feel something warm against my belly.

Beneath my shirt.

Maddox's other hand is still around my waist, and I smell his sweat. Hear his laughter rumble through his chest, one hand still above his heart, the other clenched around the knife.

But I'm frozen.

Leaning against him, blood oozing around the blade, I force myself to look up. To meet his gaze.

And with his hand around my arm, barrel of the gun to my stomach, I can't move.

Behind me, I hear nothing.

Sense nothing.

It's just me and Maddox, locked in some sick sort of stand-off, too close to one another. So close, I want to fucking puke.

His lips pull up into a sneer, and I think about how much his eyes are just like Maverick's, maybe his hair, too, but there's nothing else about my brother that reminds me of this sick fuck of a man.

I notice too, though, his skin is turning pale.

Sickly.

I didn't stab near his heart, on the wrong side, but it's getting to him all the same. Even so, I know it doesn't take much effort to pull a fucking trigger.

My throat feels like it's closing up as his fingers dig into my waist.

"You're a fucking bitch," he says, and I hear the floor creak behind me. His eyes dart past me, narrowing into slits.

*"Don't.* I think we all know by now it's in my best interest that Sid Rain is dead and buried. If you keep coming, you'll only give me more incentive to put her out of my misery."

"How could you?" I ask him, taking the attention off whoever is moving at my back.

He seems to slump more fully against the door, and I shift with him, the gun warm against my skin, just over the J carved into my flesh.

Something like grief seems to take over from my anger, the adrenaline leaving my body, a bone deep heartache in its wake.

It would've been nice to have a parent who cared. It would be nice to know what it means to love. *Really love.* I don't regret things I've done, who I am. But that security some people feel in the arms of their parents? I think that would have been really nice.

Me, Jeremiah, Lucifer? We didn't get that. We never got *any* of that.

"How fucking could you?" I ask him again, my grip on the knife sweaty, my heart thundering beats of agony in my chest.

Maddox just stares at me, his lips growing pale too.

"You just gave me up?" I ask him, my voice breaking. "You gave me up, and you let them…" I take a shaky breath. "You let them keep Jeremiah in that…that fucking *cage?*" I search his eyes for any sign of regret. Remorse.

And I think I see it.

His features seem to soften, his brows raised, mouth pulled down into a frown instead of a sneer. His hold on me doesn't let up, and that gun is still to my belly, but he seems to be…breaking.

"Did you ever regret it?" I whisper quietly, because I have to know. Before one of us dies, I have to know if all that pain he caused me, caused Jeremiah…all in the name of some pedophile ring for a cult with too much fucking power that still felt the need to corrupt the only people that can't fight back, I need to know if he ever got a bad night's sleep over it. Over me. Jeremiah. "Ever wish you could take it back?"

He stares at me for a long moment.

I think I know the answer by the haunted look in his eyes. With my hand on his arm, the other on the knife still hilt-deep in his chest, this close to him, I wonder about his own life. Who made him? Was it as bad as who made me? As bad as him? *Worse?* Where did the 6 start? Did they always want to be monsters, or did they want to change the world once upon a time? When does power corrupt? Is it from the beginning, or does it fester like a slow-moving poison?

How does it ruin?

When?

All these questions racing through my mind, I don't notice for a second that he's moved the gun from my belly. I don't notice until he brings it up to his head and pulls the trigger.

I jump back from him, a scream leaving my throat as I turn away, warm flecks of blood over my face and neck, that knife left behind in his chest.

My stomach cramps are worse, the pain as bad as the pain in my head, in my chest as I try to catch my breath. Arms come around me, and I inhale pine and nicotine, my chest heaving with dry sobs that don't come out as more than a gasp. No tears, because I'm beyond them.

And not just for Maddox.

But my stomach hurts so bad.

*So fucking bad.*

I think I might be bleeding, something warm and wet between my thighs and—

"This is all your fucking fault."

Jeremiah's words make my blood run cold. I freeze in my husband's arms as they tighten around me.

I pick my head up, trying to breathe, taking in shallow inhales, panting exhales.

Jeremiah is behind Lucifer, his eyes on me, hard and cold and full of hate. He doesn't step closer, but I still tense in Lucifer's arms, my hands balled into fists against his chest.

"This is all *your fucking fault.*"

And then he moves.

# CHAPTER
## Forty-Seven

**JEREMIAH**

I SEE him let go of her. Push her to the side.

My pulse is pounding in my head.

I clench my fingers around the knife. Sid thinks she's the only one who ever went without one.

We both know that pain. The panic of always looking for the next attack. Terror over even the idea of being backed into a corner you can't get out of.

I won't let that happen to me again. Or her.

And Maddox might've put himself down like a fucking coward, but this asshole is still here. *And he's going to try to take her from me again.*

He's unarmed, scanning the room with a broken expression on his face. I know it well. Probably exactly how I looked when he left me in that goddamn cage.

The only person I give a fuck about is Sid Rain. And I might have let her have a goodbye. Might have let him fuck her against me, because otherwise, she'd never get over his skinny ass. But now I know for sure that when I walk out of this room, Lucifer Malikov won't still be breathing.

I step close to him, into the dim lights of this disgusting room, Maddox's dead body slumped against the wall, half his head fucking missing. It doesn't bother me. Death has been a companion since I was a child.

Sid is calling my name softly, and I wonder if she's torn between running to him, running to me.

*I'll have to fix that problem for her.* From now on, she'll only have one place to fucking run to.

Lucifer snaps his head up, his gaze on mine. For a second, there's no recognition, and I realize just how horrible he looks for the first time. I have no idea what the fuck she sees in him.

There are circles beneath his eyes, his skin is so fucking pale, and he looks...gaunt. A shell of a man. I guess that happens when you lose your soul as a teenage boy.

It happened to me, too, but it made me stronger.

Lucifer let it turn him into a fucking pussy.

I smile at him and step close through the foyer, empty save for us, and the dead fucking body. But even though it's empty, this entire house is a shrine to debauchery. I know what they did here. It smells like marijuana and alcohol as my nostrils flare, my heart pounding hard in my chest. That, and sex. And not just from me.

*Who else fucked her?*

But I block all of that out.

I block it all out because right now? It's just me and him. And I've wanted to get my hands on him for a long, long time.

His jaw clenches as I approach him, and he lifts his chin, his eyes hard on mine, until they flick to the bandana around my throat.

He doesn't have a weapon, Sid's knife is lodged into Maddox's chest, and the gun is on the other side of the room.

He could have something hidden in the pockets of his shorts, but considering he doesn't have a shirt on, I can see a lot. A lot more than I care to see, really, but it'll just make the ways I break him all the more satisfying.

"That's cute, J," he says, cocking his head as I stop a few feet from him, flexing my fingers around the knife. It's in my steady hand, but I might have to switch it over. I don't really mind if killing him is messy.

In fact, that's what I'm counting on.

He gestures toward me with his index finger, pointing at the bandana. "Did my wife buy you that?"

I inhale. Exhale. Count to three. I'm not ready to kill him just yet. I want to play with him, first.

"She want you to feel included?" he taunts me, and this time, he steps closer.

Sid bites out his name, but she doesn't move. Almost as if she knows we need this. As if she knows I need to *fucking kill him*.

Rage washes over me, making my jaw tick, my vision almost blurring, but I force myself to focus on him. Force myself to not let him get under my skin. Not until I'm ready to get the fuck under his.

"Or she just want you to look more like me? Like the brother who *knocked her up?*"

"Lucifer!" Sid hisses, her voice angry on my behalf.

*Beautiful.*

I ball my unsteady hand into a fist, but I still wait. Wait until he comes closer. Wait until I can go for his fucking jugular, just like he's going for mine with every word he speaks.

I hate the fact that I share anything with him. I hate that *he* knocked my sister up. I hate that I share a father with him, even if Lazar *is* dead.

He let me rot in that cage, too.

And just like that, standing here in the midst of chaos when I should be killing him for *her*, Lucifer Malikov, my half-brother, inches from my face, I'm back there again.

*My back hurts.*
*Everything hurts.*

*My stomach is hollow, a constant ache that the bread and wine they bring me won't sustain.*

*I pull my knees into my chest, wrap my arms around my shins as I shiver, head resting against my knees.*

*It's dark in here. So dark, I can't see my body, but I can feel pain in every inch of it. They don't beat me here. They don't hurt me that way.*

*They just…leave me.*

*I think of my mother. The bruises around her face. The men that came to use her. Threaten her. Terrify her.*

*I think of watching after Sid. Locking her in my room, even when she screamed for our mother. Even when she tried to hurt me, to crawl out. Even when I had to stuff a pillow over her face to muffle her screams. Because I knew…I knew they'd come for her.*

*We got on the same plane.*

*We went on to different lives.*

*She begged for me, in that office where they pulled us apart, before I woke up in here, in this hell.*

*My heart hurts, thinking of her. Of where she is. If she's here.*

*For years, I've lived here, under this roof. Watching my older sisters be fed and cared for and loved and I…was nothing.*

*Less than nothing.*

*Only the one sister, the one who pities me, only she's whispered anything of kindness, but it feels like a special kind of pain, too. Because even she isn't brave enough to let me out.*

*When I do get out, I'll wrap my hands around her throat all the fucking same.*

*Since my seventeenth birthday, a week ago, I've been in this cage. The same one they first put me in, when I was eight.*

*Nearly a decade later, and it's only gotten worse. It's not tall enough for me to stand. Not long enough for me to stretch my legs out.*

*I start to shake, pressure on my bladder from the wine they gave me.*

*But there's no room in here…there's no room for me to relieve myself, and I've tried to go through the bars. I've pissed on the floor of this basement and I can smell the sharp scent now, and something worse.*

*An anguished, broken sob leaves my mouth.*

*My throat is dry, and the cry comes out hoarse.*

Someone save me.

She would. The sister that brings me food. Whispers that small word of comfort. *Sicher.*

*Where is she?*

*"Please." The word is a whisper, and no one is here.*

*No one is here.*

*No one will come.*

*Pati.* Latin.

*To suffer.*

*The Forgues chanted it to me all night, a single, red candle lit in their hands.*

*To suffer, so I can be born again. Become the son they need. The missing link in the 6.*

*I'm the holy one, they told me. I'm the cure. The answer. But I have to be scrubbed clean first.*

*I grit my teeth, my stomach growling, my bladder physically aching.*

*I can't do it.*

*I can't...*

*I let go. I can't hold it. Warmth seeps from me, surrounding me on this cement floor.*

*Another sob escapes my throat.*

*I think of the last time I saw my mother. Broken. Beaten.*

Dead.

"YOU REMEMBER WHAT IT'S LIKE, DON'T YOU, PRICK?" Lucifer whispers, leaning close to me, his breath against my ear.

I close my eyes tight, pushing the memories away. How long have I been standing here? How long has he been talking?

*Why is he still alive?*

"Alone in that cage, exactly where you belonged?"

I see red behind my closed eyes. I hear my own screams. I smell my own filth.

And something else too.

The ways I paid them back for all of it.

The news reported I shot them.

A smile curves my lips. *I would've never let them go that easily.*

My eyes fly open, thinking of how good it felt to have them broken underneath me.

I'm going to do the same to him.

I grab him by his hair, drop the knife, and reach for the gun holstered behind my back. His eyes widen in shock. He should've paid better fucking attention. I went for it when Maddox had Sid, but I couldn't get a clear shot, and he was too busy getting ready to throw himself at her that he didn't notice.

"I have, up until this point, resisted breaking your fucking jaw against the floor. Do you think that's because I can't? Are you really that idiotic?"

"Jeremiah, please don't," Sid begs me, her voice raw.

I don't listen. No one listened to me when I begged. *No one fucking cared about* me. And this fuck? He could've saved me.

He doesn't speak, because I have a gun in his mouth. Tends to shut people up.

"You should've fucking left her alone. You should've crawled back into that miserable church you belong to and sucked your friends' dicks and fucked. *Off.*" I shove the gun further down his throat and I have to hand it to him. He doesn't even flinch. "But you didn't, did ya, *prick?* You couldn't leave her to the one person who has always loved her." I push the gun further back, hear it hit his molars. His eyes are watering, but I don't stop. "Now I'm going to fucking kill you, raise your goddamn kid, and teach it to call me daddy, you piece of shit."

I don't let him go.

My finger is on the trigger.

I want to end it now, but it would be too easy. Too good for him. I let him beat the shit out of me up on that balcony, after Sid had found out the truth. Because I deserved it. I deserved to hurt for her.

But I'm done with that.

Now I want to kill for her. So many people.

Maddox and Elizabeth were first.

But the next person on my list? He's right fucking here.

Still, a bullet is too good for him. With a snarl, I pull the gun out of his mouth and toss it across the room behind me where it clatters on the floor.

I hear Sid whimper, see her coming closer.

Changing my grip to Lucifer's throat, I haul him up, glaring up at him as his eyes narrow, he takes great gulps of air now that the gun isn't down his throat, and his hands come to my neck, too.

"You left me in that cage, Malikov." I try to keep the venom in my voice. "You fucking *left me.*"

I see that pity flicker in his eyes. Pain?

*I hate that.*

My chest is heaving as I walk us both backward, slam his head against the fucking wall while he glares up at me, his hands still around my throat.

I lift my fist, ready to break his fucking nose, but he doesn't take his eyes off of mine.

Or his hands.

Something in me…shifts as I stare at him.

As I think about him down in that basement, when I begged him. When I pled with him.

For some reason, I think about his stepmom. After I got out. When I was supposed to be one of them, I saw her.

*Pammie.*

She was always touching him. Her hands in his hair, calling him pet names, and he always looked…pissed.

But he kind of always looked like that. I didn't think

anything of it, when the Unsaints started letting me around them, after the Forgues were nothing but blood and bones, burned in a fire I hadn't actually kept going.

I told the police that, but Lazar Malikov stepped in at that point.

They let the fire rage.

It swallowed that mansion whole.

I don't even think they got the remains.

But Lucifer's words, about what I did to them, before he pissed on me...*maybe they did know.*

As I think about it, about what I went through, I think about Sid Rain.

My sister.

My fucking soulmate.

He would've fed her to his father. He would've offered her up as a sacrifice.

My grip loosens on his throat, and his on mine, his eyes still connected to my own.

"You left me," I say again, my voice broken. "You fucking left me." I shake my head, watch as his eyes widen, like he's surprised I'm bringing it up. *"Brothers don't do that."*

And as he lets go of me completely and Sid is silent, both of them thinking maybe that I'm not so fucked up. That I got out of that cage with my soul intact, or my mind, too. Forgetting for just a split second that I'm not a fucking sociopath, I bring my fist down on his nose for the second time today.

But *this time,* I hear it break.

And goddamn, does it feel good.

*But I'm not done.*

Sid is screaming my name, and I see her rushing toward us, but I don't care.

He brings his hand to his bleeding nose, but his other arm comes up and hooks around the back of my neck, drawing me closer to him. We're nearly the same height, but Lucifer is lean.

If he thinks he's going to throw me to the ground, send us stumbling back and somehow get out of this alive, *he's fucking stupid.*

I shoot for his throat, slamming him against the wall.

Blood is pouring over his lips, down his pale skin, bright red and vibrant.

I duck out from under his hold, hauling him back from the wall and to the floor.

He catches himself on his palms, rising back up to his feet, but I'm already there, hooking my leg behind his, shoving him backward.

This time he hits the ground.

His head connects with the hardwood.

He lies on his back, dazed, blinking up at me as I come to stand over him, his nose still gushing blood.

I'm breathing hard, crimson on my knuckles, and a lightness in my chest that I haven't felt in a long, long time.

But Sid is here.

She's shoving me. Screaming at me.

I'm not paying attention to her.

I can't even hear the words she's saying.

I shove her aside, hear her as she hits the floor. See his eyes narrow on me as he tries and fails to get up.

I hate this man more than I think I hated even the Forgues. They're dead. Buried. Burned.

He still got to breathe.

Not now, though.

That's fucking over.

I squat down over him as a hand comes to his nose, one to the floor as he tries to push himself up. I untie the bandana, smiling at him as his eyes narrow.

I grab his throat again, knock his head back against the floor as he tries to sit up. A groan leaves his bloody mouth as my hands leave him. I smooth out the bandana, folded into a triangle as I cock my head, watching his chest heave beneath me.

"You know, I wasn't sure why the fuck you guys wore these things." I hold up the bandana, one hand on each end.

He's wincing, clearly in a lot of pain.

It would be a shame if I put him out of it just yet.

"But now I get it." I shrug, watching his eyes close, so much blood on his face it's kind of hard to make out his features now, the way he's lying sending the red trailing down into his eyes, too.

What a fucking mess this guy is.

"It's just another weapon." His eyes widen, but before he can react, I thread the bandana beneath his neck, then criss-cross it over his throat as I lean down close to him as his mouth opens, and he tries to breathe.

*Good luck, fucker.*

His hands come to my shoulders, digging in, but he's too weak.

He's always been too weak. For my sister. For the Unsaints. For the breath he fucking breathes.

I enjoy the way his pale face turns red, nearly matching the color of his blood.

"I'm going to enjoy fucking your wife for the rest of my life. I'm going to enjoy whispering to *your child* just how awful their father was." I smile at him, close to his face, feeling nothing coming from his nose. His open mouth.

The pressure against my shoulder grows weaker, and he's barely holding onto me.

"I'm going to enjoy picking off every last fucking one of your—"

"Jeremiah."

I freeze, my words cut off, but I don't loosen my hold on the bandana, even as my hand shakes. Even as that tremor cuts through me, reminding me exactly what kind of person my half-brother is.

Footsteps echo behind me.

I hold my breath, refusing to look away from Lucifer, because I want to see him fucking die.

"Let him go," Sid begs me.

I see Lucifer's blue eyes shift to look up at her.

I see her bare feet, her slender legs.

I don't let go of Lucifer as he slumps back, his eyes fluttering closed, his mouth open, like he's trying to form a word.

A fucking word he doesn't deserve to say.

I lean closer. "What was that, *prick?*" I snarl at him. "Go ahead. Give me your last fucking word." I cross the bandana tighter, see his jaw tense, his brows furrow, but his hands drop by his sides.

It won't be much longer now.

But Sid squats down.

She holds something to my head.

Warm.

As I turn to look at her, she adjusts the barrel of the gun, forcing it against my temple. Her eyes are wide, panic etched onto her face, but her aim is steady, Lucifer's body between us.

"Let go of him," she says, her tone nothing but fucking ice.

Those words stab in my gut, because I don't want her to want him. I don't want her to give a fuck about him.

It's me and her, and it's always been me and her.

*Always.*

Still, I loosen my hold on the bandana.

Enough that Lucifer gasps.

I don't let go though, because I need him dead.

*He has to fucking die.*

Something in Sid's face gives, like I can see the relief flooding through her.

But she darts her gaze to him, and I do, too. See he doesn't move. He's too weak to do a fucking thing.

"Let go of him," she pleads again. She hasn't moved the gun from my head. "J, if you love me, *let go of him.*"

I don't want to.

I don't want him to live.

I don't want him to get her.

But I think about him standing in front of Maddox, between me, her, and the gun.

My chest tightens. I swallow down a lump in my throat.

And after a long, long moment, I slip the bandana from beneath Lucifer's neck and stand, pocketing it.

"Lucifer," Sid whispers, letting the gun clatter to the floor as she crawls over him.

My stomach heaves.

Not just because of that.

Because there's blood.

There's blood on her inner thigh, I can see from here, her body over his, her ass in the air.

"Sid," I choke out, and she glances over at me, her hands cupped around her husband's face as she sits on his chest. "Sid, are you bleeding?"

She swallows, her face pale, flecked with blood from Maddox.

And as she reaches a hand between her legs, I hear the last word Lucifer tried to say.

"*Lilith.*"

# CHAPTER Forty-Eight

**SID**

I DREAM OF THEM BOTH.

Jeremiah is darkness. Cold fury. But I'm burning up, and his arms around me keep me grounded, keep me from turning to ash completely. He's been there since the beginning, hurting me. Saving me. Always both at once, never one without the other. I didn't know, for a long, long time, that the things he did to me were to keep me safe.

But he's never quite been able to keep me safe from his own hands. His own corrupted mind.

Lucifer is hell. Hot fire, burning every inch of me, keeping my own fire going inside of me. He fans the flames like my own personal demon. Satan himself, holding my hand as I turn into his Lilith, creating chaos and havoc wherever we go. With each other, always keeping the blaze of our misery alive together.

We're all the same, the three of us.

Born from demons, haunted by devils.

Our minds are black rot, our souls poisoned before we could even talk.

We didn't have a choice in the evil we became.

And I never had a chance to not love them both. Brothers forever at war, I only wanted to be the white flag.

But I'm not that.

I've never been anything so pure.

I only get one, because they'd kill each other before they shared me.

*But I can't let either of them go.*

# CHAPTER Forty-Nine

## JEREMIAH

"SHE WON'T GIVE YOU UP."

Those words are like a knife. The way he speaks them. The truth ringing through them. The way my stomach twists into a knot because for once—seeing Maddox's hands around her, that gun to her belly, and feeling the steel of the barrel against my own head as she tried to save him—for once, I don't take pleasure in that thought. In the monstrous ties that bind us to each other. Our broken past. A mom that wasn't really.

Fathers that...

I swallow down that lump in my throat.

They're both dead now.

The 6 still exist, but maybe with Elijah's wife back, free from harm—on my command—and with Maddox dead, maybe things will get better.

I'm probably fucking delusional, but even so, when I turn to look down at my half-brother in the hospital bed, his deep blue eyes glaring at me, I know he wouldn't let them hurt her. Not again.

Never again.

He was willing to die for her.

Just like me.

He would've let Maddox pull that trigger with the gun against his head if it meant keeping her safe. And when Maddox had the gun to her belly, Lucifer was going to throw himself at her. He would've died with her.

But she...she's having a baby with him. She loves him. It makes me feel sick, and I kind of want to puke thinking about it, but what settles me is that I know...*she loves me too.*

She's probably the only person in the world who ever has.

Ever will.

Giving her up...

"It's going to kill me," I finally say. My voice breaks and I hate it. That it's happening in front of him, of all people. But the nurses wanted me out of Sid's room, and I wouldn't usually give a fuck what anyone wants, but there's already enough cover up happening in this hospital right now that I didn't want to push my fucking luck.

Besides, Lucifer is the only one who would understand.

"It's going to fucking kill me and you..." I lift a finger, coming to stand by the side of his bed. Even with an IV for fluids in his arm, a black eye, nearly shattered fucking checkbone, he still clenches his fists, sits up straighter like he'll fucking kill me if I come any closer.

Yeah. He won't let anyone hurt her. But even still...

"You can't keep doing drugs," I say, leaning down close, jabbing my finger into his chest. It's easier to reach for the anger. It keeps me from fucking falling apart.

A muscle feathers along his jaw and he glances down at my finger in his chest, but he doesn't touch me.

"You can't keep fucking her over like that."

"She's fucked me over, too—"

"When she's scared. When she gets in too deep," I explain, dropping my hand, straightening and running a hand through my hair. "She fucking loves you. It's why she left. She was terrified. Not of fucking Maddox." I pinch the bridge of my nose, close my eyes and take a breath. I still don't look at him when I keep going, explaining the way my beautiful sister's soul works. How they fucked us up. "Of you. She was terrified because you were fucking losing your mind and she just thought..." I dig my nails into my palms, that tremor starting up again in my fucking hand. "She just thought it was better to leave than get left."

He doesn't say anything, and I dart a glance his way.

Think about killing him all over again.

Then I remember the feel of the gun against my head. Her crawling over him, holding his face in her hands. How she charged at Maddox, for him. For her. For *us*.

He looks down, his eyes swollen, his nose probably permanently disfigured. I can't find it in me to give a fuck about that as he twists his hands together, his breath shallow beneath the hospital gown.

Maverick is in the hall with the redhead, and the rest of them are with Elijah. At that fucking church.

I think about the bandana in my pocket. About driving there now and wrapping it around each of their throats.

I'm still considering it.

It was the plan, all along.

But as with all my plans that have Sid Rain in my orbit, it's all fucked up now.

"Is that why?" he finally asks me, picking his head up, his eyes locked on mine. The blinds are closed, but light streams in anyway as the sun rises, and it dances across his gaunt, pale face, the shadows beneath his bruised eyelids. "She left because she was scared of me...leaving her?"

"That, the 6, and she was probably fucking scared of *you*. I hate to be the one to tell you this, but I think you've got a couple of fucking screws loose in that fucked-up head of yours." I'm at the foot of his bed as I deliver the words, and I see his jaw tighten.

Then he seems to relax against his bed, inclined so he's

sitting upright. He rolls his eyes, and I almost want to laugh, but despite what she might see in him, we aren't friends.

We'll never be friends.

After today, we'll never be fucking anything.

My heart threatens to shatter as I think about it, and I can't really breathe.

"You're legitimately insane," he mutters under his breath, turning his head to the side and closing his eyes. "So don't give me any more mental fucking health advice."

A smile pulls on the corners of my lips, but I bite it back even though his eyes are closed. Fucker.

"And why'd you fucking do that?" He suddenly sits up, apparently too fast, because he winces as his blue eyes connect with mine. "Why'd you fucking mark her? How could you fucking—"

I hold up my hand, palm facing him. "You marked her too."

He leans back again, but his eyes are still narrowed as I shove my hand in my pocket, clenching it into a fist, not wanting to feel the tremor return.

Not wanting him to see it.

"She won't give you up," he says again, and I hear the vulnerability in those words. I don't much give a fuck about it, but I know how he feels. Like he can never quite have her completely.

She's feral.

She's not one to give into anyone, to surrender her heart. We both have pieces of it, but I don't think either of us are strong enough to take the whole thing.

That kind of pain hurts. It's different from anything else in the world. Loving someone with your entire being, and only being returned a sliver of it. The sliver is like a knife through your chest. You almost want to pull it out completely, drop it, turn and run. It'd be better than the agony.

"She will never stop loving you." He says those words with

anger, his jaw clenched as he stares at me in this sterile room. Big enough for a few beds, because he's a goddamn fucking Malikov.

Something I should've been.

These are things I should have had.

But I think of Pammie hanging all over him when we were teenagers and my skin crawls.

*I don't want that.*

Neither of us got anything good out of being born what we were. Him rich and spoiled, me the product of a drug addict, poor and lacking.

We both got fucked.

So did she.

But enough is enough. She deserves happiness. It's not in my nature to share. It's not in my nature to surrender either.

But for her...*I'd do anything.*

I swallow down the lump in my throat, both hands in my pockets as I look down at the white floors of the hospital room, inhaling the antiseptic smell, and that undercurrent of something like rot. I hate hospitals.

I hate a lot of things, actually.

She's the only thing I never have. Not really.

"I know," I finally say, my head still bowed as my gaze connects with his. I take a jagged breath in, knowing I might fucking collapse as I say the words, but I'm good at resurrecting walls. It's the only way I've learned how to survive.

She's the only one who ever managed to tear them down.

*Just for a moment.*

"I wanted to kill you, you know." I don't phrase it as a question. I'm sure we're both aware of what we feel for one another.

His eyes harden, but he doesn't speak.

"I hated you. I still do, actually," I tell him with a soft smile.

He doesn't return it.

"I can't stand the thought of her living a good life with you. Of you two…" The emotions clog my throat, threatening to choke me. I grit my teeth. Bite the inside of my cheek, so the physical pain can distract me from the fucking agony. "Of you two having a life. Me on the outside. Her…forgetting about me. What we went through together. How I never stopped…" I take a shuddering breath, unable to look him in the eye anymore. "Never stopped loving her. All those years. Nearly two fucking decades. I never stopped."

He just keeps staring at me, not a trace of emotion on his face. For once, though, it doesn't piss me off. I know this armor well. I've worn it myself most of my fucking life. I just keep talking anyway, knowing if I don't get it all out now, I probably never will. If I don't tell someone—and I don't think she always believes me, even if she understands me, sometimes, she's so full of self-loathing, she can't see all the ways I fucking adore her—it'll stay festering inside of my skin. Poisoning me from the inside out.

"The idea of you taking her, when I knew what you've done…" I bite my tongue so hard, I taste iron, but it's the only way I can keep going. Keep fucking talking. "I know what you did to me." My voice is hoarse as I stare at him, slipping my hands from my pockets, curling my fingers around the foot of the hospital bed, the plastic bumper bending and warping under my hand. "You left me in there, and I couldn't…I couldn't fucking let you do something like that to her. And your dad…*our fucking dad* sent me to kill her. And you too. And I didn't, but you…" My eyes are filling with tears. I swallow down the knot in my throat, trying to draw breath in my fucking lungs, but fuck, it's hard. It's so goddamn hard. I shift on my feet, taking another breath. "I thought you would have killed her. Until tonight…"

I notice his eyes are red too, gleaming with tears. I notice that lump in his throat as it bobs, the veins in his neck straining against his skin, his knuckles blanched as he clasps his hands tight together.

"You would've taken that bullet for her. And before that? I saw how you looked at her. Like it was…" Something wet falls from my eyes, warm down my cheek and I hate it. I hate him. I hate her.

I hate that I don't fucking hate them at all because I understand them. Both of them. They're just like me. I'm them.

We're all fucked.

"Like it was the last time. Like you were going to let her go, *if it made her happy.*"

He's chewing his cheek, tears falling down the pale planes of his face as his chin quivers, but he doesn't look away from me. Doesn't bother trying to hide his grief or deny the truth of my words.

"You're a fucking dick," I say, and he laughs, wiping the back of his hand over his eyes. "You're a piece of shit, and I swear if you don't stop fucking using, I really will kill you." He's still laughing, but it's kind of hollow. We both know it's true. "But you love her, and she fucking loves you, and the baby…"

He drops his hand to his lap, curling his fingers into a fist. I think about the scar across his palm. About the scar on hers.

The one on her belly too.

My name.

At least she'll have that.

"The baby is yours, and you need to be there for them."

He's nodding, his hands twisting in his lap again as those tears fall from his face. "Yeah," he croaks out. "Yeah…I know. I know." He says the words more like he's saying them to himself, and I know that feeling so well. Trying to convince yourself you'll do better. Be better.

But unlike me when I'm talking to myself, I think he actually means it.

"She's okay," I tell him, even though I know he knows. "But she's going to need you." Maverick came in here first without a single glance at me, to tell him exactly that. I know he loves her, too. I know he's been a far better brother than I could have ever been to her.

But I tried.

And that's what I say now. "I tried." My hands are shaky against the bumper on the hospital bed, but it's not from the tremor. Not from what the Forgues did to me. Instead, they're trembling from the same reason my head hurts. My body. The reason my eyes feel achy, my pulse flying from what's coming.

It's the grief that's making me shake. Threatening to send me spiraling.

I've been here before, when she ran from me. From them. I've felt this pain.

I almost didn't survive it. I think I won't now, either.

"I tried really hard for her, but I'm just not..." I shake my head, "I'm just not what she needs."

"But she loves you," he says, as if that excuses anything. As if that means we can keep playing this game between the three of us. Keep fucking each other over, nearly killing each other over something like that.

Love.

That's not real love. I'm not even sure what real love is. I've never felt it, save from Sid. She'd take both of us if we'd give her that. But I'm too selfish.

So is he.

I can't make her choose in this war.

"I love her, too, and when I'm gone..." I can barely say the words, the pain in my chest overwhelming. "I want you to make sure she knows that. Let her talk about me. Fucking...let her grieve."

He nods. "I will," he promises me, choking on the words from his grief. "I will."

And he doesn't ask where I'm going. He doesn't say

another word, and neither do I when I lock eyes with him and nod, and for a long, long moment, we hold each other's gaze.

I see his pain. I think he sees mine too.

I see what they made him into, but I see something else, beyond it. I see how he tried to fight against it. How he still has a heart, even though they tried to carve it right out of him. And like mine, his beats for her.

*Just her.*

I don't need to say any of that and neither does he. So instead, I nod once more, tap my hand against the edge of the bed, clench it into a fist, and turn around, walking out of his room without a glance back.

# CHAPTER Fifty

### SID

WHEN HE COMES IN, he brings the heaviness with him.

Jeremiah has always been impossible to ignore. Not just to me. *To anyone.* He's impossible to look away from, tall and fucking gorgeous as he is. He commands a room without saying a word.

And for me?

I've always felt like I've orbited around him. Like he held my entire world. Even when I ran, I felt his pain at finding me gone.

And those years we were apart?

I missed him, too, even though I had thought he'd terrorized me throughout my life because he was insane.

And he is.

But so am I.

That's why, when he comes in my room, an IV in my arm to hydrate me, I tense, and not from fear. Even after what he did to Lucifer, I'm not afraid of him. I don't think I'm even…angry.

Lucifer stabbed him.

They've both fucked with one another long before I was around.

Instead, I'm rigid from something else.

Because that grief that comes with him is palpable, like a thunderstorm inside this sterile room.

I fuck around with the buttons on the remote to my bed, inclining it so I'm sitting up. I'm exhausted, but I feel fine, physically. The bleeding was unexplained, but the baby is fine, and once more, I felt guilty that Lucifer didn't get to see the ultrasound, didn't get to hear the heart whooshing.

I felt even worse when a nurse asked about the J carved into my stomach.

I told her to mind her own business.

It wasn't that that made me feel guilty.

It was thinking of the scar it'll leave behind. How Lucifer might want me to tattoo over it, fuck, he might try to carve it out himself, but...*I want it.*

And as Jeremiah sits on the edge of my bed, the entire fucking thing dipping with his weight when he grabs my hands, holding them tightly in his, I know that might be all I have to remember him by.

I was wrong.

Lucifer won't leave me.

Or maybe he will, when he gets discharged. Maybe he'll be gone too.

But so will J.

I can see it all over his face, and I want to beg him to stay. I want to throw myself into his arms as his thumb runs over the top of my hand, the needle jammed in a vein. He's careful to avoid it.

So fucking careful.

So gentle.

Something he's only ever been with me.

Thinking of him doing this with someone else makes my stomach twist into knots. My mouth is dry, and I want to say something, to stop him from talking, but I can't get the words out.

Something bad is about to happen.

My heart is going to shatter all over again.

"Baby," he says, his voice broken. He glances down at our linked hands, the morning sun peeking through the cracked blinds at my back. There's a tray beside me, a cup of ice cubes in it, and I want to reach for it. I want to do something with my hands besides hold his, knowing he's going to get up and walk out.

He's going to leave me.

"Don't leave me." I blurt the words out, fast and in a rush.

His eyes hold mine, searching. I see tears welling in his own, beautiful green gleaming through the pain. So much fucking pain he's lived through, it's amazing he's able to be gentle at all.

Amazing, and heartbreaking, because he's going to go through more.

"Baby," he says again, "I think we both know I have to."

No. *Don't leave me.* I want to scream it. I want to scream at him. Shake him. Hurt him. Keep him here.

*Don't you dare fucking leave me.*

Panic threatens to wash over me, and he glances down between us, at my stomach, covered by the starchy white sheet and the paper-thin hospital gown. Aside from the question about his name branded into my belly, the nurses and the doctor haven't asked about what happened to me. To us.

Maverick, I think, had something to do with the fact that they haven't pried.

He came to me first, wrapped his arms around me. Ella did too.

And he didn't seem at all upset that our dad is gone. We didn't talk about it, but if anything, he seemed...lighter.

Maybe because Elijah's wife is back, although she doesn't even seem to know who took her. A girl, she said. A girl, but she covered her face with a skeleton mask.

*Seems fitting.*

It's something to worry about later, but she dropped her back off at Sanctum's doorstep. Well, the gate. Edith said a man hauled her out, that's what Maverick told me. A man, because she felt his size as she scratched at him. Heard his voice telling her to calm the fuck down as he set her down by the gate. But he bound her arms and she had a blindfold over her face.

She heard the engine of the car. Then it pulled away, and she had to wait until Elijah came to Sanctum to meet up with the Unsaints again.

But she's okay, and now there's more questions than answers.

In this moment though, I don't care about any of that.

All I care about is my heart breaking.

All I fucking care about is where he's going to go.

"Don't leave me," I say again. "You can't…you can't do that."

He's still staring at my belly, and I know he's thinking about the baby. Seeming reluctant to do it, he tears his eyes from there, meeting my gaze, and I see a tear clinging to his lower lash line.

He squeezes my hands tighter, our fingers threaded together.

"I don't want to." He runs his tongue over his teeth, staring at me. "You know that, don't you, baby? I don't fucking want to."

My heart is beating too fast in my chest. So fucking fast, it's scaring me. But I'm not hooked up to a pulse monitor, and I'm glad, because I can't deal. With doctors, nurses. I couldn't fucking deal.

"Then don't," I plead with him. "J, please——"

He leans in close to me, stealing my words as he angles his head. His gaze dips down to my mouth and I inhale his clean scent, sucking in a breath.

Then his mouth is on mine, and my lips part for him

without hesitation. His hands come to my face, then one threads through my hair. I grip his arms, feel his hard muscles flex as I cling to him, tears falling down my cheeks, salty on our lips.

He's crying too, and as we collide, I try to memorize this. His taste, fresh and minty and fucking perfect, because he's tried to keep everything that way. For so long, he was in darkness. Filth and decay.

I embed the way his fingers feel against my face, tangled in my hair, into my mind. The way he groans against my mouth like he just can't fucking get enough of me. The way he takes and gives and how my heart flutters when his tongue twirls around mine.

The hand on my face trails down to my throat, over my breasts, and he moans against me, but that's not where he stops.

Instead, he slips his hand up the gown, over my thigh, past my hips, right above his initial carved into my skin.

Goosebumps break out over my body as he runs his thumb over the healing cut.

Finally, when I feel like I really can't breathe, he pulls back, fingers still threaded in my hair.

"I love you, baby."

I bite my lip, a swell of emotion making it hard to think, let alone talk, but I know if I don't say it, I'll regret this for the rest of my life. I have this strange, crushing feeling that where he's going, I won't be able to follow. "I love you too, J. So much. I love you so fucking much."

"I know," he says simply, his full, beautiful lips turning up into a smile. "I know you do. And that's the best thing anyone could have ever given me, you know that?"

I can't let him leave.

*I fucking can't.*

"Where are you going?" I whisper instead, because I've already begged him. Already told him not to go. And I know when Jeremiah makes up his mind about something, he doesn't stop. He won't let anyone change it.

I haven't accepted it yet.

I don't quite believe it. Don't think that soon, he won't be following me. Won't be stalking me.

The thought almost makes me smile, and he must see it, because his own lips pull into a small smile. "What're you thinking about, beautiful?" he asks me quietly, his breath caressing my mouth.

I know he didn't answer my question, but I kind of don't care. I kind of don't want to hear his answer. How it might shatter my heart.

"I was thinking…" I trail off and he leans closer, his lips grazing mine in the whisper of a kiss.

My eyes flutter closed, and I try to get myself the fuck together to finish my sentence.

"I was thinking that you're a complete fucking psycho," I whisper honestly, dissolving into laughter that only serves to twist my heart further. I force myself to open my eyes as I feel my lips brush against his with the words.

He blinks at me, then laughs too, delicious and husky, a sensual sound that sends warmth flooding to my core, right beneath his hand still on my bare skin.

I should feel bad about it, and maybe I do a little, knowing my husband is in the room next to mine, still recovering.

But these are stolen moments of time. Moments that'll end too fucking soon, and I don't let the guilt plague me.

Because if I don't enjoy this, if I don't drink every inch of Jeremiah Rain in, I'll regret it for the rest of my life.

Nearly two decades spent hating and loving him, running from and to him.

I think it'll take at least another two to get over him.

"I am," he says finally, agreeing with my assessment of his mental health. He drags his fingers through my hair, tucks a lock behind my ear. "Remember that time I fired a gun at your head?"

And then we both dissolve into laughter, because the truth is, we're both fucking insane.

After a moment, though, the smiling and laughter trail off, and we're together in silence.

He bows his head over mine, our brows together as he grabs my hand again, one still splayed over my belly.

"I love you, and I never want you to forget that. And there's something else I never want you to forget."

I hold my breath, trying not to break down as I stare into his beautiful eyes.

"I never want you to forget that you deserve it. *My* love. *His love.*"

My stomach churns with his last words. My heart is pounding so hard, it hurts.

"You remember I once told you that you deserve the world, baby?"

I close my eyes, squeezing them tight as tears spill down my cheeks again. I remember it. I've never forgotten it.

"I mean it," he whispers, his lips grazing mine again. "And I don't have to burn it down. Lucifer will give you everything you could ever want, in your wildest fucking dreams."

The tears fall faster, my chest rising and falling as the sobs break through, clawing up my throat.

"And if he doesn't," he says, pressing his soft lips to my cheeks as I keep my eyes closed, scared to look at him for the last time, "I'll fucking kill him, okay, baby?"

I don't laugh at that.

Mainly because I believe him, but also because I don't want to see him for the last time. I'm not ready.

Not yet.

Not until I know.

"Where are you going, J? *Where the fuck are you going?*" The words come out strangled, a faint whisper laced with the darkest grief.

He licks my tears, drags his mouth over my cheek until his tongue flicks along the seam of my lips. But when I open my mouth, suck in a breath, he doesn't kiss me. He just tells me the truth.

"Far from here, baby."

"The Order of Rain?" I manage to ask, clinging to him, my nails digging against his hard muscles.

He laughs and despite my heart breaking, I can't help but smile at that laugh. "Come on, *sis*. The Order goes where I go."

I knew he would say something cocky like that.

He slides his hand from under my gown and he wraps his arms around me, scooting awkwardly onto the bed as he lifts me up, careful with the IV, and holds me in his arms.

I twist around and my own arms are around his neck. He's cradling me like a child, and in this moment, I feel exactly like one, scared to death to leave the only family I've ever known.

"You don't need me anymore, Sid, baby," he says, as if he's reading my mind. "You're so strong. The strongest girl I've ever met." He nuzzles his nose against mine and another strangled sob leaves my lips, but I try to keep it together, try not to lay my head against his chest and sink into a dark, dark grief I'm not sure I'll ever recover from. "It's time to fucking fly, Sid Rain."

He wraps me up in his arms, my head against his shoulder as I cry, and I think he is, too, his shoulders shaking, warm wetness against my neck.

"It's time to fly, baby, and you and Lucifer and this kid? You're all gonna rule the fucking world."

I can't speak. How do you handle twenty years of loss? How do you move on from someone you spent your earliest moments with, someone that protected you with their own body, their own life, as much as they could?

How do you wrap up hate and love in a pretty little goodbye?

How do you let go?

I cling to him, gripping his shirt in my fists.

"Maybe me and you are it in another life, yeah, baby?"

*Yeah. Maybe then.* But I don't say that. Instead, I just let the tears fall and hold him tighter.

We only have this life, J.

*We only have this one.*

# CHAPTER Fifty-One

## SID

HE'S SLEEPING, just like he's done the past two days. He has his wrist over his brows, the sheets pulled down to his hips, his bare chest rising and falling steadily, those beautiful scars over his torso making my chest tighten.

I'm awake, just as I've been for nearly two days now.

Two days since Jeremiah left me in that hospital bed. Since Maverick helped Lucifer hobble over to my room when it was all over, helped him get into my bed.

He's still bruised, his face still swollen, but he looks better.

In fact, he looks perfect, because that's how he always looks.

On our nightstand, there's no coke. No fucking straws, either. Mayhem cleaned the house out while we stayed overnight in the hospital as a precaution. At least, that's what the doctor said.

We were fine.

I think the precaution was a payoff from my brother so he could rid our house of drugs.

Save for the cigarettes, and the lighters downstairs on the kitchen island.

One thing at a time, I guess.

I sink down into the couch under the window in our bedroom, the curtains pulled closed, only a slice of light spearing the room.

I bring my knees to my chest, which is becoming increasingly harder to do, and wrap my arms around my shins.

If I close my eyes, I can still smell him.

Feel him.

Hear his beautiful laugh.

Lucifer promised me he didn't know where he was. I called Nicolas. I called *him*. I just wanted...another goodbye.

But I think he knows what I've come to learn about goodbyes.

No matter how many times you say it, the end result is the same. Someone still leaves, and it still hurts like hell.

Another clumsy word on the tip of our tongues can't save us from that kind of pain.

I glance down at the ring on my finger. A black diamond in the shape of a rose, a black band, too. Despite the hole in my heart that Jeremiah left behind, I smile at that ring.

At the one I see on Lucifer's ring finger, too. A matte black band carved with a skull.

My husband.

The words feel good now when I think them. Think of how I'm here with him. He's coming down from all the fucking coke, and I know it's hard. It's why he's sleeping. Why I've tried—and failed—to cook so many meals and ended up throwing in the metaphorical fucking dishtowel and letting Ella handle it all.

I rest my chin on my knees, staring at Lucifer stirring in our bed of black satin sheets, gray pillows.

He's so fucking beautiful it sometimes hurts to look at him.

But other times, I can't look away, like now.

He rubs his fists over his eyes, slowly sits up, and he's looking around in a daze, like he's searching for something.

*For me.*

I clear my throat softly, and he whips his head in my direction.

When our eyes connect, a smile pulls at the corners of his beautiful mouth. His top lip is bigger than his bottom one and it looks so fucking adorable, it takes an effort for me to stay right where I'm at on this black leather couch.

"You should've woken me up," he says, his voice thick with sleep. "I thought you wanted to run this morning."

I smile at him, picking my head up as he leans back against the headboard, running his hand through his curls. He drops it by his side, and I take in his abs, his chest, his perfect pale skin.

"I do," I tell him. "But you said you were taking the week off."

He tips his head back and laughs at that, raspy and throaty as he stares at the ceiling.

Reminding me of Jeremiah. *His brother.*

"Baby girl. I'm not going back to work for a long, long time," he finally says, dipping his chin and holding my gaze.

His eyes are so startling, contrasted with his pale skin, his black curls, they take my breath away.

"You're my priority. And the baby, too." His voice softens with those words, as he dips his gaze lower, to the loose white tank I'm wearing, nothing else but underwear. "Speaking of, come sit with me, *mama.*"

That word sends warmth coursing through me, and after a minute of him staring at me in expectation, I get to my feet and cross the room. Before I can crawl onto the bed, he's leaned up, grabbed me by the waist, and hauled me against his chest, his arms wrapped tight around me as he leans against the headboard, kissing my cheek and squeezing me close.

Then his hand slips under my tank, resting against Jeremiah's initial.

I tense in his arms, not breathing.

He laughs against my ear, his breath on my skin. But it isn't a pleasant laugh. There's nothing warm in that raspy rumble.

And when he flips me over, coming on top of me as my breath leaves me in a rush, I'm not at all surprised at the fury in his gaze as his finger digs into the healing wound as he yanks my shirt up.

*There he is. My husband.*

"You let him do this to you?" he asks me quietly, tracing over it with his index finger, but his eyes are boring into mine. He's blocking the sliver of sun at his back, and his features are shrouded in darkness, but that blue of his eyes is so damn vivid, it's startling.

I don't think I'll ever get used to his beauty.

"Lucifer, I don't—"

"Answer the fucking question, Lilith."

I bite my cheek, glancing down at his finger on me, my hands gripping the sheets beside me. "Yes," I tell him. "I let him do it."

He stares at me a moment, as if he's looking for the truth. Trying to decipher it from my fucking bullshit.

"You know what I should do, don't you?" he asks me, leaning down closer.

"What you threatened at Ignis?" I counter. "That didn't work out so fucking well—"

He grabs my throat, silencing me as he leans even closer and I can smell the pine scent of him, tinged with nicotine. "Baby girl," he warns me, "since when have you ever known me to just *let things go?*" He glances down at his finger over my brand. "Especially when it comes to *my feisty fucking wife?*"

He reaches over me, his long, lean arm flexing as he grabs something I can't see from the nightstand drawer.

I tense even before I hear the snick of the blade.

Before I feel it cold against my skin, right over Jeremiah's initial.

*His name.*

J.

Jeremiah and Jamie. A beautiful, broken boy that I couldn't save how I wanted to. But he saved me, in the end.

"Lucifer," I whisper, gripping the sheets so hard my hands shake. I glance down, see my swollen belly. I'm showing now, due August seventh.

I have another scan next week, because I missed the full anatomy scan. Didn't see the gender.

But I'm glad, and I told them in the hospital not to tell me.

I wanted Lucifer to be there for that.

But now…

"Don't," I tell him.

He runs the flat side of the blade over my belly, making it jump. He glances down, and I see his face soften as he stares at the baby.

If he stays away from the coke, if he keeps a regular sleep schedule, and maybe if I stop breaking his heart…he'll recover from the psychosis.

He spoke to a psychiatrist at the hospital.

Maverick was in the room, per Elijah's orders. He told him nothing other than that he'd watched his father die.

His nightmares the past two nights have been non-existent. He's clung to me but hasn't spoken much. Mav and Ella have been over, and they told me it was normal, apparently. Because of his withdrawals. He's just lethargic, lacking energy. Probably craving blow, but he hasn't said anything about it to me.

We're back to building our walls.

He's back to acting angry when he's really just…scared.

Scared I'll run. Scared I'll break his heart again. Maybe scared the 6 will come for us all over again.

Mayhem told me Maddox was buried next to his father.

Another one down, but with the investigation into who took Elijah's wife, who stalked me in the woods behind Jeremiah's house and got my pictures—the thought makes my skin crawl, knowing someone was watching me who I didn't know —who killed a dancer at Jeremiah's club, and the retaliation against Maddox's suicide hasn't come.

But then again, he did it to himself.

I have no doubt one of the three of us would have killed him in that cabin in the woods, but the fucker didn't even give us the chance.

Lucifer angles the knife so the sharp side is against my skin.

I tense, but I don't look away from him. "I know you don't want to do this."

"You think I want another man's name on you, baby girl? You know better than that."

I reach up, cup his face with my hand, taking in the beautiful curve of his cheekbone. "Your baby is listening right now," I tell him quietly, my thumb stroking over his bottom lip.

His eyes widen, his already-pale face turning ashen as his throat bobs.

"You want them to hear their father threatening their mother with a knife?"

He blinks down at me, but he doesn't move, one hand pressing into the mattress, the other still holding the blade to my belly. Then he says, "Did you tell Jeremiah just that when he made you bleed?" There's venom in those words, but there's pain too.

I feel it, not just from him. From me.

From thinking about what he went through while I was gone.

His eyes find the scar on my brow for a second. "I made you bleed too, yeah, baby girl? But that's because you're mine. You're mine to do whatever the fuck I want with, because at the end of it all—all the fucking pain, all the agony, the goddamn tears and blood and bruises—I'll always put you back together." He leans down close, presses a kiss to my mouth. "I'll always be here for you. I'll never leave you. I'll never fucking run from you, Lilith, like you did from me." He drags the knife softly over my skin and I suck in a breath, my hand going to his shoulder, my other one, too, holding onto him. "I might make you cry. I might hurt you, just as bad as you hurt me. But that's the difference between us. When it gets hard, I'm not going to run. And you fucking left me when I needed you. So, don't think for one fucking second you're going to manipulate me into *not* carving any trace of him off of you."

I dig my nails into his skin, prepared to fight him off if he tries. I'm glaring up at him, holding my breath as he speaks.

"Because it's not about him. It's never been about him. It's about *you, Lilith. Fucking* you." An anguished groan escapes his lips and he throws the knife across the room. It hits the window, then clatters to the floor as I flinch, trying to catch my breath.

"It's about how you always chose everyone but me." He pushes back, away from me, sitting on his heels, raking his fingers through his hair before he drops them down to his thighs, his hand over his Unsaint's tattoo and all the scars along it, his boxer briefs the only thing he's wearing. "You always ran away from my pain, while all I wanted to do was fucking hold yours. Hold you. Keep you together."

His words cut deep.

I sit up slowly, thinking of all the ways I fucked him over. The ways he's fucked me too.

"Lucifer," I whisper, reaching my scarred hand out, the one with the black ring. He looks up at me, full of mistrust, shadows under his eyes, his face still healing from Jeremiah's fists. "I'm sorry," I tell him, and I mean it.

I really mean it.

I don't regret the time I had with Jeremiah, but I can understand how that fucked up my husband. And I know he knows why I ran, and I know he's used to this life. The threats. The rituals. The freaky shit.

I'm not.

And his nightmares…the way he acted like he couldn't stand the sight of me sometimes…it hurt.

"I'm sorry for running, but I'm not anymore."

He swallows as he takes my hand, threading our fingers together. "Did you hate me?" he asks quietly. "Did you think…maybe that I was…broken?" He looks down at me with wide blue eyes, and he looks so vulnerable, something in my chest seems to crack. Just like that night I ran down the stairs, trying to find him, soothe his nightmares, I feel a rush of protectiveness toward him that I don't think I've ever felt for anyone else, save for Jeremiah Rain.

"What?" I ask him, shaking my head, my lip trembling. "Of course not. You never thought that about me—"

"You're not," he says quickly, and I shift forward, on my knees too, so our legs are brushing against one another. "You're not broken. You're perfect, Lilith. You're fucking perfect for me. I just…don't know why it took you so damn long to figure it out."

*I still haven't.*

"I don't deserve you," I say out loud, exactly what I'm thinking. "I don't think I…" I trail off as Jeremiah's words get stuck in my head. *"I never want you to forget that you deserve it. My love. His love."*

"You think, because of what happened to you, what they did to you, that I'm not gonna be yours for the rest of our fucking lives?" He yanks me forward, swings his legs over the bed, his feet hitting the floor as he pulls me into his arms, cradling me just like Jeremiah did.

The last time I saw him.

"Because make no mistake, baby girl, when my time is up…*so is yours.*" His hand comes to my throat, one around my back as he holds me close, my legs dangling over his lap. His fingers close around me, and he kisses me, long and hard, his teeth dragging out my lower lip. "And until that day comes, you're fucking stuck with me, baby girl."

I kiss him back, sitting up straighter, my arms wrapped around his neck as he steals my breath with his mouth, his fingers on my throat.

And when his other hand comes between my thighs, slipping underneath the edges of my shorts, I know that we're both insane.

And I wouldn't have it any other way.

"No matter what you've done, no matter what you do, I've been wrapped around your fucking finger since I saw you at that intersection," he says against my mouth, his fingers pushing into my pussy as I gasp, my lips brushing his. "The only thing I could fucking think about was, *when do I get to knock this crazy bitch up?*" The pad of his thumb circles my clit while I clench around his fingers.

His tongue dives into my mouth, but then he pushes me back on the bed, pulling his fingers out of me like he just can't fucking stand that being the only thing inside of me.

He yanks down his boxers while I pull off my underwear.

I go for my shirt, but he grabs my wrist, then pushes me down against the pillows.

"No," he says, a bite in that word. "If you don't want me to carve that out of you, baby girl, keep your shirt on." But he lets go of my wrist, takes the strap of my tank top in his hands and pulls, ripping the fabric on one side, then the other, shoving it down so my swollen tits are exposed, his hands gliding over them, twisting and pulling my nipples.

I gasp, my back arching as he strokes his cock, positions it against my entrance.

"You should've never let another man touch you like that. You should've never fucking let him put his hands on you at all, baby girl," he whispers, his hand finding my throat again as he shoves into me, not giving me time to adjust.

He props himself up on his elbow, his free hand splaying along my stomach between us as he fucks me so hard my head hits the headboard. "This is *my* baby. Me and you, Lilith. *This is us.*"

He buries himself inside of me, his hand still on my throat, the other going to the headboard as he leans down, bites my neck so hard I cry out, my hands going to his throat too, trying to push him off of me.

He doesn't stop.

I know I'm bleeding.

I know he can taste me in his mouth, and I know that's exactly what he wants.

He pulls back, pulls out of me as he does and I gasp with the loss of him, craning my neck up as he glides his tongue down my body, sucking on my nipples, biting too.

Then his head is between my legs, his hands on my ankles as I bend my knees, planting my feet on the bed.

"Always so fucking wet for me," he murmurs, his words against my pussy.

I run my fingers through his hair.

"You're mine, baby girl. Fucking mine." He licks me, teasing, pulling my clit into his mouth as I gasp, his eyes on me. "If you ever let another man touch you like he did, like my fucking brothers did…if you ever let someone that close to you again…" He turns his head, bites the inside of my thigh, my fingers knotting in his hair as I gasp, see blood on his lip when he pulls away.

"I'll fucking kill them, until all you've got left is me." Then he dives down, pushing his tongue inside of me, gripping my thighs hard enough to leave a bruise as I gasp, calling his name.

He pulls back, and I try to push his head back down but he just laughs, resisting me. Then, staring right at my pussy, he spits on me, warm saliva dripping down my slit, before his gaze meets mine again. "You're my fucking wife, Lilith. Mine, and goddamn, I'm yours. Don't forget it again, yeah, baby girl?" He pushes two fingers into me as he waits for me to answer him.

I clench around him, then nod. "Yes," I gasp out, "I'm yours, Lucifer."

He smiles at me before he dips his head back down and starts torturing me all over again until I'm moaning his name. Then he crawls up me, pushing into my throbbing pussy, groaning my name as he fucks me. *Lilith*, like a chant, his hand around my throat like that'll keep me here. Keep us together.

I think this time…it just might.

"DID YOU MEAN IT?" HE ASKS ME THAT NIGHT. I'M IN HIS LAP, his hands on my hips, the blankets pulled up to our chin as we sit on the couch in the living room, empty cereal bowls on the coffee table, a horror movie neither of us are watching playing.

We're healing, going through motions to living, but our hearts, our minds…they're probably elsewhere.

I pick my head up from his shoulder, twist around to stare into his eyes. "Mean what?" I ask him, confused. Tense. Everything has been one explosion after the other with us, I'm not comfortable. I'm not scared of him, but with Jeremiah so far, and his protection gone, I just feel…out of sorts. There's a literal ache in my chest from J's absence, and the only thing that makes it feel remotely better is looking at his initial in my skin.

But seeing my husband's face now, his dark brows furrowed, his eyes glued to mine, I know that if I had been forced to choose—if Jeremiah hadn't made the choice for me —right here is where I would want to be.

I love them both. I probably always will.

But living without Lucifer…I think it would be impossible. For both of us.

"When you said I was your…" He glances down, between us, one hand coming to my belly, slipping under the hem of my tank top, his fingers cold as they splay against my skin. "Nightmare?" he finally finishes with, whispering that word as he looks back up at me through his long lashes. The TV is on low, the screen flashing along his face, and I see the fear there. He doesn't bother trying to hide it.

Like he's trying to open up. Trying to be vulnerable.

"When you said I wasn't your flinch?"

At that word, my breath catches in my throat and I close my eyes, my hands fisted under the blanket, in the fuzzy velvet.

He leans closer and I feel his breath against my ear when he whispers, "It's okay, baby girl." Despite the words, I hear the pain. "You can feel how you like. I don't want you to hide anything from me, Sid." He drops his head, pressing a kiss to my shoulder, his full lips against my skin as he slides the thin strap of my tank top down my arm with his teeth.

Warmth flushes through me, but I open my eyes, wanting to stop him.

We communicate with sex, but it's not enough. For me, for him. We have to find ways to talk without fucking it out. Afterward, fine. But I know he wants more from me. He always has.

I wrap my arms around his neck, twisting further, swinging my legs on the couch. He smiles, one hand still on my tummy, the other around my back as he holds me to him.

My heart races in my chest as I think about the past year and a half. How our lives changed completely. The things he gave up for me, and the things he's tried, in his own way, to fight against. How he felt when he lost track of me on that Halloween night, and then Noctem, when I ran.

*He loves me.*

I think I've always known that.

But I'm not sure if he's always known my own truth. "I

love you, Lucifer," I tell him honestly, my eyes searching his as his hands tighten around me, on my hip and my belly. Over our child. "I've loved you since before we were married." I didn't want to feel it then. I didn't want to be so vulnerable, but I knew if I ever had to live without him, it would be a hard, painful life. I wanted to keep them both, and my love for Lucifer doesn't negate my love for Jeremiah, but Lucifer…no matter what he's done, *he's my person.* "And you've always been my flinch. That night…" I swallow down the lump in my throat, the broken tone to my voice as I close my eyes tight and he brushes a lock of hair behind my ear, his arm wrapped around me. "And every night after," I finally finish on a hoarse whisper as I open my eyes.

When I do, he's smiling at me, his white, straight teeth and that dimple in his pale face the most beautiful thing I think I've ever seen.

He presses his forehead to mine, his thumb drawing small circles on my belly. "You mean that?" he asks me, his voice so, so quiet.

I smile back at him, inhaling that pine and nicotine scent that I wish I could bottle up and keep forever. But I guess since I have him, I don't really need a bottle. "I mean it," I promise him.

"You think you can be happy with me?" I see his throat bob as he swallows when silence, save for the movie neither of us are paying attention to, spreads between us.

I bite my lip, my fingers running through his curls, my arms still wrapped around him. "I know I can." There's conviction in those words, because I mean them. If he stays clean, if he lets me breathe, lets me talk, lets me *be me*, he could make me the happiest girl in the world. "I am, when you love me for me," I add truthfully. "I love everything about you. I just want you to love everything about me, too." My chest tightens with that confession, and his thumb stops trailing my skin for a moment, his body rigid beneath me.

I tense up, too, worried I've said the wrong thing then pissed at myself for worrying about something like that. If I want transparency between us, he needs to let me live, just like I said.

But after a moment, he relaxes, pulling me even closer until my head is against his chest and he's cradling me like I'm a child.

"Okay," he says softly, staring down at me, "but *do you* love when I do coke?" There's a hint of a smile on his lips, and I punch him playfully on the arm, rolling my eyes and shaking my head.

"Of course not you fucking fool, but that's not actually *you*—"

He shrugs, cutting me off, still smiling as he holds my gaze. "I don't love you letting other guys touch you. I don't love you flirting with them, or, to be fucking honest, talking to them, but I can get over that last one if I have to."

A heavy weight seems to settle back on my shoulders and I look away from him, at the blanket over our laps. "You didn't seem to mind when everyone took turns with me at Ignis."

His grip tightens. "That was different. A one-time thing. *An initiation.*"

I roll my eyes, but give him another truth. "I'm not going to fuck anyone else." I bite the inside of my cheek, trying not to see it. To think about him fucking Ophelia at Liber. My face turns hot, and it's not from embarrassment. It's anger. *Pain.* "But I don't want you to—"

He slips his hand from under my shirt and grips my chin, lifting my gaze to his. His eyes are fierce, the blue seeming to darken in the reflection from the TV screen. Every word is serious when he says, "Never again, Lilith." He angles his head, his lips hovering over mine, his breath fanning my face. "I'm only yours. I'm sorry for what I did." He swallows, his thumb caressing my jaw, his mouth so close but not quite there. I clench my thighs together, and remind myself we need to *talk*, not just *fuck*. But he's so damn hot and so damn close.

And when he's promising to be just mine?

I want to ride him right here, but I dig my nails into the tops of my hands, still wound around his neck, and wait.

"But I'll never speak to her again."

I open my mouth to tell him that's okay, but he kisses me then, his mouth open on mine, his tongue flicking along the seam of my lips.

I part for him and he groans in my mouth as I squeeze him tighter, drawing myself closer.

He pulls back and I'm panting when he does, a wicked little smirk pulling at his own lips.

"I don't care if you were going to say it's fine. It isn't fine. I already told her," he says quietly, and I arch a brow, not knowing they spoke. "She wanted to see me in the hospital," he admits quietly, holding my gaze, as if he wants me to know nothing happened. That it didn't mean anything. "Mav wouldn't let her."

A small laugh escapes my mouth and I know it's petty, but he's my fucking husband. *Not hers.*

"I answered her call, though, told her our friendship had to end."

My stomach twists into knots as I pull back to take him in better. "And?" I press, wanting to know.

He shrugs. "She started crying. I told her you were my wife, the mother of my child, and you, *baby girl*, come before anyone else in the fucking world."

My breath catches, my heart pounding painfully in my chest. "Really?" I whisper.

He rolls his eyes like I'm crazy. "*Obviously.*" His smile widens. "And I bought you a stupid fucking car, by the way."

My brows raise high on my head, and I sit up straighter, twisting and adjusting my stance so I'm straddling him, my knees on either side of his hips.

He laughs, his hands skimming up my arms as the blanket falls behind me. "Damn, if I had known that would get me laid like this—"

"Shut up," I mumble, swatting at his chest, both hands against his bare skin. "You always get laid, baby."

He bites his lip as he stares up at me. "True," he concedes. "Because you're fucking perfect." He drops his hands to my ass, squeezing me.

"So, about this car..." I tilt my head, waiting.

He laughs again and the rough sound sends a chill down my spine. "It's just like mine, but gray." His head is tilted back, that vein in his neck looking extra kissable. Maybe...bitable? "But seriously, I don't..." He swallows, glancing down between us, my thighs around him as his hands grip my ass. "I don't want you going places that could get you hurt. And it has a tracking device, but so does mine." He shrugs, looking back up at me. "It's in an app on your phone, upstairs."

I cup his face in my hands, leaning down close to him. I know I should argue with him. Maybe tell him he's fucking extreme, but the fact is...it kind of makes me feel safe. Letting him take care of me. Track me. *Protect me.*

"I love you," I tell him, my nose against his. "I love you so much, baby."

He's quiet a moment, staring up at me through the curtain of my hair. "I love you too, baby girl," he finally says, and I can hear the emotion thick in his voice. "More than anything in this stupid world."

# CHAPTER
## Fifty-Two

LUCIFER

SHE'S in my lap eating cereal, and Maverick has his arm slung around Ella across the table from us, his expression serious as he stares at me.

I smack the side of Sid's hip, and she groans my name in annoyance, which just makes my dick hard.

I know she can feel it too, the way she sighs, like she's exasperated, but I know she can't get enough of me.

Two weeks since Maddox died, and I swear to God his fucking body rotting in the ground has made everyone happier. Lighter. Full of…something like goddamn joy.

If it weren't for Mav sitting across from me like someone pissed in his fucking Corn Flakes—I don't have those, Sid is eating something fruity because we both know it's the superior cereal—I'd be having another great fucking day.

It's been over two weeks since I last used, and I'm not even thinking about it anymore.

Not usually, anyway.

Sometimes, I catch sight of that scar on my wife's growing belly, and I want to drag a blade around it, cut it the fuck out, bump a line while I do it.

But I let it go, because our baby growing inside of her is

the most beautiful thing I've ever seen in my fucking life. I place my hand over her belly now, my chest tightening thinking about it.

Being a father. Her, a mother.

She's already so perfect. She'll be even better then.

I haven't heard from Jeremiah Rain, and sometimes, I think he might be dead. I don't think I care.

But sometimes...I wonder if I do.

A few nights, Sid has cried over him, and while it pisses me off, seeing her so emotional over another man like that, I just let her, holding her as she does.

I don't really understand their bond, but I know Jeremiah had Maddox in his car, bringing him here to kill for her. I know he killed Elizabeth Astor too.

For her.

"We have Council tomorrow," Mav says, tearing me away from thoughts of *him*, and Ella rolls her eyes which makes me smile, but Mav must see it because he reaches his hand down her shirt and grabs a handful of her tit.

She flushes red, twisting to glare at him, but he just keeps talking to me, his hand still down her shirt as Sid cracks up in my lap, her legs dangling over mine under the polished wooden table.

I slip my hand between her thighs, unseen by them, and that shuts her pretty little ass up. All I hear is her sharp intake of breath, then the loud crunch of cereal as she shoves a spoonful into her mouth, staring down at the nearly empty black bowl on the table.

I grab her hip and keep my eyes on Mav. "I'm not going."

"You can't just not go, Luce, fuck." His hand slips out of Ella's shirt and he raises his arm from around her as he brings it down to the table, clasping his fingers together. "My dad is fucking dead," he says, and I hear the pain in his words. He doesn't mention his mom, and I know that one hurts a little more.

He might want to deny it, but even Brooklin cried. I was there when he told her, at Ezra's house.

Ezra seemed relieved too, but curiously, Ezra hasn't seemed too upset about who kidnapped his mom. Never seemed that bothered by it at all.

But they took pictures of my wife, so as soon as I find out who the fuck it was, I'll kill them too.

And that's how I know Maverick knows that his parents' deaths are…what needed to happen. Otherwise, he would've killed Jeremiah at the hospital.

He didn't, though.

We let him go.

"The rest of them…" Mav runs a hand over his hair, and I see my wife's name and want to fucking kill him all over again.

But she's mine.

She's in my lap.

She's not going to run again.

We've been talking. *Really* talking. And fucking, of course, and sometimes we still scream at each other and sometimes she acts like she hates me, but I know she doesn't mean it.

I know she loves the fuck out of me.

"The rest of them are decent," Mav says, and I laugh so hard at that. Even Sid snorts, shoving her empty bowl away from her as she leans back against me, my hand still between her thighs, one still on her hip.

"Good one, *bro*," I tell Maverick, shrugging. "You can go. Let me know what they discuss."

"Don't you want to know who the fuck stalked Angel?" he asks, like that's her name. I guess to him it is, but doesn't really seem to fit to me.

I reluctantly move my hand from cupping her pussy over her shorts, wrap it around her chest, feel the swell of her breasts beneath my forearm as I kiss her cheek. She's no angel. She's my fucking little devil.

"Yeah," I tell Mav honestly, "and if you find out, you can let me know, okay?" I kiss my wife again, her fingers around my forearm, clinging to me. I see the lights overhead reflect off that black diamond around her perfect little finger and even though we have the scars, it feels like Jeremiah fucking Rain corrupted that shit, and I'm glad I got her a ring.

She deserves it.

That, and so much fucking more.

Mav rolls his eyes. "You know they'll make you come if you don't—"

I sit up straighter, my arm still slung around Sid's chest. She presses her nails lightly into my skin, like a warning, but I don't give a fuck anymore.

"They let him threaten my wife." I don't say his name, because he doesn't deserve to be remembered. He doesn't fucking deserve to be spoken of, ever again. This is the last I want to say about it. "I have enough fucking money to buy the goddamn world without working another day in my life. If they want to throw the occasional murder my way, fucking fine. So be it. But until I'm good and goddamn ready," I rap my knuckles against the table, "I'm done. They can come." I smile at him, his eyes hard on me, and Ella glancing at the ceiling, probably wanting to be anywhere but here. "I'll fucking kill them if they touch my girl again, but they're *more than fucking welcome to come.*"

Maverick clenches his jaw, that tattoo pulling down as he glares at me. "I need you back," he says quietly, and Ella glances at him, sidling closer, and no doubt putting her hand on his thigh under the table. "I need you back because I can't do this alone."

Sid stiffens in my lap. Her fingers are still wrapped around my forearm, but she leans forward a little. "Why go?" she asks her brother, and I stare at him, waiting for him to answer the fucking question. "Why bother?"

Ella's eyes dart to Sid's. "You can't just give up the 6," she says, surprising me. "We all know that's not how it works."

I always knew she was smart and not just good at sucking my dick.

Mav wraps his arm back around her shoulder, pulling her close, and she smiles up at him. He's smiling too, but then his eyes find mine again and the smile is gone. "We could make it better, if we wanted," he says quietly.

I bark a laugh at that. "And if we don't?" Because I don't fucking care. Like Cain once said, someone else can handle that hero shit. It's not for me. My son doesn't need a hero. My wife, either. She's not one. He won't be one, I'm sure of it.

I'm fine with that.

Villains get shit done. Heroes are a great distraction from the bloodshed behind the scenes. The hard work that's *necessary*. Not every life deserves to be saved.

"You don't want to protect anyone else from going through what Angel did? What *he* did?"

I tense with those words, and I know my wife isn't breathing in my lap.

I hold her closer, a warning and a comfort.

"Nah," I tell Maverick. "I don't have time to give a fuck about anyone else right now. My family is my priority."

"And what if that happened to your son?" Ella chimes in, and I want to ring her fucking neck. "What if someone took him, sold him off to be used?" She darts her gaze to Sid, blushing as she does.

Sid, for her part, is silent, until she says, "If someone touched my son, I'd fucking gut them," and my dick grows hard all over again.

I kiss her neck, smile at Maverick. "That part," I tell him.

He rolls his eyes. "Don't you want to know if they've got any other kids being abused right fucking now? Being used as fucking sex toys, just like Sid? Being throat fucked and—"

"Shut the fuck up," I snarl, holding my wife tighter, as if

squeezing her hard enough to cause pain will stop her from hearing the reminders of her past.

"Exactly," Mav says. "You don't want to hear it, but it could be happening. And it's up to us to fucking do something about it."

For a long moment, no one speaks.

And when I ask, "Baby girl, you wanna burn that shit to the ground?" I don't. I really, really don't. It might make me a fuck, but I already know that.

What I want is to keep my wife safe. My kid safe.

I want her by my side, all the time. I want to tuck her against me, never let her move without me knowing about it.

I never claimed we had a healthy marriage, but fuck if it isn't exactly the kind of toxicity I want.

"Yeah," she finally says, twisting around to stare at me, her big silver eyes locked on mine. "I do."

I hold her gaze for a moment, biting my lip.

Then I sigh, looking to Mav.

"You heard her." I shrug, rolling my eyes. "Guess I'll go fuck shit up at Council again after all."

Mav laughs, but he's looking at Sid, and when he says, "Except it'll be at a new location," I can *feel* the happiness radiating off of her. "Someone burned down Sanctum."

*Jeremiah fucking Rain.*

I guess we are brothers, after all.

THAT NIGHT WE'RE WOUND UP IN EACH OTHER IN OUR BED LIKE we always are, exhausted from a run in the forest while it was still light outside. She kept up really well, and I cut our mileage in half, not wanting her to overexert herself.

She claimed I was being overdramatic. It wouldn't be the first time, and probably won't be the last. Not with this girl.

"You miss him, baby girl?"

She picks her head up from my chest, facing me. She looks nervous. Hesitant.

I reach for her hand, thread my fingers through hers, our scarred palms touching. "It's okay, Lilith. You can talk to me."

She glances at our joined hands, and my stomach twists into knots, anticipating what she might say. But she's told me she loves me more in the past few days than she has our entire relationship.

Whatever she feels for Jeremiah, I know she loves me, too. And while I don't want to share her love, I feel better, knowing she wants me.

"It's not…" She starts to say, then trails off, still staring at our joined hands. The lamp on her side table is on, a book of poetry she was reading face down to save her page. I had grabbed it from her hands, tossed it there before we fucked after our run. Now I feel a little bad about it, but *not too bad*. She takes a deep breath. "He was just there…when I needed him." She bites her lips, glancing at me. "He was always there."

I swallow down my anger. My jealousy. Instead, I try to understand. Mav was that for me, always there. Ophelia, in her own way, but my relationship with Maverick more mimics hers with Jeremiah than anything I ever had with O.

I take a few moments to respond, ensuring I'm composed. Letting her know I really do want to hear everything her pretty little mouth has to say.

Finally, I'm able to speak without cutting words. "I'm here now, baby," I tell her, my eyes searching her gray ones. "I'm here now. And you just have to trust me. That I'm going to take care of you, Lilith. Take care of our kid too." I bring our joined hands to my lips and kiss the back of hers, see her soft smile. "Always," I promise her, dropping our hands to my chest. "You'll never need anything, baby girl. Not anymore."

# EPILOGUE

## JEREMIAH

*THREE MONTHS Later*

It's pouring rain at the coast when the message comes through. It's an unknown number, and I know if I were to call it, no one would answer. It'll probably never be used again. It's a burner phone. A piece of shit.

I know, because I bought it.

"Let me see!" Ria squeals, bouncing up and down on her toes on the deck of the beach house, the awning covering us from the summer storm.

"Let him have his moment, damn," Nicolas says with a laugh, and I see him wrap his arm around Ria, hug her close.

She graduated after all.

Lucifer Malikov's father has a science building named after him at Alexandria University. *My* father, although thinking of it that way still makes me feel sick, but it's good I have that connection. Lucifer put in a call, and Ria had her diploma. We guarded her at graduation, then of course, we had to come here.

But the 6 are busy looking for whoever killed Cindy, stalked Sid, abducted Edith.

Maverick never asked how I knew about Lucifer's psychotic break.

I knew because Ezra knew.

And Ezra told someone that's done a lot of work for me. But I called them off of it, after Sid went to the hospital.

Paid them a fuck load of money, too. Never met the fuck, but some of the deadliest criminals in the world operate on the dark web, which is how I found them. Cindy and Cory's deaths were to keep the 6 off of my ass. I didn't authorize them, but I found out afterward, and it worked out pretty well.

The killer was good.

"Let me *see!*" Ria screeches again, jerking me back to the present.

I run my thumb over the screen of my phone, see the healthy baby boy with a skeleton beanie on, minutes old as Sid Malikov holds him close.

That anger I have toward Lucifer softens a little. Or rather, I don't care about it. Our hatred. The way we'll never be close.

The way I think I'd give up just about anything for Sid to love me like she loves him.

My throat tightens, and I take in the boy's big blue eyes, his red cheeks, his mouth open in a wail.

I see Sid grinning from ear-to-fucking-ear. They're at home, in their big bed, black sheets, and Lucifer is beside her, his arm around her and his face lit up, the happiest I've ever seen that piece of shit.

He's not even looking at the baby in her arms.

He's staring at Sid, holding her so close it's a miracle she can even breathe.

Another message comes in, a close up of the baby's face. Fucking adorable, and I hate babies.

But it's the next text that undoes me.

The rain pounds on around us, the waves choppy just a few feet from us, the beach stretched out in either direction, as far as the eye can see. My mom told me her sister lived here. She had a daughter. Eden. My cousin.

I think about that as I read the message.

*Family I never had.*

**Lucifer: Rain Malikov is 6 pounds, 6 ounces. Small, but he'll grow.**

I stare at that message for a long, long time, until Nicolas's hand comes to my shoulder.

I flinch, and he steps back, bringing Ria with him when my eyes connect with his.

But that means it's time.

The baby is safe. Sid is safe. Lucifer will keep her that way.

And I told her once I couldn't live without her.

I meant it.

I force a smile at Nicolas, which he must find odd because he asks, "You okay?" before he takes the phone and Ria snatches it out of his hand, oblivious.

She's scared for her family, but I told her the 6 are distracted right now. Too many loose ends, the whole fucking blanket unravels, and a few threads get forgotten about.

"Yeah," I lie to Nicolas, "I'm fucking great." I force myself not to smile again, because he's staring at me like I just lost my fucking mind.

Of course, I lost that a long time ago.

"I'm going to the gym," I tell him.

"It's fucking pouring—"

I cut him off with a look, and he seems to remember he works for me and not the other way around when he nods, looks down at the phone. I see that slow smile curving on his lips, him and Ria lost in the beauty of a baby.

*Rain.*

I let myself into the beach house through the sliding glass door, grab my keys and head downstairs, out the back door.

It takes me five minutes to get to the warehouse. I've always had an affinity for scoping those out, every city I'm in, it's one of the first things I look for. The opposite of the crate in so many ways, with the same sort of security walling me in. Some things you never get over, I guess.

The parking lot is empty. I own this place, but I'm the only one who knows about it. I grab the gun from the glove compartment, type in a text to Nicolas but don't send it just yet.

When I'm inside the empty building, I flick on the overhead lights, watch them spark to life in rows.

It's hot in here, which is unsurprising. I can hear the thunder flickering beyond the walls of the warehouse, and I stand against the wall, close my eyes.

All I see is her.

She's what I've seen behind my closed eyes for two decades.

Seems fitting she's here now, with me in the last moments.

I thumb the safety on the gun, pull my phone from my pocket, count to three.

Then I send that text to Nicolas, close my eyes again.

Her. *Her.* It'll always be her. Nicolas knows better than to tell her, but I think Lucifer knows. When I left his hospital room, I think he knew.

Dropping the phone—the sound echoing in the warehouse —I hold the gun under my chin and take a deep breath.

All this fight, and it wasn't for nothing.

It was for her.

I feel a sense of peace at that. That I was there in the beginning, and in the end of my life, I helped her by doing just this.

My finger is on the trigger, and I'm surprised the way my heart picks up speed, like I'm nervous.

I've wanted to die for a very, very long time.

Without Sid by my side, there's not much to live for.

Still, my mouth goes dry, my hand starts to shake.

And it's my good hand. My right hand.

The one without the scars. The damage.

But I'm still shaking, and my knees feel weak.

I know how to push past fear though. I swallow, take another deep breath. And just as my finger twitches on the trigger, I hear a voice, and at first I think it's in my head.

"*Sicher.*"

I keep my eyes closed, wondering why the hallucinations have to start *now*. Very unfortunate timing.

"But that was a lie, wasn't it, Jeremiah?"

My eyes spring open as I slowly lower the gun, turn my head.

Only to see a ghost.

The gun slips from my hand.

The sound makes me flinch as I turn to take her in. The bluest eyes. So blue, they seem unreal. Her hair is long and dark down her back, nearly blending in to the all-black she's wearing, a gun in her hand. There are tattoos along her collarbone, edging up her neck, down her arms, over her hands.

"And you don't get to kill yourself," she whispers, stepping closer.

There's no fucking way.

"You know, you taught me to like the darkness. *The ruins.* And you?" She smiles, dimples flashing in her pale face. "You ruined me." Another step, and she's aiming that gun at my gut, the barrel against my shirt. "*Surprise.*" She flashes a wider smile at my shock. "You should really check into your hitmen before you hire them, Jeremiah."

"Kameron..." It's the only thing I can think to say. The last time I saw her, she was underneath me, *dying.* Her father— Francis—was crawling to her.

And I was hurting her.

My mind is spinning as I stare at someone that should be long dead. Then her words hit me. "L-Lazarus?" I ask her, incredulous, shaking my head. "How—"

"Roman is dead, by the way," she over talks me. "But he was really useful, leading me to you."

My mouth drops open.

"And you never did want to pry too much, how I knew what went down with the 6." Her lips curl at that last word as my stomach twists into knots. "Did you think I was just a really, really good hacker?" She laughs, and it cuts like a knife.

This can't be real.

*This can't be fucking real.*

I clench my hands into fists, glancing at the gun on the floor, but it's closer to her than me, and she's still holding one, aimed right at me.

"You know they don't have cameras. The only thing that was ever in that church was a phone line." Her smile is wicked, her teeth slightly crooked as she stares at me. "But Ezra…" She sighs, shrugging. "He's a really, really good source of information. Damaged enough to trust me, *just like I was to trust you.*"

She cocks her head, her blue eyes flashing. "But you're damaged too. A boy of ruin, you're going to your grave. And when I'm done with you," she leans in close, standing on her tip toes, her lips at the shell of my ear, "there won't be much left of you to bury."

# ACKNOWLEDGMENTS

First thank you always goes to you, my readers. I somehow got the best fucking readers in the world, and I never take that for granted. I wake up grateful for the sick and twisted minds I've met on this journey.

Thank you to Abby, Christina, Kandace, and my wife—Taylor—for beta reading. Also for loving these crazy fuckers as much as I do. I had a lot of doubt writing this book. You girls eased those doubts and I appreciate you more than you know.

Liza James. Wow. I don't know what I did to get you in this universe but damn, I'm glad the world brought us together. Thank you for listening to me rant, rave, and freak the fuck out on a daily basis. A duo, us against the fucking world.

Ash. I don't always like myself, but I see so much of me in you, and I never dislike YOU, so… I'm not entirely sure where I'm going with this, all I know is that I think I love you.

Thank you to Amy Briggs for being a kick ass editor, but also not judging me too harshly with the bullshit I write. And for your funny comments…they help me see through the tears.

Thank you to Samantha La Mar for loving Jeremiah, growing my team, and KICKING MY ASS ABOUT TEASERS BECAUSE I SUCK AT THAT SHIT. Keep shining.

Thanks to Books & Moods for getting these headings RIGHT, and being there when I'm losing my shit.

Dani E. I didn't know if putting your full name in here would be too weird. The songs you send help me write all of my books, literally. Thank you for being fucking awesome, there from the beginning, and also when I go to NC, we're meeting up. Sorry, we just gotta.

Elijah. Thank you for being there, always. I appreciate you more than you know. Love you.

My family, specifically my husband…thank you for putting up with my antisocial tendencies, the insanity that descends on my brain when I'm writing, and loving me despite it all. You have no idea how much I love you.

My reader's group, Order of KV. Wow. I LOVE YOU GUYS SO DAMN MUCH. I try to read every single comment in that group, and it's like we're all soul mates in there.

Cult Sluts. You are ONE OF US. Hashtag Kiza.

I feel certain I forgot someone, because I have so many amazing people that for some reason, really like me. I love you, too, whoever you are.

# ABOUT The Author

K.V. Rose is an author of dark romance. She lives with her family in Toronto. She's usually drunk on coffee or rum. Sometimes both at one time. You can find her on social media nearly everywhere at AuthorKVRose. She also hates talking about herself in third person, but this is the last sentence so, whatever.

▼

pinterest.com/authorkvrose
instagram.com/authorkvrose
facebook.com/authorkvrose
goodreads.com/authorkvrose
authorkvrose.com
order of kv

# ALSO BY
## k.v Rose

Made in United States
North Haven, CT
28 November 2021